AF557800

Ananda

Also by Karan Madhok

A Beautiful Decay: A Novel

Ananda

an exploration of cannabis in india

karan madhok

ALEPH

ALEPH BOOK COMPANY
An independent publishing firm

promoted by ***Rupa Publications India***

First published in India in 2024
by Aleph Book Company
7/16 Ansari Road, Daryaganj
New Delhi 110 002

The Publisher unequivocally states that it does not endorse or promote any views, opinions, or content expressed by the Author related to drug use. The views and experiences presented in the book are solely those of the Author and do not reflect the Publisher's opinions. The book is intended strictly for entertainment purposes. The recounting of drug use experiences or any discussions related to drug use are fictional or based on the Author's personal experiences and should not be construed as advocating or encouraging drug use. The Publisher expressly disclaims that the content of the book, including discussions of drug use, should not be considered as legal, medical, or any other professional advice. Readers are encouraged to consult appropriate professionals for advice and guidance regarding any legal, medical, or related matters. Readers are advised to exercise critical judgement while interpreting the content. Any actions or decisions taken by readers based on the book's content, including discussions of drug use, are entirely their own responsibility, and the Publisher shall not be held liable for any consequences arising from such actions or decisions. Readers are reminded that the use, possession, or distribution of drugs may be unlawful and subject to criminal prosecution under applicable laws.

The Publisher recommends that the book is intended for mature audiences. It may contain content that could be unsuitable for minors, and parental guidance is advised. Any external content accessed by readers is beyond the control of the Publisher, and the Publisher shall not be liable for its accuracy or legality.

By reading or using the book, readers acknowledge and accept the terms of this legal disclaimer. If readers do not agree with any part of this disclaimer, they are advised to refrain from accessing or using the book.

The views and opinions expressed in this book are those of the author and the facts are as reported by him, which have been verified to the extent possible, and the publisher is not in any way liable for the same. The publisher has used its best endeavours to ensure that URLs for external websites referred to in this book are correct and active at the time of going to press. However, the publisher has no responsibility for the websites and can make no guarantee that a site will remain live or that the content is or will remain appropriate.

ISBN: 978-93-95853-39-2

1 3 5 7 9 10 8 6 4 2

Printed in India.

For Laila / Layla

Contents

The Seed

'...a numbing of pain sensation, an alteration of memory, a change in appetite...and of course, that phantasmagorial feeling of bliss. Bindaas. Ananda....'

I remember the first time the bhang hit.

I was eighteen, almost exactly twenty years ago as I type these words today, on a train to New Delhi. It had been less than a week since I had graduated from high school, and I was visiting a close friend in Patiala, Punjab. We decided to celebrate our farewell not with famed Patiala peg, but with a bhang lassi: a cool beverage infused with the paste obtained by grinding the leaves and stems of the cannabis plant. Standing outside the train station, we clinked our tall glasses together, gulped down the bitter beverages, and waved goodbye.

In the train, I sat on a metal bench of the airy general compartment, allowing the late-afternoon summer breeze to soothe me through the open windows. I'd picked up a copy of Archie Comics from the platform—*Jughead's Double Digest*—to keep me occupied for the approximately five-hour journey. I leaned back on my seat, relaxed, alone among a crowd of other travellers.

And then, the universe dilated. I found myself stuck on a single panel of the comic book, barely able to read the speech bubble. It may have taken years before I finally turned the page. It may have been a couple of minutes. Through the hubbub of conversations in the packed compartment, I could single out the train's steady chug, as it hurtled forward on the track, as if each thump matched my heartbeat, or as if my heartbeat willingly amended itself to synchronize with this new rhythm of the world. I would later learn that this reaction is hardly uncommon: scientists have discovered that, within the first few minutes of inhaling marijuana smoke (or the half hour it took for me to digest it), a normal person's heart rate (70 to 80 beats per minute) may increase by 20 to 50 bpm. It may even double in some cases. It's as if the body's circulatory system had hired its own personal DJ, remixing a classic, evergreen Bollywood track into a club item number.

I took a sip of water. Someone excused themselves as they brushed past my knee. 'Bhaisaab,' they said, and the word echoed in my head, haunting every other sound I heard with its sampled remix. *Bhaisaab...bhaisaab....*

Soon, it felt like my heart was beating faster than ever, as if it was rushing away, eager to leave the rest of me behind.

Another sip of water. Bourbon biscuits. A cup of hot chai from the vendor that walked past. Blurry faces and distorted voices. The smell of the Indian countryside. Smoke and dung and fertilizers.

Finally, I put the comic book down. I allowed myself to be taken.

I don't know how much time passed before my heartbeat slowed down again. Outside, the afternoon shut down its shutters, transforming into the twilight of the evening.

I was on the cusp of a transformation, too, in the twilight of time before adulthood. At eighteen, there was nothing more exciting than the blank slate of the future, one that allowed me the freedom to colour it in, however I wished. I felt then that my world-view had been left incomplete, that there were ways of seeing and experiencing the world which I had ignored. There were thoughts inside me that I hadn't heard out loud; there were filters of my own gaze that I hadn't yet experimented with.

It felt terrifying at first; but I imagine that it would be terrifying for any winged creature to take their first flight. It felt like freedom.

I arrived in New Delhi safe and sound that evening, met another friend at the station, and went over to his house. I spent most of the night in a goofy, joyful daze, playing FIFA 2003 on his desktop computer. The 'high' tapered away just as exhaustion kicked in, and I gradually collapsed into a comforting cloud of sleep.

The main psychoactive ingredient in cannabis is tetrahydrocannabinol or THC. THC's successful coup of our system is based on its chemical structure, a structure fundamentally similar to anandamide (ANA), which is a fatty acid neurotransmitter found in our brains. It was the Israeli organic chemist Raphael Mechoulam (1930–2023) who first described anandamide in 1992, and if the name sounds slightly familiar, then it should be: anandamide takes its moniker from the Sanskrit-root word ananda, which means joy or bliss. It is an endogenous ligand (a binding substance created within our body). ANA participates in our endocannabinoid system to bind our cannabinoid receptors—called exogenous ligands—receptors that already exist in our body, and are responsible for physiological processes such as appetite, pain sensation, mood, and memory.

THC, then, in its similarity to ANA, works as an undercover agent, essentially disguising itself in those binds of our endocannabinoid system. It takes over our neurotransmitters, activating—or boosting—the mental functions for those particular physiological feelings. Users of cannabis may feel a numbing of pain sensation, an alteration of memory, a change in their appetite*...and of course, that phantasmagorial feeling of bliss. Bindaas. *Ananda.*

Looking back at that trip from Patiala, I remember the giddy sense of excitement I'd felt downing that glass of bhang lassi. The drink had an earthy taste to it, as small morsels of undissolved bhang paste still swirled in the liquid. It was unpleasant, but tolerable. But then again, this wasn't exactly a wine tasting ceremony. We drank in a hurry to consume as much as we could without tasting it. More importantly, we rushed out of a teenage paranoia that we were breaking a taboo—or worse, breaking the law.

---

*Many more Bourbon biscuits followed.

I should've known better. Marijuana, in its common recreational form, is *seriously* illegal in India. However, it is permissible to consume bhang, which has been a cultural staple in much of the country for thousands of years. Cannabis, or ganja, grows with feverish freedom across India, unshackled by the rules of law or social guidelines. In its easy accessibility, the plant is about as Indian as a cup of masala chai or filter kaapi. Former Narcotics Commissioner Romesh Bhattacharjee has claimed that the plant is cultivated in nearly 60 per cent of all districts in the country.

In my mid-twenties, I had put my wanderlust to its biggest test: I quit my correspondent's job with the *Times of India* in Varanasi, and left home with only a hiking backpack as my companion for a modern-day Bharat darshan. What followed next were eighty-six days on the road, during which I travelled in trains, buses, and automobiles, spending most of my nights sleeping in overnight trains to save on boarding. I found cheap guest houses and ashrams around the country to lay my head, and relied on the kindness of old friends to lodge me. In these three months, I ended up setting foot in eleven different states, dozens of cities, eating a variety of food, hearing a symphony of different languages, and testing the waters of true, unstructured freedom.

India is massive, but more than its size, it is its complexity that truly harkens a feeling of awe. I discovered the people and places in the country impacted by the gravitational force of the cannabis plant: from large-scale cultivations and illegal trafficking, to bhang-laced beverages, hemp textiles, and cannabis used as spiritual sacrament.

Ganja, charas, marijuana, weed, vijaya, bhang, pot, grass, hemp, maal, sab kuch milta hai.

Now, over a dozen years later, I hit the road again, this time with a specified purpose to explore some of our country's rich history and cultural relationship with this ancient plant. I trekked up to the grand valleys of ganja in Uttarakhand and sought a cult strain of charas in the mystical Himalayan hamlet of Malana. I chased a mythical strain of 'gold' weed in Kerala and found the epicentre of India's cannabis smuggling rings around the tribal regions in Andhra Pradesh and Odisha. I discovered trade, festivals, spirituality, and addiction in Manipur and Nagaland. I spoke to lawyers in Delhi and connoisseurs in Mumbai. I consumed films, music, celebrity scandals, and all varieties of pop culture influenced by ganja. I met ascetics in Haridwar and Varanasi, scientists at the forefront of cannabis research and development in Lucknow, industrialists hoping to profit off the plant, activists fighting for decriminalization and legalization, and doctors investigating the plant's medicinal benefits.

I was often alone—on jeeps, on buses, on flying machines, on trains—following my sense of curiosity, chasing a shot of my own bliss, chugging along on the tracks, station to station. I found myself looking at the passing world out the window as much as I fell deeper within, excavating parts of the self that had been hidden by the dust of daily life.

And, on any long-distance train journey, the odds were always high to find a carpet of naturally-growing ganja outside the open window grills in the countryside, as ubiquitous in the India as the train tracks themselves.

Malana Cream

'…when this charas is finally smoked, it's a rocket ship buzzing into the brain, a feeling of elevation, Superman meeting Shiva to lazily amble across the great Himalayan peaks…'

I'm on time at the Kasol bus stop. Ten minutes early, even. The organizer had already arranged my tent and other amenities at the campsite in Kheerganga, so I carry only the minimal requirements in my backpack.

As usual, I choose to occupy the very back of the bus. It's where I have the best vantage points of the comings and goings of other passengers, where I feel that there are no surprises behind me. A diverse array of passengers climb aboard: old men and young ones, men in kurtas and men in shirts, women with large duffel bags, mothers with their toddlers.

The bus sputters to a start, honking around the blind corners. From its horn emerges a familiar setlist of short melodies; or to be more precise, a thoroughly unmelodious cacophony of brass instruments, loud enough to awaken hibernating Himalayan brown bears, discordant enough to ensure our bus is heard approaching for kilometres on ahead.

And despite this noise, the crowd, and the terrifying sway of the vehicle every time it speeds around a blind turn, I feel relaxed. I'm alone again, free for a short solo holiday, back among the mountains I so love, breathing the clean air, surrounded by the lush forests and clear horizons.

And, oh yes, the faint, slightly sweet, slightly oily, slightly pungent smell of charas.

That intoxicating waft is nearly unavoidable here, in the cafes, in the fields, by the river, in the buses, all around Parvati Valley in Himachal Pradesh. These hill stations—thousands of feet above sea level—are infamous for nurturing what many consider to be some of the best charas in the world: the Malana Cream.

Named after Goddess Parvati—the god Shiva's first wife—Parvati Valley is one of India's most fertile grounds for charas production. The alpine climate here provides ideal conditions for the sativa species of the plant, producing charas that is in high demand all over India and abroad.

Charas is a cannabis concentrate, similar to hashish but made from the resin of live cannabis plants that grow wild across North India. Malana itself is a tiny village near Kasol where the 'cream' is regarded for its particularly high purity, and thus, particularly high potency. Some estimate that this village—which has achieved mythical status among weed smokers—produces about 500 kilos of hashish every year. The ascendence to its gates is a short hike from Kasol, its darshan a sort of teerth yatra among aficionados of all forms of cannabis: weed or hash, bhang or ganja or charas. You can smoke it, you can drink it, you can eat it. You could probably do a lot more.

Did I say, 'aficionados of all forms of cannabis'? Stoners. I mean stoners.

My bus from Kasol started on time, more or less, but there are delays and stoppages on the road further ahead to Barshaini, a village just about an hour's drive up the road. It is the farthest I can get on a vehicle before the trekking trail up to Kheerganga. Delays are only part of the natural ecosystem here, the price to pay for making motorable roads around the highest mountain range in the world. The road zigs and zags, spiralling upwards around long bends and sharp corners. The bus sways and chugs over its throttling engines, filled to the brim with locals hoping to make their stop at villages on the way.

It's the type of journey that would make many suffer from motion sickness, a sort of stubborn whirlpool swirling from one's head to one's stomach, volatile with the threat of vomit. But not me; I'm accustomed to these roads, to the altitude thousands of metres above sea level, to these rides around and up, a serpentine coil higher up the mountains. I have lived much of my life in the Himalaya. After the Partition in 1947, my paternal great-grandparents planted new roots in a small village called Kandaghat, near Simla in Himachal Pradesh. My grandfather grew up here, and my father was born here. In the 60s, work opportunities moved my family down to the Gangetic Plains, to Varanasi in Uttar Pradesh. This is where I was born and raised for part of my life. My parents and extended family have lived in Varanasi (or Banaras) for over fifty years. But I'm now a non-resident Banarasi, dropping in to see family and friends only a couple of times a year.

Varanasi is an ancient city of spirituality, of politicized religion, the city of cremation and death and mukti, the city most beloved by Shiva. It's also a city teeming with government-approved bhang stalls allowing mere mortals to spend their days in a tizzy of Shiva's favourite sacred plant.

In Class 5, my parents shipped me away to the Himalayan regions, to the touristy town of Mussoorie in Uttarakhand. I was a ten-year-old, depressed to be away from my mother's daily embrace. But soon, I embraced it all: the freedom of being away from home, the mighty beauty of the mountains, the lush deodar woods, the myriad colours of those autumn sunsets, the bright twinkling night skies, and the jittery cold winters. Mussoorie has stayed with me all my life, and serves as my second home now, even in adulthood.

Every trip up these winding roads from the plains floods me with a sea of emotions. The first sight of the Himalaya is always breathtaking, and the fresh air hands the breath right back. But the romance of the hills also fills me up with a sense of dread and guilt:

visiting the Himalaya is more convenient now than ever before for outsiders—like me—who choose to visit the hills for holidays, or even to make them our homes. The ease of movement—inwards and outwards—has provided some with economic benefits, and words such as 'development' and 'modernization' are often used to celebrate the accessibility of places otherwise esoteric to city folk. And yet, the same rush to development is contributing to much of the destruction of this fragile ecosystem. In Parvati Valley, for example, a number of hydropower projects near Barshaini and Pulga have added more grotesque man-made oddities to blemish the natural splendour of the region. In recent years, climate-related cataclysmic events have increased exponentially, both in their volume and their impact. Heavy rains, landslides, mudslides, infrastructural damage, land subsidence, death, and destruction.

Each such Himalayan destination is a Schrödinger's steel chamber, and the beauty of the hills is the live cat left with decaying radioactive substance. The serenity of this region is based on whether we open the steel chamber to experience that very serenity; our visit kills the cat, introducing the same pollution that we escape from in the city to this untouched natural environment.

My bus from Kasol is one such pollutant, adding small puffs of smoke to the pristine air, engine noisily sputtering through the Himalayan silence. Motorbikes, scooters, and jeeps beep past as we go further upwards.

Only fifteen minutes into the ride, we crossed Manikaran, a small pilgrimage town that sits in a valley below the highway, by the banks of the Parvati. Here, the bus comes to an unexpected stop. No, it didn't stop to pick up and drop passengers, or for the driver or conductor to take a susu–potty break, or because of police barricades or toll taxes. It stops because, in front of us, occupying the thin space of the highway up the mountain, lies a large goods truck on its side, like a fallen beast, hunted down by predators.

The conductor of the bus is an older man with youngish features—grey hair and smooth cheeks, a creased forehead, and nimble childlike limbs—who saunters to the back of the bus to make his announcement in Hindi (with a strong Pahari accent). 'Niklo sab log. We can't go any farther. The bus is going to turn around and head back. Stay on if you wish to return; or walk forward if you wish to go ahead.'

I grab my backpack and bounce off the bus. My boots land on the hard tarmac, and I continue my ascent on foot. The winding mountain road disguises itself, offering blind curves as I move forward, so that I can only visualize the future for the next few hundred metres, until I have to snake around and turn from right to left, and then left to right, uncertain of what lies ahead. For the first few kilometres, it is all more or less the same: monstrously tall Himalayan peaks on one side, and low drops beyond the parapet on the other. The highway is narrow but well-paved, and my shoes feel the warm, coarse gravel of the road. The soles of my feet ache for the first half hour of the walk, but soon, the pain becomes a natural extension of myself. There are intermittently-spaced stone barriers on whichever side that overlooks the valleys below. There are poplar trees, and willows, and robinias, and deodars.

I check the time on my phone every few minutes or so. 9:53, 9:56, 10:00, 10:05, 10:08.... I'm worried about this delay in my plans. I would arrive late in Barshaini, and be late to start the *real* hike. I worry about how late it would be before I arrive at Kheerganga, how much of the daylight I would lose to dusk. I check my phone again. 10:12.

I haven't worn a wristwatch since college, since I was old enough to have my own mobile phone that serves as a timekeeper. And with each glance at my device, each digital flip of a minute, I can only concentrate on my delay. Even in a trip where I owe my time to no one but myself, I feel betrayed by the collapse of structure.

My trip to Parvati Valley was supposed to be just a short, four-day getaway, and I was determined to make the journey feel random, spontaneous, to allow myself the freedom to sway and change, to drift wherever the wind leads me. And yet, I yearn suddenly for some predictability, to hitch a ride, to get to Barshaini on time, to bring some order to the randomness.

I have walked far enough from Manikaran to escape all sounds of human humdrum. The mountain road is serene and bucolic, the air even cleaner than it was half an hour ago, the sky even bluer. I have been accustomed to being alone, even in the company of hundreds, of thousands, tens of thousands; but now, walking up on the highway, the sun shining bright in its own ascent towards noon, I'm truly, physically, alone, too. It's a strange sensation in our country—now the most-populous nation on Earth—to be the only one in sight, even if it's just for a brief murmur of time. For a moment, it feels as if the highway is all mine, and all of the Himalaya, and the northern plains, and—why not?—everything south of the Deccan as well.

Finally, I hear a rumbling sound, getting louder, closer. From around the corner behind me, I see a white jeep-taxi, ploughing up the highway. I stick my hand out to get the driver's attention, and the vehicle slows to a halt. There are men and women packed in the passenger seating in the back of the jeep, eight or nine of them. One young man sits alone on the rooftop.

'Where to?' the driver asks.

'Barshaini.'

'Hundred rupees,' says the driver. 'But there's no space in the back.'

'Rooftop?' I ask.

'Dekho, that is up to you, OK? But if someone stops us, it's your problem.'

I shrug. 'Sure.' I climb the ladder in the back up to the roof rack. The man already seated here nods, and I nod back. He seems to be in his mid-twenties, resting in a reclined, confident posture of *I-couldn't-possibly-give-less-of-a-damn-about-the-world.* I cross my legs and sit, feeling the cylindrical metal bars under my butt.

I feel a cool mountain breeze as soon as the jeep stutters to a start, an immediate relief under the mid-morning sun. I have triumphed against chaos; I would start the trek in time, and as a bonus, enjoy the slight thrill of this little crime, seated on the roof of a moving vehicle.

'Lighter hai?' the man besides me asks. With a flick of his thumb, he makes the universal sign of igniting a light. 'Smoke up,' he says, the 'up' direction offering a clear distinction from the tobacco-only act of simply 'smoking' a cigarette or a bidi.

'Haan, haan,' I answer him, and offer a small gas lighter out of my backpack. He, in turn, fishes out his own ingredients, including a sticky black ball of charas between his thumb and index fingertips. There's rolling paper and a cigarette from which to sprinkle some tobacco, as a mixer.

When it's ready, he puts the joint to his mouth, lights it, covering the flame with his other hand to shield it from the wind gushing by us. He puffs in aggressively to ensure that the burn sticks. After a couple of tries, it does.

I know what will happen next. An exhilarating rush to his head. A thump on his forehead that first jolts him, and then, in the quick instant that follows, relaxation. His eyes droop and cheeks feel heavier. He smiles at nothing, a smile that tells me that he has found that brief shot of bliss. Blood cells in his head seem to evaporate up to the clouds, floating up past the layer of meninges that wrap around his brain. He takes another puff, inhales it deeper into his lungs, and exhales slowly.

Like a Trojan Horse, the THC in cannabis mimics the anandamide to give our brain more of the same thing it already has. The substance has often been described as a duplicate key to unlock into the body's anandamide receptors. It's a cheat code of sorts, a shortcut to exhilaration.

The world is filled with those seeking this extra, exhilarating bliss. The United Nations estimate that, as of 2021, about 4.3 per cent of adults consume cannabis. According to the World Health Organization (WHO), cannabis is by far the most widely used, cultivated, and trafficked 'illicit'* substance in the world, with ten times more users than other popular controlled substances, like cocaine or opiates. In 1985, a significant national decision—the Narcotics Drugs and Psychotropic Substances (NDPS) Act—branded the substance 'illicit' in India, too.

In recent years, the central government has intensified its crackdowns of the cannabis trade around India, and made the lofty announcement of making the country 'drug free' by 2047—the 100th year of our independence. The government has claimed to have arrested thousands of individuals and destroyed over 82,000 acres of cannabis cultivation across the breadth of the nation since 2020.

That is enough weed to fill up half of Mumbai.

On the moving jeep, I lean against the luggage bar behind me, careful not to lean too far back and lose my balance. We are zooming ahead now, and the sun beams streaming down make me feel lethargic. I lose track of time.

I ask the man where his home is, and he says that he is from a different region of Himachal Pradesh. He says that he's just travelling. I say I'm doing the same.

I fish out my phone to take photos of the passing woods and the mountains. Then, I take a photo of myself; it's a necessary celebration for this moment of unexpected joy, which arrived like a blind curve of the mountain highway, and soon, hummed away again, like the honks of passenger buses since past, leaving behind only faint echoes drifting in the Himalayan wind.

*Their word, not mine.

The jeep stops for me at Barshaini. I pay the driver, and nod a silent goodbye to the man on the rooftop—who has also got off to head on foot in the other direction.

I have a new road ahead of me, a path I must tread on foot for a few hours, up a somewhat strenuous hike up to Kheerganga. There's a dam here at Barshaini on the Parvati River and, nearby, I see several groups of other young men and women strapping on their belongings to set off on the same trek. I know that, at the summit, there will likely be a busy campsite, a complete antithesis of the type of solace I seek. I make sure to take off before the other hikers can gather themselves, to have more time to myself untethered from the rest of them. I strap my backpack tightly, and I walk.

Feeling a rush of excitement, I strain myself to climb faster, rushing up the thirteen-something kilometres to the destination. A lifetime of trekking around the Garhwal region of Uttarakhand also gives me some advantage with the terrain, as well as a confident spring in my step. I know how to pace myself. I know how to balance my steps on each surface I encounter: sharp dry rocks and loose gravel, clear footpaths, and wet stones under small cascades of water.

When I arrive at the summit a few hours later, the campsite is spread out across large grassy patches of (mostly) flat land, where the organizers have already prepared tents for the visiting trekkers to stay overnight. My tent is in the far corner, away from the 'mess' area and the popular hot water springs. It's a two-person tent, the smallest they could arrange for the only solitary traveller. I've brought my own snacks for the night, with my own arrangements for entertainment: my music, my books, and a clear view of the moonrise over the cold, black night. My only request to the organizers is for a hot cup of chai.

I imagine that if the Malana Cream hits in a place like this, one could ask for little else.

About 3,500 metres above sea level, Kheerganga is famous for its hot water springs, which are believed to be therapeutic in a spiritual sense, with the necessary jadoo in the water that cleanses sins as much as it cleans the physical form. According to popular folklore, Kartikeya—the son of Shiva and Parvati—lost a great race to his brother, Ganesha, and chose a life of self-exile and meditation in the mountain. He couldn't be found for a few thousand years, until Shiva himself formed a stream of kheer (rice pudding) to bring Kartikeya back. Hence, the kheer ganga.

It won't surprise any student of Hindu mythology that Shiva's son chose these specific Himalayan valleys for his seclusion. The mythologies are ripe with stories of Shiva and his particular affection for cannabis—stories that continue to shape the ganja/charas/bhang consumption habits of Shiv bhakts up to the present day.

And I'm hardly surprised by Kartikeya's yearning for seclusion. I often pursue the same solitude. Trips like these are a chance for me to encounter my own self, a physical manifestation of the metaphysical 'trip' that stoners take far into the recesses of their own mind, seeking deep contemplation, seeking bliss.

I have frequently enjoyed the freedom of solo travel, of choosing an itinerary without debate or consultation, of getting up and going on my own schedule, of the brief, non-judgemental comfort of new people. In India, it is no secret that this is a certain privilege granted to men like me—a privilege extended less often to women. It is the freedom to stray, to spend nights without worry next to strangers on sleeper trains, to walk down unfamiliar lanes without the fear of a second shadow, to plan without much stress of serious consequence. I also have the double privilege of some financial stability, the stability that allows me to be unstable in my whims. It has allowed me the time and the risks of being on the road, to risk being late, to risk getting lost.

The risks, rewards, and unpredictability of travel has often served as the key to unlock my personal endocannabinoid system, the rush of anandamide. It's that feeling after you run a marathon and sit back on a mound of green grass, red-faced, sweaty, and relaxed. That feeling after an orgasm, bodies untensed. It's a breath of fresh air after being submerged underwater.

I have 'settled down' in recent years, getting more comfortable planting my roots, working and writing, marrying and fathering. But I have continued travelling alone: there was always something I found enticing about being far away from the expectations of social constraints. I crave the high of the road all the time, not to escape from the stresses of life, but to escape its utter dullness.

Every so often, these journeys would bless me with experiences that would take my breath away: waterfalls above McLeod Ganj, beaches at Puri, shared conversations on the train, moments that would keep me present in time and place—away from the distractions of the past and the future, of other places, or other interfaces on my phone screens. It would be a feeling not entirely unlike that of a hallucinogenic high, the soma that our ancestors claimed to drink in the days of Vedic scriptures. A type of meditative bliss found through a return to nature, and the resins found in nature's very gift to humanity: the mountains, the skies, the wildlife, and the cannabis plants which we have cultivated for millennia, in an ancient search for our own form of amrit—immortality—or at least, its best-possible imitation.

The moonrise at Kheerganga makes it all worth it.

After a night of peaceful sleep in my tent, I leave early the next morning from Kheerganga for my return to Barshaini. I catch another shared jeep back to Kasol.

From, here, I begin my exploration of the ananda in earnest. The following morning, I arrange another taxi towards the Malana Hydro-Electric Power Plant, and up to the small highway village of Jari. I set off on foot once more, for another short trek zigzagging through a crest between the peaks, and then up the mountain again, until I arrive at the little village which has long been known as the nucleus of Indian hashish: Malana.

There are a number of legends about this place. Rumours and hearsay, folklore and rural myths. Some claim that Malana is one of the earliest democratic communities in the world. Some believe that the villagers here are descendants of Alexander the Great's army. Some say that the sacred tongue spoken here, Kanashi—a mixture of Sanskrit and Tibetan dialects, one of the rarest languages in the world—is a dialect spoken by mythical rakshashas, forbidden to all outsiders. Some say that, merely weeks after a birth in the village, newborns undergo a strenuous test where they are sprinkled with ice cold water on a chilly moonlit night, so they may prove their mettle under the harsh environmental conditions.

The survivors carry forward the village's legacy.

From this little hamlet of mystery and history also comes the beloved Malana Cream.

There are thousands of acres of land in Himachal Pradesh's Kullu district dedicated to the cultivation of cannabis, attracting visitors from all over the world to catch a whiff of that enchanting, clay-like local maal. This 'maal'—*stuff*—has been the subject of films, documentaries, and numerous journeys of self-investigation. It has been a recipient of the Cannabis Cup in Amsterdam, awarded to the world's best hashish.* It has been referred to as 'the charas piece de resistance'.

I find myself completing the final part of the journey on foot, a few hours' trek up the mountain that will finally bring me to Malana, 8,700 feet above sea level. A heavy blanket of mist greets me up this route, and soon, the peaks of Chandrakhani and Deotibba on each side envelop the path under gloomy pockets of shade. The mist turns into a soft drizzle, and the drizzle into a shower of rain. I find cover under a half-tattered canopy on the bend.

---

*I'm not expecting to see this prestigious honour advertised on any 'Incredible India 2.0' tourist brochures soon.

Fortunately, the showers are over quickly; they are merely a passing welcome—or a warning—from the burdened grey clouds. I continue my walk.

Soon, signs of civilization emerge: local shepherds with their flock, and tourists finding shade under the roof of a large slab of rock, openly smoking a joint. Then there's a stop for snacks: thukpa and Maggi and chai. I ignore the temptations and keep climbing. The destination is near.

There are no motorable roads up to Malana: the terrain, of course, has made construction difficult, but there has been resistance from the locals, too, who are still grasping to the last straws of keeping the rest of civilization at bay. The reason to stay a little delinked may be the state government's own doing, hoping to keep alive the mystique of this land. In 2023, there were finally signs of a thaw: residents of the village sent a memorandum to the state's Revenue and Horticulture minister to connect the village via ropeway 'to ease the life of villagers and promote tourism'.

It's no secret that the present disconnect to major motorable roads also limits quick access by any authorities planning a surprise raid on cannabis farmers and smugglers here.

In Malana, I'm greeted by a row of homes built with mixed architectural styles. There are newer constructions in brick and mortar with tin-sheet rooftops, built after a devastating fire in 2008 that burned many houses down. Some of the original small abodes erected in the wooden kath-kuni style are still around, made using a technique that is indigenous to this region, where structures are built using alternating layers of wood and stone masonry, designed specifically to better withstand natural calamities.

A kath-kuni temple sits in the middle of the village square, three storeys high, with each level a little wider than the one below. It has astonishing balconies with intricate wooden carvings on the ledges and the balustrade above. I'm told by an elderly man here that I'm prohibited from touching the temple; I feel no specific compulsion to test this prohibition.

The temple is in honour of Jamlu Devta, the beloved sage of Malana who is the central force of the village's cultural gravity. Jamlu is the regional name of Jamadagni, a rishi from Vedic times, who—according to local myths—landed in ancient Malana as per the advice of Shiva. Here, Jamlu clashed with the rakshasha*/asura king Banasura, and their conflict was finally resolved with a compromise to share the political and civic responsibilities in the village: Banasura would be in-charge of administration, and Jamlu of the judiciary. Even to this day, a village priest in Malana is appointed as the caretaker of Jamlu's shrine. Cannabis seeds are made as offering to Jamlu Devta here.

The citizens of Malana boast of having practised democracy for thousands of years, before the city-states in ancient Athens or any modern British/French/American models. The local administration in Malana still claims to be independent from the polity of the rest of the district and state. The village chooses its own administrative leaders, all under the guidance of Jamlu (through a chosen 'medium' of the head priest).

Around August every year, Malanis celebrate the Shaun festival, where the village priest sets a tree alight in the village square, and dancing and singing commences around the burning pyre. There is a sheep sacrifice, before the party really sets off. 'The men in the village drink alcohol and smoke Malana cream for the duration of the festival, dance and play music into the night,' writes Carly Clarke, in her 2014 photo-essay, 'and the women are allowed to watch.'

Allowed to watch? This is ironic, because the women of this region traditionally have a closer, more tactile relationship with the cannabis crop. While the men may gather and distribute the plant,

*In Hindu mythology, rakshashas belong to the demon class. But unlike the Western demonization of that phrase, the rakshashas are just another race, like the devas (gods)—not better, not worse, just different. Sometimes, gods and demons fight; sometimes, they don't.

it is the job of the women farmers to rub the resin off the buds, an act of mushing the fruiting tops of the plant into its 'cream' form.

A thousand-some years after the scriptures that first mention tales of Jamlu Devta, more travellers allegedly arrived here, this time from distant foreign shores. The conquering Macedonian king Alexander the Great crossed the Indus River to enter ancient India, and local legends claim that his army found their way through the mountain mist up to Malana. Some say that that Macedonian king himself came along, looking for herbal cures for his many ailments. There is no historical evidence of this, except stories passed down over about 2,500 years. Elders in Malana may still allege that the villagers are descendants of 'Sikander's' army, who intermixed with the natives.

Stories like these have helped to build a narrative of superiority for the people of Malana, as a kingdom of spiritual democracy, as a race descended from great warriors, and a region gifted by nature—or the gods—with natural cures for all of the world's ailments. Fresh mushrooms bloom in the farms surrounding the village. Valuable herbs like artemisia and cinchona have been found here, too.

The most lucrative of all, of course, is cannabis. Combine the Himalayan climate, fertile soil, and frequent rain, and one gets the ideal conditions for cultivation. Much like the tales of Jamlu and Alexander, the lore and lure of cannabis in Malana has existed for centuries, with locals intimately familiar with the plant, using it as a means of medicine, recreation, nutrition, and a number of practical day-to-day purposes, too, including ropes for tying livestock, baskets, clothing, etc.

In interviews with locals in 2018, journalist P. Krishna Gopinath learned that the cannabis's commercial potential wasn't discovered until the 1970s, when cultivation began here with the specific purpose of profiting off this beloved crop. Gopinath writes, 'Malanis tell the story of Glenu, an Italian who stayed in the village and taught them to make charas using the "hand-rubbed" technique.'

Other journalists have claimed that, while the wild plant was being used in the Kullu district for centuries, it was the involvement of 'outsiders' that made locals realize its commercial value.

A decade after Glenu's visit, national forces eventually interfered with the hidden lives of the Malanis—and of millions of more Indians for whom this herb had been a common part of daily lifestyle, ritual, recreation, and trade.

In 1985, the Indian Parliament enacted the Narcotics Drugs and Psychotropic Substances (NDPS) Act into law, officially prohibiting the production, manufacturing, cultivation, possession, sale, transport, storage, and/or consumption of a number of narcotics, including cocaine, heroin, LSD, opium, methadone, and, of course, cannabis.

In Section 2 of the NDPS Act, cannabis (hemp) is defined as:

(a) charas, that is, the separated resin, in whatever form, whether crude or purified, obtained from the cannabis plant and also includes concentrated preparation and resin known as hashish oil or liquid hashish;
(b) ganja, that is, the flowering or fruiting tops of the cannabis plant (excluding the seeds and leaves when not accompanied by the tops), by whatever name they may be known or designated; and
(c) any mixture, with or without any neutral material, of any of the above forms of cannabis or any drink prepared therefrom.

By this definition, the 'illegal' components of the plant are its flowering/fruiting tops and its resin. The buds. Excluded from this definition is the actual stump of the hemp plant, which is a useful crop for a variety of industrial and commercial products. More recently, the Supreme Court also clarified that selling or possessing ganja seeds is not prohibited under the NDPS Act. Outside the Act, the legislations of the Juvenile Justice (Care and Protection) Act of 2000 and individual state laws also determine punishment regarding cannabis in India. No state has the power to amend the NDPS Act to decriminalize other forms of cannabis for recreational use; they may only regulate the illegal forms of the plant for medical, scientific, or industrial purposes.

Notably missing from this policy is any preparation of cannabis in the bhang form. States in India are allowed to make their own ruling on bhang under this national guidance. Under the full legal purview, bhang should not include flowering tops of the cannabis plant or its resin—the parts of cannabis high in THC content, the parts of the plant most responsible for getting you high. And yet, any bhang consumer knows fully well that this edible drug (whether mixed in your milky summer beverage or a sugary dessert) will leave one mind-numbingly intoxicated, sometimes for a whole day, with elation, a pacing heartbeat, a ravenous appetite, and paranoid jitters.

A 2019 survey published by the Government of India's Ministry of Social Justice and Empowerment concluded that about 2.8 per cent of Indian citizens reported* having used cannabis in the previous twelve months, the majority of whom used the substance in its bhang form.

Some of the cannabis from the Himalaya—or grown at licensed farms in Uttar Pradesh—end up being the supply for the special government-licensed bhang shops found in holy cities (usually, any one of Shiva's favourite vacation spots) like Varanasi, Jaisalmer, Pushkar, Mathura,** and more. Legal bhang is also procured from

---

*OK, but who is really, honestly telling the government—the *government*!?!?!—their weed habits? My unscientific conclusion is that the real number could be much higher.

**In late 2022, Mathura police alleged that 500 kilos of cannabis stored in local police stations was consumed by rats. 'Rats are small animals, and they aren't scared of the police', deadpanned a local court.

cannabis plants that have been confiscated in major drug busts, or from the wild hemp—grown without any industrial specificities—collected from the hillside.

With the 1985 NDPS ruling, the cultivation of this natural, indigenous plant was suddenly declared criminal. Almost overnight, farmers and users of all forms of cannabis around India were now seen as law-breakers. A crop that had been part of India's cultural tapestry for millennia was branded as contraband.

In Malana, however, little changed for a couple of decades, and the business of charas only saw a bigger boom. Perhaps it was because of the relative isolation of the region, and an unspoken agreement between villagers, local authorities, and politicians not to meddle with their affairs. Or perhaps—as the primary and most-abundant crop here—the Malanis simply refused to allow the laws of the outside world to define their livelihood.

While popular charas strains are produced in other areas of Parvati Valley, the 'Cream' from Malana is literally the cream of the crop, something of a cult favourite across India and around the world. It has enticed domestic and foreign travellers to wander up this way in search of the mythic high. It has been smuggled and sold at exuberant prices. If a Malana resident earns around ₹500 for a tola (a tola is equivalent of 10 grams) of the Cream, the same would cost around ₹5,000 in New Delhi. Abroad, a 'T' might cost three or four times that.

The annual monsoon season is critical for cultivation. When it rains, the plant produces THCA (tetrahydrocannabinol acid) as it matures and its buds grow. But it's the next strike of sun around the second half of September (after the rains) that gives the Parvati Valley hashish its psychoactive qualities. Now, the cannabis produces the delta-8-THC; like Superman, it uses solar energy for its powers to transform into the best charas in the world.

For outsiders who've encountered the purest, untainted form of Malana Cream—also called 'Black Gold'—the experience usually begins with a brush with its soft, clay-like texture, instantly providing a comforting mush when rubbed between the fingers. At its purest, the sticky substance will feel like soft modelling clay. If you let it get too cold, it becomes hard as stone and difficult to crumble. When it's just right, it will grind down like soft powder, leaving your fingers greasy and sticky, nail plates stained with dark charas residue. A mere whiff of the blackish/brownish soft block is a minor high of its own.

It has been claimed that the THC content of Malana Cream is about 30 to 40 per cent, some six or seven times more than that in regular natural ganja that grows in India. And when this charas is finally smoked, it's a rocket ship buzzing into the brain, a feeling of elevation, Superman meeting Shiva to lazily amble across the great Himalayan peaks.

Once upon a time, the dense forests in this part of the Himalaya were popular mainly for being the 'apple belt' of the country. Today, small towns, hamlets, and even undefined clearings amidst these woods have become a major draw for unregulated cannabis tourism. Wild growth of the four-to-five-feet high stalks of the cannabis plant are scattered across the valley's hillsides and plateaus.

For young Indian stoners—particularly those from a background of some privilege—the expedition up to the Kullu district is almost like a form of initiation, an exciting escape from the comforts of home, trading the farmhouse parties around Delhi for tattered tents under the naked mountain skies. Some are transformed by the magnetic mixture of the charas and the serenity of these places; some are drawn back here often, leaving their sitzmarks on the local culture; some choose to migrate here permanently.

One such journey was imagined in the 2014 film *M Cream*. Directed by Agneya Singh, the film features a group of early twentysomethings who take a road trip from Delhi to Parvati Valley in search of the fictionalized village of Mababajagal—inspired by Malana—to find the holy grail of charas. It's a rare Hindi film openly exploring the lifestyle of India's privileged stoner community. On the way, the four friends fall into deep philosophical tangents, dwelling upon themes of purpose and purposelessness, democracy and activism, responsibility and lack thereof. They encounter Tibetan-in-exile communities, chance upon a hidden hippie commune for a no-holds-barred rave party, and assist the cause of villagers who seek to protect their forests from the construction of a government-approved resort. The young protagonists smoke and drink and trip out on 'acid', and they lust for each other, and they love each other, and they grow up.

The film lacks a sense of real focus—more vibes than purpose, more journey than destination—but, perhaps, its waywardness serves as a commentary on the waywardness of the typical 'charas tourist' to Parvati Valley, too: young people seeking escape from the weight of the world and the burden of expectations placed upon them. Despite its flaws, *M Cream* captures at its heart the type of young Indians most attracted to the lifestyle of the mountains, a lifestyle that they—*we*—exoticize as the 'other', and a lifestyle *we* can't get enough of...just as long as we have the option to return to our urban comforts whenever we wish to do so.

Yet, decades before films like *M Cream,* the Kullu district had already become popular for foreign visitors stumbling upon these hidden Himalayan pockets. They have been coming from all around the world—still alight with the last embers of the hippie counterculture of the late 60s—soul-searching, maal-seeking. Communes like the one portrayed in *M Cream* still exist around this region, although they are much depleted in recent years due to the attention they've received from local authorities, the curiosity of domestic tourists, and the slowdown of international tourism that followed the Covid-19 pandemic.

Kasol is hardly on the poster of any itinerary designed for the average international tourist visiting India, far from the 'golden triangle' of Delhi, Agra, and Jaipur, hardly a draw like the financial centres (Mumbai, Bengaluru), the spiritual havens (Varanasi, Amritsar), or the relaxing getaways (Goa, Kerala). It's not connected by rail, and the nearest airport in Bhuntar only welcomes a couple of arriving flights each day. And yet, word-of-mouth and circumstance have always attracted a steady drive of tourists.

The most common foreign presence here is of the Israelis. The touristy parts of Kasol are filled with several cafes and guest houses catering to Israeli customers. Falafels and shakshuka galore. Floor cushions and colourful tie-dye bed sheets hanging from the walls and ceiling. Signboards and alternative menu cards in Hebrew. Lo-fi trance beats. Absolutely killer hummus. And if the ambience is chill enough, chillums and joints passing from hand to hand, enveloping the space under a heavy cloud of charas smoke. Before ever visiting the region, I had heard rumours that some of the Israeli establishments here even had a 'No Indian customers' policy—but during my visit, I didn't chance upon any such place myself.*

How did Kasol get to be known as a 'Mini Israel'? Most able-bodied Israeli adults have to complete three years of mandatory military service. It is tradition, then, to mark the end of this service with a holiday, a long-term sojourn somewhere away from home. In conversations with several Israeli travellers in Parvati Valley (as well as in McLeod Ganj, Varanasi, Pushkar, Goa, and elsewhere), I discover that India is a particularly attractive option for an economical trip: providing an escape to solitude and peace—on a budget. And for some, yes, that peace comes with access to the popular charas, too. Ahimsa and ananda. The Chabad House in Kasol was opened by Rabbi Dani and Rivka Hila Winderbaum in 2004, providing activities and services to Jewish backpackers

*Or perhaps, as an Indian, I was never intended to chance upon them.

in the region, including Shabbos meals, Torah studies, a Mikvah (ritual bath), emergency assistance, and aid for those suffering with drug abuse.

Kasol is a charming little hamlet, if one can avoid the traffic logjam of the main, motorable road. It's a starting base for a number of hikes and treks around the region, to other villages, hot springs, temples and gurdwaras, and fabulous sunsets against the snow-capped peaks. A short walk away from Kasol, across a suspension bridge and through a dense jungle of pine trees, lies the hamlet of Chalal, which is a favourite of tourists looking for a sense of adventure, and a home to many festivals and raves. People come for the charas here, but they stay for just about everything else. Another popular destination is Tosh, a village situated on a hill close to Kasol, filled with green pastures, Israeli-themed cafes, and scores of like-minded visitors looking for a higher high.

For every visitor 'imported' to the region, an exponentially-high proportion of the charas is exported out. The hashish from Parvati Valley is the favoured strain of choice for much of North India, and is particularly popular in New Delhi—where its distribution finds its true economic boom. It is also estimated that charas worth nearly ₹1,000 crore is smuggled out each year to Western Europe, Scandinavia, and Israel.

The highest quality maal would, of course, be the 'pure' Cream. But much of the charas in distribution in the plains is spiked with inferior strains, oils, caffeine, detergent powder, shoe polish, glass, battery acid, other drugs, or a prescription sedative called benzodiazepine, which could lead to dependence or addiction to sedatives. Some growers or dealers may spike the weed with rat poison to avoid rodents, who are attracted to the seeds.*

There is no sign of authenticity in a contraband item. No brand name on the plastic wrapper. One must simply trust the

---

*YIKES!

middlemen on their word. Spiked charas in India usually feels powdery, or leaves a strong black imprint (signs of shoe polish) when crumbled between the fingers. Spiked ganja may have excessive seeds or be brownish in colour. The smoke itself will feel metallic and rough going down the throat, while leaving behind a stinging aftertaste.

Instead of a blissful high, the adulterated maal can be a precursor to a nightmare, resulting in dizziness, throat pains, sleep disturbances, nausea, and in the worst cases, severe illnesses, infections, and hallucinations. Some of these adulterations could even result in bronchitis, asthma, or permanent lung scarring.

Untampered Malana Cream rarely reaches south to Mumbai, Bengaluru, Goa, etc., or beyond Indian shores. While cafes as far as the Netherlands boast of featuring the Malana Cream, most of the hash entering European borders is from Morocco.

Meanwhile, Kasol has earned the nickname 'Amsterdam of India' for a borderless connection it shares with the Dutch capital—some 6,000 kilometres apart—in its affection for the cannabis plant. The influx of tourism is a major economic boon to Kasol's local economy. The easy availability of charas is often an open secret, even if the area doesn't legally have a 'tolerance policy' for selling weed like the coffee shops in Amsterdam.*

In recent years, there has been some positive momentum to realize the economic potential of the vast supply of cannabis

---

*In response to nuisance caused by the excessive crowds, Amsterdam banned outdoor marijuana smoking in its red-light district in February 2023. Despite some misconceptions, cannabis was only 'tolerated' in the Netherlands since the 1970s, in a policy known as gedoogbeleid, where the sale and use of the product was still illegal, but authorities chose not to prosecute lawbreakers for small amounts. From December 2023, however, cannabis has been grown, sold, and consumed legally across the Netherlands for the first time as part of a four-year trial run known as the wietexperiment (weed experiment). Officially sanctioned companies have been allowed to cultivate and supply marijuana in eleven municipalities. The 'experiment' will assist the government in keeping a closer eye on the supply chain to the coffee shops and determine if legalization will help reduce crime rates.

across Himachal Pradesh, particularly as the state faces grave economic challenges, a debt rising into the thousands of crores, and unemployed individuals turning towards illegal trafficking. According to some police reports, nearly '80 percent of the youth' have been involved in possession and the trafficking of drugs in the Kullu district alone, leading, of course, to many more arrests under the NDPS Act. The local police have also hinted at a 'nexus' between peddlers, some politicians, and international drug mafias—all working in the backgrounds, unseen by most eyes that gaze upon the picturesque serenity of this valley. There are over 20,000 hectares of cannabis under cultivation in the Kullu Valley alone, and thousands more in Chamba, Kangra, Mandi, Shimla, and Sirmaur.*

Moreover, Himachal has also seen the rise of more serious substance abuse among the disenchanted and disenfranchised young: 'chitta', a dangerous, adulterated cocktail of heroin and other drugs like trimethoprim and megaloblastic. Officials have claimed through seizures of the drug that chitta consumption in the state has spiked nearly five times in recent years. In Punjab, which has been hit harder than most states with the chitta menace, farmers and agricultural experts have called for allowing the cultivation of cannabis to curb addictions to the harder substance.

In his case for cannabis decriminalization in Himachal Pradesh, law professor Khagesh Gautam has argued in favour of the potential of legal cannabis-related tourism in the state. It is an industry, Gautam writes, 'that exists peacefully and operates efficiently right below the radar of legality, and yet is beyond the reach of our tax laws'. He adds that this move could help generate employment opportunities for the young of Himachal Pradesh, from cultivation and production to import, export, and more white-collar jobs, too.

---

*How much is 20,000 hectares? Combine all the terminals of New Delhi's Indira Gandhi International Airport, then make ten duplicate copies, then fill it all with cannabis. And now, imagine all the 'terminals' that the police haven't yet discovered.

Similarly, Himachal-based cannabis activist Haneesh Katnawer told me over a phone interview that, 'People [in the region] are smoking up in coffee shops, like Amsterdam. You should just be able to go into a shop and buy it. Tax it. Remove the policemen. This tourism of tax-based cannabis will be very profitable for HP.'

In November 2021, the former chief minister of Himachal Pradesh Jai Ram Thakur had said that the state was 'seriously considering the cultivation of cannabis in a controlled manner'. BJP minister Ramesh Chand Dhawala—formerly an MLA of the town of Jwalamukhi—leaned even further in, calling cannabis a 'Ram baan aushadhi', a medicine that removes all obstacles, like the arrow of god Rama. Dhawala added that 'a single drop of oil obtained from hemp can boost immunity, cure innumerable diseases, prevent heart blockage, and reverse memory loss by activating dead cells.' Thakur's successor as HP's chief minister, the Congress politician Sukhwinder Singh Sukhu, said in a media roundtable event that cannabis is not a 'nasha' (intoxicant) but a medical boon.

In the summer of 2023, the Himachal government announced a massive anti-drug drive to destroy cannabis and opium cultivation in a number of districts. Around the same time, however, the state government formed a panel to explore the possibility of legalizing hemp cultivation. A group led by the Himachal's Revenue Minister Jagat Singh Negi visited the Centre for Aromatic Plants at Selaqui in the neighbouring state of Uttarakhand, where industrial hemp cultivation was legalized only a few years prior. In a report submitted to the state's chief minister, the panel recommended amendments to the 1985 NDPS Act to develop standard operating procedures of cannabis cultivation in Himachal, create a seed bank to fund research and development, and hire specialized excise staff to regulate and moderate cultivation. The proposed protocol suggests that agricultural universities in the state will conduct research on medical cannabis, while any cultivation outside of designated areas will be punishable.

'The step will not only benefit farmers economically, but also generate about ₹500 crore revenue for the government,' said Negi.

In September 2023, Negi announced that the state government had begun preparing a policy on hemp cultivation for its medicinal, industrial, and scientific use. Cheering on this decision, the BJP MLA from Mandi district Puran Chand Thakur said that, if legalized, '[Cannabis] will provide income to thousands of unemployed youths. This will also be the beginning of the end of the drug mafia in the state.' Shimla-based advocate Deven Khanna, who had filed a public interest litigation in the high court in 2018 seeking direction about non-narcotic cultivation of cannabis, added, 'If legalized, cannabis will overtake the state's apple industry in terms of revenue.'

And lo and behold, a chamatkar! In September 2024, the state assembly accepted the government's proposal to legalize controlled cultivation of cannabis for medicinal, scientific, and industrial purposes—close to the Uttarakhand model. Nevertheless, a string of NDPS cases and arrests continue in Himachal Pradesh for now. Around 4,000 kilos of charas have been seized in the state in the past decade. Just a month after Negi announced Himachal's interest in a cannabis cultivation policy, the state's police launched a major operation in the Manikaran valley—the same region where a wounded bus had forced me to deboard my ride—to 'find' nearly 150 acres of forest land under illegal cannabis cultivation. The forest department was asked to destroy the nearly 3 lakh ganja plants found in this operation, plants that could have been used to help farmers transition to the legal side of the business down the road. Thirty-four individuals were arrested.

The demand for the Cream has inevitably led to international notoriety for the once-idyllic Malana village. Matters had got so out of control that, in 2017, the village parliament—part of the self-professed 'oldest democracy'—got together to evoke the spirit of their deity, Jamlu, for a solution. The chosen medium announced

Jamlu's absolute decree: he had 'ordered' Malana be shut to all visiting tourists. 'The deity did not want any of the villagers to rent out their property for running guest houses and restaurants,' said Malana's panchayat pradhan to the *Hindustan Times*. 'He has forbidden everyone from doing this, and those violating his orders will have to bear the brunt of his curse.' About a dozen guest houses were closed. Photography in the village had already been banned earlier that year.

Even as Malana has somewhat loosened these restrictions since, visitors won't find easy accommodation in the village. During the Covid-19 pandemic, Malana claimed to have zero cases because of its self-imposed isolation.

The Cream, however, has kept flowing, immersing users in its happy haze, absorbing into their skins, boosting this lucrative trade, while also turning farmers into imprisoned criminals.

In the spring of 2022, I spoke to Priya Mishra, who is in her early thirties, who was recently based in Malana, and has described herself as 'Asia's first female Cannabis activist'. Mishra is the founder of the Hempvati platform, and speaks with impassioned, dithyrambic declarations when discussing the positive aspects of cannabis and industrial hemp. Around 2011, she was diagnosed with late-stage tuberculosis, an infectious and potentially-fatal disease that mainly affects the lungs. She told me that hospitals in Mumbai took her 'for a ride' for several months, and the synthetic drugs she was prescribed only ended up torturing her with worse side effects. Respite from the pain finally came when a friend offered her a joint to smoke.

'I laughed so much that I puked,' she told me when we first spoke over the phone. 'But I fucking slept like a child when I smoked [cannabis]. And then, I had the "eureka" moment.'

Managing the pain with cannabis, Mishra's condition slowly

improved, so much so that this new lease of health made her determined to invest her life into learning and spreading the message of the plant's healing powers. 'Cannabis saved my life,' she said. 'There is medicinal, agricultural, recreational, educational, religious benefit to it...I know that, once the laws change, it will help serious patients. Cancer, AIDS, TB patients.'

When she moved to Malana, Mishra ran a youth centre for dozens of local children, many of whom have suffered the collateral damage of the cannabis trade in the region. She mentioned that several of her contacts in the village have been arrested and detained. 'There is a "brother" of mine in Malana whose kids I teach—he has spent three years in Tihar jail already, because a distributor in Delhi gave up his name as his source for the charas.'

Mishra hinted that there are many more cases like this, which is why her long-term hope is for complete decriminalization of cannabis. 'Which means that all the people who have been previously jailed will be expunged, too.' Decriminalization would remove all criminal sanctions against the substance; even if ganja remains illegal, a person using or possessing some amount wouldn't face criminal prosecution.

'The government is scared [of this process],' says Mishra, 'because many people have a taboo about it. But the prime minister has to say something on the open stage. If he can go through with demonetization, he can go through with decriminalization [of cannabis] too, can't he?'

The 2013 documentary *Goonj: The Empty Call*—directed by Adhiraj Bose and Nishad Sen and starring acting legend Naseeruddin Shah—explored the issues around cannabis cultivation in Parvati Valley. Shah begins by talking about India's democratic values, about the right to choose—and more specifically, India *not* guaranteeing this right for all of its citizens. 'If alcohol or nicotine—which are thought to be more harmful—can come under the purview of "personal choice", then why not charas?' Shah asks. The documentary further argues that if there is to be criminalization of the drug in the state, the local farmers need alternatives that should be at least as rewarding as cannabis.

And cannabis has numerous rewards, way beyond the recreational high. Like all living beings, the plant is much more than one thing. Depending on the specific part of the plant (flowers, leaves, or stems): it can be rolled-up and smoked, stirred into sweet summer beverages, dissolved into medicine as a painkiller, pickled as a dinner supplement, tied as a leash around the neck of cattle, or threaded into T-shirts.

In Kangra—a district in Himachal Pradesh about six hours' drive away from Kasol—a couple of cannabis activists found an unlikely use for the plant: sanitary pads. Until a few years ago, Haneesh Katnawer (a Kangra resident and former engineer) and Suman Sodha were volunteering to help with the Great Legalization Movement (GLM), the largest major initiative yet to lobby for cannabis legalization in India. Armed with this experience, Katnawer and Sodha found themselves back in Himachal Pradesh, looking for new possible applications for the plant. In 2021, they helped design the first 'Hemp Hut' in Kullu, made from the hemp fibre once removed from the longer stalks of the plant. They had realized that this clean, cheap, readily-available, and biodegradable substance could have a practical use for female hygiene products, too.

Hemp is resilient, moisture-absorbent, and anti-bacterial, and it would prove to be an ideal candidate. Katnawer and Sodha travelled from village to village, teaching women to stitch the sanitary pad and training them to train many more women in turn. At the time of the pandemic, their co-op organization also began to provide N95 face masks, stitched from cannabis fibre.

'We started looking at cannabis from a different perspective,' Katnawer told me over the phone. 'We wished to work with struggling marginalized communities here. So many are getting jailed because of their involvement in cannabis.

'It was important for us to show that there are alternative ways to use the plant.'

Malana is rinsed from the recent rain showers. The rickety wooden structures are gleaming under the morning mist. The painted homes offer a dim glow of colour: reds, pinks, and light blues. When the fog clears to let the afternoon sun shine down, many men who are here for construction projects walk to the town square to bask under the warm glow.

I take a chakkar around the main 'lower' village and some of the farms, greet the villagers, and drift away again.

On the trek down, I make a stop at the thukpa and Maggi spot I had seen earlier. Upon closer inspection, I notice that on the shop's sign—next to the illustrated face of a chubby, moustachioed chef—are the following words written in marker pen: 'No Entery: Out of Countrey Pepol in Resturent.... Only Indian Entry in Resturent'. The same messages are repeated elsewhere on the sign, underlined, and circled. Then, written in Hindi, too: 'Angrez ko aana sakht mana hai'.

I'm shocked by this striking, open call for segregation. But I'm Indian, and I'm hungry, so I order Maggi for myself. Make it a double. No added vegetables, just a little ketchup from that plastic squeezy bottle, with old ketchup residue sticking around its neck. There's a slight chill in the air, even as the warm sun rays have punctured their way down through the mist. And when I get that first taste of the piping hot noodle, the spicy odour cracks against the crisp afternoon breeze, and I'm transported back to my youth—as if the masala in the noodle* is my own version of Proust's madeleine, never failing to evoke the hungry little child in me. I'm back tasting that deliciously unhealthy gluten in primary

*Which may or may not be MSG; or my favourite desi-fied Japanese word: ajinomoto.

school in Varanasi; I'm back in my teenage years in Mussoorie, huddled around pots of Maggi and Wai Wai in the kitchen of my boarding school, sharing bites with my classmates; I'm a lazy adult, saving time and effort by mastering the easy art of boiling water for processed cup noodles, adding layers of stress to my digestive tract; I'm in a college canteen with my friends in Bhubaneswar; I'm at a highway dhaba in Punjab; I'm in a small Naga village. I have found such glimpses of capitalism even in the most far-flung parts of the country: packets of Maggi on the shelves, shop signs sponsored by Coca-Cola, giant hoardings advertising a matrimonial website endorsed by M. S. Dhoni, highways to nearly every district, roads to nearly every city, motorbikes that can drive up to almost any village.

I end up spending about a week in Parvati Valley, and I often have no network connectivity on my phone. When I eventually upload the photographs from the trip on my computer, I name the folder 'Airplane Mode'. High in the mountains and disconnected.

But, a few years later, when I look up for Malana on social media again, there were live Instagram streams of tourists at the village. Every disconnect would soon be tethered. Every hint of mystique from this place of pioneering democratic sages and Alexandrian aspirations would be lost, withering under the heat of illumination. Until it became just another village in just another part of the country.

It's tempting to mystify Malana and its mythologies through the filter of the Cream. It's easy to see what attracts souls from all over the globe to the pleasant embrace of the Kullu district. The environment helps, of course, but the anandamide of the brain makes magical new connections under the effect of the local charas. Being stoned is a shortcut to real forms of mindfulness and meditation—to the oneness with the surroundings that Bodhisattvas seek, a feeling of being truly present in the *here* and the *now*, of breathing deep and separating oneself from all other superfluous sensory distractions. Sometimes, those distractions can be a creaking, aching spine, a sharp pain in the stomach, the tingling of a grave disease. Sometimes, those distractions can be the heavy burdens of life itself: of unfulfilled duties, of unatoned regrets.

For too long, I've been uncomfortable with these burdens, too. I spent many of my formative years in boarding school, and then, away from home in college. While this experience forced me to become self-sufficient early in my life, the self-sufficiency leaned heavily on the *self*; I was happy performing the bare minimum to be in charge of myself, and myself alone. While keeping intact some of the emotional connections with close family and friends, I refused to offer myself as a dependent, as someone who would be there for my loved ones when they needed me the most.

I've found it easy to stray away from family—a man's desperate attempts to leave the mainland, to become an island. Even in marriage, I had found someone who shared my sense of self-sufficiency, someone who *wanted* me in her life, but didn't *need* me in it. She would be fine—more or else—without me.

And then, our daughter was born.

Suddenly, I had to reckon with a wave of responsibility the size of a damn tsunami, threatening to uproot me from everything that made me, *me.* Here was someone that actually needed me to survive, to thrive, who needed to be nurtured, to be guided in the right direction, but to be allowed the space to make decisions of her own.

It was the first time that I could truly imagine the potential weight of my *absence.* As in, the father-shaped hole for every day that I would not be present in her life. I've had to leave the island, swim back to shore. Or, at least, learn to share the real estate on my island with a few more people.

And yet, I crave the occasional escape. Now, I still make time for those untethered freedoms, except that they have to be artificially manufactured. They are planned and scheduled, with a return date in sight, with a ringing alarm in my mind to ensure that I always remain cognizant of passing time.

Time dilation is usually the first sign that the 'high' has hit. On the strongest strains of the Cream, time seems to change—relativity in action—as the few seconds it takes you to read a sentence seem to stretch and expand under the force of an inner gravity, until you experience the light-speed firing of the neurons in slow motion, until it feels like you're in a waking dream, where the streaming services of what some believe to be the larger illusions of life—the Maya, the Matrix, the Simulation, whatever—briefly seem to pause, till each sound reverberates back within itself, where the recursive loops of the software code is laid bare, bugs and all.

Sometimes, cannabis makes us see the world as it really is, instead of through our individual filters. These are filters that tell us to ignore some truths for the greater good, the human defence mechanism that allows us to hold false beliefs, even in contradiction. These are our filters of self-deception.

But once the veneer of adventure wears off, once the high dips back down, one can't help but acknowledge the *ordinariness* of it all. One eventually seeks the high all over again—to recall that new perspective, to experience time and space through new senses. A hyperaware brain is wired like a chaotic chowk in an Indian marketplace: scooters and autorickshaws and cars and buses and pedestrians and bicycles and cows entangled haphazardly without order or direction, honking in panic, cursing and crashing, and still, always on the move. Sometimes, it helps to sweep the path clean. To glide down an empty highway, listening to soothing sitar music. To take a break from ourselves.

I've scraped my bowl of Maggi clean and now I'm back on my feet again, back on the path, leaving that cloud of mystique behind. Even for all its own unique customs and traditions, Malana is very much a real Indian village, with real human motivations and real challenges. It's a place of agriculture and worship and trade. It's a place where the young blast music on their mobile phones, where they aspire for life in bigger cities: for better educational opportunities, for stable jobs, for a chance to see the world they've already seen on their screens.

The imagined presence of Jamlu watches all. The village's protector-deity has been worshipped and exalted here for generations. When he is honoured with the gift of cannabis seeds, the villagers make a natural dalliance of Malana's spiritual and economic identities. For Malanis, Jamlu Devta has been a self-preservation mechanism, one that grants them some sovereignty to make their own decisions, and allows them to skew laws under the guise of faith.

Malana is but one, tiny village, but this guise of faith and spirituality has played a crucial part across India in its contradictory handling of the ganja issue. The substance that lands hundreds in jail is the same that is celebrated for its ties to spirituality. The plant that has gained notoriety in international smuggling rinks is the same consumed casually by many bhakts of Lord Shiva.

The gaze of the gods makes the gaze of the laws a lot more flexible.

In the scriptures, it was Shiva's advice that led Jamlu up to Malana. Now, leaving behind Jamlu's territory, it's Shiva's footsteps which I follow to the banks of the holy river, to understand the ancient theology and scriptures that still dictate India's response to cannabis, skewing time and history with each mind-mesmerizing puff from a chillum.

Vijaya

'...No gem or jewel can touch in value bhang, taken truly and reverently. He who drinks bhang drinks Shiva...'

With the sharp end of a small, crescent-shaped knife, he chops the ganja, quickly cutting the sticks off, letting the little seeds—each smaller than a grain of rice—fall to the ground. He lifts the remaining bud and rubs it in the palm of his hand (In Sanskrit, ganja* literally means 'compressed female buds'). The size of a small pebble and easy to conceal, he rolls and crumbles it like clay, or a piece of putty.

He rubs and kneads it all together strenuously with his right-hand thumb, until the disparate flower tops of the cannabis plant triturate into one muddy, beautiful mush, until the lines of his palm are further lined with the ganja's greenish residue. He packs this mush into the open chamber of the chillum.

The chillum is his smoking pipe, dark brown and made of some form of soft stone. It's about the length of the man's hand, and he wraps his long, wiry fingers around the conical tool. The man sits shirtless in the shade, a few feet away from the afternoon sun blazing down by the banks of the Ganga, here in the holy city of Haridwar. His hair is thick, long, and grey, forming serpentine coils over his head, and then down to his shoulders. The only item of clothing he wears is a plain white lungi draped around his waist. He is, however, decorated with a plethora of other accessories, from

*The Merriam-Webster dictionary defines ganja as 'a potent and selected preparation of marijuana used especially for smoking'.

the prayer mala around his neck to the gold rings on his fingers. The same fingers now grab the chillum as if it were a fat cigar, or a phallic lingam made in honour of Shiva.

There are other 'babas' like him who sit on the steps nearby, legs folded one over the other: two holy men to his right, one more to his left. There is a small brazier ahead of them, powered with wood and little blocks of burning coal, carrying soft fumes of smoke into the sky. The heat sends the sweat pouring down their chests, till their greyish chest hair begins to glisten. But they are unperturbed. Occasionally, one of them will get a beep on his mobile phone, creating a fantastic juxtaposition of asceticism and global connectivity. Sometimes, they smile or wave at passing faces. One of them keeps his eyes low, staring down below, as if he's looking into the earth in deep, silent contemplation.

Then, the baba with the chillum uses a pair of rusted, metal tongs to place a small piece of coal over the chamber, right above the ganja mush. He uses a piece of cloth about the size of a pocket handkerchief to wrap around the chillum's stem. He takes a deep breath, raises the chillum up in obeisance to the imagined Shiva, and utters out an honorary, magic mantra.

'Har Har Mahadev.'

It's ready.

He has one fist enveloped around the cloth, and the other hand below it to form a little tunnel of space to smoke through. He raises the pipe to his mouth and takes a long toke, *inhale*, and he holds it, and holds it, and then, follows it up with small exhales, out his nose and the sides of his mouth, each releasing wondrous grey puffs. His eyes dilate, his calm visage turns even calmer.

If I didn't know any better, I would have been completely perplexed: how is a clearly illegal substance being consumed so openly, by so many, and in full view of the authorities? In full view of the gods?

But I *do* know better—and here, the view of the gods easily supersedes the view of law enforcement. In India, such religious devotees are often offered a layer of protection under this smoky cloud.

The sadhu passes the chillum to his right.

It's hotter than usual this time of the year in Haridwar. There are a few dozen ascetics who walk naked, or near-naked (with just a thin lungi wrapped around their privates) towards the holy river. They blow conch shells and chant 'Har Har Mahadev' at the top of their lungs. Some of them thrust swords up into the sky, and many take deep inhales of their chillums before generously passing the ganja to whoever walks beside them. Many of them have painted their faces and bodies ashy white. Some devotees sit around the temporary encampments near the river. Prayer materials—from photos of Shiva to beads to bronze plates and turmeric powder—lie around them, close to the burning brazier. Orange flags wave in the breeze. Ganja smoke sweetens the air. Sometimes, a helicopter passes low above the city's old streets, a surreal sight, showering fragrant marigold and jasmine flowers. Pilgrims take a ceremonial dip in the river. Devotional music blares out of the speakers.

The crowds keep growing, bigger and bigger, until there is hardly any room to walk, hardly any room to breathe. Most of the inner lanes of the city are open only to foot traffic. All the hotels and dharmshalas in town are packed to the brim. Visitors drudge along for hours among the dense crowd, with barely enough space to step forward, as they slowly head towards the river.

It was the season of spring festivals. Yellow flowers and kites in Punjab for Vasant Panchami. The bamboo dance after harvest, as Mizoram celebrated Chapchar Kut. Mango leaves and rangoli patterns that welcomed visitors in households in Karnataka during Ugadi. Myoko in Arunachal, Shigmo in Goa, Gangaur in Rajasthan, all leading up to the great North Indian festival—

Holi—when there would be a rave of colours, a fiesta in honour of birth, growth, and the gift of life.

But in 2021, this season of life-giving colours was blotted with the urgent red splatter of death. The second wave of the Covid-19 pandemic punished India unlike any other tragedy in recent history. Reports claimed that over 2.5 lakh lost their life in the spring and summer of 2021—but it is widely accepted that the real toll of Covid-related deaths was much higher than the skewed official counts. Up to ten times higher. Patients took their last breaths on stretchers outside hospitals in Delhi, waiting for a bed that would never be available. For those at the frontlines—doctors, nurses, ambulance drivers, emergency services—there was hardly any rest. Families said goodbye to their loved ones on video calls or from behind the imperious wall of cold glass barriers.

When the government failed to provide the most basic of requirements—oxygen—citizens did what they do best in our country (or what they do worst, depending on one's privilege and perspective): they took matters into their own hands. They hustled for oxygen cylinders and tussled for oxygen concentrators. Social media was flooded with urgent requests for blood and oxygen. For once, Facebook had more obituaries than conspiracy theories. There were retweets hashtagged with the name of the nearest major town and the eerie alphabets of blood types. *Help, if you can!* Crematoriums ran out of firewood. Kabristans and graveyards fell short of space to bury the dead. Hundreds of discarded bodies floated up to the banks of the Ganga, swollen corpses on the swelling river.

Corpses? No. People. Fathers and mothers, husbands and wives, children and friends, lives unfulfilled.

We all lost someone.

And it was at the precipice of this incoming, infectious disaster that India once again hosted the largest-ever gathering of humanity, the Kumbh Mela, that saw the pilgrimage town of Haridwar—also by the banks of the Ganga—inundated by over 9 million visitors.

The Kumbh Mela is a major Hindu festival, held every twelve years at four holy riverbanks across India: Prayagraj,* Nashik, Ujjain, and Haridwar. Pilgrims believe that the sins of all those who bathe in the rivers here are cleansed, providing a means to prayascitta (atonement) for past mistakes. The exact date of the Kumbh is determined by astrological movements; it was the same astrological rationale that actually preponed the Kumbh by a whole year—to 2021 instead of 2022—when 'Jupiter moved to Aquarius and the Sun entered Aries'.

It wasn't just the astrologers who were appeased by this decision: the Haridwar fair was also a precursor to the legislative assembly elections in the states of Uttarakhand and Uttar Pradesh. The rest of the country went back into lockdowns, distanced from each other, spending each night in anxious hope that they and their loved ones will make it through this spring of sadness, sleeping to the searing sirens of ambulances rushing past all night. Meanwhile, this mela of millions kicked off as planned.

The Haridwar Kumbh turned out to be a major super-spreader event. Two weeks into the fair, more than 2,000 attendees had already tested positive. Many returned home carrying the virus, and soon, the spread accelerated around the country. It was when India's healthcare infrastructure began to suffer a catastrophic collapse that the prime minister finally pleaded attendees to mark the rest of the mela as only a 'symbolic' event. The congregation ended soon after.

Under the commanding dogma of religion and ancient customs, scientific reasoning hardly had a chance.

The Kumbh Mela is credited to the eighth century philosopher Adi Shankara, who was said to institute large religious gatherings to promote scholarly discussion and debate. With a few exceptions, various forms of this mela have been a staple of the Hindu astrological cycle for over a millennium. But the myth of the Kumbh

---

*RIP Allahabad. You had a good run.

goes back even further in the story of Indian history. These myths are the reason why, even today, as holy men camp alongside the banks of the Ganga, a smell of purifying incense and jasmine flowers comes infused with that magnetic, strong stench of ganja. These myths ensure that the drinking of ceremonial bhang remains an important component of religious custom. It is this force of ancient mythology that continues to seep into modern Indian culture: sometimes enriching it, sometimes haunting it.

It's a story worthy of the greatest superhero cinematic universe.

First, there were the great celestial battles. Gods vs antigods, devas vs asuras. And like Thanos overpowering the Avengers in *Infinity War*, Mahabali led the asuras to a victory over the gods. After the violence came diplomatic negotiations, and Vishnu—the Preserver—suggested that the devas come to a cordial understanding with their eternal rivals. It was decided that both sides would join forces to churn the great Ocean of Milk of Hindu cosmology, Kshira Sagara. Its purpose was to yield amrit, the super-drink, the great elixir of immortality. This churning—known as the Samudra Manthana—would become one of the most consequential events in ancient Indian mythology.

But there was a side effect. The churning also produced a lethal poison, halahala, otherwise known as kalakuta (black mass)*. In another version of the story, the poison was released from the mouth of the serpent king while the devas and asuras were busy with the Great Churning. The halahala produced toxic fumes, polluting the air, choking even the eternal superbeings; it was the type of toxin with the power to destroy all that existed in the universe.

*Honestly, halahala is the most badass word for 'poison' in any known language, the second-most badass being kalakuta.

It was in the face of this doom that the gods turned to Shiva, the all-powerful god of destruction himself, burdened with the divine responsibility of ensuring that the wheel of time keeps spinning. Shiva saw the poison and didn't flinch: he consumed the halahala, saving all of creation in the process. The venom drenched his throat with a blue hue; he's been known as Neelkantha (the blue-throated one) ever since.

Thanks to Shiva's valour, the battling celestials could shift their attention back to the amrit. The god of medicine—Dhanvantari—appeared with a kumbha (vessel, or womb) to carry the amrit away. The temporarily-reconciled devas and asuras turned foes again, setting off into another mighty battle. The devas turned to the eagle-like divine bird Garuda to fly away with the nectar of immortality; their aim was to drink the nectar all by themselves.* No sharing with the antigods.

Garuda's escape, however, was not without an incident. Some say that four drops of amrit spilled on Earth from the kumbha at four different places: Haridwar, Prayagraj, Trimbak, and Ujjain. Some say that the gods *chose* to temporarily hide the kumbha—with its nectar of immortality—in these locations. The four spots hence became the four destinations of the Kumbh Mela, originating the belief that a bath by the river here will grant immortality beyond the Hindu cycle of rebirths—that is, immortality beyond the painful curse of mortal life. True moksha.** Nirvana.

The spot where the amrit fell in Haridwar is called Brahma Kund, right by the popular Har ki Pauri (Footsteps of the Lord) ghat. It is perhaps the most sacred place in the city. It's also in a near-constant state of mania, a crowded festival of devotees chattering and bathing. Crowds walk past the wet stone slabs near the river,

---

*One of the greatest things about ancient Indian mythology is that there is little ethical distinction between the good and the bad, gods and demons, asuras and devas.

**'Moksha' is also the name Aldous Huxley gave to a fictional mind-expanding psychoactive substance he invented for his novel *Island.*

or across the muddy banks of the water, passing by leftover food and prayer flowers that have been casually strewn away. There are hawkers selling balloons, snack carts offering golgappas and chhole-puri, elder Brahmins holding the audience of their young devotees, beggars asking for alms, and many naked bodies, unashamed of their warts and scars and portly paunches, all here to experience the divine.

Back to our story: Garuda had taken off with the amrit. But there was still the problem of Shiva's throat, burning bright blue with halahala. One of the attempts to cool this burning involved a special jari booti, a herbal cocktail grown and cultivated from the cannabis plants of our very Himalaya: bhang.

One version of the story claims that the spilled amrit led directly to the creation of the hemp plant, a miraculous impregnation of the Earth. In his 1893–94 paper 'On References to the Hemp Plant Occurring in Sanskrit and Hindi Literature,' the Irish administrator and linguist in British India, George Abraham Grierson, wrote:

> [Cannabis]...was originally produced, like nectar from the ocean by the churning with Mount Mandara, and inasmuch as it gives victory in the three worlds, it, the delight of the king of the gods, is called Vijaya, the victorious. This desire-fulfilling drug was obtained by men on the earth, through desire for the welfare of all people.

There is another ancient narrative that celebrates Shiva's tryst with cannabis, a story more suited to a light-hearted comedy rather than a summer blockbuster. The mahadeva needed some time off from his family after an argument.* He wandered into a field, and—exhausted from the hot sun—slept under a cannabis plant. When he woke up, he tried a little bit of the fresh ganja and was rejuvenated. The experience changed his immortal life. Cannabis

*I'm not saying that I don't relate.

became his favourite little avocation, and thus, the favourite of every Shiva superfan (Shaivite). Shiva is known as a god of immense strength—sometimes, even dangerous strength—and it has been believed that the discovery of cannabis helped him focus his powers better, to harness it for the good of the cosmos.

Man creates god in his image. And the men who created the mythologies of Shiva found in this deity the perfect do-everything toolkit, a Swiss Army Knife Superhero, a Transformer that could sometimes morph into a cosmic dancer (Nataraja) and sometimes a wayward beggar. Sometimes he is the lord of cattle (Pashupata), and sometimes he takes an androgynous form (Ardhanarishvara). His mythology has been continuously customized and updated—a Wikipedia page of unlimited edits and almost no verification checks—until he became the type of god that allows everyone to attribute whatever they wish to him. And thus, they attribute whatever they wish upon themselves, too. If Shiva does it, then it's the right, dharmic thing to do—and Shiva does absolutely everything right.

Shiva is also considered by many to be the lord of hippies and stoners, of bhang trips that lead one into intense bouts of self-reflection and meditation, of the 'Sadhu Baba' stereotype that includes near-naked ascetics seated by the riverside, hair knotted in unwashed dreads, a life spent watching life pass by with the words 'Bam Bhole' or 'Har Har Mahadev' on their lips before taking each long puff of marijuana from their chillums. There is even a popular rolling paper brand in India called 'Shivaay' named after him.

In his 'Note on the Religion of Hemp' as part of the report of the Indian Hemp Drugs Commission (1893–94), James M. Campbell, the CIE, Collector of Land Revenue and Customs and Opium, Bombay wrote on this subject:

> The Hindu poet* of Shiva; the Great Spirit that living in bhang passes into the drinker, sings of bhang as the clearer of ignorance, the giver of knowledge. No gem or jewel can touch in value bhang taken truly and reverently. He who drinks bhang drinks Shiva... The mere sight of bhang cleanses from as much sin as a thousand horse-sacrifices or a thousand pilgrimages... He who drinks wisely and according to rule, be lie ever so low, even though his body is smeared with human ordure and urine, is Shiva. No god or man is as good as the religious drinker of bhang.

In my hometown Varanasi, a city Shiva allegedly promised never to desert, religious festivals are often celebrated with a mind-altering trip in homage to the great stoner-god. Holi is incomplete without celebratory gulps of bhang-infused lassi or thandai drinks. Shivratri—the Night of Shiva—is another festival celebrated with much pomp among Shaivites. Some fast on the day, some meditate, some worship Shiva's lingam, and some get really, really high. For many yogis and ascetics, bhang serves not as a drug of delusion but a medicinal supplement to strengthen their focus, to aid one's concentration in the art of meditation, to clear one's mind completely, to get in touch with that slippery spark of divinity. To be Shiva.

American psychiatrist Timmen L. Cermak, who specializes in addiction medicine, wrote for *Psychology Today* about his visit to India, and learning about how mythologies around Shiva shed light on the relationship between marijuana and the mind:

> The world, including ourselves, is in constant flux, constant reformation through destruction and recreation. All learning is a process of unlearning and relearning, forgetting and gathering new experience. Shiva [the destroyer and creator of Hindu mythology] symbolizes this constant flux.

*Of course, he's also the god of poetry.

> Because endocannabinoid receptors are concentrated in specific brain areas, THC especially alters our experience of memory, appetites, time, emotions, and very importantly our sense of novelty and awe. Sights, sounds, and ideas are perceived with an added sense of newness, as though never seen before (jamais vu). Routine stimuli are perceived differently, like how a black light illuminates a poster differently. A rose is just another rose until its unique fragrance and stunning color are attended to and absorbed. Synesthesia, the flowing of perceptions from one sensory system into others, spreads visual and auditory stimuli through the body as thrilling kinesthetic energy. For example, unexpected electronic notes in Pink Floyd's music can resonate beyond mere sound into bodily sensations.

Now, lest the other deities feel a little left out, Shiva isn't the only god to be associated with bhang. As popular mythologist Devdutt Pattanaik has pointed out, offering or using bhang is part of many rituals at Vishnu temples around the country. When I visited Puri, a coastal city in Odisha popular for the Jagannath temple (Jagannath is considered to be an avatar of Vishnu), I saw that bhang was sold legally in government-approved shops, and that many openly consumed cannabis around the older parts of town. Sites associated with Krishna—another avatar of Vishnu—like his hometown Mathura or the city of Nathdwara also offer bhang with government (and spiritual) approval.

And then there's Krishna's elder brother Balarama—the god of architecture and farming—who is often depicted with a naga (serpent) and farm-related items like a plough and a watering pot. It is traditional for the Balarama statue in Puri (and elsewhere) to be bathed with bhang.

Bhang is popular among the customs of other religions in India, too. The Sikh Nihangs refer to cannabis as Sukhnidhaan, or Sukha parsad, which means 'giver of peace', consuming it especially during the Holi-adjacent festival of Hola Mohalla. The 1894 Indian Hemp Drugs Commission's report stated that the Sikh holy city of Amritsar is 'not only a great market for bhang as well as charas, but it is the headquarter of the Sikh religion, and the former drug is largely consumed by followers of that faith. It seems to be a regular drink or refreshment with the visitors to the Golden Temple.'

In Tantric Buddhism, the *Mahakala Tantra* prescribes cannabis and some other psychoactive plants for medicinal purposes.

Now, in the inevitability of ours being an incredibly online nation, there are websites from where one can legally order bhang, too, including in edible forms as cookies, chocolates, laddus, or just as powder.

This two-faced attitude towards cannabis—sometimes seen as a tipple for celebration and relief, sometimes as an unspeakable taboo—is just one of the many contradictions of modern-day India. We are a country that worships the same river that we routinely pollute, revere the same Himalayan ecosystem that we actively desecrate, where sexual freedoms are frowned upon, but Shiva's lingam—a delightfully rude phallic symbol—is erected in temples across the country and worshipped by millions. It's a nation where our educational institutions churn out geniuses of modern science and technology, while our politics and cultural practices remain enamoured with scriptures and mythologies from centuries ago.

One of those scriptures is the Atharva Veda, a collection of 730 hymns divided into twenty books, all comprising to make one of the most important spiritual storehouses of knowledge, which continues to influence modern spirituality over 3,000 years after they were first conceived. (Composed in Vedic Sanskrit, the Vedas are some of the oldest scriptures in Hinduism, and among the oldest surviving scriptures of any kind.) Sometimes called the 'Veda of magical formulas', the Atharva Veda—likely compiled around 1200–1000 BCE—is so much more, filled with instructions of rituals of lifestyle and worship, with philosophy and incantations, with recipes for herbal medicine and potions to cure maladies both human and divine.

These texts are really, *really* old. Older than the Iron Age, older than the *Iliad* and the *Odyssey.* Like the other Vedas the Atharva was mainly composed by groups of rishis. The roots of Ayurveda—an alternative system of Indian traditional medicine and healthcare—are also credited to this scripture.

And it is among this treasure trove of knowledge where one finds the most explicit salutation of our cherished cannabis plant. In Hymn 6 of the Atharva Veda—a hymn translated to English as 'A prayer to all Divinities and Sanctities for deliverance from distress'—Verse 15 states:

> पञ्च राज्यानि वीरुधां सोमश्रेष्ठानि ब्रूमः।
> भर्गो भङ्गो यवः सह ते नो मुञ्चन्त्व् अंहसः ॥
>
> To the five kingdoms of the plants which Soma rules as Lord we speak.
>
> Darbha, hemp, barley, mighty power: may these deliver us from woe.

The Sanskrit word 'भङ्ग' above was translated as 'hemp' by Ralph T. H. Griffith, but any reader of the Devanagari script can see that it actually reads as 'bhang'.

The verse references the drink of soma, a mythical nectar of immortality considered to be a synonym of amrit.* Soma, here, is crowned as the ruler of the 'five kingdoms' of these great plants, a list that includes darbha (*Desmostachya bipinnata*, a sacred natural preservative), bhang, barley, and sahas (a word that literally translates as power/courage; but the exact identity of this plant remains unknown). All five of these herbal supplements—real or imagined—

---

*So, for those keeping count at home, the elixirs of immortality are amrit/soma, the deadly poison is halahala/kalakuta, and the refreshing drink of relief and joy is bhang (cannabis).

were meant to 'deliver us from woe'.

(Soma would later be popularized in English literature by Aldous Huxley in his classic dystopian 1932 novel *Brave New World*, where it is used as a recreational drug to numb citizens into frivolous joy and complacency.)

If being in the council of these five sacred plants isn't enough, cannabis was also exalted with a worthy designation: vijaya. The word—which means conquest, victory, or triumph in Sanskrit—was the name given to Arjuna's chariot in the Mahabharata. Some Sanskrit dictionaries have defined vijaya as: 'Cannabis Sativa...or the tops of the plant used as a narcotic.'

Thus, marijuana isn't just the deliverer of joy and the vanquisher of foes—it is also, literally, related to the grand celebration of victory.

In a 2021 essay arguing for the legalization and taxation of cannabis, bestselling mythological fiction writer Ashwin Sanghi mentioned that, during the tenth century CE, cannabis was called the 'food of the gods'. In Indian culture and scripture, the intoxicating bud has been given a number of other pet names, including: siddhi (accomplishment/attainment), virapatia (hero-leaved), capta (light-hearted), trilok kamaya (desired in all thrarshinis), harshini (rejoiced), and, of course, ananda (bliss). Hindu medicinal books have also given this plant a plethora of adoring alternative 'urfs', including bahuvidini, madika, madini, madu, ranjika, and on and on. Each name describes a plant that was much beloved—and one that left its users with a feeling of victory and joy.

In February 2017, Gujarat became one of the latest states to legalize bhang by removing it from the list of 'intoxicating drugs' covered by section 23 of its Prohibition Act. Pradipsinh Jadeja, the state's minister for Home and Prohibition said:

> Bhang is consumed only as prasad of Lord Shiva. The state government has received complaints of misuse of prohibition act against those found drinking bhang. Hence, keeping

> in view the sentiments of public at large, the government has decided to exempt bhang from the ambit of Gujarat Prohibition Amendment Act. *Bhang is less intoxicating as compared to Ganja*!*

With the Vedas and victory in mind, law student Prashant Sharma submitted a petition in July 2019 to the Delhi High Court, seeking direction from the authorities to allow the medical use of *all* forms of cannabis. 'In certain Vedic rituals,' the plea noted, 'cannabis stems were thrown into the yagna (ritual fire) to overcome enemies and evil forces. According to Vedas, cannabis is referred as a source of happiness, joy giver and liberator.'

The petition was dismissed.

And so, this tossing and turning continues in modern India, where our view towards the plant takes a step back for every step forward. This push and pull causes a modern-day churning of its own, much akin to the churning that the gods and antigods tussled with in the mythological tales.

That nectar of immortality—amrit—remains elusive; but in cannabis, our earth blessed us with a worthy consolation prize.

I can't hear the word 'amrit' without thinking of my grandfather.

Born in 1930 to a Hindu family based in Gujranwala—now in Pakistan—Amrit Lal Madhok migrated with his family in 1947, the summer of India's Independence and Partition. His family was among the millions of Hindus and Sikhs that crossed the border to India, while millions of Muslims drifted the other way to Pakistan, and to the country that has since become Bangladesh. Estimates say more than a million people died in the riots and genocide on all sides of the border during the year that followed Independence.

---

*Emphasis (and surprise) mine.

A teenaged Amrit and his family, however, survived to make it to Kandaghat.

For tens of millions of South Asians like me, this is a familiar origin story. And like so many, Amrit was raised by the burden of this violence—but also with the spirit of freedom and survival—as he restarted his displaced life as a stranger in a new republic.

Amrit's household was enriched with poetry and art, and he carried the love of Urdu sher-o-shayari with him his whole life. Later, the poetic tradition influenced his academic and professional decisions too: he studied Persian language and History in the 1950s and was eventually sent to Tehran (Iran) to learn and teach the language. Upon his return to India in the 60s, Amrit, his wife, and children, moved to Varanasi where he received a PhD at the Banaras Hindu University (BHU) and became a professor of Persian, Persian History, and Urdu.

It was in his forays as a poet, however, that Amrit adopted what many Urdu shayars call a takhallus, a nom de plume: Ishrat. Ishrat is an Urdu term that translates as 'joy' or 'delight'. My grandfather immersed himself into the more epicurean pleasures of life—particularly music, poetry, and alcohol—and his addictions became both the art that lifted him and the burdens that were borne in his verses. He published nearly a dozen books in his lifetime on Iranian history, literary criticism, and Urdu shayari. Outside of his academic work, he published his ghazals in Urdu literary magazines.

Amrit had chosen ishrat and ananda, two terms in Urdu and Sanskrit respectively that convey similar emotions. It was also a marriage of the Ganga–Jamuna Tehzeeb of Hindu and Islamic language and culture that my grandfather cherished and celebrated. Even today, an inter-faith mushaira is regularly held in Varanasi in his honour, bringing together many of the country's best shayars—from all religions—for a social gathering of ghazal, poetry, and humour.

Ishrat died in 1989 in his late fifties; the last five years of his life were the first five years of mine. Nearly thirty years after his death, I translated some of his ghazals into English for the first time. His poetry continues to give him life after life, an immortal amrit through verse.

No, he isn't exactly the reason why I yearn for ananda—but my grandfather confirmed that this yearning runs in our blood.

I come from an upper-caste and relatively progressive Hindu/ Sikh household. Religion was introduced but not enforced. Social drinking was the norm, while smoking cigarettes was considered taboo. The uncles and friends who smoked at social occasions were tolerated, but frowned upon. Anything deemed a narcotic was an unthinkable offence.

Growing up, I remember the plots of many Bollywood films featuring stereotypical notorious villains whose primary vocation was to smuggle 'brown sugar' (heroin) and be a general menace to society. My earliest exposure to ganja or charas was somewhat influenced by the popular 1971 song 'Dum Maro Dum' from Dev Anand's *Haré Rama Haré Krishna*. Watching the old clips of actress Zeenat Aman in a den of smokers and hippies, ganja felt like a choice that accompanied a vagrant way of life. This perspective was further confirmed by the actual sadhus, vagrants, and foreign hippies I would see around the old gullies and ghats in Varanasi: a chillum in hand, smoke in the air, long tangled hair.

Now, these scenes find their urban parallel in the bedrooms of many young Indians, passing joints with one hand and gaming on their mobile phones with the other. Ashtrays overflowing with cigarette butts and spliffs, empty bottles of Kingfisher Strong that became ashtrays, too, bongs containing stale green water, lighters lost between cushion seats, empty packets of potato chips, and half-torn visiting cards that make for the best roach material. Smoke clouds the room, hardly anyone moves, hardly anyone speaks. Complete bliss.

Well, *some* may call it bliss; my father, a workaholic who is forever haunted by the *drip-drip-drip* of time's hourglass, would call it a waste of a life.

The Atharva Veda is considered a scripture for the Hindu religion, much like the other Vedas, as well as the Upanishads, Puranas, Itahasa, Manusmriti, the epics of Ramayana, Mahabharata (which includes the Bhagavad Gita), and more. The spiritual significance of these texts is in itself an ephemeral concept; Hinduism isn't one religion but a conglomerate of a thousand different ways of life and beliefs rooted in the subcontinent, all of which just happened to be forced under the same umbrella a few hundred years ago to formulate an easy definition of who a Hindu is—and who a Hindu *isn't*.

But once a religion has been created, denoted, and politicized, there's no looking back, is there? And in the context of religion, the word 'scripture' is granted magical superpowers: the power to build and destroy communities, the power to define social structure and class, the power to create laws and topple governments. It doesn't matter how outdated, insignificant, or dangerous the scriptures might be; if they're ancient, they're untouchable.

To me, this rationale has never made sense. Despite growing up in the city of temples—or perhaps *because* of the heavy weight of religiosity shackling Varanasi around its ancient ankles—I grew up questioning the idea of divinity, of religion, and the gods. My encounters with different faiths had me wondering if any organized religion could truly answer all the questions about the universe, about why something exists—rather than nothing at all. And here I was in the heartland of Hinduism—in one of the world's oldest and continuously lived-in cities—and the unquestioning dogma of these ancient rules could only make me wonder...*is this really all there is?*

If the scriptures say so, must it be true?

Hinduism is the most weed-friendly of the world's major

religions. But, if it says in the Atharva Veda that bhang is a magical herb, then must we simply accept it as so? If the ancient stories narrate to us that Shiva turned to cannabis after saving the universe, is that enough reason for the rest of us to do the same? There has hardly seemed to be any need for further logical assessment: the scriptures gave us all the excuses we ever needed.

In my travels and interviews while researching cannabis in India, I met several individuals fighting for its legalization: activists who seek to protect unjustly imprisoned villagers and tribals, industrialists hoping to swipe a share of the massive potential profits of hemp, and healthcare practitioners propagating the plant's considerable medical benefits. And far too often, the proponents of the plant evoked the spiritual excuse—*it was written in the Vedas*—to support their argument.

I've almost had to defamiliarize myself from the tendencies of my own country, to the Indianisms I have so far taken for granted. I've come to digest the scriptures more as a history of mythology, rather than strict and meticulously written instructions on how to live a spiritual life. It's clear that the benefits of cannabis have been recognized and celebrated for almost as long as we have had recorded human civilization. It is undeniably fascinating that the forefathers dignified 'vijaya' in its many forms—and it is proof that our modern taboo towards the plant is all a grand mistake.

We live in a country where many modern laws continue to reference back to the shastras. The story of the churning is partly responsible for the exemption of bhang from the NDPS Act; it's also this story which helped create our willing deference to anti-science customs, customs that allowed an event like the Kumbh Mela to be held at the height of a national healthcare crisis. It is the delusion that now sees citizens clashing over scraps of supposedly holy land, and the same delusions that turn any confident forward movement of India into reverse gear.

We are always rewinding far into the past for reason, for blame.

Back to previous governments, back to colonial rule, to the Mughals, the Indo-Aryans, to words written and uttered eons ago.

It just so happens that most of the best weed in India is found near the abodes of god.

I visit Haridwar for the second time a year after the Kumbh. This is a city completely devoted to the spiritual aspect of tourism, from the big statues of Shiva greeting visitors at the train station to the strictly vegetarian decree for food across town. By the ghats of the river, half-naked and fully naked adults take a dip, being cleansed by and sullying the same patch of water. The main ghats here are much cleaner than the ones I'm familiar with in Varanasi; people visit with the explicit purpose to swim, change, and encamp nearby. Men, women, and children take a big dip and jump back up, with excited smiles on their drenched faces, almost akin to scenes from a Christian immersion baptism.

There are holy men by the ghats here, taking in deep puffs from their chillums, for whom the very first hit will be enough to jettison them away, like a rocket being propelled by an explosion of colours. The THC from the smoke will go down into their lungs, seep into their bloodstreams, and flow up to their brains, where it will successfully emulate the chemical structure of anandamide. A heightened feeling, an elevation of self.

If the stuff is strong enough, the real 'reward' is what will follow. The most potent strains of cannabis can reshuffle one's relationship with time, providing a desired break from the regularly scheduled programming of life. The rest of the world moves along as it has always done; but internally, one feels like the distances between moments have been further separated into infinitely smaller moments. It's not that we physically move slower than usual; we are instead able to grasp hold of these microseconds—between seconds—that we otherwise take for granted. We fastidiously experience each iteration of forward motion from the present, into each immediate future. Vivacious vivace music slackens to a lazy lento; speech is long-winded and distorted. One catches the distance between sounds, between the splash of the oar hitting the water, the long descent into the underwater world, its cheery escalation, the smooth skim of the blade over the Ganga's surface, then repeat, then repeat.

Time is stretched, allowing one to dive inside, to drown in the river of time; not desperate for air, but happy to explore, to revel in this distortion. Reality moves forward frame by frame, like watching clips of a motion-capture film that make the larger movie come together.

In Buddhist philosophy, the definition of life is often given as the change of one unalterable moment after another: normally, our species moves along at a brisk pace, hardly noticing the small increments of these changes; but with our brain fused with this new release of anandamide, we confront our consciousness and our morality at each step, experiencing each change, beat by beat. It's as if the atomic structure of the world has been fully revealed, as if the smoker themselves—glowing with an inner phosphorescence—has pulled apart dark matter and nestled into its nooks, crannies, and gullies.

It can be frightening. It can also be enlightening.

The ascetic hands the chillum to the man on their right, like a bewitched baton. The seconds that pass feel like forever. And another day so passes.

For some habitual users of cannabis, the high can become all there is. There's no low any more, just a gliding volplane, or Garuda soaring comfortably over the earth. A threshold gets crossed, and a return journey becomes near-impossible. It's the new forever normal. The focus falls on the slight uptake in the mild summer breeze, instead of the larger passing season. A whole Mahabharata in the mind, a brief history of humanity and civilization, every damn night.

How can a mere plant produce such magic? Cannabis is a form of weed, the type of plant that can grow almost anywhere without human intention or interference. But the weed doesn't merely transform into psychoactive cannabis—smokable, edible—by accident. In Haridwar, the maal that ends up getting stuffed into the chillums of recreational users likely stems from the vast acres of land in the fertile Himalayan foothills elsewhere in the state, from hidden green fields in rural regions, cultivated by a legion of local farmers, cut and pressed and sold to drifting middlemen, transported across district and state lines, into the hands of legal bhang outlets or street-level dealers, before it's purchased by consumers, where one life cycle is smoked away, and another one begins in the smoky vapours.

Big Bhang Theory

'...It grows everywhere, and it grows however the hell it wishes to grow, wild and untamed by farm-hands and lab-coats, free even from the destructive interference of wild animals, uncaring for your human designations of percentage points and legal acts...'

It had been an extended period of penance as I waited for the right season of harvest, for the ideal village in the ideal valley, to earn the trust of the guides shepherding me forward. It had been a long drive further away from urban civilization, a trek up another hill, and a hidden crevice by the hillside that took us on a detour and back up under the sun again.

And then, I arrive at the motherlode.

Acres upon acres of the greenest, cleanest weed I have ever seen, over bugyals (meadows) coruscating golden in reflection under the afternoon sun, stems that are ten, twelve feet tall, with leaves and buds that bloom above to even greater heights. The meadow is surrounded by glaciers, resting at an altitude of over 2,100 metres above sea level. Each plant here in Uttarakhand's Urgam Valley is generously well-endowed, grown naturally with little or no human interference, with flowering tops of the female plants so rich with trichomes that one can hardly help but simply reach over and rub a little resin off.

Praveen,* the 'bhang collector' who has led us here, tells me that the local maal is called sulfa. He tells me that it's the best in the state of Uttarakhand. I'm aware that it's some of the best in the world.

*Not his real name—I'm not telling you that.

I can hardly believe that I made it. Accompanying me today are a half dozen college students from Mumbai—all nineteen, twenty-year-olds—who are staying in the district for a month-long study of the organic farming and social conditions of the region, as well as the potential of industrial hemp. At the meadow, some of the students rip off the leaves from the cannabis stems and take dramatic photographs with the great mountain ranges in the background. One of the young women makes an Instagram reel of the experience, enhanced with the soundtrack of the theme song to the Netflix series *Narcos*.

'You guys should cherish this,' I say, suddenly feeling like the responsible elder, giving an unsolicited advice to the youth. 'It's not the type of thing you'll get to see often in your lifetime.'

In 2016, Uttarakhand became the first Indian state to introduce a policy for the industrial farming of hemp. 'Hemp', for the practical purposes of this policy, is the low-THC version of the cannabis plant, the type that can potentially be used for industrial purposes—fibres for textiles, ropes, etc.,—rather than as an illicit, psychoactive substance. Growing in wild thick shrubs without much restraint across the hillside of this state, the crop is colloquially referred to as, simply, 'bhang' (not to be confused with the usage of bhang elsewhere in this book, referring to *only* the legal parts of the plant as defined by the NDPS Act).

Only farmers native to the state can procure a licence to legally grow industrial hemp in Uttarakhand. The license process, however, can often be a Kafkaesque headache of bureaucratic roadblocks, dead ends, and U-turns. Let's say, you, Dear Industrious Uttarakhandi Farmer, have found the right plot of land, paid off the right people, ordered the seeds, and now have that elusive hemp-farming licence in hand. It's a maze of trouble that you've had to suffer just to grow a plant that could grow naturally, without any active effort, in your own backyard. Well, there are more webs that await disentanglement. The new law in Uttarakhand is extremely specific: only varieties of the plant with less than 0.3 per cent THC are allowed to be legally grown, and only for 'industrial' purposes. The '0.3' number is borrowed from the Agricultural Improvement Act of 2018 of the US Department of Agriculture—which deemed that only a product sufficiently weak in THC would be free from the burden of being deemed a 'controlled substance' (i.e., an evil drug). Keep it below that miniscule amount, and you're helping to usher in an exciting new industrial revolution; go up to 0.4 per cent, and...Sorry bhai, you're now a mini drug kingpin.

The natural state of cannabis in this region is far more psychoactive, with THC levels reportedly between 5 to 10 per cent. Even for farmers with the best of intentions, it is damn near impossible to even determine if the seed will produce a low-THC crop, much less have any influence on lowering the THC levels themselves.

The sulfa that I discover in Urgam Valley is unrestricted by the shackles of policy and botanical chemistry. It's too strong to be legal; and yet, despite occasional crop destruction exercises by the local authorities, its existence is too persistent to be completely eradicated.

It had taken some convincing to urge Praveen to guide us up here. He—and many more in the villages below—are more paranoid than usual about any outsiders visiting to enquire about the popular local crop; just two weeks before my visit, there had been a police raid from the district headquarters, where many bhang crops were cut, fields were burned, and suspected farmers were arrested.

But, I wonder, how much could they possibly destroy? Cannabis grows everywhere here. Praveen tells me that wherever I see the droppings of a goat, I'll soon see a bhang plant.

And there's goat shit everywhere, too.

Uttarakhand was officially formed in 2000 when I was a teenager in Mussoorie, after being carved away from my state of birth, Uttar

Pradesh. In the decades since, there has been a mixed political and social reaction to this decision, but no one can deny that Uttarakhand—with its unique lifestyles, cultures, languages, and pilgrimage centres—has its own distinct identity.

I have returned to Mussoorie often as an adult; and yet, I felt that I had barely scratched the surface of this state. So, my journey to further discovery began at the crack of dawn in a cramped, bumpy jeep.

First, I'm driven to the sight of the slow-rising September sun from Mussoorie to the state's capital, Dehradun. Here, I catch a shared jeep near the railway station, which takes me nearly nine hours from the Garhwal region of Uttarakhand to the Chamoli district in Gairsain,* much further east. Nine hours are spent thus, as I ache to stretch my legs in the crowded middle row between other passengers. The driver blasts sappy Hindi and Garhwali love songs from his audio system. Usually, I would plug in my earphones to listen to my own music; but on this dusty, long journey, I can't help but nod my head and tap my feet to the car stereo, too. We drive across narrow highways that cut forward in a dizzying spiral, across the Himalayan peaks, on bridges crossing over holy rivers, and overtaking buses often filled with Hindu pilgrims touching bases of every holy shrine** on the way further ahead to Badrinath, which is one of the main pilgrimage stops of India's Char Dham (four abodes). A visit to all four of the dhams is supposed to guarantee moksha, salvation, release from the cycle of reincarnation, and the agonies of life.

A special highway has been under construction here for years to connect a great number of holy sites; for now, however, rubble

---

*There are three main administrative divisions in Uttarakhand: Garhwal, Gairsain, and Kumaon (west to east). Not all parts of the state are equally well-endowed with the ideal conditions for bhang.

**Uttarakhand is known as Devbhumi—the land of the gods—for the great number of Hindu pilgrimage sites across the state.

and broken roads greet us for major chunks of the journey, with multiple notices on road signs warning us of landslides raining down loose rocks over passing commuters.

The Chamoli district is also part of the Nanda Devi National Park—a UNESCO World Heritage Site—where, in February 2021, a large avalanche of rock and ice caused flooding across the district. Flash floods followed in the Rishiganga and Dhauliganga rivers, and across several dams and hydropower plants. The flooding left over 200 people in the state missing or dead, and is considered to be one of the biggest disasters to occur in the state since its creation.

This is a region highly vulnerable to the whims of nature, and the continuing human encroachment has only taunted nature's vicious backlash. Construction of highways, buildings, and the rise of footfall have made the conditions more perilous. Anthropogenic climate change has threatened the balance of the Himalayan ecosystem.

I visit Chamoli a year and a half after these floods. My stop is Pipalkoti, a town in this district by the banks of the Alaknanda River. It is here that I settle as my temporary home base for some local research and further exploration into nearby villages.

Pipalkoti is a highway town, serving mostly as a rest stop for the passing pilgrims. My primary contact here is the Alaknanda Ghati Shilpi (AAGAAS) Federation, a local NGO which has been working to help support the development of rural communities in the region, from disaster management and bio-tourism to organic farming and bamboo craftwork. For over a decade, their chairman/ founder Jagdamba Prasad Maithani has also been a major proponent of industrial hemp, and has helped support artisans and craftspeople who work with hemp-based fibre—a largely under-utilized natural resource.

I descend the rocky path on the side of the highway and down through a botanical garden, which leads the way to AAGAAS head office. Wild cannabis plants grow abundantly here on the hillside, a sight about as common as any wildflowers and millets.

Maithani, now in his late forties, was born in Pipalkoti. His father served in the 1962 Indo-China War, before finding himself stationed as a caretaker at Pipalkoti's PWD Dak Bungalow, one of the many British-era guest houses built in India's outposts for travelling dignitaries and officers. As a child, Maithani saw a variety of VIPs pass their way through this guest house, including former prime ministers Indira Gandhi, Morarji Desai, and V. P. Singh, as well as Edmund Hillary, one of the first men to scale Mount Everest. The experience was exciting, but, Maithani adds, seeing his father spend his years as a subordinate to higher authorities strengthened his own resolve to never work for anyone but himself. 'These VIPs used to seem very ghamandi (arrogant),' Maithani says. 'My father was a chowkidar at the guest house, and had to compromise a lot in front of them. So, in my mind a thought settled back then: I will not be a "Yes Boss" person. I decided I'll do my own work, no matter how small it might be.'

Years later, after securing his undergraduate and Master's degrees in Dehradun, any ambitions for crafting a life in a bigger city were interrupted by a calamity back home. In the spring of 1999, Pipalkoti and other regions in Chamoli were hit by a severe earthquake, one that took over a hundred lives and demolished thousands of homes. Maithani got involved with a local NGO to help generate employment for victims and survivors—and soon, his efforts gave birth to the AAGAAS Federation as it stands today.

Hemp, bhang, cannabis—whatever you wish to call it—was absolutely everywhere, nature's multipurpose gift. But for many like Maithani, there was an initial taboo towards the plant. The illicit business of bhang as an intoxicant—in the form of charas/sulfa—had already been active here for decades. 'When I was a kid,' says Maithani, 'the stereotype I understood of bhang is that it's only a nasha (intoxicant). The Pahadi people had a way of cursing someone, where they would say, "I hope that bhang weeds grow in your farm and destroy your other crops!" And if bhang grows in your farm, then it was assumed that you would be abusing it, and no one will be there to support your household any more.'

Maithani's perspective first shifted when he began to look for sources of fibre used by local villagers, many of whom were already in the trade of ringal basketry, a popular bamboo basket-making craft in Uttarakhand. Along with the local Himalayan nettle,* bhang surfaced as a surprising option. 'Then, around 2003–2004,' Maithani says. 'I came across shepherds in the snowy regions of the mountains. They were wearing shoes made of sheepskin, but the ropes around the shoes were made of bhang. I was shocked—*rope made of bhang?* I learned that it is used as the thread to wrap together the whole shoe. It is of sturdy quality and didn't slip in the glaciers and snow. It's called chhapet.

'Then, my mother told me that the genda (rope to tie around the neck of cattle) was also made of bhang. Of course, we knew that for some people there were cultural and religious connections, too.'

In conversation with others in town, I was also told that it had once been customary for the poorest residents in the region to wear clothes made from bhang. It was the cheapest option for many, and those clad in hemp textile were once called bhangali.

As Maithani gleaned more knowledge about the crop that grew copiously in his own backyards, he began to believe in what he calls the 'revolutionary scope' of hemp. Much of AAGAAS's work has been in trying to convince local farmers to understand that there is more than 'charas' to the cannabis plant. 'Why not sell the stem? The seeds, the fibre? All of these things have no THC issue.'

Local hemp, along with the Himalayan nettle, makes for much of the fibre that is regulated by Uttarakhand's Bamboo and Fibre Development Board. At the beginning of winter, the hemp itself

*Careful with this one; even a brush of nettle against one's skin can leave a painful sting for hours.

(the stem) is separated from the flowers of the cannabis plant. It is cut and chemically treated, till it takes the form of a semi-fibre. This is further cut and sent for 'combing', where the bits of fibres are separated. By spring, the fibre is ready to be made into thread, which will be used for weaving purposes. The fibre is sent off from Pipalkoti to a nearby village, Mangroli, where it is woven into baskets and other handloom, providing a steady vocation for locals—particularly women—from this region. A similar process of collection takes place for hemp in Bhagheshwar, Uttarkashi, and other areas in the state, too. When I visited the Fibre Development Board office and workshop in Pipalkoti, field coordinator Ashish Prasad told me that about 40 per cent of the collected hemp can be 'saved' for weaving. One kilo of hemp would make about 400 grams of thread—about a T-shirt's worth.

AAGAAS is involved in the earliest stages of this process, buying the hemp fibre or seeds from local farmers to resell to other organizations. The cost of seed, Maithani says, has increased three or four times in the past few years; the stem/fibre by almost ten times. 'The villagers used to burn the danthal (stalks) earlier for their chulhas at home,' he says. 'Now, even that is going for fifteen to twenty rupees a kilo. So naturally the farmers are seeing the potential. They're realizing that they don't need to do the "do number ka kaam" (selling the illegal parts of the plant) and still earn money.'

Maithani stresses that an environmental revolution could be ushered with a more liberalized policy on cannabis, too. Hemp is particularly successful in sequestering the carbon dioxide in the atmosphere; one hectare of industrial hemp absorbs twenty-two tonnes of CO_2 per hectare.

AAGAAS have also helped some farmers navigate the labyrinth of Indian bureaucracy to legally grow the plant. It's an expensive and complicated endeavour, even beyond the current licence fee of ₹1,500 per hectare, which can be applied for at the Centre for Aromatic Plants of Uttarakhand, the nodal agency for granting hemp farming licenses in the state. This agency, however, is only in the state's capital, Dehradun, an inconvenient distance (as I recently discovered myself) from other far and wide districts. Farmers must get a no objection certificate (NOC) from the forest department (even for their own private land). They have to chase down excise inspectors, contact patwaris (government officials) to conduct a survey of the land, and fill up a great deal of paperwork.

The Indian Industrial Hemp Association (IIHA) were the first to begin legal cultivation of industrial hemp in Uttarakhand. Since then, they and similar organizations have consulted for potential investors with some of the scientific background about the industry, including testing for cannabinoid content, soil and water analysis, quality testing, certification, etc.

For the common farmer, however, even getting the process started can cause a headache that not even the world's most-relaxing weed would help subside. Take the example of Dehradun-based Sanket Jain, a descendent of a family of farmers in Uttarakhand who once cultivated sugarcane, rice, wheat, and other regional crops. 'We belong to the Uttarkashi area,' says Jain in a phone interview, 'and in our district, during the snowy seasons when there are no other vegetables, people prepare a chutney made of bhang, mix it with lassoon (garlic), and eat it with chapatti. In the coldest couple of months of the year, this is the only option as a 'vegetable', and it has been very important for the survival of people there.' In some villages in the Garhwal region, many people use hemp seeds to season the food, as an alternative for salt or pepper.

Inspired by the potential of industrial hemp, and particularly his ambitions in hemp-based textiles, Jain applied for a cultivation licence in 2018. But he would soon be caught in the holds of a bureaucratic morass. For the next ten months, Jain's documentation was sent from the district collectorate to the district excise office, from where he needed a NOC, after which a letter was prepared and sent to six different departments, including excise again, the revenue office, and the forest department. The letter would be passed through the hands of more patwaris, and be subject to more inspections. Since the cannabis crop is not registered under the definition of 'horticulture' by the Department of Agriculture and Farmers Welfare, banks are more likely to refuse loans to farmers hoping to get started in their investments. There are no other government schemes offering targeted help specifically for hemp farmers. Then, there's the fear of the narcotics bureau, who could bring down their hammer at any wavering spike of THC. And, since India still doesn't have its own low-THC seed wildly available, farmers have to import the seeds from abroad, a process that requires permission from the Directorate of Plant Protection, Quarantine and Storage in Faridabad (Haryana), where a sampling of the seeds will be checked for defects and potential viruses that could infect India's indigenous crops. And only then, if the stars align and Lakshmi showers her blessings for the umpteenth time and Mercury is not in retrograde...import might be allowed.

Phew.

'There are many problems for the common man—the local farmer—who wants to be in the industry, but isn't able to grow the hemp,' says Jain. 'One needs time, resources, and money to go to every different department. The [hemp] policy came to Uttarakhand in 2016....' Eight years later, only a small number of people have been successful in getting the licence.

Jain spoke from experience of seeing how the government once helped farmers, like his own forefathers, get started in the sugarcane business. 'In the 1970s, when this industry began to flourish in India, the government had a full sugarcane policy, where they decided on a minimal sale price and gave hundreds of crores of rupees loan to people who wished to establish factories. When the government wants it to be so, things can happen in a smooth way. But right now, it's all moving at a very slow speed, and there is hardly any industrial hemp cultivation.'

I'd spoken to Jain in the winter of 2022, four years after he'd first applied for the licence. It took a little more patience and penance, until finally, in late 2023, Jain's company signed an MoU with the Veer Madho Singh Bhandari Uttarakhand Technical University to begin hemp cultivation on his patch of land near Bageshwar for industrial, medicinal, and research purposes.

India has usually been on the backfoot of such changes, taking the lead from foreign countries—particularly the US—instead of moving forward with the scientific reasoning that fits our own natural conditions. An increase in allowable THC percentage would make it easier for more of our indigenous, wild cannabis to be considered legal under the industrial guidelines.

Back at AAGAAS, Maithani believes that there is an urgent need for a new agrarian solution, and one of the first steps should be for Uttarakhand to have an officer solely appointed for the duty to oversee hemp licences. 'There should be one officer in-charge in each district, whose job is to have all the knowledge about bhang farming,' says Maithani, 'someone who understands that the farmers aren't just growing charas, someone who doesn't have his own feeling of a taboo. And of course, local policemen should have the knowledge, too, so they don't make trouble for legal hemp farmers.'

For the past several years, a new generation of villagers have abandoned their farms and homes in search of economic opportunities in urban regions, often working as day-labourers at construction sites or in the state's budding tourism industry. Hundreds (some say thousands) of villages in the state became 'ghost villages', with migration leaving behind a quiescent silence of padlocked homes, classrooms without children, and farms descending into decay.

At AAGAAS, I also meet one of Maithani's employees, Dilwar Singh Negi, who hails from a nearby village. Decked in an all-blue tracksuit, Negi is missing a left arm, which he had lost in a road accident after coming under a speeding truck. The accident left him with dwindling job opportunities, until he was employed by AAGAAS.

Negi offers me a handful of hemp seeds from a small plastic bag. 'From my village,' he says, and we both munch on it like I would eat from a packet of fried moong dal. It's tasteless, but—I'm told—excellent for my health.

Negi is one of the caretakers at the nursery here, and, like many from the region, is aware of his community's deep-rooted relationship with cannabis/hemp. 'The change in law has hardly helped the local people,' Negi says. 'There has been no difference to our lives. People from outside are coming in and grabbing our lands. All I care about is that our future generation of villagers and farmers come back home and find a reason to invest in the farms here.'

And yet, bureaucratic hurdles and legal misunderstandings have continued to delay the full potential of the industry. Out of the hundreds of farmers who approached AAGAAS, Maithani has been able to list only a few dozen from the state who have been successful in obtaining the hemp-cultivation license. According to the Department of Revenue, cultivation of cannabis without licence can lead to 'rigorous imprisonment' of up to ten years and a fine of up to ₹1 lakh. The 'production, manufacture, possession, sale, purchase, transport, import inter-state, export inter-state or use of narcotic drugs and psychotropic substances' also carries the penalty of a maximum six-month imprisonment, a ₹10,000 fine, or both, for what is defined as a 'small quantity'. Larger, 'commercial quantities' (defined as 1 kilo for charas and 20 kilos for ganja), can lead to 10–20 years in prison and a fine up to ₹1-2 lakhs.'

A little spike in THC can make all the difference. With fear of incarceration, financial penalties, and the threat of crops being destroyed, many farmers—even after obtaining the licence—have to navigate a thin line between sustenance and crime.

Let's thicken that thin line a little, shall we? Time for some science!

Cannabis is a genus of flowering plants in the Cannabaceae family, and there are three recognized species within cannabis itself: *Cannabis sativa*, *Cannabis indica*, *Cannabis ruderalis*. Most of the cannabis that is smoked (or ingested) in various forms of ganja is a crossbreed of these different species. And within these forms of cannabis lie further wonders: there are about 483 known compounds (or 'natural components') that have been isolated and/or identified within the plant.* India's NDPS Act does not discriminate about the type of cannabis (indica/sativa/ruderalis) that is restricted.

Out of all of these subsumed compounds and cannabinoids, the ones that matter most for our discussion of ananda are tetrahydrocannabinol (THC) and cannabidiol (CBD). THC is the 'psychoactive' compound, i.e., the *good shit*. It was first isolated in the 1960s by Raphael Mechoulam, the same doctor who would describe and name anandamide in the early 90s. The higher the percentage of THC in your weed, the higher you'll get.

CBD, the other primary extract of the plant, is usually the more popular herbal/medicinal component of cannabis, suggested for anxiety, pain management, cognitive conditions, etc.

CBD will help you smell the wet grass under your feet; THC will find you a pillow among the clouds.

When THC levels are low enough, one finds varieties of cannabis that are usually classified as 'hemp', which is already a highly lucrative industry worldwide, used for textiles, paper, biofuel, ropes, body care products, seasoning oils, animal grains, fibre, and on and on. It is considered by many to be the sustainable-growth crop of the future.

For better or worse, you won't get stoned by wearing a T-shirt made from hemp.

---

*This is the most I've actively cared about botany since high school.

Now, for those who *do* wish to get stoned, the varieties of sativa and indica are the most common species denominations that one is likely to come across—or sometimes, a hybrid of the two. In 1753, the Swedish botanist, zoologist, taxonomist, and physician* Carl Linnaeus published *Species Plantarum*, a work that gave birth to nomenclature of modern plants (he would be known as the 'father of modern taxonomy'). In this text, Linnaeus classified the '*Cannabis sativa* L.' ('sativa' means 'cultivated', the 'L' is to give credit to himself). A couple years later, French evolutionary biologist Jean-Baptiste de Lamarck described a new species, '*Cannabis indica* Lam.' The word 'indica' is classical Greek or Latin for 'of India' (or how we may say in Hindi: 'India ka'). '*Cannabis ruderalis* Janisch' was identified in 1924 by the Russian botanist D. E. Janichevsky.

Very broadly speaking, indica is responsible for the 'chill-at-home' high, sativa for the unfettered 'let's-go-on-adventure' high. Ruderalis, bechara, is a mere muggle, low in THC, stripped of most superpowers.

Sativa is usually found in hotter drier climates, including parts of Africa, Central America, and West Asia. Indica is South Asia's gift to the world, usually growing in the dry mountainous regions of India, Pakistan, Afghanistan, and as far west as Turkey. Some believe that the 'purest' version of Indica is the Hindu Kush, named after the 800-kilometre-long mountain range to the west of the Himalaya, stretching from Afghanistan to Northwest Pakistan and into Tajikistan.

To cultivators, 'indica' generally means a shorter, and broad-leafed plant; sativa usually has narrower leaflets and takes a longer time to finish flowering. Despite its resonance with our country, there is much more to India than indica: the cannabis that grows in the Himalaya generally has wider leaves, while the leaflets get narrower as one ventures south.

---

*Sounds like a long LinkedIn bio.

There are some in the cannabis industry who describe the different types of cannabis not by their species but by their 'chemovars'—a breakdown of the strain by chemical composition. Many botanists believe that there is, perhaps, just one species of cannabis—sativa—but with strains bred to enhance different cultivars. Type I has a higher composition of THC, Type III is more CBD-dominant, and Type II, in the middle, is a close combination of both.

Are you keeping up with the dualities so far? The THCs and the CBDs, the sativas and the indicas? The buds and the stems? There's one more important factor, something that ties the cannabis plant (and a whole lot of other vegetation) closer to animals like us: sexual identification. As in, male weed and female weed. This is going to sound familiar, but the male cannabis plant's only purpose is to produce pollen, to pollinate the female plant. It has no psychoactive functionality. All that 'high-power' comes courtesy the ladies of the marijuana world—the Madam Ganjas—that produce the flowers which are ultimately used for recreation or medicine, for the THCs and the CBDs. One could also grow a hermaphrodite cannabis plant, which is capable of going both ways, so to say: to pollinate and get pollinated.

Like hormonal teenagers in boarding school,* the male and female plants are usually raised separately to induce a process called 'parthenocarpy' in the fruits of the females, which helps increase the production of the cannabinoid resin. If male plants are allowed to be grown nearby, it will lead to pollination and seed dispersal. The seeds attract rats and other pests, for which the farmers may spray pesticide, and thus, contaminate the plant down to the granular level.

Cannabis doesn't need much chaperoning to grow, but a little attention to detail can go a long way to obtain the best results. Botanists and horticulturists will recommend that the plant is grown in soft (friable) moist soil, well-fertilized by manure rich in cow

*I'm speaking from personal experience here.

dung.* Seeds should be sown by the end of the monsoon, and are usually ready for transplanting by September or October in the North Indian climate. At this point, a farmer will cut down the male plants, leaving behind only the 'madi' females.

The presence of even a few male 'staminate' plants can damage the crop: the females have to be allowed to come to maturity into their full, glorious bloom over the new few months.**

When confronted with the pure, rational science of it all, cannabis is hardly different from the other common flowering plants in the world, from lilies and oleanders and lantanas and mallows. It produces seeds, fruits, has a common life cycle, and can be used for medicine, agriculture, and industry. Roses are red, violets are blue, and Mary Jane is as green as spring.

While cannabis' reputation often precedes itself, it has long been necessary for us in India to confront it scientifically, botanically, for its properties and benefits, just like much of the rest of the world has done in recent decades.

A central government-funded campus in Lucknow has been doing just that.

In the 1800s, Nawab Saadat Ali Khan II of Awadh or Oudh established a royal garden in the city. Later, Mirza Wajid Ali Shah—the last king of Awadh—dedicated the garden to his favourite queen, Sikandar Mahal Begum. The Sikandar Bagh became a centre for British horticultural activities. Later christened as the National Botanical Gardens, it was adapted by Independent India's Council of Scientific & Industrial Research (CSIR) as an establishment for plant science research. The transformation to its present-day form took place in 1978, when the gardens were renamed as the National

---

*Another material where India faces no shortage.

**So many women are feverishly nodding as they read this.

Botanical Research Institute (NBRI) with the mandate to study and support plant diversity in India, conservation, bioprospection, and more.

And, a couple centuries after the Awadh royals ruled and romanced in these gardens, the NBRI launched the country's most-intensive cannabis research and development programme. In 2018, the institute successfully obtained the first-ever licence to cultivate cannabis for R&D purposes initially for Uttarakhand—where much of the actual cultivation is held—and then in their home ground in Uttar Pradesh. It is here in the state's capital of Lucknow, barely a ten-minute drive down the heart of the city from the chief minister's office, where the institute has been hard at work studying and producing several potential varieties of the cannabis plant.

Speaking on video from his office in Lucknow, Saroj Kanta Barik—then-director of the NBRI—presents the calm, unassuming face leading some of India's most-progressive investigations of cannabis. In his late-fifties, Barik is bespectacled with a greying, receding hairline. Originally from the tiny village of Gourpur (population: 817, as per the 2011 census) in Odisha's Baleshwar district, Barik was instrumental in launching the NBRI's cannabis niche programme within the botanical gardens in Lucknow. Uttar Pradesh is currently among four Indian states/union territories—along with Uttarakhand, Manipur, and Jammu and Kashmir—with permission for R&D for cannabis.

'You know this name, "Cannabis indica" itself says that it is a plant of our own indigenous origin,' says Barik. 'That's how you find it in Ayurveda and many traditional medical systems of our country, particularly for pain management. Of course, during Shivratri or Holi, it is used for its psychotropic affect... That's a different story....'

Barik laments that 'international movements' have caused a ban on what has been a traditional medicine in India. (This was before a recent U-turn. A number of scientists abroad are now studying and developing cannabis strains with targeted THC content for medicinal and industrial use.) 'Until the Narcotic (NDPS) Act is relaxed, our main concern is to develop a strain which will not harm people,' says Barik. 'Say that we are able to produce something today of 0.2, or 0.1, or even zero per cent THC, and suddenly, the level shoots up to 1, 2, 3 per cent—then the farmer will simply be arrested! So, we have to be very careful.'

The NBRI began research work on *both* low and high-THC lines: the former (<0.3 per cent THC) is usually high on fibre; the latter (>0.3 per cent THC) is useful for medicinal purposes. But Barik's fear is that Indian cultivators, short of finding that magical 'under 0.3 per cent' strain, will continue turning to imported varieties. 'If they (foreign cultivators) are maintaining low-THC content, it's not guaranteed that we'll be able to maintain the same THC in our conditions, in our soil, in our climate. I would request that we should wait for a while, and when our own lines are ready—a few years down the line—we will be self-sufficient, and we should produce it in a large quantity.'

Barik's hope is for the rise of our own indigenously lab-created, made in India strains,* ones that don't affect our biodiversity or negatively impact the local ganja. By the time he ended his tenure at NBRI in late 2022, Barik told me that the institute had produced six 'lines' with the desired traits of low-THC. They will now need to be maintained and kept clear of any containments for a number of generations, before it can be asserted that these varieties will remain stable for farmers who choose to cultivate the seeds.

Back in 2017, the jumpstart to NBRI's cannabis R&D programme was provided by a private enterprise, the Bombay Hemp Company (BOHECO). In a public-private partnership, BOHECO lent support to the NBRI on a genetic breeding project, with the hope to produce strains that can be later applied to cultivate cannabis for commercial and medicinal use.

---

*Atmanir*bhang* Bharat.

BOHECO is a conglomerate with its fingers in a number of sticky green pies, including partnerships with government-run scientific institutions, hemp-based textiles and fabrics, health and wellness centres, and more. Their medicinal products are sourced from the cultivated or collected hemp in Uttarakhand, ending up as hemp seeds for metabolism and weight loss, or oils for creaky bones and chronic discomforts.

In a Zoom interview in early 2022, Yash Kotak, one of the co-founders of BOHECO, told me that, despite Uttarakhand being the first state to roll out a commercial hemp policy, the science hasn't kept up. 'There is no right kind of uproot, germplasm, or seed variety that a farmer can grow that is approved by the Indian government,' said Kotak. 'The policy reads that you have to have less than 0.3 per cent THC seed. Now, who has that seed? No one has that seed.'

In India, cannabis grows everywhere, and it grows however the hell it wishes to grow, wild and untamed by farm hands and lab coats, free even from the destructive interference of wild animals, uncaring for our human designations of percentage points and legal acts. The 'under 0.3 per cent' seeds don't magically appear out of thin air and drop around the hillside. They must be bred, germinated, artificially created.

Meanwhile, on the other side of the globe, a bill was introduced in the US Congress to raise the limit for THC in legal industrial hemp from 0.3 to 1.0 per cent. In September 2022, Costa Rica implemented this change swiftly, providing production licences for higher THC cannabis cultivation. As India copy-pasted our policy from the US, there is hope that any development across the oceans would soon be mimicked in the Himalayan foothills, too.

There was a ray of hope by the end of the 2022 monsoon season. Four farmers in Bageshwar—a district in Uttarakhand about 150 kilometres south of Chamoli—were able to grow hemp with less than 0.3 per cent THC in a half-acre patch of land. I meet

Maithani in Pipalkoti just a week after this news from Bageshwar. He glows with optimism, because successful implementation of these new, 'legal' seeds could finally metamorphose the fortunes of so many farmers hoping to turn the green grass into greener profits.

Tourist buses packed with pilgrims pass by Pipalkoti day and night. Some tourists stop for the steaming kulhad chai by the highway, some for a quick lunch, some to stay overnight at a hotel or guest house, before continuing further towards Badrinath. I stay in one such hotel for three nights, a short walk away from the AAGAAS nursery. The accommodation is simple, down to its bare bones: Hot water is available only for a brief period of time around 4.30 a.m., giant spiders hang from the ceiling, occasionally lurking down the wall of my bathroom, and, much to my chagrin, non-vegetarian food is a mere myth. Opposite my hotel is a residential children's school, perched and spread out on a beautiful steep hillside. Every morning I'm woken up at 5 a.m. sharp (missing the hot water window) by a loud and spiralling siren, which rings like a frantic fire alarm. Its purpose is to wake the schoolchildren up for their morning activities. I go back to sleep until the next alarm, an hour or two later. A cold bath ensues.

On my very first night at this hotel, while sitting in the common dining area, I notice an elderly couple. Husband and wife, both in their early seventies. The husband is incredibly extroverted, speaking to all of the hotel staff, and as many of the passing guests who have the time to sit and form a bardic circle around him. He has silvery white hair, beady eyes behind oval-rimmed spectacles, and spends each evening in a black Carolina Panthers sweatshirt, with its hood pulled up over his head. Seated on a plastic chair outside the hotel's main entrance, he sings old songs to himself. *Aaj jaane ki zid naa karo*, he croons the first time I see him. *Don't insist on leaving today.* His wife sits inside in the dining area, smiling to herself, relaxed amid the evening rush of incoming guests.

When our respective dinners arrive, the couple invites me over to share their table, and their khichdi, and their stories, too. They tell me that they are originally from Nagpur, and plan to spend an entire month in Pipalkoti. They are ardent followers of the spiritual leader Osho,* and this hotel is run by an Osho bhakt. Only then do I notice photos of the late, bearded mystic, framed and propped up around the dining area and the corridors. Since the husband's retirement from government service, the couple has spent a month or two at various 'Osho hotels' like this one every year, all over the country.

For the next two days, whenever we cross paths in the evening, the man tells me about his life, his work, his favourite foods, the long walks he has taken around Pipalkoti, his children and grandchildren, his philosophies of life. All this while, his wife—a short woman with a slight hunch—speaks only occasionally, in a soft voice, sometimes rolling her eyes at her husband's gregariousness.

I don't mind the company, and actually begin to look forward to dinners with them. When I casually suggest my plans to explore the Valley of Flowers—a popular national park of flowery meadows a couple hours' drive away—the man finds a new outlet for his energy, spending the following morning doing as much research as he can for me (mostly through YouTube travel vlogs) to offer a palette of suggestions. There is the longer option, of a multi-day trek and overnight camps in the valley. Or there is the quicker disruption: a helicopter ride to a popular point in the hills, a short trek, and a helicopter back to motorable roads that same evening.

I'm not overly enthusiastic about either alternative: the former would take more time than I have at my disposal for this trip; the latter seemed needlessly expensive and against the very spirit

---

*Real name: Chandra Mohan Jain, who started a new religious movement and was famously deported from the United States in 1984.

of exploring the picturesque park. I tell him I'll mull over my decision; he tells me he's ready to accompany me on the helicopter if I commit.

And even if I don't, he is able to solve a smaller problem for me: the cooks at the hotel—now well-acquainted with him—have offered to make us an omelette for breakfast. Ah, the modest, delicious egg, almost as forbidden as its fully grown non-vegetarian progeny in these holy lands.

After the sinful morning omelette, I'm back at the AAGAAS nursery, where I'm introduced to the undergraduate students from Mumbai who are keen to accompany me on my bhang-discovery trip that day. We share a jeep up to Urgam Valley, an area which consists of a few small hamlets about 15 kilometres ahead from Pipalkoti. Our driver is Vibhas,* in his mid-twenties, who drives dangerously uphill on the winding roads, seemingly unperturbed by the threat of falling rocks from the hillside or veering off the edge down the khud (ravine) on the other. Vibhas keeps one eye on the road and the other on his phone, playing the role of a DJ, clicking past YouTube advertisements to play the next Punjabi hip hop song. I'm in the passenger seat beside him, convinced that I will die to the fucking 'Skip Ad' button.

We arrive at the valley almost two hours later, thankfully unharmed. Suddenly, the hue by the mountainside changes into a lush shade of green. There are large shrubs of cannabis everywhere by the roadside, most 2 to 3 feet tall, and a few more than twice my height. From a distance, they almost look like the cypresses in Van Gogh's paintings. When we stop to take photos, Vibhas ensures us to stay patient. 'There is a lot more ahead.' Overhearing my conversation with the students, he tells me that he was stung by a bee under his eye while riding on a motorbike just two days ago. Immediately, his mother had prepared a paste of bhang, applied it on

*Name changed.

the sting, and *whoosh*, like a cantrip, the pain magically disappeared, leaving him even without any physical sign of swelling.

Beyond bhang, Urgam is a fertile region for many other crops, particularly the region's local rajma, which is sown around the same time as cannabis. Farmers cultivate potatoes, dhan (a form of rice), and mandua (millet) in the opulent barsaat/monsoon season, and wheat in the summertime.

Like many such Himalayan settlements, one of the big draws of Urgam Valley is a temple. The Kalpeshwar Mandir here is dedicated to a folk legend from the Mahabharata, where one of the five forms of Shiva were revealed in five different 'Panch Kedar' sites; Kalpeshwar—as the name suggests—is where the god's hair appeared.

Nothing about a Shiva temple here, surrounded by swathes of fertile cannabis, is surprising to me. It doesn't shock me when some locals mention that the holy men who sit at this temple boast of having access to the best-quality sulfa* found in the state—the type enjoyed far and wide, beloved by the highest of connoisseurs, including (I'm told) a former chief minister.**

Past the trees and through a cave jutting out the smooth face of the mountain, I enter the temple first, and find one such holy man to confirm or deny the legend of the local maal. He has an old, creased face, with a long grey beard that reaches up to meet his thin, grey hair; and more, thicker dreadlocks of hair on his head. He sits cross-legged on a small carpet on the floor, and answers each question with a slightly cantankerous sneer. 'Well, I have an ancient name,' he says. 'But I'm known as Moni Baba.' For Moni Baba, when the topic of the local bhang is broached, his primary concern is of quality control. The younger dealers from the region, he says, are only sending the 'kachra maal' (trash stuff) of charas

---

*The 'sulfa' here, by the way, is not related to the abbreviated form of the sulfonamides group of antibiotic drugs.

**Allegedly.

out to the cities, ersatz substitutes of the good stuff. In the past, many wayward stoners and dealers have approached him and other priests directly for the source of the best sulfa, to which Moni Baba's response has been: 'Bhaago yahan se!' *Scram!*

We thank the ascetic and scram away from the mandir. In a nearby village of Lyari, Vibhas introduces us to Praveen, a recent school graduate who does odd agrarian jobs. Praveen's side hustle is collecting bhang: he spends a few hours a day rubbing his palms over the fruiting tops of the cannabis vegetation in and around his village, picking from the plants that grow wild on the hillside. An hour of palm friction can produce enough sulfa for a few hundred rupees. The same amount will likely sell for ten times more in New Delhi.

Praveen now leads us on a forty-five minute, gentle uphill trek, through smaller settlements, past giant shrubs of unclaimed cannabis,* past much more vegetation and exotic flowers—including lots of rajma—until we reach a wide-open expanse, and then take a sharp right turn into a shaded path, hidden from view, beneath the steppes, through a creek, across a thin footbridge of unsteady rocks, and then, back up another hillside to that aforementioned motherlode: acres and acres of cannabis planted intentionally for the purpose of a large-scale sulfa trade. This part of Himalaya is categorized as having 'sub-tropical' climate, featuring a heavy and often reoccurring monsoon season, from June to September/October, when plants grow to produce the flowers that carry the resin and seeds.

We spend a little more time up on this steppe, looking even further up the steep incline at dozens (hundreds?) of more square plots of cannabis cultivation, reaching hundreds of metres high up to the mountain ahead. Praveen demonstrates to us how to rub the

*On the way, Vibhas points at a particularly full-bloomed cannabis plant, growing in the backyard of someone's hut. Its leaves are fat, full-bodied. 'It's like the one you see in Wiz Khalifa videos,' he says.

resin off the flowering tops. His palms work with expert speed and efficiency, like a Stone Age man rubbing two sticks together to make a fire. The shoot of the cannabis plant—where the hemp comes from—is as strong as a thick rope; we find it almost impossible to uproot it with our bare hands.

Among the amalgamation of smells in this valley—hay, manure, and a slight wet whisper of monsoon—there is a familiar aroma of fresh ganja: fruity, muddy, and lightly intoxicating.

And then, it's time for us to leave.

Our final stop in Urgam Valley is a visit to Minkal Makhandwal, who is the gram pradhan—head of the village council—at Lyari. Besides her leadership duties, Makhandwal helps run a small family business, offering homestay options, and organizing treks and outdoor sports for visitors. The new highways to Badrinath have increased tourism to Urgam, too, and helped reverse some of the mass migration out of villages.*

We meet Makhandwal at her store, a small, rectangular space stacked with winter clothes. Like much of the nearby area, the hillside immediately next to this shop is inevitably bountiful with giant shrubs of cannabis. But Makhandwal, perhaps disillusioned by the negative use of bhang in the village, or still stirred by the police raid across Urgam, objects to any suggestion of the growth of industrial hemp—and its potential economic benefits. 'It shouldn't be legalized,' she says. 'Bhang is not a good thing. It has caused a negative impact on many of our generation. The biggest thing is that if it's legalized the production will increase. If production is increased, the generation which is already getting bad will get even worse. I want this to end, first and foremost.'

There is nuisance, she adds, for the other popular crop—rajma—which shares its cultivation life cycle with that of cannabis. Farmers are often forced to endure the inconvenience of sifting out any

---

*Many migrants also returned home from larger cities after the Covid-induced shutdowns.

intermixed parts of the bhang plant out of rajma, a process that adds to their labour.

'But,' Makhandwal adds, as if to cover her bases, 'this is the land of Kalpeshwar. So, even if you cut the crop off, it will grow again by itself, naturally. It is just that way. I know that it's a gift from Lord Shiva, so nothing can change it.'

On the bumpy drive back to Pipalkoti, Vibhas—who has overheard my conversation with Makhandwal—asserts that the pradhan hasn't told me the truth. 'Bhang is really the main business here, and the most profitable,' he claims. 'They just don't want to admit it to you.'

The drive is bumpy and rocky, full of puddles, across narrow passes where we hope to avoid traffic incoming the other way. When back on the main highway, Vibhas points out a number of small dhabas, where—beyond the ubiquitous chai and Maggi—one can also surreptitiously purchase some of the local sulfa. It is rubbed into the charas form, producing little slate-coloured twigs of hashish.

The Urgam Valley is only one example in a nation filled with this infamous plant. There are many more varieties of ganja that grow naturally around Uttarakhand alone, including the *Cannabis indica* found in the valleys at India's borders with Tibet and China. Nanda Devi—which at 7,816 metres is the tallest mountain peak located entirely in India—is also known to shelter the highest* cannabis found in the country. The Indian Landrace Exchange describes some of the famous Indica found in villages like Malari and Tapovan to have mango and cherry-like flavours that make 'you want to bite down on the bud itself'.

Similar reservoirs of ganja, often hidden from the eyes of local authorities—or simply ignored by them—exist all over the country. In many cases, even the risk of cultivating this illegal crop hasn't

---

**highest*

deterred farmers in the face of economic desperation. In October 2023, police in Maharashtra's Yavatmal district discovered cannabis cultivation in about 20 acres of farm land, camouflaged to grow between cotton and toor (pigeon pea) crops in villages like Ghonsara and Bargwadi. Nearly a dozen quintals of cannabis (valued at around ₹25–₹30 lakh) were seized and six farmers were arrested.

But, uprooting the plants didn't quite address the root of the social conditions in this region. Yavatmal, located on a plateau in east Maharashtra, has the unfortunate blemish of being known as the epicentre of India's farmer suicide crisis: thousands of local farmers have died by suicide due to agrarian and related economic distresses over the past few decades. Weeks after the police crackdown in Ghonsara and Bargwadi, farmers in the district handed over a memorandum to the divisional commissioner, demanding a 'symbolic' official sanction from the state government to grow cannabis, in light of the meagre returns from the usual crops like cotton, toor, and soybean, rising debts, and unseasonal heavy rainfall that further deteriorated agricultural output. Cannabis could fetch up to fifteen to twenty times higher returns than cotton. A farmer named Prakash, whose father was taken into police custody in this case, told reporters that, 'We are ridden by debts and need money to meet farm expenses. So growing cannabis was the easiest way out.'

Easy may seem like a strange turn of phrase, considering the risk of detention, fines, and/or imprisonment. But in Indian conditions, the cultivation of ganja is *easy* in the natural order of things, as common as rice or millet, or cotton or jute. Whether it is intentionally nurtured or a product of the natural environment, whether grown for profit, or—as some would believe—a gift of Shiva's divine intervention, cannabis has been a part of the natural ecosystem for centuries.

It's been almost as omnipresent as civilization itself.

Recently, cannabis had a reckoning with its own ancestry, one that crucially reshaped our understanding of the plant's origins—the inception points from where it first began its dalliance with humanity.

In a 2019 study, a research team from the University of Vermont reviewed more than 150 fossil pollen studies to trace the birth of wild cannabis 28 million years ago to the highest plateau in the world, near the Qinghai Lake in modern-day Tibet. Then, time passed, tectonic plates moved, landmasses changed positions over the earth's core, and the weed spread its wings. A 2021 study concluded that humans first began to intentionally cultivate the plant about 12,000 years ago in modern-day China: for food, for medicine, and likely to get high, too.

All existing strains of cannabis in the world will likely find an 'ancestor' source in East Asia from this early Neolithic period. This conclusion, the researchers add, has been supported by pottery and other archaeological evidence from the same period discovered in present-day China, Japan, and Taiwan.

This latest revelation counters the long-held belief that the first cultivation of the crop was along the steppes of Central Asia, in regions which are now Mongolia and Serbia.

Wherever it was first 'born', cannabis is considered to be one of the oldest crops cultivated by humans. Older than our countries, older than any of our surviving organized religions, older than any modern language.

Archaeological evidence for the burning of cannabis has also been found in the Romanian kurgans, over 5,000 years ago. The first documented use of cannabis may be attributed to the pharmacopoeia of Emperor Shennong from around 2800 BCE. Shennong was a mythical Chinese ruler who is known as the 'Divine Farmer' and the father of Ancient Chinese medicine. Egyptian historical texts like the *Ebers Papyrus* (c. 1150 BCE) mention the use of cannabis for the medical treatment of inflammation and pain. Around the fifth century BCE the Greek historian and geographer Herodotus described hemp vapour baths used by the ancient Scythians.

It has been suggested that cannabis was used by Proto-Indo-European tribes in the Pontic-Caspian steppe (the steppeland stretching from the northern shores of the Black Sea) in ritual ceremonies—customs that eventually extended south to modern-day India during the Indo-European migrations. The cultivation and consumption of cannabis is believed to have been introduced in the Indian subcontinent between 2000 BCE and 1000 BCE by the invading Aryans.

One of the most revealing discoveries was made in the 1970s by Soviet archaeologist Viktor Sarianidi, who found a basin containing cannabis dating back to the second millennium pharmacopoeia at a shrine at the Bactria-Margiana Archaeological Complex (in modern-day Turkmenistan). In his wide-ranging 1980 text *Marihuana: The First Twelve Thousand Years*, Canadian scholar Ernest L. Abel claims that the link between the Indo-Aryan 'soma'* (mentioned in the Vedas) and the concoction of 'haoma' from the Zoroastrian/Iranian religious text *Avesta* suggests that the drug made its way down to the subcontinent with the ritual knowledge of the Indo-Iranians, 3,000 to 4,000 thousand years ago.

As new civilizations and Vedic cultures thrived in northern India, it is safe to presume—based on the surviving scriptures of that time—that cannabis was accepted and celebrated as an important medicinal and recreational supplement.

In circa fifth century BCE, Siddhartha Gautama renounced his kingly life for an ascetic's life, until deep meditation offered him his great awakening and enlightenment. Buddhism was soon born. In the text *Lalitavistara Sutra* (possibly third century CE), it is claimed that Siddhartha—now known as the Buddha—ate a grain of hemp

---

*The same soma that the Atharva Veda crowned the ruler of the five kingdoms of plants; the same soma that was repurposed by Aldous Huxley.

every day as part of his austerities. (In Mahayana Buddhism, the Buddha is also depicted holding a bowl of 'soma'.)

By the eighth century CE, the Sanskrit-language medical text *Sucruta Samhita* mentioned bhang (supplemented with some other drugs) as an anti-phlegmatic. Cannabis has also been named in Indian texts like *Tajnighuntu* and *Rajulubhu*, where, aside from its benefits in clearing phlegm, it is suggested for patients struck with gonorrhoea, those who need to stimulate their appetite, and, not unimportantly, those suffering from excessive flatulence.

And, inasmuch as cannabis became a fundamental part of the culture in the subcontinent, religious borders would be blurred again with traditions and preparations of the plant stemming from Arabic and Islamic cultures. One such preparation is 'kief', deriving from the Arabic kēf or kīf, which means 'pleasure'. Kief is a powdery substance sifted from leaves or fruiting tops of cannabis, either to be consumed in that form or produced in cakes of charas.

In the last sections of the *Baburnama*—the memoirs of Babur, the founder of the Mughal empire—the emperor, in poor health, turned to various pain-killing substances for relief, including opium, wine, and majun.* Known as 'Modern Society's Oldest Edible', majun or majoun is a traditional Egyptian treat which includes honey, nuts, dried fruits, and cannabis. It produces 'extatic [sic] happiness, a persuasion of high rank, a sensation of flying, voracious appetite, and intense aphrodisiac desire.'**

In the *Storia Do Mogor*, a seventeenth/eighteenth century first-hand account of the Mughal empire in India, the Venetian writer and traveller Niccolao Manucci made some vivid observations about the rise of cannabis use among the Muslim populace of the time:

> So accustomed are the Mahomedans to intoxication that the poor people, who have not enough funds to procure

*Sounds like a regular Thursday night for some people.

**Yes, yes, yes, yes, and yes.

> spirits, invented another beverage, called in the language of this country bang (bhang). It is nothing else than leaves of dried hemp ground down, which intoxicate as soon as it is taken. Aurangzeb also wanted to suppress this disorder. He therefore appointed an official under the title of matucib (muhtasib), whose business it was to prevent the use of this beverage or of others similar to it. Not a day passed that on rising in the morning we did not hear the breaking by blows and strokes of the pots and pans in which these beverages are prepared. But, seeing that the ministers themselves also drank and loved to get drunk, the rigour of prohibition was lightened by degrees.

There are numerous tales of warriors in India turning to bhang not for relief but for a little shot of courage—akin to the stereotype of medieval European soldiers (or pirates) taking a swig of ale before a big battle. There is a popular account that involves Guru Gobind Singh, the seventeenth century warrior and the tenth and final Guru of the Sikhs. In the heat of battle, Gobind Singh's soldiers faced a marauding elephant from the enemy ranks. Then, like Popeye the Sailor Man super-powered on his spinach,* one brave soldier consumed a blend of bhang and opium, and found the mettle to slip under the elephant—and kill it.

We are barely scratching the surface. Even as cannabis was once 'imported' to India, it has since been adopted and become as Indian as any other of our imports through the course of history—much like how the British-era tea plantations have now made us into the world's proudest chai-drinking nation.

In a 1957 report produced for United Nations Office on Drugs and Crime, scholars I. C. Chopra and R. N. Chopra** argued that, as the cannabis plant grew under different climactic conditions in

---

*Someone needs to investigate the THC concentration in Popeye's spinach, too.

**The Chopra duo feature often in India's ganja history.

the Indo-Pakistan subcontinent, it took on a different variation in its appearance from its forefathers. 'Those variations at first may give the impression of separate species,' Chopra and Chopra write. A uniquely, South Asian species.

> In India the plant is found growing wild throughout the Himalayan foothills and the adjoining plains, from Kashmir in the west to Assam in the east. It has become acclimatized to the plains of India and grows even in the warm climate of southern India, producing its narcotic principles.

According to the Chopra and Chopra report, the highest quality yields of charas resin were obtained from plants grown in present-day Xinjiang (the autonomous territory claimed by China). The resin once served as an important article of trade between Central Asia and India.

Thus, this plant links thousands of years of humanity and progress across the continent. It has been present around every major development of human society since our species decided to settle down with the invention of agriculture, and since we decided to look to all the joyous yields in the ground beneath our feet. The plant links migrations, movements, languages, kingdoms, religions, old civilizations, and new ones. Now, it can be found growing naturally on every continent on Earth except Antarctica. If, in a particularly heady mind trip of ananda, one experiences a dramatic shift in perspective—the skewing of time and space—where minutes feel centuries long, don't panic. It is only the plant's way of giving us a taste of its own journey, each toke a time machine capable of offering a macroscopic view of history, of 12,000 years across landmasses, continents, and oceans of the world.

Pipalkoti is about a 36-kilometre drive away from Joshimath, another town in the Chamoli district that usually serves as the starting point for visitors to the Valley of Flowers, the Hemkund Sahib gurdwara, or onwards to Badrinath. The town—oft-visited by pilgrims—is also of strategic importance for its proximity to the border with China.

Not long after the catastrophic floods of 2021, locals in Joshimath had noticed small cracks appearing in their homes. Something was brimming under the earth. The cracks spread; steady at first, and then quickly, like an epidemic. This was the result of land subsidence, a gradual sinking of the ground, which can occur as the earth is hollowed out of the mineral resources, gases, and water from under its surface.

Much of Joshimath is built on an unstable foundation. Surrounded by two rivers, environmentalists have warned that such Himalayan cities could be particularly vulnerable 'to earthquakes, landslides, and erosion'.

In September 2022—around the same time I visited Pipalkoti and Urgum Valley—an expert study had flagged the rapid sinking of Joshimath, likely due to the mixture of natural catastrophes and unregulated construction. Environmental experts blamed the construction of the National Thermal Power Corporation's (NTPC) Tapovan Vishnugad hydropower plant, which is being constructed on the Dhauliganga River. Land erosion here has been worsened by the tunnels build for this project.

Over the next two months, hundreds of more man-made structures in Joshimath started to develop severe cracks, and then, began to sink into the ground.

The Earth, it seemed, had had enough.

By January 2023, parts of the city were declared 'high danger' zones and hundreds of families were evacuated, abandoning their homes. Over a hundred families were given temporary shelters and accommodation in Pipalkoti. Locals like Maithani helped organize aid efforts to host the new migrants.

Meanwhile, the cracks and subsidence spread across other

Himalayan towns—Karnaprayag, Uttarkashi, Nainital, Mussoorie—buckling under the weight of over-construction and over-population.

I wonder what this destabilization—of the earth, and the people who occupy it here—would mean for the grand economy of cannabis? Will the cultivation model change? Will there be a short supply in the coming seasons? Would that translate to higher demands and higher costs? Or would the displacement in Joshimath and other Himalayan towns turn more people towards the cultivation of bhang: a crop that can grow easily and abundantly even in the most challenging environments?

Scientists have said that the stretch of highway from Joshimath to Rishikesh—is likely to get increasingly vulnerable to landslides due to the removal of natural vegetation and slope destabilization.

The night before I take that same highway back to Dehradun, I have evening chai with the elderly couple at my 'Osho hotel'. The man is ebullient, as usual, and a little disappointed that I couldn't find time to visit the Valley of Flowers. He's excited to tell me details of the best masala dosa at the bazaar near the bus stop.

I have little to contribute but polite nods and smiles, before excusing myself for the night. The man still has a few more questions for me—about my purpose here, my work, my travels ahead. From the corner of my eye, I see his wife give him an unspoken nudge, communicated in the language of a couple that has shared nearly half a century of their lifetime together. But I'm able to translate this tiniest flicker of silence for its complex intended emotion. She wants him to leave me alone, to not bother me too much, as if she has figured something out about me, as if she knows that—despite the company I temporarily keep—I am here to specifically be alone. That I'm running away from something.

Or maybe, I have completely misunderstood the gesture, and it was just a nudge to wrap up their dinner.

It doesn't matter, though: for it was the emotion I inevitably projected upon myself. I'm suddenly stumped with this thought, because I'm not sure if I am running at all. I would only figure that out when I *stop* being away, if I pause for an honest confrontation with self.

I have a jeep to catch early the next morning, and I leave the couple like I leave everyone: ghosting without a long goodbye. We are never going to see each other again. Why waste time on a dramatic farewell?

The front two rows of the Bolero jeep to Dehradun are already packed. The driver motions me to the back, making room in the dicky. He moves some of the luggage to the rooftop and folds down the seats in the rear. The last thing left on the floor here is a small bag, the type of plastic jhola used for rice. In a rush to sit inside, I almost step on this jhola, but the driver frantically stops me. He picks up the bag and opens it to reveal a small, white, baby goat curled up inside.

Once discovered, a young woman in the front takes the goat and cuddles it in her arms. It belongs to her and five of her family members squeezed into the front two rows of the vehicle. The woman holding the goat tells me that his name is Ramu.

At the next few stops, a couple more passengers join me in the dicky area. Soon, there are ten of us squeezed in the eight-seater jeep. Plus, the goat.

Cramped between the seats, my backpack, and the jutting legs of the men seated near me, I strain to find meaning in all of this. A larger metaphor, perhaps. Is the little goat a reminder to me of myself, a creature far outside of its own comfort zone, thrust into a preternatural mechanical and industrial age, wary and scared of the world, blissfully oblivious to the incoming complexities of life?

Or is it just a fucking goat in a jeep?

As we ride forward—humans and Capra—I watch packed buses dashing past us, up the other way. It's astonishing to me that this jerky, kutcha road is frequented daily by so many pilgrims, who seem comfortable testing the laws of physics as they sway and bend around every corner, until they reach the temples of their beloved deities.

These are the same roads traversed for the transportation of the local bhang, too. While much of it is smuggled out illegally—collected by men and women like Praveen in Lyari, who pass it on to their emissaries on the road, who transport it to collectors and dealers in high-demand urban areas—some of this bhang also finds its way through official channels. It is stuffed in big bundles—like hay—on the back of ten or twelve-wheeled carrier trucks, marked by the state to be sold for a variety of purposes: to licensed hemp companies for food, textiles, and other materials; to government-approved (recreational) bhang shops; to the growing sector of cannabis-sourced health and wellness products in India.

Under the guidance of the government's Ayush ministry, some of these health and wellness companies turn the wild herb into easily-marketable, low-THC medicine, which are then distributed to clinics, hospitals, or—with an approved doctor's prescription—directly to patients around the country. Cannabis-based medicine is still in its very nascent stages in India, and the very first physicians to truly explore the *legal* application of the medicine are practitioners of Ayurvedic medicine—vaidyas—who are merely reintroducing this ancient herb now in a new package.

To unwrap this new package, I would have to travel far south, leaving the Himalayan peaks for the southernmost state in the country. A few months earlier, I had spotted an advertisement from an Ayurvedic hospital on the back page of a news magazine. Tucked deep in the lush forests of Kerala, this hospital announced the use of a new cannabis-infused treatment as part of their therapies and procedures. I found their contact details and emailed the CEO. The promise of a new adventure beckoned.

Kerala had once been a significant place of interest for cannabis connoisseurs. If the northern states offer the charas of Parvati Valley or the sulfa in Uttrakhand, Kerala has completed the polar balance of sorts with its own offering: a near-mythical strain of ganja called the Idduki Gold.

As we travel towards Dehradun, Ramu is well-behaved, and doesn't make a mess. About forty-five minutes into the journey—not long after we leave Chamoli district behind—the woman holding him requests the jeep driver to stop on the side of the road. There is a man standing here by the hillside of the highway, perhaps another relative of hers. The woman gives the goat a kiss on its forehead and passes it out the window. Everyone waves goodbye to Ramu. And we're off again.

Idukki Gold

'...a majestic extinct dinosaur, a beloved anti-hero in these parts, the ganja of God's Own Country, the manna of the Malabar Coast, the soma of the South...'

I have the time for long train journeys. Visakhapatnam to Palakkad, from India's east coast to the southern state of Kerala out west. Bay of Bengal to Arabian Sea. Twenty-two hours on my A/C 3-tier berth.

I'm scheduled to arrive in Palakkad early morning, where a taxi will pick me up and drive me deeper into Kerala's countryside. My destination is an Ayurvedic wellness retreat on the highway on the way to Cherpulassery. Launched in 1989, the retreat—with a Malayalam name that translates to 'Flower Garden' in English—welcomes patients suffering from chronic ailments, like autoimmune disorders, gynaecological conditions, dermatological issues, etc., who have turned to India's ancient holistic system for healing and relief.

Our country has a long history of alternative healthcare, including the tenets of medicine shared in the Atharva Veda, the *Sucruta Samhita*, and more. India even has an entire government ministry—Ayush—formed 'with a vision of reviving the profound knowledge of our ancient systems of medicine'. Ayurveda is the first tenet of Ayush. Yoga/Naturopathy, Unani, Siddha, and Homoeopathy follow to create the little acronym.

Ayush is also the ministry that regulates medicinal cannabis in India as Ayurvedic medicine.

Despite cannabis's scriptural links with ancient medicine, only a minority of Ayurvedic practitioners openly utilize the plant in actual treatment. The legalities and nuances of the NDPS Act prohibit research and distribution of medical marijuana—even if, unofficially, most Ayurvedic vaidyas (physicians) will agree to the plant's benefits.

This is where the wellness retreat, or ayurvedasram, near Cherpulassery differs. In February 2022, the management of the ayurvedasram officially announced AyurCann, a combination of Ayurveda and cannabis, to be used in their wellness programmes for pain, stress, and sleep management. 'Experience the powerful combination of our Ayurvedic treatments,' says their website, 'and the use of premium blends of Cannabis Leaf oils, serums, and supplements in their processes.'

I knew I had to be there.

Known as 'God's Own Country', Kerala has unmatched charm: lush forests, white sandy beaches, canals and lakes that make up the breathtaking backwaters, Malabar parottas and beef curries. For stoners, however, Kerala has an added layer of folklore. For decades, the state was responsible for blessing us with 'Idduki Gold', a strain of particularly strong weed cultivated in the hidden jungles among the Cardamom Hills in the Idukki district. The greenest, cleanest high, so green that it might even turn golden after a few hits. The kind of weed that Indians from all other regions spoke of in reverent whispers, the kind of weed that could briefly transport any user back to the tea plantations and the backwaters, to colourful sunsets and coconut trees.

I'd known by now that the Idukki Gold had been reduced to more myth than reality. Over the past decade or so, authorities had demolished swathes of the illegal cultivation and driven much of the trade out of state. Still, like a honing beacon pointed at the holy 'golden' grail, I knew I had to investigate for myself. Idukki would be my final destination in Kerala; but the discovery of the AyurCann programme convinced me to take a little detour on my way there.

The train down south is a blend of linguistic delights, a little taste of true Indian variety, from Telugu and Tamil to Kannada and Malayalam, and, of course, the Hindi and English that I'm familiar with. I don't mind the slow passage of time, or this circumstance where I must stay mostly rooted in my coach, around my upper-side berth, for nearly a whole day. I carry books and music and a healthy dose of my anandamide receptors. People-watching piques my interest and helps pass the time, too. The train rumbles past the countryside, crossing villages, green fields, arid lands, lakes, rivers, and the cacophony of cities by the major platforms. We keep moving, one sip of chai at a time. The five-rupee Styrofoam cups now cost ten rupees. The ten-rupee cups go down as easy as a quick shot of whisky or a toke from a chillum. The next time the chaiwallah makes his way down the coach, I ask for another one, and then another.

Sometime in the afternoon, I am awoken from a nap on my blue Rexine berth to a phone call. It's from Jishnu Raveendranath, the CEO of the ayurvedasram where I'm headed. Raveendranath is expecting me to arrive the following morning, but there's been some drama: he informs me that, just the night before, Kerala's excise department raided the ayurvedasram's campus and confiscated all their cannabis products—down to the last sample. 'They want to run their own tests,' he says.

I am crestfallen and a little confused. There continue to be misconceptions and misinterpretations regarding the curlicues of nuance in the NDPS law. For some, it's a simple healing plant; for others, it's a 'capital-D' Drug. The fruiting tops/flowers of the plant are illegal, but not the stump of the hemp plant and the paste of the leaves.

Remember, cultivation of cannabis is legal in Uttarakhand as long as the THC level in less than 0.3 per cent. These cannabinoid products are legally cleared by Ayush. Many companies targeting low-THC oils and medicines—like BOHECO—have hit the 'health and wellness' market in India. The products are only available with a doctor's prescription; and the doctor could be a practitioner of any of the branches of Ayush, like the Ayurvedic vaidyas I am on my way to meet in Kerala. High on CBD, these medicines won't get you wasted like THC, but they'll find a way to relax and relieve your system. The impact of CBD is more gradual, and many users may only feel its effects after days or weeks of consistent use.

These BOHECO medicinal products, including oils, serums, and seeds, found their way from Uttarakhand to Kerala, to the ayurvedasram for their AyurCann therapies. And the same products were seized just days before my arrival. No doubt, the subtle distinctions of legalities—the percentages of THCs and CBDs—were lost to the overzealous excise officers.

In recent years, Kerala has been especially strict in its clampdown regarding offenders of the NDPS Act. The state is often a transit point in the smuggling route of narcotics like MDMA, LSD, as well as cannabis. Drugs are often seized entering the state from Karnataka, Goa, Tamil Nadu, Andhra Pradesh, and Telangana, en route abroad, perhaps to Sri Lanka, Maldives, or beyond.

In Tamil Nadu, the district of Nagapattinam has been identified as one of the key routes for smuggling ganja (and other substances) to Sri Lanka; Tamil Nadu police have claimed that large consignments of the substance are often transported from Telangana and Andhra Pradesh down to Nagapattinam, before being smuggled out by sea. Through 2023, the Sri Lankan Navy seized over 3,700 kilos of what they referred to as 'Kerala cannabis' from smugglers attempting to cross international waters.

In January 2022, Kerala police seized 460 kilos of ganja being smuggled in a goods lorry at the Perambra village in Thrissur district. Once the home of the Idukki Gold itself, Kerala is now finding imitators of its finest brand of weed coming in from Andhra Pradesh and Odisha. The Perambra incident was claimed by police to be the biggest ever such seizure of drugs in the state.

Over the years, the state's 'war on drugs' has produced some moments of comic absurdity, too. A couple of youngsters celebrated World Environment Day on 5 June in the best way they know possible: by planting cannabis on the roadside in the Kandachira village in Kerala's Kollam district. Just two saplings: one 60 centimetres long, the other half its size. The excise department acted immediately:

> It was Kollam Excise Special Squad Circle Inspector I Noushad who got tipped by a witness of the incident. He was also told that a young man 'addicted to ganja' had led a few others to do the planting on World Environment Day. 'Let this plant grow here,' the men apparently said before planting the two saplings there and taking photos of it on their phones. These ganja lovers have however not been caught yet.

My salaam to these young heroes. This should be an annual tradition. I can hardly imagine a befitting ode to Mother Earth.

Of course, India is as diverse as its landraces, and not every place in the country has the same visceral reaction to the plant. One community's poison is another's pickle. And for much of history, many other parts of the country have embraced ganja—or at worst, have been nonchalant towards its recreational use.

But it took only a few decades to reverse thousands of years of friendly relationship, turning the inspiring into the illicit.

Sometime around 1,500 years ago, rulers of central and western India—the Rashtrakuta and the Kalachuri dynasties, along with other wealthy folks of the region—patronized the construction of the temples at the Ellora Caves in Maharashtra's Aurangabad district. Now considered a UNESCO World Heritage Site, the complex features Hindu, Buddhist, and Jain temples, said to be carved into the rock between 600 to 1000 CE. The most impressive of these is the Kailash Temple—in Cave 16—featuring the largest single monolithic rock excavation in the whole world. The temples at Ellora are such an outstanding feat of human engineering that the History Channel show *Ancient Aliens* decided that they may have been proof of something supernatural, suggesting that aliens likely taught the builders and provided ancient scientific devices to give shape to these mammoth, beautiful structures.*

The truth, of course, is hardly that sensational. Engineers of that time needed no superpower to create the great structures and wonders of the world; their innate, human wisdom was enough—along with a whole lot of indentured labour,** and donations from the rich who apparently didn't know what else to spend their money on.

There was one other secret ingredient that kept the 'magic' together: *Cannabis sativa*. In a study conducted by M. Singh and M. M. Sardesai, it was found that cannabis—in the form of raw hemp—had been admixed in the ancient clay plaster used in the construction of many of the temples at Ellora.*** Hemp, it seems, has been a valuable ingredient to prevent the caves from rapid degradation—even a millennia and a half later.

One can assume that the local term at that time for the plant was the Sanskrit word found in the Vedas, bhang. The first known use of the term ganja, however, is attributed to the Merrian-Webster dictionary in 1689, some eighty years after the British East India Company first landed in the subcontinent. The plant may have been new to the British, but the locals had already been familiar with its recreational and medicinal uses for thousands of years.

By 1798, the East India Company—in dismal financial state and in the face of bankruptcy—enacted a new law directed towards hemp products (ganja, charas, and bhang) in India. 'No one was

---

*If you leave the History Channel to its devices, it will find aliens in your Thalassery biryani.

**Allegedly.

***The composite material is known as 'hempcrete'.

permitted to manufacture or sell hemp drugs without first obtaining a license from the Zillah, the administrative office set up to collect such revenues.' There were costly licences for farmers and wholesalers for growing, storing, buying, and reselling the stock of ganja plant in every step of its life cycle before it reached the consumer. The taxation took its biggest hold on a 60,000-acre tract in Bengal called Ganja Mahal.*

The term 'ganja' found its way into English literary use (perhaps for the first time) in Philip Meadows Taylor's 1839 novel *Confessions of a Thug*,** considered to be the most popular novel about India presented to the English-speaking world, before Rudyard Kipling wrote *Kim*. For Taylor—and by extension, many of his Western readers who were exposed to this 'foreign' drug for the first time—ganja, associated with miscreants, gangsters, and lowlifes, was excitingly taboo.

> Taylor writes, 'Peace!' said he, 'no brawls: it is disgraceful and only fit for drunkards and smokers of ganja; listen to me. Surfuraz Khan, you are no boy, and ought not to let your anger have sway; listen, and hear what our young jemadar has been about, and I swear by Bhowanee I think he will yet put us all to shame.'***

But if Taylor was essentially exploiting the stereotyped notoriety of cannabis smokers, another European man was simultaneously working on the most in-depth and influential study of ganja ever done. That man was William Brooke O'Shaughnessy, an Irish physician who had found a job with the East India Company after helping with the development of an intravenous fluid therapy to

---

*The Palace of Weed.

**The novel also popularized the use of 'thug' in the English language, a term that would be appropriated, reappropriated, and misappropriated for subsequent centuries by everyone from Tupac Shakur to bigoted politicians.

***p. 115.

combat the ongoing cholera pandemic in the 1830s. A graduate of Edinburgh Medical School, O'Shaughnessy landed on Indian shores in 1833 with a distinct interest in the medical properties of plants. Based mostly out of Calcutta, his encounters with cannabis laid the early groundwork for the plant's therapeutic benefits from the prism of Western medicine.

After years of research and clinical trials in Bengal, O'Shaughnessy presented the paper 'On the preparations of Indian Hemp or Gunjah (Cannabis Indica)' in October 1839,* while serving his role as assistant surgeon and professor of chemistry at the Medical College of Calcutta. The paper would receive wider audience in England after appearing in the *Provincial Medical Journal* in 1843.

O'Shaughnessy recommended cannabis as a sedative for the central nervous system for diseases like tetanus, hydrophobia, migraine, and convulsions. He also commented on the plant's botanical characteristics, chemical properties, popular uses, cultivation, recipes (with bonus details of popular forms of preparation and consumption). He details experiments conducted on both animal and human subjects**.

Based on the notes of a certain Mr McCann, the local deputy superintendent of police (DSP) at the time, O'Shaughnessy writes:

> [T]he gunjah consumed in Bengal is chiefly brought from Mirzapore and Ghazeepore, being extensively cultivated near Gwalior and in Tirhoot. The natives cut the plant when in flower, allow it to dry for three days, and then lay it in bundles averaging two pounds weight each, which are distributed to the licensed dealers. The best kinds are brought from Gwalior and Bhurtpore, and it is also cultivated, of good quality, in a few gardens round Calcutta. In Jessore, I am

---

*Between this paper and *Confessions of a Thug*, 1839, was truly a marquee year for ganja visibility.

**Subjects controversially included fish, vultures, storks...and children.

> informed, the drug is produced of excellent quality and to a very considerable extent of cultivation. In Central India, and the Saugor territory, and in Nipal, churrus is collected during the hot season…

O'Shaughnessy finds references to the medicinal use of ganja from the studies of scholars in the Arabic and Persian world, too. He waxes lyrical about the historical nomenclature and uses of the hemp plant in India:

> Its synonymes [sic] are 'bijoya,' 'ujoya,' and 'joya,' names which mean promoters of success; 'brijputta,' or the strengthener, or the strong-leaved; 'chapola,' the causer of a reeling gait; 'ununda'*, or the laughter-moving; 'hursini,' the exciter of sexual desire. Its effects on man are described as excitant, heating, astringent. It is added that it 'destroys phlegm, expels flatulence, induces costiveness, sharpens the memory, increases eloquence, excites the appetite, and acts as a general tonic.'

O'Shaughnessy's conclusion was as clear as they come:

> The preceding cases constitute an abstract of my experience on this subject, and constitute the grounds of my belief that in hemp the profession has gained an anti-convulsive remedy of the greatest value. Entertaining this conviction, be it true or false, I deem it my duty to publish it without any avoidable delay, in order that the most extensive and the speediest trial may be given to the proposed remedy.

The paper was a sensational hit worldwide, the nineteenth century botanical equivalent of going viral. More than 100 follow-up articles were published by European and American medical journals before the end of the century about the therapeutic use of Indian

---

*Ugh. These anglicized Indian spellings.

cannabis—including one by John Russell Reynolds, a physician to the royal household during the time of Queen Victoria, who wrote: 'Indian hemp, when pure and administered carefully, is one of the most valuable medicines we possess.'

One of the most memorable cases that O'Shaughnessy pursued was of a certain Hakim Abdullah, a patient who had been bitten by a rabid dog and was beginning to show symptoms of hydrophobia (rabies), considered a near death-knell decades before the development of a vaccine in the 1880s. O'Shaughnessy passionately detailed Abdullah's suffering, writing, 'Never can I forget the indescribable horrors of the paroxysm which ensued.'

Although death was near, O'Shaughnessy succeeded in providing Abdullah some respite by the administration of regular hemp resin; for days, Abdullah awoke with painful paroxysm, but found relief through the medicine. Five days after first encountering O'Shaughnessy, Abdullah passed away. Reviewing the tragic demise, O'Shaughnessy wrote:

> [I]t seems evident that at least one advantage was gained from the use of the remedy [hemp]—the awful malady was stripped of its horrors; if not less fatal than before, it was reduced to less than the scale of suffering which precedes death from most ordinary diseases. It must be remembered, too, that in this, the first case ever so treated, I possessed no data to guide me as to the dose or manner of administration of the drug...but next to cure, the physician will perhaps esteem the means which enable him 'to strew the path to the tomb with flowers'.

Meanwhile, as O'Shaughnessy was helping Western physicians comprehend the painkilling and other healing properties of cannabis, there was another narcotic that, frankly, commanded much more of Britain's interest and attention. By the 1800s, the 'drug of the century' for the British empire was opium, 'freely available to the British population and so popular that the government went to war to prevent the prohibitionist Chinese disrupting the trade.'

In 1842, China signed the Treaty of Nanjing, ending the First Opium War and ceding Hong Kong to the British. The treaty also relaxed restrictions of the opium trade into China. The sale of the narcotic flourished, as opium—a derivative of the poppy plant grown in India—became the second-largest source of colonial revenue for the East India Company. In his 2021 book *Opium Inc.*, Thomas Manuel writes that the British were 'enabling the longest running drug deal in the history of the world'. Opium was illegal in Britain itself, but the Company's policies paved the way for addiction crises to emerge in both China and India.

As the colonial drug trade flourished, tensions rose between economically frustrated Indian poppy ryots (farmers), their zamindars (landlords), and the colonial administrators. These tensions fuelled the larger, widespread Indian uprising—also known as the Sepoy Mutiny or India's First War of Independence—in the summer of 1857. Historian Utathya Chattopadhyaya recently argued that the taxation of cannabis was among the reasons that local rebels were emboldened to revolt against the British. 'Cannabis was the key to challenging the legitimacy of Indian sovereignty,' Chattopadhyaya said.

It took nearly eighteen months, but the British were able to suppress the revolt, formally end the Mughal empire in India, and transfer their rule from the East India Company to the British Crown. By then, the Company had already adopted the Opium Act of 1857 to give tighter control over the private cultivation and free trade of opium. And, in the process of tightening their grip over their opioid cash cow, ganja was dragged into the drama, too. The various forms of hemp were further formalized and recognized as narcotics—rather than substances of great cultural, recreational, and medicinal significance for the Indian population.

Since the earliest days of civilization, the subcontinent had passed under a variety of leaderships and kingdoms, Mughals and Marathas and Sikhs and Nawabs and Mysoreans and Company and Crown, all without any real criminal prohibition of the plant. But, by the 1870s, the colonizers shared a distaste for cannabis and its users—most of whom were poorer Indian subjects. The customs and practices of cannabis became tied to 'low-brow' culture, and thus, became another way for the British to prop themselves up as the superior race.

In an 1872 survey, a colonial administrator in Burma even said that 'most of the acts of Mutiny of 1857 were undertaken under the influence of bhang, charas or ganja'. This is a claim terribly difficult to fathom: anyone who has ever been high knows that even the lightest task is akin to a Herculean chore—whether they have been asked to undertake a dangerous military expedition or open the door for the pizza delivery-wallah. Perhaps, the weed was different back then; or perhaps, the path to ananda truly did enlighten dormant minds and help inspire some brave souls.

If this indeed was the case, I'm happy to grant some credit to cannabis for planting the seeds of revolt, for lighting the first spark of Independence. All the plant needs, then, is a little rebranding. *Marijuana: Smoke the Reefer of Revolution!*

It's just after six in the morning when the Visakhapatnam–Kollam express lets me off at Palakkad. The sun inches its way out above the coconut trees, and within seconds of being driven out of the train station, I'm left breathless. The drive is green and verdant. The hillocks are dense with forests and wildlife, and little ponds and lakes nearby add an extra shot of blue serenity to the day.

I'm finally at the ayurvedasram.

The campus is airy and spacious, surrounded by the shade of coconut, banana, and mango trees, with a permeating smell of exotic oils. This place could hardly have existed anywhere else but Kerala; I already feel comforted, exultant after a long train journey to be within this hidden lap of nature. I'm given a double room that faces picturesque ponds and gardens just a short walk away. The bedroom is simple and clean, with white sheets and white pillow covers and white towels. Then, there is a back door that opens into a private therapy room. It has a wooden therapy table (droni), shelves full of massage oils, and a shower space.

Patients visit this ashram for weeks on end, for wellness procedures like Dhanyamla Dhara (for arthritis, inflammatory conditions, muscular sprains), Karana purana (ear pain), Shashtika Shali Pinda Sweda (for serious neuromuscular diseases and certain autoimmune disorders), and much more. I learn that the AyurCann cannabis programmes—for pain management, stress management, and sleep wellness—are usually two to three weeks long, and cost close to ₹1 lakh per patient.

Over a simple breakfast of idli and disappointingly bland sambar, I also learn that patients are encouraged to closely monitor their sleep and minimize all 'strenuous' activities—activities that include internet use, 'intense discussions', and sex. Outside food is strictly prohibited, leaving me wary of more flavourless sambars and rasam and boiled cauliflower to come.* The chai, however, is probably the best I've had in years; there must be something special in the milk.

I'm the only one checked in here who is not a patient. Apart from mealtimes, I hardly see any of the other patients on campus: I assume that they're busy with their various treatment activities. Many of them are from foreign countries.

I take long walks around the ashram, to the surrounding woods, to the yoga and meditation hall, and to the main office, where I finally meet Jishnu Raveendranath, and his father P. M.

---

*'Cleanse' diets aren't ideal for passionate carnivores.

S. Raveendranath, the ashram's founder. Father and son are both dressed in collared shirts with traditional kaili mundus wrapped around their waist. Both have tilaks smeared over their foreheads, remnants of the morning prayer. And both speak to me in fluent English. The elder Raveendranath—known popularly as Vaidya Ravi—got his early immersive learning in the Ayurvedic system in the 1980s under the tutelage of his guru, Vaidyamadham Valiya Narayanan Namboodiri. While Ravi was working in Kerala's remote Attapaddi area—'the Silent Valley'—with a number of tribal groups, he got a clearer revelation of his own aspirations. He hoped not just to practise Ayurvedic healing, but to also devise and prepare his own medicine to target each specific ailment. He founded this ayurvedasram in July 1989, soon after Namboodiri's passing. In 1994, the ashram moved to its current location near Cherpulassery, and has expanded here since. The campus also houses the ayurvedasram's own manufacturing unit, where they produce hundreds of their own products, including oils, tablets, powders, and *aah,* and that very excellent tea.

Ravi, who is in his early sixties, is slow and deliberate when he speaks. 'We get patients with all kinds of complaints. Both for chronic illnesses and acute conditions. Usually, Ayurveda is known only for chronic illnesses, but we want to educate people that if they come to us at the right time, we can treat the beginning of the disease itself.'

'One of our mottos is, "Let Ayurveda be your first choice of treatment",' adds Jishnu, who is the twenty-eight-year-old CEO of the company his father founded. 'Allopathy has its own role to play, and so does Ayurveda. We can coexist. We don't have to degrade other systems.'

Ravi says that, from his experience, the initial application of the AyurCann procedures began with patients suffering from a number of neurodegenerative disorders, including Alzheimer's disease, Parkinson's disease, Huntington's disease—conditions that are caused when nerve cells in the brain or peripheral nervous system lose function and begin to die. Small globules of various CBD formulas are administered to supplement the larger treatment plan. Studies have shown that the molecular mechanisms associated with CBD can have a beneficial effect on patients suffering from Alzheimer's, Parkinson's, etc. The process of decay may be slowed, but it can never be stopped.

At the ayurvedasram, cannabis-based medicine has also been used to treat patients with sleep disorders or severe pains. Until recently, hemp oil, seeds, and powders were used to prepare food and drinks for some patients.

There are many other conditions, for which Ravi says that the research is ongoing. He remains wary of any iatrogenic side effects. 'We are very careful about using the cannabis in a limited way. The patients should know and understand the medicine they are getting, and give us their consent.'

Cannabis treatments are also far more expensive. A CBD muscle relief oil will cost around ₹900 to ₹1,000 for a 50-millilitre bottle; a 'normal' 450-millilitre bottle of similar oil would only cost around ₹350.

Ravi hopes that more cancer patients will choose to turn to cannabis as a form of pain relief. 'It's all about awareness,' he says. 'They're not usually aware that Ayurveda deals with such things, too. Now we have to create awareness about Ayurveda first, and then, about the importance of cannabis.'

The different schools of medicine—Western and Indian, modern and Ayurvedic—have often been on polar ends, with some mistrust, some ignorance, shaded by histories of politics, colonialism, science, and religion. Cannabis, however, is a bridge between these schools of thought: it is treasured in the ancient Indian scriptures that formed the basis of Ayurveda; and in the West, its medicinal properties have been somewhat 'rediscovered' by progressive medical research in recent decades.

Ayurveda specialists have noted that the moderate use of the plant can work as a stimulant for the nervous system, as a powerful aphrodisiac, or a sedative. When marijuana is used in any Ayurvedic formulas, it is assumed that it has been 'purified' (referred to as 'shudha bhang'). Of course, any habitual or frequent use of cannabis leads to an imbalance in the Ayurveda-recognized physiological forces of the body—vata, pitta, and kapha—leading to issues in digestion, sexual potency, and mental health.

Then, there's the International Institute of Cannabinoids, which claims that bhang has long been used in quasi-official Ayurvedic treatments:

> Fresh leaf juice (bhang) is also used to treat dandruff, as a preventive measure against parasites in hair; also in cases of earache, and against bacterial inflammations and infestations of the ear. The juice is also diuretic, and therefore is used in treating inflammations of the bladder and kidney stones. Dried leaf powder is applied on fresh wounds to promote healing (new granulation tissue development). A poultice of crushed fresh leaves is used on the skin in cases of different skin infections, rashes, neuralgias—for example erysipelas, Herpes zoster, Chickenpox, eczema, etc.—to diminish pain and itching. Combined with other herbs, bhang can be used against diarrhoea...With digestive herbs (like cumin, fennel, anise...) bhang can be excellent for stimulating appetite and digestion; with aphrodisiac herbs and foods (almonds, walnuts, sesame seeds, saffron...) it becomes an excellent aphrodisiac.

Researchers of modern medicine have explored the efficacy of cannabis products for treating epilepsy, insomnia, chronic pain, and pain related to cancer. In 2018, the US Food and Drug Administration approved a drug for the first-time containing a substance derived from marijuana, an oral medication for the treatment of severe forms of epilepsy—Lennox-Gastaut syndrome and Dravet syndrome—for patients as young as two years old. With a prescription, this medicine is now available for patients to import in India, too. And in early January 2024, an Indian pharmaceutical company launched cannabis-based medicine to treat seizures in toddlers associated with these syndromes.

'We know that, throughout history, [cannabis] was used as a medicine,' says Ravi. 'For us, whenever we wanted to do something [with cannabis], we wanted to make sure that we do it completely legally.'

The illegal—or let's say 'unofficial'—prescription of bhang-related medication is nothing new in India, particularly for vaidyas and physicians practising alternative health care systems. A month after my visit to Kerala, I would meet a vaidya from Punjab who claimed that he was medicating and curing patients for nearly every ailment with some sprinkling of cannabis and a little pinch of hope.*

Jishnu admits that if vaidyas *were* using cannabis as part of their Ayurvedic treatments, they were doing so without publicity or drawing any attention upon themselves. For the father–son duo at this ayurvedasram, however, the priority was to take advantage of the nuanced legalities of cultivation and distribution in India to finally bring the plant back into the mainstream of Ayurvedic medicine.

'BOHECO is getting their plants from the legal sources, from the government's own collection centres,' says Ravi. 'We are only using BOHECO's propriety medicines, which are accepted by the Ayush department. You often read in the paper, that someone has been arrested with 10 kilos, 15 kilos of marijuana. So, people get confused. As an established and respected Ayurvedic centre, we have to be very careful. We are worried about that. Nobody else is doing this [legally] because of fear. We don't have that fear, but we don't want to confuse people.'

---

*Allegedly.

And yet, confusion ensues. The ayurvedasram manufactures all of its own medicine, *except* those originating from cannabis. Kerala doesn't give out licences for manufacturing cannabis-based products. Only a few months after the AyurCann programme was launched, once the state's excise department caught wind of the ayurvedasram's activities, they reacted by confiscating their BOHECO products.

Like many others I have come across in my journey, Ravi is tepidly hopeful for a future where the plant loses its stigma. 'There should be *some* control over the cultivation, because it can also be misused,' he says. 'But the problem is, whenever you have regulation, you open it up to corruption. My idea is to have regulated use of cannabis just like any other potent medicine. And the regulation has to be responsible. They should spend their energy on that, instead of seizing all the products.'

Ravi seems cautious, speaking without a hint of rancour even when criticizing this raid, even as the excise department had subjected the health retreat to something akin to a high-profile drug seizure. To him, it is all a misunderstanding, which he hopes will be resolved soon enough.

But months pass; the misunderstanding remains unresolved; Jishnu told me in mid-2024 that they their appeal was still lagging in the high court, and the AyurCann programme hadn't resumed.

There are others hoping to profit off the marriage of Ayurveda and cannabis in the state, too. Another cannabis-focused healthcare start-up recently announced a partnership with the Amrita Vishwa Vidyapeetham in Vallikavu, where they will be conducting clinical trials for cannabis-based medicine on menstrual cramps.

After speaking to Ravi and Jishnu, I spend the rest of the day at the ashram, allowing myself to slow down to the pace of the place, taking long walks, reading thick books, swaying to the rustle of the trees, watching the moonlight reflect off the placid lotus ponds.

This little system recharge is essential; the next morning, I'm packed and out the door before the earliest rays of the morning sun for another journey. A shorter train trip within Kerala from Shoranur to Ernakulam (Kochi). The boxy Jan Shatabdi train is packed to the brim, and the tropical climate gets hot and humid early in the day. At least the open windows allow for a relaxing breeze to flutter through from between the window bars. I grab on to my backpack and a small, stroller suitcase, and I feel like I've almost packed my whole self in, made myself small enough to fit into any space between the thousands of faces that pass by on the trains, the stations, the buses, the winger jeeps, the airports.

These are the times that I end up feeling envious of the plant. Cannabis is one of the sturdiest weeds on Earth, capable of surviving in a great variety of conditions, spreading its wings over thousands of years, partly entrenching itself in the planet's history, millions of years older than my own species. Despite the ferocity with which some attempt to eradicate it, it perseveres. It travels light, grows wild, follows no rules.

It's free.

India didn't win its freedom after the revolts in 1857–58. But, the mutiny lighted a ninety-year slow burn against the empire. The opium trade continued, and so did the legal consumption and regulation of ganja. But, every road to regulation features a couple of short cuts, and Indian ganja farmers, too, found their way to grow undeclared crops, conceal production numbers, and give rise to criminal organizations.

By the late nineteenth century, the reputation of cannabis in India continued to evolve for the British government. Was it a narcotic that drove people insane? Was it a medicine to help ease the pain of torturous physical suffering? Was it a cure for ancient ailments? Or was it, simply, a mild tipple to be enjoyed recreationally at the end of a tiresome day?

The use of cannabis was so common and prevalent in India that the British government created the Indian Hemp Drugs Commission (IDHC), on the request of the House of Commons. The purpose of this committee was to 'ascertain whether, and in what form, the consumption of the drugs is either harmless or even beneficial as has occasionally been maintained.'

In an essay analyzing the work of historian James Mills, the academic Sebastiaan Broere wrote:

> In the imagination of the British colonial population, hemp came to be related to insanity, violence, suicide, indolence, and immorality. Some, for example, claimed that satis—women who committed self-immolation, usually at the funeral pyre of their husbands—or those who ran 'amuck' consumed hemp before performing the act.

For the British authorities, the substance remained closely tied with crime, in its continuing 'thug' associations. Soon, it would become synonymous with mental health, too. Cases of alleged insanity—from asylums in Calcutta to Dhaka—would be attributed to the use of ganja smoking. Scholar and psychiatrist Amritranjan Basu said that these cases were used 'to construct the narrative of a special category of mental illness called "Indian hemp insanity".'

'Insanity,' writes Broere, 'came to be understood as an inevitable consequence of cannabis use.'

As an activity closely tied to Indian spirituality, British missionaries in India also disapproved of the use of cannabis. Led by William Sproston Caine, the under-secretary of state for India lobbied the government to form the IDHC. The commission conducted a seven-month study of cannabis in India in 1893, and by 1894, presented the first of the eight-volume, 3,000-page report about its findings. This report was the most comprehensive study of cannabis yet anywhere in the world, featuring everything from the work of O'Shaughnessy, the plant's religious observance (particularly among Hindu Indians), and its true impact on the health of frequent users.

The commission's findings, however, would disappoint Caine and other anti-cannabis advocates. After examining the evidence, the report acknowledged the substance's beneficial medicinal qualities, and then commented separately on the plant's effect on physical, mental, and moral nature:

> In regard to the physical effects, the Commission have come to the conclusion that the moderate use of hemp drugs is practically attended by no evil results at all.
>
> ...
>
> In respect to the alleged mental effects of the drugs, the Commission have come to the conclusion that the moderate use of hemp drugs produces no injurious effects on the mind.
>
> ...
>
> There is no adequate ground for believing that it injuriously affects the character of the consumer.

Clean chits all around, as long as one respects the functional term here: 'moderate'. Moderate use is rarely cause for alarm: a moderate drinking habit, moderate amounts of screen time, a moderate interest in pornography, a moderate amount of sugar in one's diet, vagerah vagerah.

Elsewhere in the same report, the commission noted that the criminalization of cannabis would 'deprive the very poorest of the population of the use of a narcotic to which they have always been accustomed'. The British government followed the commission's recommendation and instead of prohibition, an Act was passed in 1896 to license retailers and tax all aspects of the cannabis trade: preparation, transport, trade, imports, and exports.

A few decades later, India was amidst the throes of a long-winded freedom struggle. In the spring of 1930, just around the time that Mohandas Gandhi and his followers set off on the salt march as an act of civil disobedience, the British government also enacted the Dangerous Drug Act, identifying cannabis under its definition. Despite this label, however, the drug still wasn't specifically criminalized.

Globally, the reputation of cannabis oscillated between beloved and bedevilled. In the US, closely following the hysteria of anti-marijuana sentiment, the 1937 Marihuana* Tax Act was passed. Cannabis was classified as the highest Schedule 1 drug—like heroin—with no accepted medical use. Some others, however saw through the sticks and seeds for the blooming flower: in 1938, Indian hemp was called a 'Billion Dollar Crop' by *Popular Mechanics* magazine, a prediction that holds remarkably clear-eyed and prescient almost ninety years later.

And then, the political maps of the planet changed rapidly. For the second time in a handful of decades, the world went to war. There were genocides. There were innovations. There was the bomb, and then, the second bomb. Back home, activists and freedom fighters revved up the Quit India movement—violently, non-violently, politically. There were famines, there were deaths.

There was freedom.

The Republic of India was officially born in August 1947. A tryst with destiny. There was Partition. Displacement. More death.

A new Constitution was soon written for a young country. New laws—and, for cannabis, a continuation of the status quo.

In 1961, the United Nations Economic and Social Council convened a conference of seventy-three nations in Manhattan, New York, which came to be known as the United Nations Conference on Narcotic Drugs. The convention placed strict restrictions on the cultivation, trade, and use of cannabis. While the world chose a more conservative and suspicious outlook toward the plant, the Indian delegation at this time—representing a culture with deep-

*The prevalent spelling in US Federal documents at the time.

rooted social and religious ties to ganja—opposed these restrictions. India's objection partly stemmed from the traditional use of the lower-THC bhang, an objection that was supported by our once-brothers-turned-foes Pakistan, as well as by Myanmar. A compromise was reached: India promised to limit the export of hemp, and furthermore assigned a twenty-five-year grace period to outlaw all non-medicinal and non-scientific use of the plant.

And in 1985, a year before the twenty-five-year timeline expired, the Indian government under prime minister Rajiv Gandhi passed the famous/infamous Narcotics Drugs and Psychotropic Substances (NDPS) Act. The bill was introduced in Lok Sabha on 23 August 1985, debated over the next few days, and enacted into law by 28 August. Much of this one-sided 'debate' was actually about opium, with cannabis once again being categorized among harder narcotics because of lazy misunderstandings. In many instances, speakers confused the substances for each other. In his book *Cannabis Indica: Perception vs. Potential*, professor of constitutional law Khagesh Gautam wrote that the MPs arguing for the bill had little to no understanding of the effects of addiction, abuse, and (recently debunked) gateway drug theories in regards to cannabis. Some even made unfounded connections between cannabis and terrorism.

The bill passed in both houses of Parliament and was laid on the table of the Lok Sabha as the NDPS Act on 14 November 1985. For the first time in history after thousands of years of common cultivation and use, the Act defined cannabis and outlawed it—with the exception of bhang. It's ironic that these laws are based on the promises of the 1961 UN treaty which, in itself, has since been amended and replaced.

I was born just a year before the NDPS law. From the days of *Chitrahaar* on DD National to viral reels on Instagram, I have already witnessed drastic transformations in the country. I often ruminate over how my generation—and the ones that have followed—have experienced the rapid speed of change around us: rushing forward from black-and-white to technicolour to 4K HD, zooming past economic liberalization, the creation of new middle and upper classes, the complete disruption and domination of new technology, revolutions in science and medicine, and an abrupt farewell to the analogue way of life. The changes have also paralleled the evolution of law and regulations, adapting to the challenges and innovations of the new millennium.

And yet, the once-predicted 'Billion Dollar Crop' has stuttered to launch in the very country which it calls home. Nearly forty years after the NDPS Act, this is still the law that—with only a few minor amendments—remains in effect today.

When I travelled around the country alone in my mid-twenties, I often found myself drifting from place to place, train station to train station. Apart from a few appointments with old friends on the way, I had no set itinerary, no purposeful schedule for my time, no destination to research, no plot to chase, no pots of gold at the end of the rainbow. Even now, I struggle to convey what I had once been in search of, because I'm not sure if I ever found it. It could have been a yearning for a new environment, a thirst to educate myself about unexplored parts of my own country, to experience the world instead of simply theorizing about it. Or, it could have been a search for something within myself, an examination that would only have been possible if I was alone, untethered to family, friends, and community who had come to know and define me.

Being 'alone', in this instance, is more of a state of mind, for solitude is a rare privilege in our over-populated country. In my travels, I was often surrounded by the gazes of strangers without recognition or expectation. This, I know, is its own form of solitude. I yearned for what Sartre had defined as the 'being-for-itself', where I could simply exist without playing a role, without skewing my personality for its impression upon others, where I would be less tempted than ever to act in bad faith.

And so, I kept drifting. My personal mantra for most of these destinations was: *I'll get there and figure it out.*

Years later, as I take yet another train alone to another new destination, I begin to encounter my younger self again, the drifter who—albeit temporarily—feels comfortable in uncertainty, with the ability to negotiate and navigate almost any new environment without prior preparation. I'm reintroduced to this version of myself, one who had long been hidden in the backrooms of my personality, a version that I had tamed to keep up appearances, for the expectations of family, romantic relationships, marriage, and fatherhood, to make a certain impression in professional settings, to embody an alternative avatar.

On the train to Ernakulam that morning, I feel that yearning to simply *be*.

I fall in love with Kochi within hours of laying my backpack down at a homestay. I'm at Fort Kochi, a charming, historical neighbourhood in the city's south-west. Within this one segment of a city contains multitudes, a living history that presents the future as much as it celebrates the past, a minor miracle of culture and architecture. It's a sleepy old town, a bustling beachside, a humming postcard that spans centuries.

Fort Kochi was the first European fort on Indian soil, annexed by the Portuguese in the early 1500s. But this was not before Chinese traders and fishermen also landed on the shores, allegedly giving the region its name (Co-chin means 'like China') and popularizing the Chinese fishing nets which are still in common use. With every passing century or two, the multicultural hue of Fort Kochi got even more colourful. There were Portuguese Catholics, there were the Dutch, there was the kingdom of Mysore, the British Raj, and finally, the governments of Independent India.

Today's Fort Kochi is an agglomeration of all these influences—

and more. There are museums celebrating Indo-Portuguese history, a Dutch cemetery, Syrian churches, synagogues, Jain and Hindu temples. Added to this mix is the fusion of quaint modern-day commercial enterprises, from teahouses and hotels to beachside shacks and art museums.

Tourists holding popsicles walk on the beach under the humid afternoon sun along the Arabian Sea. Fishermen in their lungis set up the famous Chinese nets. It smells of fish everywhere. Street cats lie lazily within eyesight of the fresh catch, waiting for the slightest opportunity to scavenge.

I find a beachside shack, order a strawberry milkshake, feel the sea breeze, and watch the lazy, orange sun slowly descend over the water in the horizon.

Back in my homestay that night, I catch a glimpse of myself in the mirror. The man who stares back seems almost like a morphed version of me, like someone caught me looking into a funky face-distorting photo-app. I realize that I've hardly seen myself for days, whether in a mirrored reflection or through the front-facing 'selfie' lens of my phone camera. My photo gallery is filled with photographs of places I've been to, places that exist *without* me. Beaches and train coaches and platforms, sunrises, chai in Styrofoam cups, mango trees, moonlit nights, and the many people I've met and interviewed on the way. But I don't take photos of myself; my personal presence is a blank. I'm my own ghostly memory.

I'm in my late thirties now. My cheeks are thinner, beard and hair steadily growing silver,* darker circles under my eyes, a few more wrinkles on my forehead. I expect this older reflection to set off a sharp notice of my mortality, a descent into existential abyss, an anxious confrontation with self, a reminder that each passing day is a day closer to death. And when I'm gone, I'm gone. No reincarnations and heavenly gates. Just an eternal vacuum, sans

*Well, they're turning white, but I find it more consoling to write 'silver'.

my consciousness. And my descendants will die, and all records of existence will vanish, and the very Earth will be baked and blasted by the sun, leaving behind nothing but light years of ghostly silence.

But that anxiety barely brushes the surface of my skin before skipping away. Instead, I feel a flight of mosquitoes landing on that very skin, bringing me back to the present. I smother myself with mosquito-repelling Odomos cream, legs and feet and arms and neck and my cheeks, too. I have always felt as if this species held a personal vendetta against me. Some researchers have found that mosquitoes gravitate to human body odour abundant in carboxylic acids, like butyric acid, which is produced naturally in our body, but also occurs in milk products like cheese, yoghurt, butter, etc.* The solution to this issue—i.e., the opposite of carboxylic acids—is any odour rich in eucalyptol, which the American Chemical Society says is found in tea tree oil...and *Cannabis sativa*. The hope is that this discovery may help in fighting vector-borne diseases, particularly in endemic regions in India and elsewhere, with a more targeted response—and another potential use of the cannabis plant.

In my homestay, the Odomos hardly helps. The mosquitoes keep coming back, undeterred, puncturing bits of me for tiny doses of their own ananda. A short moment of ecstasy, procreation, followed by a swift death. A month or two for them, a handful of decades for us.

(In the travels from my younger days, I used to tell myself that all I needed to survive on the road was a 1. Clean toilet and 2. Odomos cream. Now, I've updated that list: 1. Toilet, 2. Odomos, and 3. Decent Wi-Fi. The triangle of expectation, however, rarely tessellates together in perfect symmetry.)

That night, lying alone on a new bed, in yet another new city, I plug in my earphones and close my eyes, and, exhausted after another long day, I wonder how I could isolate and fool myself—

*No, this information is not going to make me cut down my murg makhani or milky chai intake.

temporarily—into believing that this is really all there is, that life matters only for the present moment, that in a burning world, I could simply insulate myself in the haze and never seek clarity again.

In 2013, the director Aashiq Abu brought together a group of veteran actors of Kerala's film industry for the Malayalam-language stoner dramady, *Idukki Gold*. The plot features five former schoolmates who reunite in adulthood and reminisce over youthful nostalgia, when they spent much of their time in the pristine mountains around Kerala's Idukki district, drinking alcohol, and savouring the region's beloved creation: the eponymous local ganja.

A disclaimer before the film covers all the legal complications, before the fun is set to begin: *We don't support the use of any drugs. Usage of drugs will lead to impotency or even death. BE CAREFUL!!!**

Unlike much of mainstream Indian cinema, which has flinched in the face of marijuana use, *Idukki Gold* comes shrouded under a cover of cannabis smoke. Ganja dominates the experiences of the characters, and eventually defines their friendship together. Much of the film is thus based in flashbacks, to a time when this strain of ganja grew abundantly in the Idukki district.

By the time I make my first visit up to the mountains, however, a lot has changed. Most of the cannabis farms in the hidden forests of Idukki's Cardamon Hills**—or Yela Mala—have been seized, burned, demolished. The famous Idukki Gold landrace of weed is now probably extinct.

Nowadays, the most popular export from Idukki is not the cannabis leaf, but tea leaves. After one night in Kochi, I find myself on an early morning bus to Munnar, up towards this idyllic land of

---

*Perhaps I should've copy-pasted the same disclaimer at the beginning of this book.

**The name comes from the cardamom spice grown here, which also supports the growth of pepper and coffee.

tea plantations. A popular draw for tourists, Munnar is nicknamed the 'Kashmir of South India'. The drive is on a beautiful ascending hill road up the Western Ghats, among dense forests of rubber and pine trees, and across the Periyar River. Four hours later, acres upon acres of tea gardens are revealed, leaves shining almost golden under the morning sun. I have the window seat, with the shutter pulled wide open, feeling the cool mountain air.

With plantations even at 2,200 metres above sea level, Munnar has some of the highest tea regions in the world. The first tea estate is believed to have been set up here by the Scotsman Baron Von Rosenberg in 1879. Today, there are more than fifty tea estates and gardens in and around Munnar, including the famous Lockhart Tea Museum and Factory. Tea is for sale everywhere, along with local spices, homemade chocolates, and honey. The weather is mostly pleasant during my visit, lush and green; I learn that, in the monsoon season, much of this region will be under torrential, heavy rain. So much of the topography here looks like it could've been the setting of Tolkien's imagined Shire (I half-expect to see barefoot Hobbits popping up and around the teahouses, stoned on pipe-weed). The climate is much cooler compared to the heat and humidity of Kochi. These are ideal conditions for harvesting tea—and cannabis, too.

Of course, I try the tea, binge-drinking all day as if each cup was a little shot of soma. It tastes crisp, with a slight creaminess to it, sweetish even without adding sugar. I imagine that the local strain of extinct weed probably shared the same flavourful qualities: crisp and fruity, a delightful head-trip.

There are many local legends to the inception of the Idukki Gold, a strain that landed in the forests of Idukki in the 1980s. Also nicknamed Neela Chadayan*, the weed was possibly a hybrid of two different strains. Journalist Bobins Abraham, in interviewing

---

*In 2023, twenty-eight-year-old Akhil Kavintarikath, a writer from Kannur, won the Kerala Sahitya Akademi's literature award for his short story collection named after the local brand of cannabis, *Neelachadayan*.

some of the expert growers from the region, estimated that the strain was likely 80 per cent of Indian origin, and 20 per cent foreign.

Abraham wrote his report in 2017, years after much of the cultivation of the plant had halted. That year had also been marked by a rainfall deficit, which hurt the production of the main cash crop in the region—cardamom—and led some farmers to test the waters with cannabis once again. However, Abraham told me more recently that the cannabis cultivation in Idukki is 'next to nil'.

So, arriving in Munnar so long after the last of that beloved 'blue curly', I almost feel like I'm a marijuana-palaeontologist. Two decades ago, thousands of acres of land in the outskirts of Munnar had been dedicated to the cultivation of cannabis, in dense jungles which sometimes ran into the unmarked borders of neighbouring Tamil Nadu, and regions near Mathikettan, Thodupuzha, Kattappana, and more. Many of those areas now belong to local tribes, or are protected by the forest department, including the reserve at the Pampadum Shola National Park. Several tribal villages here are now closed to outsiders; Edamalakkudy, a remote village, became the first tribal panchayat in Kerala. The forests that formerly played host to cannabis cultivation cannot be visited without permission from tribal seniors, the forest department, the state police, and after crossing many more bureaucratic hurdles.

About 10 kilometres from Munnar, the nearby forest has also been taken over by the Eravikulam National Park, which is closed when I visit for the animals' breeding season. If the cannabis isn't protected here any more, at least other species are, including the endangered Nilgiri tahr (goat of the blue hills), Nilgiri langurs, tigers, leopards, wild dogs, and giant squirrels. I'm told by locals that panthers are also sighted in the open grasslands, far away from the touristy encroachment of humanity.

I'm part of that touristy encroachment, too. I spend an afternoon and evening familiarizing myself with Munnar, with the aforementioned cups of tea at the famous museum, strolling up and down the somewhat-busy city centre, and around photogenic little hillocks around town. Everything in Munnar rushes at me in a form of a sensory overload, everything feels vivid, vibrant, alive, as if I'm in the first-person point-of-view video game, exploring a new graphic environment created solely for my experience. I hear the rumble of each passing car engine, fall into the abyss of the space between each letter on billboard advertisements, and ponder joyfully at every item of food I consume. Each spoonful of sambar-dipped idli tastes like the greatest dish ever conceived. If I concentrate, I can see the idli not as a fluffy rice cake, but as an organism of active throbbing cells, spicy lentils in a state of elemental flux.

I take a bite and combine the energies. The arrow of time splits and splits again, branching out within the morsels of vacuous space between seconds. I'm invited into possible parallel universes, a choose-your-own-adventure story that is being dictated in real time.

A 2012 study for the *Psychopharmacology* journal investigated the acute effects of THC on time perception in frequent and infrequent cannabis users, concluding after tests on forty-four subjects that THC doses can increase 'internal clock speed as indicated by time overestimation and underproduction'. For habitual users of cannabis, the borders between real and unreal can become blurred, bringing us back to those age-old philosophical concerns about truths and illusions, metaverses and universes, maya and atman. The perception of time and sensory diffractions turns reality over its head.

But, one could argue that even our 'sober' realities are a form of illusion, too. We see what we wish to see and sense what we wish to sense. Where two people could be in the same restaurant, sharing the same plate of idli, and yet taste two entirely different dishes.

One of the best examples of this is the idea of the brain's pantone, or how our eyes perceive colour. We all see the same green on that cannabis leaf, but that colour itself is an illusion, stimulated by reflected light teaching our brain how to interpret each shade of green (or a shade of gold, or curly blue). For most of us, the perception of every instant of reality is performed too quickly for us to ever notice the firing neurons of our brain. But, under the blissful, mind-expanding high, the inner-workings are slowed down, not fully revealed but exposed with more clarity. Some senses are enhanced, while others get blurred, like a macro-focused camera that leaves the background in a haze.

Frequent, heavy marijuana use can leave the dependent individual longing for this haziness, or with a scrambled gaze offering new pantones with which to view their world. The 'old' perspective of reality around us is simply not as interesting any more. Perhaps, ganja is an addiction the way that travel might be an addiction: that yearning to experience a different world, that rejection of familiarity, a motivation to remain unsettled, to get up and go again. Or, perhaps, the addiction is merely a longing for a break from the norm: a new coat of colour on the house, a new flavour of ice cream, an extramarital relationship after years of monogamy.

In the cruel doldrums of predictability, we crave for every day to feel special—if only in our heads. It's why the world is so memorable for children, for whom every minute feels longer, every experience is something new, each day an opportunity to learn and dramatically refresh oneself. So many of us 'grown ups' continue to seek a sense of daily wonderment which has been snatched away by the shackles of adulthood. Sometimes, we wish to be unsure and uncomfortable again, to revel again in the joys of bewilderment and curiosity. Life can feel simply too absurd, too meaningless without it.

Now, when the THC receptors collaborate with our anandamide, they are not answering any deeper questions about existence; but perhaps the bliss is enough to numb the pain of this existential crisis, to provide sensory distraction from the daunting, sober reality.

I think of the songs we hum, the films we watch, the books we read, the livelihoods we chase, the families we love, the mechanics of biology that keep us alive, and I feel smaller than ever in the grand scheme of things.

And thus passes another night.

And then the morning calls. The clouds clear, the sun peeks in through the curtains, a cup of tea jolts the dulled senses.

I have set up a time to meet Munnar's DSP this morning, the most senior police officer here. I walk up the short incline to the local police station, accompanied by little else but a long silence, disturbed occasionally by trucks from a nearby construction project blowing dust in the otherwise pristine air.

Busy with what is described to me as only an 'incident' in a nearby village, the DSP K. R. Manoj is a little late arriving to the office. He has a round face and a proud, Chevron moustache—bushy and jet-black—the chosen style of facial hair, I've noticed, of many men in Kerala. In thick-accented English, he tells me that he has only been posted at Munnar for the past couple of years, long after the days of ganja cultivation in the region.

Now, Manoj is confident—almost aggressively so—that those days are over. 'We have five police stations in this area, and four of them are connected with the Tamil Nadu border. There is no cultivation, no information. Zero. There is nothing. Nil.'

(Similar claims have been made in Tamil Nadu, too; in July 2023, the police claimed that the state had maintained 'zero' ganja cultivation in the past five years.)

Manoj asserts that, one of the main reasons for this absolute shutdown in Idukki is the increase in mobility. 'You see, there is a lot of forest area here, forest covering. And there are *all* animals here—except lions.* The place is highly cut off. Even the police couldn't go that deep into the jungle before. But, nowadays, mobility has become very easy: we can easily get information and make an arrest.'

'This area is quite peaceful,' he adds with a smile. 'Not so much of a problem. It's going good.'

---

*Supercop Manoj is also a master of hyperbole.

(It wouldn't stay good for too long: two months after my visit, three police officers working at this very police station would be accused of leaking information from a work computer to 'extremist' organizations. Manoj would be directed to conduct a probe over this issue and submit a report to his seniors. A few months later, the accused officers would be transferred to different districts. I interviewed a number of officers and support staff during my visit, but none who were named in this probe.)

While Manoj couldn't offer many more details about the heyday of cannabis cultivation in this district, he did introduce me to two civil police officers—Aneesh Kumar PR and Shaju MM—who had witnessed much of the 'action' first-hand. We converse between languages and translations: I can speak in English and Hindi, but not in Malayalam, which is their mother tongue; Kumar knows some Hindi but not English; Shaju can speak in English but not Hindi. Both have lived in the region for nearly thirty years, with Shaju spending twenty-seven of them on the force.

We're seated in an empty room in the station, one used for meetings, perhaps, or for interrogations. Before we even speak of any specifics, both officers double-down on their superior's credo: Do you notice, they ask me, how peaceful it is here now?

While Munnar has long been a mostly peaceful destination—a draw for tourists and honeymooners—danger and drugs once lurked in the surrounding dense forests. Kumar estimates that, at its peak, ganja cultivation likely encompassed approximately 2,000 acres of land in Idukki and the borderlands by Tamil Nadu—or, the equivalent of 500 cricket grounds.* The mitti (soil) here, says Kumar, is perfect for cultivating, with cool weather and a decent amount of rain. The closest farms were 60 to 70 kilometres away from towns like Munnar, with no motorable roads. These jungles

*If you fill every One-Day International cricket ground on Earth with ganja, you will need at least another Earth of similar ODI grounds to fit all the ganja that once grew in Idukki.

are deep, dark, and mysterious. In January 2024, fourteen members of a police team who were combing through the forest for cannabis cultivation got lost in the woods overnight, before a rapid response team rescued them the following morning.

Kumar suggests that, apart from the tribals and local villagers hired to cultivate the crops, there were also several Tamil-speaking middlemen involved in the process from across the state border. The larger organization was led by drug-trafficking groups from elsewhere: Kochi, Calicut, Thiruvananthapuram, or Tamil Nadu.

The local farmers were instructed to work on the fields, while remaining virtually disconnected from the outside world. Under the opaque cover of the forest, they had all they needed to insulate themselves and their weed. The middlemen gave them enough ration (rice, vegetables, and alcohol) to last the season. They hunted and gathered whatever other meat and vegetables they needed. They had all the ganja in the world in case they wished to get high on their own supply. Their only task was to take care of the ganja fields, and when the buds were ready, the farmers would cut and pack the 'gold' for the middlemen, who would then hike back down from the mountains and spread its golden tresses far and wide.

To get to these hidden hectares of cannabis, local police officers like Kumar and Shaju traversed for hours into the dense forest on foot, long before motorable roads connected some of the way. 'And when we went by foot, they [the farmers] could easily spot us from their elevation,' says Kumar.

'There was a lot of violence at that time,' Shaju adds. He has a big, found face, with a mostly bald scalp, and that Chevron moustache. He wears a smile of someone who has seen too much to bother frowning any more. 'Back then, they [the cartel] had a lot of weapons, too. It was very difficult to get to most of the land, like a Herculean task. Sometimes we had to get on all fours and slowly step up or down the mountain. From the top side of the hill, they would throw big rocks down at us. Or shoot down at us.'

Shaju spreads his palms wide and pretends to scale up an imaginary mountain, like Spider-Man climbing vertically up a building.

Things began to change drastically by the mid-2000s, when the Kerala police, the forest department, and the excise department joined hands for a multi-pronged assault on the cartels. With improved roads deeper into the forest came less privacy for the farmers. Cameras have since been installed at crucial places across the jungle. The forest department have turned much of the land into protected sanctuary zones. And the police have reached out to forge a better line of communication with the tribal population here—like the Tribal Janamaithri project—so that the locals can also serve as informants. (As part of their 'Yodhav' project to combat the supply/use of drugs, the Munnar Janamaithri police unit even produced a short film. DSP Manoj composed the lyrics for its soundtrack.)

Kumar tells me that a number of the outside middlemen involved in the trade have since left with their earnings. 'Some of them died in the violence,' says Kumar. 'Some grew older and died of disease. The rest ran away.' The cultivators were eventually overpowered, and the fields of ganja—lakhs upon lakhs of kilos of some of the best natural weed known to man—were burned.

The burning of 'illegal' crops is a particular trait of Indian law enforcement, and large-scale incinerations of cannabis farms (both wild and cultivated) routinely take place around the country. In 2011, nearly 30,000 marijuana plants were destroyed in Tripura by the Tripura State Rifles and the police. In 2018, authorities claimed to have destroyed nearly 8,000 kanals (a thousand acres) of 'bhang' cultivation around Kashmir. In Assam in early 2022, the state police made a big show of publicly setting fire to over 1,400 kilos of ganja in Kokrajhar district. Most dramatically, in early 2022, in the biggest operation of its kind, the police in Andhra Pradesh burned over 2 lakh kilos of ganja—seized as contraband—worth ₹500 crore. The operation took place at the Koduru village near

Visakhapatnam, where I imagine the fumes alone would've made any unsuspecting passing bird a little higher mid-flight.

Now, with the cartel and cultivation in Idukki mostly eradicated, many traffickers have moved up north to Andhra Pradesh and Odisha, where a 'sister strain' to the beloved Idukki Gold thrives.*

Many tourists from Kerala and beyond still visit the Idukki region in hopes of unearthing lost remnants of that mythical marijuana, reliving the nostalgia of the *Idukki Gold* film. They are adventurers on a crusade, in search of that holy gold grail of ganja. 'The Idukki Gold has become like a brand,' says Kumar, almost beaming with pride. 'Even in Andhra and other places, they are selling their product with the name "Idukki Gold". Idukki was the most powerful. Just one spoonful of the ganja would be as strong as three or four spoons of other [strains].'

And now, it's gone, kept alive only in imitation and conversation, a majestic extinct dinosaur, a beloved anti-hero in these parts, the ganja of God's Own Country, the manna of the Malabar Coast, the soma of the South.

Kerala has consistently been one of the highest-ranked states in India in the enforcement of its justice system, with a stricter police and more efficient judiciary compared to much of the country. The state's response to narcotics traffickers has been one major example of this efficiency. In May 2023, a joint investigation by the Narcotics Control Bureau (NCB) and the Navy announced a bust in Kochi of narcotics worth ₹12,000 crore—one of the largest such busts in Indian history—featuring 2,500 kilos of methamphetamine, 500 kilos of heroin, and 529 kilos of hashish oil.

Nowadays, even if the state isn't a major producer of ganja any more, weed-lovers continue to find whatever strain of cannabis

---

*Friends, this is called foreshadowing.

falsely branded as Idukki Gold to provide them their highs. The penalties are stiff, with a stringent response to any consumption or cultivation—whether it is the legally-cleared substance used at the ayurvedasram I'd visited, or the few cannabis plants found on the roadside on World Environment Day.

The stringent attitude extends far beyond ganja. Kerala was once known to have the country's highest per capita consumption of liquor, before its previous government called for an almost complete prohibition of alcohol in 2014. But history has taught us that prohibition hardly stops consumption; it only complicates matters and further endangers users to turn to illicit and more dangerous sources. And yes, alcoholism continued unabated in Kerala, regardless of prohibition. Since 2017, the Left Democratic Front (LDF) government has slowly chipped away at the policy, making alcohol available at licensed pubs and hotels.

Still, it's rare to find a spot for a glass of legal beer here.

On my last night in Munnar, I do find one such place, one with limited selections at high prices. The walls at this bar are decorated with posters of the penguins from *Happy Feet* and Richard Parker (the tiger) from the film *Life of Pi*, right next to a blown-up profile photo of its director Ang Lee. There's a four-foot-tall black-stone statue of an elephant nearby—a common sight around Kerala, like the two 'aanas' found on the state's emblem. There is no music or TV screen to disturb the establishment's solemn setting. Everything is tinged under the gaze of a dim, bluish light. Only men are seated here—mid-thirties and above—all a respectfully-morose distance away from each other.

I enjoy the occasional 'high' of drinking; but just a few, heavy sips of beer make me ponder again about the irony of it all, of consuming one legal substance instead of another, based on laws almost arbitrarily made by countries around the world. Both alcohol and ganja are substances that put one under the influence, that can provide joy and relief and relaxation and excitement.

But both can also bring about confusion, prove dangerous to young, developing minds, and threaten those assigned activities that require focus and responsibility (like driving). Yet, one of these vices is mostly socially accepted, one that makes you the life of the party or gives you some relief at the end of a difficult day; the other is spoken of more often in hushed tones—branded narcotic, illicit, dangerous, criminal.

I also think back to my conversation with the civil police officers, as they had mentioned the rise of harder drug usage in Kerala in recent years, with more of the youth turning to MDMA and LSD. Kumar had told me that, 'Ganja comes from the soil…so it would be better. But these drugs are far more dangerous. They come in all colours, all types. People have the money now, and they can swallow it easily, secretly. There's no smell, nothing. It can be in a pill form, like a powder, or even as a dessert.'

Kumar had spoken about the horrors of heroin, too, a substance behind the cause of a rising drug abuse epidemic across many regions I visited during my travels. 'With ganja, it's something for one person,' he had said. 'But heroin users share injections—so they're not only killing themselves, they're killing whoever they're sharing it with.'

From the perspective of the original NDPS Act, however, ganja is closer to the same ignoble category of the hardest drugs available on the street. Meanwhile, alcohol enjoys social acceptance in most states, sold to anyone who can offer their hard-earned money through the iron bars at a theka, openly offered at high-end cocktail parties, glugged down at sports pubs during IPL games, and taxed at high excise rates.

I take another sip of my beer. It's been a long time since I've had a drink. Or maybe, it hasn't? Perhaps the heady rush of new experiences I've had have skewed my perception of time.

Time doesn't make as much sense as it used to. But when I check my phone again for the itinerary, I remember that I'm only two days away from my flight out of Kochi, away from this comfort of unfamiliarity.

I feel I have been sitting in this blue-penguin bar for hours, but I'm not even a quarter of the way through my beer. I check my phone for messages again. Then, I play online chess, against a bot. Then, I scroll through social media, exploring anything that distracts me: sports, films, celebrity gossip, whatever makes the hour pass, whatever turns evening into night, late enough for me to consider turning in for sleep.

I can hardly let my phone sit still now. Compared to my previous trip around the country—over a decade ago—I look down at the screen all the time, unlocking it and locking it again. I know that this is a weakness, a longing to escape the present moment, to be away, to be connected with someone, anyone else.

I have learned that one of the pleasant results of a euphoric high is that it can help release one's mind from these ruts, make one observe the world with the same sense of wonder that we did when we were younger. For most of us, this version of us has now long departed: the attention span for curiosity is lost. We grow up, we specialize, we fixate on a limited number of things, our life becomes routine.

This too, I know, shall pass. I dutifully sit and finish my drink before heading back to the homestay. It's early in the night, but I have little else to do, and after a few flicks through uninteresting cable TV, I wrap myself in the bedsheet, turn down the lights, and plug my earphones gently into the pocket of each ear canal.

The music provides the background score, but the main narrative action is me alone with myself again. I've known a number of friends in the past for whom this might be the most challenging time of the day, friends who are unable to fall asleep sober, who need one last joint before calming themselves for the night. And it is true: cannabis does have the power to be an organic (and some would say safer) sleep supplement than most modern medicine. It shuts off the senses, draws the blinds inside the mind's eye, blurs the line between consciousness and dreams until one floats lovingly between both.

For some, however, sleep becomes nearly impossible unless accompanied by this supplemented bliss, without that steady, warm weight over one's head, shushing and lulling one to relaxation, the feeling of being a toddler again, pacified by the warmth of a mother's embrace. Deep breaths. The troubles of the day numbed into peace.

For me, it is this moment before sleep when I again face the most tenacious and confrontational part of myself, when I feel the emptiness of my purpose. Why am I out here again, I wonder, instead of spending more time with my family? With my daughter? Why am I skimming through so many pages of life? What is the cost of these fleeting memories and experiences—coming and going without permanence?

In the heaviest throes of a cannabis trip, some are sucked into a quicksand of paranoia, a daldal that pulls one in deeper the harder one fights to jump out to freedom. I have experienced a form of this daldal too, going down a rabbit hole of my insecurities, this sudden reminder of mortality, a faint alarm that tells me that one day I will sleep and keep sleeping.

I've thought a lot more about dying since my daughter's birth. I imagine this to be the experience of most parents, since staying alive is now more than a privilege—it's an urgent responsibility. My absence will mould her personality forever, like how the separation from my own parents—courtesy boarding school—shaped mine.

I attempt to shrug away these seeds of doubt each time my inner voice cultivates them. My hope is that those seeds will be discarded and wizen before they can truly bloom. All doubt is smoked away.

Instead, I seek a new direction. I'd come to Kerala to explore the Idduki Gold, only to find that this once-legendary strain was now all but stuff of legend. Driven away from the southern coast, the cartels had migrated towards the east, to central and eastern states where the gold would find a sequel under the cover of the dense jungles and the tribal lands of India's Red Corridor, into a region that has become the capital of the country's cannabis black market.

So, I'm on the move, too. The next bus out of town, the next walk around the stone-paved pathways of Fort Kochi, the next flight, the next trip away from home.

Sheelavathi

'...the hands that tend to the growing bud, the hands that cut the ganja, the hands that store pressed stacks of the maal in hidden compartments, the hands that pay in cash, the hands that packet the weed into small parcels, the hands that make the cash exchange with the user, the hands that roll the joint, the lips that smoke it, the mind that is blown away....'

We're in an air-conditioned room, likely the only working AC in the whole village, likely the only AC in the entire Bonda Ghati. This 'ghati' (which means incline or hill) is a hillside of a few dozen villages in Odisha, protected for members of the Bonda tribe. The Upper Bondas—with a population of just around 7,000 who live in these quiet, faraway villages—are considered to be the most-isolated community from 'mainstream' Indian society. I don't expect mobile signals or Western-style toilets here. I don't expect bottled water or even a dhaba to order a bowl of soupy Maggi.

I hadn't expected the air-conditioner, either.

I feel unworthy to be a recipient of this special treatment, to be invited into the office for lunch, eating delicious rice and chicken with a few senior members of the Bonda Development Agency (BDA). The BDA is a government programme launched to pay special interest to the concerns of this tribe—Odisha has the highest and most diverse number of Particularly Vulnerable Tribal Groups (PVTGs) in the country.

After lunch, I find time to speak to Nanddas Sheesha, one of the young Bonda men who works as an assistant for the gram panchayat at the village. He keeps his eyes lowered and talks with snappy spurts of energy, telling me of the many fellow men of this disenfranchised Adivasi group who have been caught in a menacing web of the regional drug trade. The state borderlands of Odisha and Andhra Pradesh are the heartland of India's 'Red Corridor': a homebase for armed insurgent groups, rampant with frequent violent clashes against India's security forces. Many villagers are hired as mules to smuggle out bricks of an enchanting strain of local ganja cultivated nearby, forming the backbone of the largest and most lucrative trafficking rings in the country.

That strain is called Sheelavathi.

Sheesha, twenty-three, is somewhat of an anomaly among the Bonda population. He is the first in his family to seek higher education,* studying economics in Bhubaneswar, Odisha's capital, a fifteen-hour-long drive from the Bonda Ghati. But the pandemic shut down in-person classes, and Sheesha had to return home to his village to work with the BDA. 'Sir, sir, some are studying from home,' he says. 'Some from online classes. Now, some schools have started in person, too. But there are too many in the Bonda tribes who don't have the funds to study in college any more—so they don't go.' He speaks to me in Hindi, his third language, after Remo (the language of many in the Upper Bonda region) and Odia. He adds a double honorific before every answer. *Sir, sir.*

In late 2021, a few months before my trip to Odisha and Andhra Pradesh, two youngsters from Sheesha's tribe—sixteen to seventeen-year-olds—were nabbed on a public bus, each carrying several kilos of the Sheelavathi ganja in their backpacks. When it comes to implementing the NDPS law, India's slow-footed judiciary can often turn into a model of brisk efficiency: the teenagers were immediately tried, convicted, and locked up at the district jail in Malkangiri.

In this part of the country, young Adivasis like Sheesha's acquaintances are too often caught in the crossfire of the thriving

*According to some estimates, only 6 per cent of the Bonda people are literate.

drug trade, in districts inundated by the presence of Maoist rebels, police, counter-insurgency forces, and powerful mafia. In 2021, nearly half of the cannabis-based drugs seized in India under the NDPS Act were from the Andhra/Odisha region.

When locals like Sheesha refer to the ongoings of the drug trade, they often use the passive voice, handing responsibility to those shadowy forces operating in the background, pointing at the brokers of power that command the cultivation, transport, and sale of ganja, without any specifics of who exactly these forces might be. 'They were just told to take these bags to Bhubaneswar,' says Sheesha. 'They didn't even know what they were carrying.'

There are a few other Bonda, too, he said, similarly scapegoated in the ongoing skirmish between the law and the lawbreakers, imprisoned in faraway lands: further into Andhra Pradesh, Uttar Pradesh, all the way down in Chennai. District jails around these parts of Odisha are packed with many more men and women from marginalized tribal communities like the Bonda and Didayi, all clamped down by the NDPS Act, sentenced to months, years, behind bars.

Meanwhile, the shadowy *they*—the cartel who keep the wheel turning—are hardly ever found.

Much of the actual ganja cultivation is done deeper in the jungles, away from the settlements at the Bonda Ghati and nearby towns, hidden beyond the encompassing shield of silver oak trees, inaccessible by most four- and two-wheeler vehicles, found only after long hikes through paths that criss-cross like entangled puzzles. There is also the very real threat of violence in the backdrop of this world, which makes it nearly impossible for any non-local civilian to find their way to the widespread fields of cannabis across India's Eastern Ghats.

Sheesha, the BDA administrators, and others whom I spoke to, insisted that while some of the young were getting entrapped as foot soldiers in the larger drug cartel here, they weren't users (or abusers) of the plant themselves. The intoxicants of choice here are the locally brewed alcoholic beverages. Many of the Bonda festivities incorporate the worship of natural elements: mountains, rocks, cows, trees. 'During parbo (festival) time,' says Sheesha, 'all of them [natural elements] become gods. Even a tree. Even a rock.' During the popular Chaitra Parbo, the villagers isolate themselves fully from the rest of the outside world, barring all visitors. Some consume a drink called 'salakh', made from the ras (pulp extract) of the bark of coconut or palm tree, producing an intoxicating sweet, sugary liquid. The extract is called 'gusanteb', a parbo favourite.

Alcohol consumption is a major cause for concern for many men here. 'The Bonda men have one issue,' says Sheesha, 'they get irritated over the smallest things.' This quick temper, he adds, has given the men of the community a notorious, violent reputation.

It is the role of women in the Bonda social structure that makes this community truly distinctive. The Bonda are primarily matriarchal, where women are usually the main breadwinners and organizers of social structure. Many women here tend to marry younger men—and sometimes, teenage boys—with the intention that they will be served and supported as they grow older, in a form of bonded association known as 'Gufam'.

Bonda women are mentioned in a somewhat infamous episode in Indian mythology from the Ramayana. While travelling in exile, the epic's female protagonist Sita stepped into a pond near the Mudulipada village for a bath (the pond is now called Sitakunda). Some Bonda women nearby saw the naked Sita and sniggered among themselves. Enraged, Sita cursed the women: they, and all their descendants, would be condemned to remain naked, with their heads shaved bald. Sita only gave the women a small respite—a piece of cloth from her own sari as cover.

Some 2,500 years after Valmiki composed the Ramayana, I meet a number of descendants of the originally 'condemned' Bonda women. Most are clothed in colourful saris, but their heads are bald, and their bodies are decorated with an elaborate cover of jewellery: brass nose rings, earrings, and some have orbits of huge metal rings that form towers around their necks. Some have their forearms covered under a layer of bangles, and some—continuing Sita's decree—are draped only in colourful, thin pieces of cloth below the waist.

The modern Bonda men, meanwhile, dress like they would dress up almost anywhere else: T-shirts, trousers, collared shirts, track pants, chappals. Some of them, like Sheesha, have an education and a stable job. Some find their vocation (along with the elder women) out on the farms, growing traditional crops like turmeric, ginger, rajma, and the suan bhat—a form of millet which is the principal food here, especially for community feasts. Millet has been one of the main crops encouraged by government initiatives for local farmers to cultivate as an alternative to cannabis.

This is a whole new world for me, into a life radically unfamiliar from my own.

But, let me rewind a little bit. It had taken many months of careful planning and coordination to get here, along with the generous help of local experts, before I'd packed my backpack, waved ta-ta to the last bars of connectivity on my phone, and set off on the road once again.

I land first in Visakhapatnam, popularly known as 'Vizag', a port city that finds itself tucked in the lovely confluence of space between the Eastern Ghats and the Bay of Bengal. The location provides a cool, calming breeze that often flows through this city, delivering a breath of fresh air to its residents. Vizag is in Andhra Pradesh, but lies close to the border into Odisha. It's a central hub of India's steel-manufacturing plants, a growing IT sector, a naval base, missile and submarine port, and much more. In January

2023, the city was declared the executive capital of the state and elevated to a grander political stage.

It has been called the City of Steel, the City of Destiny.

Nowadays, it's also the City of Ganja.

On my first night at Vizag, I check into a cheap hotel near the railway station, the type with narrow stairwells, chipping wallpaper, rusted window bars, and bedsheets with bite marks that could only be a sign of rodents. However, before I could even drag my tiny suitcase inside, the manager at the reception desk—bathed in neon white light—tells me that he's doing me a favour by *not* inspecting my belongings. 'The police have advised us to check everyone's bag these days,' he says. 'You don't know how many people are smuggling drugs.'

Immediately, as if to erase any hint of suspicion, I begin to unzip the bag myself. 'Go ahead and check,' I say.

'No, no,' he stops me. 'You look like a decent person.'

Decent?

I would wonder later how much the 'decency' of other travellers—and usually, other able-bodied men—would come under the scanner. How many would be forced to reveal their belongings on the mildest hint of suspicion? How many would be reported, how many arrested? By the end of 2023, the Vizag city police had seized 10,000 kilos of dry ganja and 20 kilos of hashish oil in the past two years—big numbers, but surely, just the residue that sat on the tip of the chillum, as tens of thousands of kilos of more contraband made their way past the transit points to other cities and states across India.

Just a few hundred kilometres away from the bustling cityscape of Vizag are the hills, valleys, and forests that comprise Visakha Agency: towns and villages in the Andhra Odisha Border (AOB) which are largely protected and reserved for the Adivasi communities that have long inhabited this region. These thick, forested areas also serve as cover for the Sheelavathi ganja cultivation that is then smuggled through rail and road far and wide across the country, to West Bengal, Maharashtra, Goa, Karnataka, Tamil Nadu, to Delhi and even further up north. In Kerala, it is rebranded and sold as the original Idukki Gold.

The next day, I'm off on a long road trip towards that AOB area, driving up across a remarkable variation of topography, across lush forests and arid hilly routes, past the Godavari River, into lands barely occupied, on highways hardly traversed. My destination is the border town of Koraput in Odisha, the last major district before my journey towards the Bonda Ghati. It's warm and dry on the way here, in the middle of March, away from Vizag's pleasant sea breeze.

The outskirts of Koraput are home to a number of factories of major Indian state-owned companies, including Hindustan Aeronautics Limited, the Kolab Hydroelectric power station, and the National Aluminium Company Limited (NALCO), one of the largest integrated bauxite/alumina/aluminium power complexes in the country. Towns like Koraput, here in the heart of the country, are usually rich in natural resources like bauxite, but poor in per capita GDP. For decades, activists and natives (often Adivasis) have protested the large-scale industrial mining of raw material here. This tug of war has also given rise to the violent clashes between the Maoist insurgents and the armed forces. In 2009, former prime minister Manmohan Singh stated that the rise in violence in the Red Corridor (parts of Bihar, Chhattisgarh, Jharkhand, Odisha, and more) is the country's 'greatest internal security' threat.

It's been a precarious balance for politicians in these states to appease industrial investors as well as their disenfranchised local populations; a balance, which when disturbed, has led to strikes, shutdowns, and bloodshed.

Koraput is a small, sleepy town, famous for a Jagannath temple, which is also near the guest house where I will be staying the night. Here, I wait for Akshay Sahoo, a journalist from Bhubaneswar who will join me for my trip to the Bonda Ghati the following morning. I pass time hopping from a chai shop to a coffee shop, strolling through market streets, and then, finding myself bored and uninspired, hoping for an early night's sleep.

Before coming here, I had scouted the hidden recesses of the internet to learn that there is a famous strain of cannabis—more famous in the West than in India—called the Koraput Purple. Perhaps, it's another rebranding of the nearby Sheelavathi that just happened to pass through the district. What makes a cannabis plant turned purplish* is the high concentration of anthocyanin, an antioxidant credited with anti-inflammatory effects. Some believe that the purple strains make the weed stronger; some say it's simply a more successful medication for sleep.

It's sleep that I yearn for, more than anything. None of my usual modes of distraction work that night, and I find myself weak in the sudden vacuum without messaging services, social media, or streaming videos to pass my time. It's a strange feeling to be this disconnected, especially after how I've become a slave to having the world in my hands, to the algorithms that have interpreted and redefined me. WhatsApp, Twitter**, Instagram, Wordle, sports scores, whatever. It's all so far away.

It gets quiet as soon as the sun sets outside my window. And then, it stays quiet.

I meet Sahoo the following morning and accompany him and a couple of his contacts for the final leg of this journey. Sahoo is an experienced journalist, having made a trip up to the Bonda Ghati several times in the past, usually to report on the cultures and traditions of the Adivasis, as well as to highlight their economic concerns, including alarming cases of severe childhood malnutrition. Clad in a grey collared shirt and denim blue jeans, he is perhaps a decade older than I am, and operates with a thoughtful curiosity

---

*I finally understand the context of the purple haze Jimi Hendrix once crooned about, excusing himself to kiss the sky.

**I refuse to call it 'X'.

about everyone we encounter on the way. Unlike me, he has no specific project in mind. 'I always find something when I go up there,' he says.

But when I mention my particular area of interest—ganja—Sahoo is stumped. We are seated in a taxi that takes us out of the city, and into the deeper, sparse regions in the outskirts of the district. Sahoo's confident voice changes into a quieter, conspiratorial tone. 'The Odisha government is completely in denial about it,' he says. He's not sure if he can help me in this matter—or if he even should.

This is always an obvious hurdle with such trips, where I'm an outsider at the mercy of local experts. Like Sahoo, they often turn out to be helpful in opening doors for me, but it's hard to deny that they only show the world as *they* would see it, without the new angles or perspectives that I yearn for. I end up finding myself on guard, too, growing a little more prudent than usual. This can be both a boon and a bane. Some prudence, of course, is valuable: nothing truly constructive would ever get done without it. But too much concern can rob me from the potential for curiosity. From the rush of discovery.

Sahoo hasn't yet told me any specifics, but he hints that it wasn't easy for him to ensure that I was able to visit the Bonda Ghati without any hindrance. Now that he learns that I have questions regarding the 'sensitive' issue of ganja, he advises that I remain as discreet about my intentions as possible. 'They will suspect you....'

'Suspect *me*?'

'Yes.' He explains that the Naxals have set up covert camps around these parts, and, as visitors, we are natural suspects. 'And since you're dressed nice, the BSF (Border Security Force) soldiers will probably assume that we are the leaders or organizers from the big city, who have come to provide the Naxals something. Information. Resources.'

I smirk at the 'dressed nice' comment. I'm wearing a green *Star Wars* T-shirt—a cartoon Chewbacca looking out to the world—and a blue New York Knicks cap. It's as casual as I could be, with no additional frippery; but, it is 'Western' attire, and thus, immediately, highlights me as an outsider.

And of course, I'm more than just *any* outsider. I'm an outsider who comes here from a place of relative privilege, the privilege to simply drop into another world, experience the mild discomfort and thrilling novelty of a new habitat, and just as conveniently, fly away again. One of the main concerns for me has been to avoid standing out, to avoid being treated differently, or to impose too much of myself—and my individual history—on to a new environment. This is the mentality that I have carried wherever I travelled and lived: cities like Varanasi, Mussoorie, New Delhi, Leeds, Pune, Beijing, Washington D.C., Himalayan villages, the backwaters of Kerala, beaches in Goa, on trains, by the platforms.

This plan hardly ever succeeds. I'll almost always be an outsider, and I'll never be able to escape the ignorance that comes with my 'foreignness', that impulse to exoticize any cultural variety that is novel to me. What is exotic or even momentous for me is the daily reality for so many more. For long periods of this drive away from Koraput, I'm simply stumped into silence. The most appropriate thing I could now be is an empty vessel, just willing to observe and learn.

Many of the districts that surround the Bonda Ghati in Odisha—including Koraput, Jeypore, and Malkangiri—are some of the most improvised regions in the whole state. The cultivation of ganja has helped with the livelihood of many here, the same ganja which is then smuggled out around the country.

Some reports allege that the Naxals are the 'gatekeepers' of the cartel's activities here. We pass another bend on the highway, near Govindapalli, where in 2010 Maoists killed eleven special operation group personnel in an ambushed bomb blast. Two young Bonda men were arrested in connection to this blast, and were found to be among many other Bondas that had been trained by Maoists.

Several BSF and Central Reserve Police Force (CRPF) camps in the region have been attacked in similar ambushes by Maoist forces. In 2012, a day before the then-minister of union rural development Jairam Ramesh visited Malkangiri, Naxals triggered a landmine blast in the district's Kanaguda village, injuring three security personnel. More recently, in the nearby forests around Malkangiri, twenty-three Maoists were killed in an 'encounter' by the Andhra Pradesh and Odisha police.

Hardly anyone on ground, however, uses these explosive terms—'Naxals' and 'Maoists' and 'soldiers' and 'ambushes'. Instead, I'm simply warned of 'movement'. As in, there used to be more *movement* on the Bonda Ghati until a BSF camp was set up at its summit.

At a distance, I do see BSF soldiers on patrol, armed with rifles and outfitted in full army fatigue. But any such sights are a rarity; in our bursting at its seams country, this place is a strange anomaly, with large stretches of land abandoned into a spooky silence.

We halt for a chai on the way, where I'm also treated to a frittered, doughy snack—cost ₹5—which, I'm told has the local name of 'boulder'. 'Or bomb,' Sahoo adds with a sardonic smile. And then, we continue.

At Mathili—a village known for being the hometown of Laxman Nayak, a famous freedom fighter and tribal rights activist—we shift out of our smaller car and into a Bolero jeep, which will take us on the last leg of our journey up the hill. The road up the ghati is mostly quiet and scenic, overlooking the dry valley below. We don't see any other vehicles.

It's hot outside, and when I finally step out, I feel a slight thrill in each crunch of a dry leaf under my sneakers. The sun is blinding white in the bare afternoon; there are hardly any trees for cover.

We step out in a village ahead of Mudulipada, where I'm led into a school classroom. It's here that I discover my trip has coincided with a Bonda town hall meeting. Some fifty villagers—mostly women, all in their traditional attire—sit on chairs or on the carpeted floor facing the front of the classroom. Many of these women carry their children with them, including infants wrapped in colourful swaddles. And in the front of the classroom are seven or eight members of the BDA—all men, none from the Adivasi community—who are offering a lecture in Odia—which is then translated by Nanddas Sheesha into Remo.

Through some bits and pieces that I'm able to comprehend, I realize that this meeting is part of a programme sponsored by UNICEF and Odisha PVTG Empowerment and Livelihood Improvement Project (OPELIP) to spread awareness against child marriage. Specifically, the speakers are here to discourage local women from getting married to minor boys. The BDA members stress the minimum age for marriage: twenty-one for men, eighteen for women. After about an hour, they wrap up with the announcement of incentives and prizes for those who marry legally. A young Bonda couple who has married at appropriate ages—twenty-three and twenty-two—is invited to the front to be felicitated. After garlanding each other, the BDA director offers them their gift: a brand-new sewing machine. The newlyweds smile. The lecturing men break into applause. The next such couple is offered a drying mat. There are more such mats on the side of the classroom, waiting to be gifted. Some other couples, I'm told, have been promised incentives of up to ₹30,000 to marry after the legal age. Some have been promised vocational training in skills like plumbing, sewing, mechanics, etc. Administrators line up around the young couples for a photo opportunity. More big smiles.

Later that afternoon, after we've had our lunch and are on our way back to Koraput, Sahoo reveals, with some glint of pride, how he was able to get permission for me to visit the Bonda Ghati without raising any red flags. He had told a local media contact that a 'big journalist from Delhi'—me*—wanted to spotlight the

*Yes, I laughed at this part, too.

BDA's positive impact on the livelihood of the tribespeople. The local contact got in touch with a BDA administrator, and the BDA-wallah organized this special felicitation ceremony with representatives from UNICEF and OPELIP just to put on a show for my visit. This was no coincidence at all.

The whole thing, organized for a good cause, only came together because I was bringing a new perspective into this world. I could only respond to Sahoo with a quiet shrug: a shrug of disbelief morphing into a shrug of *Well-that's-India*.

One of the young men who didn't get married as a child—and is still unmarried—is Sheesha. It's Sheesha who tells me, after the town hall, about his imprisoned acquaintances and the rising cases of Adivasi men getting caught in the crossfire of the ganja trade.

'But the people who pay them aren't caught,' says Sheesha. 'The police only catch the tribals and put them in jail.'

Far north of Odisha, on 3 October 2021, a few hundred individuals hit the streets of Tikonia in Lakhimpur Kheri, a district in Uttar Pradesh that borders Nepal. These protests were part of the larger uprising that year against the central government in response to the three new farm laws introduced in the 2020 Indian agriculture acts. Across the country, the protests had already led to bandhs, violence, and caused a searing political migraine for Prime Minister Narendra Modi and the BJP—the political party in power both in the centre as well as in the state of Uttar Pradesh.

In Lakhimpur Sekri, when some of the farmers blocked the state's Deputy Chief Minister Keshav Prasad Maurya's visit to the Banbirpur village, a speeding SUV from the convoy—a Mahindra Thar—raced towards them. Pedestrians were run over by the first car, and more were crushed by two more vehicles from the same convoy. Two of the cars involved were owned by the union minister Ajay Kumar Mishra of the BJP; his son was seen in one of the cars by eyewitnesses. Gunshots followed. In return, some of the protestors set the Thar on fire.

Nine people died, a dozen more were injured.

The incident made national breaking news, shining a spotlight on the oppressive, brute force applied to dissenters in our country.

And then, as swiftly as the news broke, it faded, shifting from the front of televised debates to the tiny tickers at the bottom of the screen. The national narrative had changed in a matter of hours. All because of a little bit of weed.

It was, indeed, that same fateful Sunday—3 October 2021—that the NCB announced the arrest of Aryan Khan, the twenty-three-year-old son of Shah Rukh Khan, one of the biggest superstars in the history of Indian cinema. The younger Khan had been picked up from the cruise ship *Cray'Ark* off the coast of Mumbai, which was the setting of a high-profile rave party. NCB officers boarded the ship disguised as passengers, where they discovered some drugs—including charas—on board. Eight individuals were detained that day including young Aryan Khan.

No drugs were recovered on Khan himself, and yet, he was levied with a number of charges including: Section 8(c): Production, manufacturing, possession, selling, etc., of narcotic or psychotropic substance; Section 20(b): On possession, cultivation, manufacture, sale of cannabis; Section 27: Consumption of narcotic or psychotropic substance; and Section 35, which presumes that the accused was in a 'culpable mental state', and thus is treated as guilty until proven innocent.

For the next several weeks, Khan was held in judicial custody, first at the NCB's office, and then, at the Arthur Road Jail in Mumbai. Despite multiple pleas by Khan's lawyers—lawyers hired by one of the most powerful private citizens in the nation—he was denied bail. The NCB's case rested upon the drugs recovered from Khan's friend Arbaaz Merchant: a total of 6 grams of charas. Or, in street slang, basically around half a tola, maybe enough for ten joints if one is feeling truly generous. It would be worth just about a few thousand rupees—give or take—depending on where the charas was purchased from.

There were also some past WhatsApp chats where other contacts—including actress Ananya Pandey—allegedly offered to 'arrange' some ganja for Khan. This arrangement (or more precisely, 'jugaad', the word Khan used) was being framed as some sort of international drug smuggling ring. In high-profile cases, *any* group of friends mentioning ganja on their WhatsApp can be interpreted as a 'drugs nexus'.

Now, of course, I'm not advocating that anyone break the law (or worse, break it on a cruise ship named *Cray'Ark**), but a mela of madness followed Khan's arrest, all because he *possibly* wished to smoke a few joints. As newspapers, televised news, and magazines hungered for the next sensational twist and turn in this case, Khan continued to spend time behind bars. He was portrayed as the symbol of all evils associated with high-profile celebrities, of spoiled 'nepo babies' of famous film stars, of a dangerous young goonda. And, in a country more polarized than ever against minority communities, he also happened to be the son of *Muslim* film star. A *Khan*. Despite unwavering support from Papa Shah Rukh's fan base, Aryan's status denied him sympathy in the eyes of much of the clamouring population, enraged by the hounding barks of TV anchors and obstreperous wildfire of social media rumours.

Some 1,500 kilometres away in Lakhimpur Sekri, it took authorities almost a whole week to arrest Ashish Mishra,** Ajay Kumar Mishra's son and the primary accused in the vehicle-ramming attack incident. Meanwhile, all around the country, farmers continued to protest, Covid cases were still a cause for concern,

---

*If anyone should be arrested, it should've been the dude who gave this cruise ship the corniest name possible.

**Mishra was released and remains out on bail at the time of writing, over three years since the incident.

violence raged in Kashmir, and the economy was still in turmoil. But little else mattered more than a famous twenty-three-year-old who'd (allegedly) wanted to jugaado a little charas for himself.

Back in Mumbai, another twist further complicated Khan's case. Now, an independent witness alleged that Sameer Wankhede—the director of the NCB behind the arrest—had surreptitiously asked for a ₹25 crore payout in return for Khan's release. Wankhede faced a probe from his own bureau.

Saner minds soon prevailed, as Khan was finally granted bail on 28 October, and walked out of jail two days later in time to celebrate Diwali with his family.

Six months later, the NCB dropped all charges against him (and five other suspects), pointing to a 'lack of sufficient evidence' and 'shortcomings' in the original probe. Khan's detention lasted just twenty-six days, but it once again put front and centre the overreaction—and deferred reaction—of both narcotics authorities and the mainstream media in such cases. Being in the limelight, Khan's case also overshadowed the thousands of young men and women arrested around the country on similarly flimsy charges of consumption, transportation, or conspiracy, while the bigger fish in the pond continue to swim untracked.

Many of those bigger fish have targeted the high-profile seaports of Gujarat for entry into Indian borders. Since 2017, the NCB, the Coast Guard, the Anti-Terrorism Squad, the Directorate of Revenue Intelligence (DRI), and the state police have seized drug cargoes worth over ₹30,000 crore from Gujarat coasts. Just a few weeks before Khan's arrest, the biggest drug bust in Indian history was made off the coast of Mundra by the Gujarat Police, worth a whopping ₹20,900 crore*. This followed the seizure of heroin worth ₹1,500 crore in April 2021. In February 2022, a ship of 'foreign

*₹20,000 crore, or $2.5 billion, is about the GDP of India's neighbour, Bhutan.

origin' was apprehended off the coast near Porbandar–Jamnagar* in Gujarat, carrying various drugs worth an estimated ₹2,000 crore, with about 750 kilos of hashish, crystal meth, and heroin.

I assume that the cargo seized is only a small fraction of the shipments that get through with safe passage. In just the span of a week in August 2023, for instance, the Customs department seized more than 250 kilos of hashish that washed up across seven beaches in Maharashtra's Ratnagiri district. The cannabis had either fallen off or had been dumped by vessels originating from Afghanistan and Pakistan.

In 2022, the NCB and the Indian Navy jointly launched Operation Samudragupta—named after the famed fourth century ruler of the Gupta empire—as part of the central government's aggressive efforts to disrupt the import of contraband through India's western coast. The operation made a major bust in February 2024 off the coast of Porbandar, where the NCB, Navy, and Gujarat's Anti-Terror Squad apprehended foreign suspects on a dhow on the Arabian Sea. They found over 3,000 kilos of charas, methamphetamine, and morphine, worth over ₹2,000 crores on the international market.

In 2021, the DRI reported the seizure of a total of 45 metric tonnes of ganja that year, with the states of Bihar, Nagaland, and Uttar Pradesh 'winning' the sweepstakes of most weed seized. In 2020—the first year of the Covid-19 pandemic and lockdowns in India—the Ministry of Social Justice and Empowerment reported an overall highest volume of drug seizures in India in the past thirty years.

In a moment of refreshing yet sad honesty, the former narcotics commissioner Romesh Bhattacharjee admitted to *India Today* that most seizures in India are only made where cannabis is cultivated.

---

*Porbandar is the birthplace of Mahatma Gandhi. Jamnagar is one of the home bases of Reliance Industries and the Ambani family, a place that become synonymous with the phrase 'pre-wedding ceremony' in 2024.

'It's the small and medium farmers who get harassed.'

And it's not just the farmers and the middlemen: much of India's 'war on ganja' focuses on penalizing casual consumers instead of the kingpins operating behind the curtains. In Mumbai, which has the highest number of NDPS cases in India, most of the individuals arrested are consumers of cannabis. A 2020 study in Mumbai by the Vidhi Centre for Legal Policy concluded that 'nearly every person arrested and convicted for cannabis consumption in the city was a daily wage worker and a slum/street dweller'.

> These drug offenders are sentenced to minor imprisonment and/or fines ranging from Rs 100 to Rs 8,000. This demonstrates how the law, though meant to be applied uniformly across social and economic strata, disproportionately targets the poor and further marginalizes the already vulnerable. This finding also mirrors a trend in the US, which witnesses a clear racial disparity in its cannabis arresting pattern....
>
> In order to arrest, prosecute and sentence a cannabis consumer, the state machinery exhausts substantial human and economic resources. The police, judiciary and correctional institutions are systematically made party to a futile exercise, the cost of which is enormous. With over 3 crore cannabis users in the country, if the NDPS Act were to be implemented effectively, with every cannabis user arrested and prosecuted, the crumbling system would cave in entirely.

Along with the heavy financial burden of enforcing prohibition and incarcerating those arrested under the NDPS Act, the Indian state also loses billions in potential revenue due to its strict regulation of cannabis cultivation and trade.

India's stern attitude towards ganja—and in some cases, a fiercely militarized aggression—is part of the reason why users and smugglers have filled up Indian prisons, and why a great number of special action teams, excise units, anti-terrorism squads, the narcotics bureau, and local police forces across the country spend enormous resources to fight in this never-ending war against our humble, ubiquitous plant.

As I'd discovered earlier, much of this apprehension is rooted in taboos held by British authorities in colonial times. But there was another major force behind the suspicious global lens cast upon cannabis: the Americans.

And like many of the ailments faced by contemporary United States, the root cause of this was linked to racism, too. In his 2020 paper, 'Racism and Its Effect on Cannabis Research', Robert Solomon argues that William Randolph Hearst (a 1920s media mogul) and Andrew Mellon (one of the investors of the DuPont chemicals company) conspired to launch an aggressive campaign to defame cannabis in the US. A 1923 Hearst paper 'reported': 'Marihuana is a short cut to the insane asylum. Smoke marihuana cigarettes for a month and what was once your brain will be nothing but a storehouse for horrid specters.' Five years later, another report on a Hearst paper directly accused India, publishing: 'marijuana was known in India as the "murder drug".' The word 'marijuana' itself originated from Spanish speakers in Mexico, but was bastardized in the early twentieth century in the US when associated with racist and anti-immigrant connotations.

Then there was Harry Anslinger, the first commissioner of the US Treasury Department's Federal Bureau of Narcotics, who, particularly offended by the lifestyle of some cannabis users, used the substance to club together seemingly every community that he felt hostile towards. He was once known to say:

> There are 100,000 total marijuana smokers in the US, and most are Negroes, Hispanics, Filipinos, and entertainers.

> Their Satanic music, jazz and swing, results from marijuana use. This marijuana causes white women to seek sexual relations with Negroes, entertainers, and others.

In 1936, the paranoid propaganda reached its bizarre peak, with the release of the Hollywood film *Reefer Madness*—originally entitled *Tell Your Children.** Directed by Louis J. Gasnier and financed by a church group, the film is a morality tale about the dangers of marijuana use, targeted at parents. A group of high school students get trapped in a web of anarchy and self-destruction after minimal exposure to 'reefer' (a joint), including a hit-and-run, manslaughter, conspiracy to murder, attempted rape, hallucinations, and suicide. (The overreaction of 'elders' in the movie to stoned young people is remarkably prescient, considering how the NCB reacted to Aryan Khan's little exposure to weed some eighty-five years later.) The trailer of *Reefer Madness* leaves little room for nuance, as a narrator dramatically announces words of fear and caution: 'DEBAUCHARY! VIOLENCE! MURDER! SUICIDE!' Spoiler alert—the trailer previews the conclusion, too: 'The ultimate end of a marijuana addict is... hopeless insanity.'

Reefer Madness is hilariously terrible, so bad that the American film critic Leonard Maltin called it 'the grand-daddy of all "Worst" movies'. The film's legacy has since become subverted: its hyperbole serves as ironic humour, and its over-the-top themes have made it a cult comedy classic—especially if one watches it stoned.

And yet, in the mid-1930s, the film achieved some of its intended impact in striking fear among many Americans. A year after its original release, the 1937 Marihuana Tax Act was enacted in the US—drafted by Anslinger—which classified marijuana as a Schedule 1 drug (like heroin) and began the period of federal prohibition of cannabis which still continues to this day. It was only

---

*And often referred to by its many other names, including 'The Burning Question', 'Dope Addict', 'Doped Youth', and 'Youth Madness'.

after the 1969 US Supreme Court case *Leary vs. United States* that the Marijuana Tax Act was deemed unconstitutional, and repealed by Congress the following year. Much of the damage, however, was already done: remember that, in 1961, the American pressure on the United Nations' Economic and Social Council had resulted in restrictions on the cultivation, movement, and use of cannabis worldwide—including, of course, hand-wringing India to promise to outlaw the substance a couple of decades later.

The decriminalization of marijuana in the United States began in the early 1970s, but it wasn't until 1996 that California became the first state to legalize the use of medical cannabis. Since then, usually following along partisan political lines, a greater number of states/territories have slowly fallen suit, and the substance is now legalized to some degree in around half the country.

Yet, there's still the other half. The criminalization of marijuana continues to play a significant role in boosting the US prison industrial complex: with some 1.7 million incarcerated, one study estimated that the US is among the two nations—along with China—to have the highest prison population on the planet. In both public and private prisons in the US, drug offenders make for nearly half of all inmates. According to the American Civil Liberties Union (ACLU), more than 6 million Americans were arrested for marijuana possession from 2010 to 2018. Just as folks like Anslinger wished it eighty-something years ago, the arrest rate has been heavily biased towards black people, who were arrested nearly four times as often as white people for possession 'despite comparable marijuana usage rates.'

Like disenfranchised communities in India, the most vulnerable or marginalized of society bear the toughest burden of these laws.

The illegal status of cannabis is particularly preferred by America's police unions. Data from the Justice Department revealed that police departments in the US earned about $1 billion in operating budgets from marijuana busts from 2002 to 2012, and over $2.4 billion in grants for drug enforcement action in 2014.

And then, there is perhaps the biggest obstacle slowing the further liberalization of marijuana policies in the US: the pharmaceutical industry. If marijuana—a natural remedy (or at least, a natural source of pain relief)—is fully legalized, more than a little pinch will be felt by America's nearly $600 billion pharma industry (the largest in the world). It is no surprise then that pharma lobbyists provided donations to about two-thirds of the American Congress members to win their favour ahead of the 2020 election.

Meanwhile, the US faces a larger epidemic: the widespread abuse of the synthetic opioid fentanyl. In 2017, the US Department of Health and Human Services declared it a public health emergency. In 2021, synthetic opioids were reportedly responsible for nearly two-thirds of drug overdose deaths in the country. Shockingly, fentanyl overdose is now the leading cause of death for Americans aged eighteen to forty-nine.

Some progressive political steps have been taken in the past regarding marijuana which have encouraged its allies. In April 2022, the MORE Act (Marijuana Opportunity Reinvestment and Expungement) passed in the house again. If enacted, it would completely remove marijuana from the Controlled Substances Act, eliminate criminal penalties for federal cannabis offenses, and expunge all past federal cannabis convictions. But MORE's future success with the senate and beyond seems unclear.

And so, despite a few decades of progressive legislation, the US continues to play a two-faced game with cannabis, all depending on where in the country one might happen to be. In California, it is not uncommon to see legal marijuana dispensaries lining the streets, where many smoke weed openly without any fear of harassment. At $3.6 trillion, California's GDP is higher than all of India's; the state collected nearly $5.9 billion in legal, recreational, and medical marijuana sales in 2023, which is about the GDP of many smaller nations in the world.

In Chicago, India-born Annu Khot became the first women of Indian-descent to open a cannabis venture. Khot—who earned her Bachelor's degree in Kolkata—has said that she first turned to cannabis after the stress of multiple miscarriages and witnessing several family members experience painful chemotherapy treatments. Her dispensary was the first of its kind in the world to be blessed by a Hindu priest.

In America's capital—Washington D.C.—just a few kilometres* from the White House, any adult can easily walk into a 'compliant gift shop' and, as per Initiative 71, purchase a pencil worth $45, just to be 'gifted' some THC-laced gummies. Meanwhile, an ounce of weed in Florida, Arizona, Louisiana, etc., could land you in prison for several years and slapped with fines worth thousands of dollars.

The international politics of marijuana played a notorious role in a high-stakes incident in 2022. When American basketball player Brittney Griner landed at the Sheremetyevo Airport outside Moscow to play for her professional club in Russia, she was detained, as customs officials alleged that she was carrying a vape cartridge with some residue of cannabis oil. Russia invaded Ukraine just a week later, an attack that dragged on all summer.** The US worked with its allies to impose harsh economic sanctions on Russia. Griner—a black, homosexual woman—was the indirect victim of this ongoing international crisis. She pled guilty to her charges and, under the harsh cannabis laws in Russia, was sentenced to nine years imprisonment in August before being transferred to a penal colony in Mordovia. Finally, in December 2022—ten months since her arrest—American president Joe Biden was able to secure a prisoner exchange to have Griner freed and returned to the United States. But the swap cost the Americans the infamous Russian arms dealer Victor Bout, otherwise known as 'The Merchant of Death'.

---

*Or 'miles', as they say in American.

**And still continues as I review this manuscript, over two years later.

When Griner was finally freed, the satirical website *The Onion* posted an article of Americans 'reacting' to her return home, which included the fake quote, 'Thank God. Could you imagine someone getting incarcerated just for marijuana?'

I couldn't help but chuckle upon reading that. Many a truth is spoken in jest.

Greenish-white smoke puffed up to the sky, polluting the clean village air. A song of fire and ganja. On a February afternoon in 2022, the village of Koduru—just a forty-minute drive from Visakhapatnam—witnessed the largest destruction of seized narcotics in Indian history. Over 2 lakh kilos of the locally-grown Sheelavathi was burned by the Andhra Pradesh police. The pyres formed plumes of smoke from the finest weed in the region, an act of destruction that mirrored Joker burning piles of cash money in *The Dark Knight*.

Speaking of cash money, the value of the cannabis burned on that Saturday totalled around ₹500 crore rupees.

The scenes were repeated in the NTR district on Christmas Day 2022; police burned 14,000 kilos of ganja which they had seized over the past thirty years.

These large-scale acts of ganja arson have been a part of the Andhra Pradesh police's special undertaking, Operation Parivartan (transformation), launched in October 2021. The intention, according to the state police, was to educate farmers to grow alternative crops in the region, including rajma, silver oak, cashew seeds, sweet orange, seethaphal (custard apple), coconut, etc., and leave the dangerous (but lucrative) liaisons with ganja behind. The state's chief minister Y. S. Jagan Mohan Reddy prioritized his vision to make the state 'drug free' ever since his party was elected to power in Andhra Pradesh in May 2019. A Special Enforcement Bureau (SEB) was set up in 2020, which operated like the armed-wing of the excise office, with a focus on combating illicit liquor, ganja, and other such black-market trades.

According to some sources, nearly 150 villages around Visakhapatnam are home to large swathes of ganja fields, with many of these tribal areas coming under the 'protection' of Maoist groups, keeping excise officers and police at arm's length. Smugglers often find creative new routes and new timings, using secret compartments in cars, oil, and milk tankers, strapping ganja to their bodies under their clothes. In one particularly dramatic drug bust in Guwahati, the Assam Police discovered 134 packets of ganja weighing over 2,600 kilos inside concealed compartments of an oil tanker. In Siliguri, West Bengal, four individuals were arrested for transporting 64 kilos of cannabis inside a coffin. They were taking the maal in an ambulance from Tripura to Bihar while impersonating the family of the deceased.

Of late, smugglers in this region have begun to use country-made boats to cross a little over 5 kilometres over the Sileru River to transport the ganja across the borders of Odisha to Andhra. Many cross the river under the cover of night to evade the police. On roadways, most smugglers use roads that pass through interior towns or forested areas to avoid tolls and police vigils.

In a creative twist, a number of individuals were busted in Madhya Pradesh for smuggling ganja through the giant e-commerce platform, Amazon. It was discovered that the marijuana was being sold on Amazon's website in India as 'kadi patta', dry curry leaves used for cooking. In another major smuggling racket, the Railway Protection Force (RPF) uncovered how cannabis was being moved from Assam to Kolkata disguised carefully inside flavoured tea packets—leaning on Assam's reputation for producing some of the finest chai in our nation.

The cat-and-mouse game in the nation's heartlands between anti-narcotics authorities and smugglers inspired the Telugu action film *Gaanja Shankar,* directed by Sampath Nandi and starring Sai

Dharam Tej as the anti-hero cannabis peddler on the run from the cops.*

In the real world, however, no 'heroism' is celebrated in this dangerous underground economy. In the first three months of Operation Parivartan, Andhra's state police arrested around 1,500 individuals connected to drug trafficking-related charges. Meanwhile in nearby Hyderabad, the capital of Telangana, a video surfaced of police officers stopping random commuters to check their phones and WhatsApp messages to search—without warrant—for the keyword 'ganja'. By 2024 New Year's Eve, the Telangana State Anti-Narcotics Bureau debuted high-tech German drug testing devices to crash the party, including the Dräeger device which is capable of checking for cannabis, cocaine, opiates, and other substances through on-site saliva or urine tests.

Back in Visakhapatnam, the journalist Sumit Bhattacharjee told me that, by his estimates, up to 80 per cent of the Central Prison in the district is filled with individuals arrested for ganja trafficking, most of whom are middlemen. 'There might be over four thousand such inmates at any given time,' Bhattacharjee said. 'They all are drivers, courier-agents, and some tribals. But not a single kingpin. Who is the main guy? Nobody knows.' The secretary of the Joint Action Committee of Adivasi Unions and Federations has claimed that most of the remand prisoners and convicts in ganja-related cases in Visakhapatnam are tribals.

A similar drive against cannabis has been in action across the state border in Odisha, too. On one single day in September 2021, the Odisha police claimed to seize three tonnes of ganja (worth multiple crores) from various vehicle checks across the state, much of it heading from Malkangiri towards Bhubaneswar. A few

* Soon after the film's trailer was uploaded on YouTube, the Telangana State Anti-Narcotic Bureau warned the producer that he could face legal action under the NDPS Act if the film glorified drug consumption and sales, and urged the makers to omit 'Gaanja' from the film's title.

months later, local police destroyed about 65,000 hemp plants in the Malkangiri district.

Malkangiri is among eight districts in Odisha which are regarded as the state's epicentres of hemp cultivation, including Boudh, Deogarh, Gajapati, Kandhamal, Nayagarh, Rayagada, and Sambalpur. Much of the ganja is reportedly cultivated near the Jalaput dam on the borders of Odisha and Andhra Pradesh—and smugglers have been known to use boats to move the drugs across the Machkund River. Police are said to receive satellite imagery from the Indian Space Research Organisation (ISRO) of pockets in Odisha where massive quantities of ganja are cultivated. Many of these areas remain inaccessible due to the presence of what the authorities called 'Left Wing Extremism'.

Controversy erupted in early August 2023 when a mob in Odisha's Phiringia tehsil burned down a local police station and assaulted a senior police official, after local cops themselves were accused of smuggling seized cannabis. Dozens of police platoons were dispatched to the site to manage the mobs, and over thirty individuals were detained after the raids.

Villagers in Malkangiri have staged protests in the past, refusing to give up ganja cultivation until the minimum sale price (MSP) was guaranteed for their agricultural produce. The district administration offered schemes to help farmers replace ganja with turmeric, but local reports suggest that there hasn't yet been an enthusiastic response to these measures.

Travelling far and wide, the Sheelavathi strain is arguably the most-desired variety of ganja now available in India. Demand for Sheelavathi across the country inflated its price to an all-time high during the New Year's celebrations to welcome 2023. Nationwide, out of the 23 lakh kilos of ganja confiscated from 2019–2023 by the NCB, more than 70 per cent belonged to the Sheelavathi strain, its popularity aided by its affordability in comparison to the significantly pricier strains of charas (like Malana Cream) found in the Himalayan regions. State police and officials have admitted that the total value of ganja trade out of the AOB region nears ₹10,000 crore per year.

I know that my work isn't being done in a vacuum, either. Everything affects the economy. I can't help but wonder if the increased attention I've given to this plant will result in a fluctuation in its cost. Or, I shudder to think, drive further police aggression towards the most-vulnerable individuals involved in its trade.

The name Sheelavathi is borrowed from a character in a number of ancient Hindu texts. Known as a chaste woman, dutiful wife, sometimes even called the 'ideal woman', Sheelavathi's tale appeared in the 1874 poetic work *Sheelavathi Naalu Vrutham* by Kunjan Nambiar. Her story was further popularized in the 1967 Malayalam film *Sheelavathi* (directed by P. B. Unni). Leave it up to a group of stoned men—I'm guessing—who had the first puff of this variety of ganja some decades ago, and (probably) wisecracked, 'Yes, she's perfect. This ganja is the ideal woman. She...she is Sheelavathi.'

Also known as 'Rajahamsa' or 'Kalapathri', the Sheelavathi is a close hybrid of the Idukki Gold. In the past ten to fifteen years, as farms in Kerala were destroyed and cultivators were arrested or chased away, production moved north with ganja experts now choosing to buy land in the AOB region.

Few individuals have chronicled the politics of ganja in Andhra Pradesh as closely as Sumit Bhattacharjee, a principal correspondent of a major national newspaper in Visakhapatnam. I meet Bhattacharjee at his office upon my return to Vizag, where even he seems surprised by the rapid rise of cannabis smuggling in recent years.

'About ten or eleven years ago, people didn't really have an idea that ganja was grown around here,' says Bhattacharjee. 'It would grow in Tamil Nadu, in the hilly tracks in areas like Salem, where the climate is cool and there's not as much crop disturbance. But there were a lot of excise raids by the Kerala police on the border areas of the two states, and the government started to do a lot of destruction of the ganja crops. The smugglers had to find a new place. and Himachal was too far. So, the Visakha Agency was chosen.'

'They found [the Agency] to be a great area,' he continues. 'It's hilly, perfectly suitable for ganja growth. The climate is cool, perhaps 10–12 degrees cooler than the city. And this is where the smugglers from the South moved to.'

The first recorded ganja arrest in this region was made as far back as 1973, over a decade before the NDPS Act. Bhattacharjee believes that 'ganja operatives' from the South assimilated with the local Adivasi communities, some intermarrying, some gaining access to land for cultivation in faraway areas without roads, cell connectivity, or electricity.

I remember first encountering this part of the country when I visited some friends in Bhubaneswar and Vizag in 2008–09. Together, the four of us took a taxi from Vizag up to the picturesque retreat town of Araku in the Agency area, driving through a shroud of cool, winter brume. We had barely settled into our hotel rooms when our taxi driver returned with a plastic bag filled with fresh ganja from a nearby farm. The maal would likely be worth tens of thousands of rupees now—but all those years ago, the farmers simply let him take all he could carry in his own hands for free.

We didn't know that it was called Sheelavathi in those days, and we didn't understand the politics between the Adivasi, the Maoists, the mafia, and the police who encounter this growing black market. We did discern, however, that this weed gave a heady yet refreshingly clean high; the type that completely opened those anandamide floodgates, but did so without even the slightest hint of a headache or heaviness caused by impure or laced maal. We named it 'Flying First Class'; as in, a feeling of soaring above the clouds in satin-clad luxury.

In the naivete of our youth, we imagined Araku to be our little secret, a hidden reservoir of India's best weed, away from the known hotspots like the charas of Himachal or the ganja of Kerala and Mysore.

Now, almost fourteen years since that first visit, Bhattacharjee confirms to me that there is nothing hidden about this place, that the ganja from Araku and elsewhere in the Agency has become the biggest political priority in the state.

'There are eleven mandals (local government areas) in Vizag Agency,' Bhattacharjee tells me, 'And all eleven became sources of ganja cultivation. It's growing everywhere. My conservative estimate is that at least 15,000 acres of land has come under cultivation.' An acre is estimated to yield about a tonne of ganja every year. 'The Maoists have had total control. Even the police don't have the dum (courage) to go deeper into these areas. The ganja is smuggled out in huge trucks and cars in tonnes. Now, we don't even report the news unless something more than 100 kilos is caught.'

Bhattacharjee and others have hypothesized that the smugglers and the Maoists have a working relationship in the cannabis cultivation and trade. 'The Maoists deny it,' he says, 'but, if they really have no connection, how can this [cultivation} happen right under their very noses? How is it possible that they don't know? They *have* to have a connection. We have written stories about how the Maoists have levied some tax to allow the movement. And in return, my guess is that the smugglers support [the Maoists] logistically: they bring them uniforms, food, and medicine.'

When I ask if the smugglers are also helping the Maoists procure weapons, Bhattacharjee is hesitant to confirm. 'The Maoists either get their weapons from Bangladesh or Nepal,' he says. 'Or from "encounter" sites, where they kill someone, and pick up their weapon.'

The 'encounters' reached fever pitch in 2018, just a few years prior to my return visit to these parts. Near the Thutangi village in the Agency area, a group of twenty to thirty insurgents ambushed the vehicles of two passing political leaders of the Telugu Desam Party (TDP): sitting MLA Kidari Sarveswara Rao and former MLA Siveri Soma. The attackers snatched the weapons from the security personnel accompanying the two politicians and then fatally shot Rao and Soma at point-blank range. It was alleged that the murders were in retaliation to the TDP government's decision to allow the mining of bauxite, black sand, marble, white stone, and other raw materials—an act that would displace the local Adivasi population and disturb the environmental harmony of the region. (Parts of the Araku Valley were known to be the operational base of influential Maoist leader Akkiraju Haragopal, aka Ramakrishna. Haragopal, who passed away in October 2021 to a kidney failure, carried a reward of ₹97 lakh on his head at the time of his death.)

Soon after the sensational murders of Rao and Soma, supporters and relatives of the two politicians—both belonging to powerful Adivasi communities—held widespread protests, blaming the local police for their negligence in these murders. Protestors in Araku and Dumbriguda burned a number of vehicles, and ransacked and set fire to both local police stations.

A few weeks later, Maoists released a statement taking responsibility for the assassinations in Thutangi, alleging that both politicians were 'looting the natural and forest resources' and had 'turned into brokers for aluminium companies such as Jindal and ANRAK.'

Bhattacharjee believes that the conspiracy runs even deeper. 'What I understand is that there was some dispute in payment of money,' he says. 'Is liye inko ura diya (That's why they were assassinated). In fact, there was a rumour that the MLA was stocking the ganja in the Araku police station. And then, people burned the police station after his death.

'It's a huge nexus. Wherever there are drugs, there is a nexus.

Now everything is done on the dark web, too, with payments in Bitcoin. What we see is very much the tip of the iceberg.'

Apart from the dry ganja itself, many smugglers out of Vizag are also producing hashish oil. It takes a small industrial set-up, with a crusher and a boiler to heat up the cannabis resin and extract the oil. When prepared, even a few globules of the substance can carry the mind-elevating energy of a full chillum hit. The oleoresinous product is much easier to conceal and smuggle in plastic containers or water bottles—in Vizag, I met a young man who had carried a 1 litre mineral water bottle filled with hashish oil on a cross-country train to sell in Bengaluru. Hash oil is a far more lucrative product: if a kilo of ganja in these parts cost ₹2,000 rupees, a kilo of the same extracted into oil could fetch up to a lakh. In a major haul in May 2023, Bengaluru police seized cannabis and hash oil incoming to the city from Visakhapatnam worth ₹6.61 crores. A few months later, a similar haul of hash oil worth crores was discovered by police in Mumbai.

Sometime around 2016, in the search for the unexplored, Bhattacharjee and his colleagues set out to the Darakonda area in the Agency. His plan was to set up a 'headquarter' for their stay in a motorable area and, from there, walk or bike further ahead with the guidance of local reporters in the villages. To his surprise, however, the contacts vanished on the day he landed; it turned out that two of those reporters had been arrested themselves for their involvement in the ganja trade.

In his explorations, Bhattacharjee eventually stumbled upon a tiny, sparsely-populated village, with very few pucca houses, no roads, and no access to public health stations. And yet, he noticed that every home there had a motorbike and dish TV access, there were bike maintenance and mechanic shops, and the local community seemed to be far more affluent than he expected. An affluence—he hinted—that had followed the boom of the ganja business. 'I asked for a Thumbs Up at a local shop, and was offered Blender's Pride whisky instead. I couldn't believe it. What is happening?' The experience, he said, helped him understand the darkness that lurked under the placid exoskeleton of these villages.

'In some places,' he stressed, 'everyone—every family—is involved in the trade.'

In another village in the Agency, Bhattacharjee says he witnessed the 'worst kind of poverty' he had ever seen. 'They didn't have food to eat, but they had ganja. The locals (Adivasis) were given a little bit of money to grow the crop. And when I asked them about it, many didn't even know what they were growing.'

Bhattacharjee often compares the Agency area to Himachal and Uttarakhand, the only other regions in India that measure up in the volumes of cannabis cultivation. In the North, however, there has been some progress in exploring an economic solution to this issue, including industrial hemp legalization in Uttarakhand and some political interest to do the same in Himachal Pradesh. In Andhra Pradesh, however, Bhattacharjee believes that decriminalizing, legalizing, and taxing this vast economy is simply out of the question for now. 'The government is not that far-sighted,' he says. 'There has only been talk of providing the farmers with alternative crops... Plus, if they legalize it, the whole gang of smugglers would be destroyed. And they don't want that, do they?'

Bhattacharjee and I can't help but let a moment of silence pass between us. A few seconds of rumination.

He says out loud what was brewing in my mind, too. 'The villagers. They are caught in this crossfire between the Maoists and the police.'

When I plan my return to the Araku Valley—more than a decade after the days of discovering the 'Flying First Class'—I'm hardly prepared to digest all that has changed since my younger days. I had only remembered the tip of the iceberg: the ganja itself. It had simply happened to *appear*, as if it was nothing but another weed on the side of the road, growing without reservation or control, accessible to all those curious enough to access it. Perhaps this was the idealist in me: someone who chose to remain innocent and uninformed, someone who chose to believe that cannabis simply *existed*—like it had done in our country for thousands of years, a gift from the Earth to her inhabitants—to provide us a sense of respite, a sense of 'otherness', something to cure us of the nausea and anxiety faced in the strenuous toil of survival.

Of course, there are many around the world who still operate with this level of freedom, those who grow their own ganja for personal use, those who hardly stray away from the gifts of this Earth, not simply consuming the cannabis but becoming a part of its lifecycle by fully immersing themselves in the natural ecosystem. But for most others, the lifecycle of cannabis follows the rest of that looming iceberg down the deep dark waters: the hands that plant the seeds, the hands that tend to the growing bud, the hands that cut the ganja, the hands that rub the charas resin, the hands that store pressed stacks in hidden compartments under car seats, the hands that pay in cash, the hands that packet the weed into small parcels, the hands that make the cash exchange with the user, the hands that roll the joint, the lips that smoke it, the mind that is blown away.

It's a tale of gore and blood, of corruption, of exploitation, of oppression, of death. Profit for some, tragedy for some others. And then—as the bud makes its final transformation to ash and smoke—there's bliss. *Ananda.*

One doesn't necessarily need the boost of cannabinoids to feel the bliss on the trip to Araku Valley. The four-hour journey from Vizag to Araku is among the most gorgeous train rides I've ever taken. I depart early in the morning from the Visakhapatnam Junction, a railway station that has become a hotspot for major ganja busts by the local police, the RPF, and the latest addition to local security: sniffer police dogs. I find my seat by the bars of an open window, and, less than an hour after departure, I feel the breeze of the Andhra countryside hitting my face, ruffling my hair, watering my eyes. We pass by lush forests and farms, and then to a view of the Eastern Ghats. There are many tourists in my coach, particularly groups of young people or couples making a quick getaway from the city. Their enthusiasm adds a little festive colour to the journey: they listen to music, they sing along, they jump off to the platforms to take photos at picturesque stops, and they yell excited *woooooos* as the train passes through a tunnel in the hills.

There are forty-two tunnels on the way—and many of my fellow passengers *woooooo* past every single one.

Soon, there's a slight drizzle outside my window, and mist rises up from the troughs of the valley. Soon, my phone loses all network—and it will stay lost for as long as I'm up in Araku. I'm hardly concerned any more. Soon, it feels like we're riding up in the clouds.

Jungles filled with silver oak welcome me to the quaint, single platform station of Araku. There are a number of honey farms on the way here, as the region is known for beekeepers and the honey industry. Araku and Agency areas are also popular for coffee production: the Arabica coffee cultivated here was awarded the Geographical Indication (GI) tag in 2019.

There's no such special indication given to the valley's other favourite crop.

As I wander around the 'thematic' coffee museum in Araku that afternoon—a little estate that looks partly like a wax museum, partly like a low-budget amusement park, drenched in the scent of coffee beans and chocolate—I can't help but wonder of the magic of the soil and climactic conditions here that allow for these two potent cravings to crop up: cannabis and caffeine.

(I also marvel at the coincidence that the world's other favourite caffeinated beverage—tea—was prevalent in Idukki, my previous stop in this ganja odyssey.)

I hire an autorickshaw the next morning to take me to the Chaparai waterfalls, a scenic tourist spot surrounded by forests about 13 kilometres from Araku city, where a wide, gentle stream of water flows down cascading steppes. But I'm not here to wet my feet in the water besides the other picnicking tourists, or to pick up a little newspaper pouch of delicious roasted peanuts on sale nearby. My hope is to build enough of a rapport with my autowallah—a tall, young man with lanky arms—to reveal to him the true intention of my visit. Between my English and Hindi, and his Telugu, our conversation is kept to a minimum. But in India, the word ganja hardly needs further translation.

Immediately, his expression shifts, as if he's scandalized. *No ganja. No ganja anywhere here.* I get the same answer when I ask others parked over at Chaparai's auto stand. *No ganja here. Everyone arrested. Everything stopped.*

Despite the illegality of the substance, any user will tell you that information about weed almost anywhere in India only requires a little persistence and daring. One needs to know to approach the right person at the right place. Sometimes, it could be a coolie at a railway station, or a dhabawallah on the highway, or the man behind the cigarette stall outside your college campus. Often, these are cash-only transactions. (Post-demonetization, it became abundantly clear that the toughest things to procure in India's 'cashless economy' were drugs, sex work, and property.) Every circle of stoner friends has their own codeword for the *stuff*, and it could be absolutely anything, an inside joke, a stray word or phrase that may sound nonsensical to the untrained ear. *Gulab Jamun. Biggie Smalls. Mango. Cream. Tuitions. Upbhog. Tauji. Mausi ke prashad.* Seeking this *prashad* is, of course, a dangerous game, and a prejudiced one, too: one inevitably finds oneself stereotyping people, reducing fully-dimensional humans into potential sources, making an assumption that the certain someone—the coolie, the autowallah—will know someone who'll know someone who'll sell you something. Most users tend to find their dealers through word-of-mouth, through secret codes, elusive men and women with vague nicknames and fickle phone numbers.

But, in a new city, a little shot in the dark is often the only option available.

And often, it works.

But even if it doesn't, the rejection is hardly ever as absolute as I faced around Araku. *No ganja here. Everyone arrested. Everything stopped.*

Perhaps I shouldn't have been that surprised. In conversation with sources back in Vizag—many of whom had access to Sheelavathi through smugglers and dealers in the big city—I had learned that there has been a heightened paranoia towards the substance in the valley ever since the aggressive policing of Operation Parivartan.

The outright denial at Chaparai makes me restless. Suddenly, I realize that I'm unable to plan the rest of my day until I have an answer to my queries. I spend the afternoon back in my hotel room in Araku. I try to read a novel I have been carrying, but now, I'm distracted, plotting, planning, thinking of anyone else I could contact. It's as if I can't focus any more until the 'ganja matter' is sorted; just the search for cannabis has plunged me into the desperation of an addict.

And even if I personally believe that the dangers associated with the plant have been highly exaggerated, there is a slow menace that accompanies many individuals whose days revolve around that desperate need for a high. This menace doesn't manifest itself in a frantic rush of the blood—a vampire biting your neck with his fangs—but a gradual build-up of discomfort, a night filled with mosquito bites, until the tingling spreads across the surface of my entire skin, until there is no more ananda in one's regular sober life, in the mountains outside, in scenic travels, in fulfilment from work, in the taste of food, in the convivial company of close friends, in the closest bonds of family.

My fortunes, however, improve later that day. I'm hopping from store to store, looking for mosquito repellent cream (my *true* yearning this afternoon) before I'm spotted again by the young autowallah who had driven me earlier that morning. At first, I fear that I've put myself at risk with my enquiries. But it turns out that my gamble has succeeded. In the gaps of understanding between our language barriers, the autowallah has had a change of heart. He reveals that there are some villages deeper into the forests, where the local Adivasis cultivate ganja under the cover of the woods and the protection of heavy Naxalite movement.

And lo and behold, a few hours later, my new friend returns from the villages in the relative guise of night and presents me with the proof I need: a plastic bag filled with at least a dozen stumps of cannabis, an amount that would likely be worth ₹10,000 to ₹12,000 back in Delhi. He says that it would be sold locally for a tenth of that cost.

I take a taxi back from Araku to Vizag the next day. I sit next to the driver, watching passively as he twists and turns down the mountainous roads. The path is lush, the air is fresh, and the warm sun lulls and relaxes me to the point of lethargy.

I hardly ever drive, often preferring to reside in places that are well-connected through public transport, easy options for a taxi, an auto, a ride-share, or—if it's convenient enough—to simply walk the longest distances.

I wonder if my refusal to drive has made me passive in other avenues of life as well. I often find myself in the passenger seat. Here, I can be free from all responsibility—even responsibility of the self. Even if I'm the one giving the directions and choosing the destination, the wheel always seems to be in someone else's hands:

the actual driver next to me, the father who guided me, the wife whose job relocates me, the editors who help tidy up my words to give them the shape they require.

Later that evening, I find myself in another guest house in Vizag, all alone, sitting in the third-floor balcony of my room, looking down at the inner alleyways, letting time pass by in yet another city. The owners of the guest house had decorated the outside walls of the building with shimmering blue and green electrical lights for Diwali, and left the lights hanging even a month later. The lights add a trippy kaleidoscope to my view of the dark night. Bicycles tinkle past carrying gas cylinders. Fruit vendors set up their thelas for the evening shoppers. And a group of young men and women—in their late teens or early twenties—walk into a residential building opposite my hotel, where they will attend night classes to prepare for their upcoming CAT exams.

I make plans to meet friends of a friend in Vizag that evening. I look forward to the company, but it's not just 'company' I'm yearning for, it's youth. For the young, friendship is such as easy concept: at school, at college, in the earliest days at work, where you and everyone else around you are still learning how to be adults, still developing as human beings. The crust hasn't hardened yet; your malleability extends to the empathy you share with each other.

As we grow older, however, social circumstances expect us to become fully formed, fully *evolve* into the person we choose to be, whom we project upon ourselves. We train ourselves to become this person, until it becomes habit, until it becomes us.

But to truly evolve, I know that I need to be more open-minded, be willing to challenge myself, and potentially, even change myself. It's a desire to blend the curiosity of youth with the wisdom of experience.

Isn't it a blessing, I wonder, to even contemplate youth and experience? To philosophize while staring at those colourful Diwali lights from the balcony? To be born in a time and place where I can actually get to grow old? To have the time to wonder how I should be spending my time? In another era, I may have been just another statistic of lives cut short by smallpox or measles before I learned how to even spell my own name. In another lifetime, I would've been sent to battle at sixteen, died on the first day, and that would've been the entire legend and legacy of Karan of House Madhok.

My friends arrive, including Radha, who is a tech entrepreneur with a small start-up in the city. They take me out on a drive around the beautiful campus of Vizag's Steel Plant, and then out to the beach at night, where there is us, and the Bay of Bengal, and there's nothing much else. Under the clear moonlight, we drink beer, we drink whisky. We speak about work, about the lack of work. Radha tells me how much he loves Vizag, that he could never leave; and, in the next breath, opens up about dread for the future, for the opportunities he has missed, of the stress of supporting his ageing mother all by himself, of the pressures to get married,* of finding some professional stability. To exhale. To relax.

Radha's days are so different to mine. My days—these days—are so different to almost anyone's I know. Days without queueing outside local bus stops, days without clocking in at an office, without lowering my eyes in subservience to an employer, without the physical labour at constructions sites, without the panic of a Monday morning, without the relief of a Sunday.

No, my days in these trips offer a kind of empty purposelessness, masked by wanderlust. Every day is chhutti. Every day is lived on my own terms. What even *is* a Monday? I've spent so much of my life building a wall around me—a kavach to guard me from others' perception of me—that now, it has become more challenging to appreciate the perspective of other people at all, to generate a real sense of empathy. And so, any new stimulation to the brain is a

*Update: Radha got married a year later!

sudden reminder of that wall, of the life I live with blinders on.

At the beach, we feel the warm sea breeze, hear the soft humming of the waves lapping the sand and receding back again under the moonlit night.

The Earth, really, is lovely—once you get to know her better.

Does being a little stoned make her lovelier? I wonder if one is stealing away from the unhindered experience of life—of a night like this—by diluting it with the slightly numbing high of cannabis. Or is cannabis a mere supplement, another boost to one's senses to add to the delight, to the sounds and sights and breezes of the night?

Even the supplement isn't permanent after all, is it? The waves recede. The sand is replaced.

And I know that, after this night, I will be replaced here, too. I will move away into another town, in the company of other faces, seeking another form of impermanence.

The past few days have been fascinating. Everything interests me more when I travel, because everything is new, unexplored, un-understood. I yearn to manufacture these bouts of curiosity much like I did in my younger years. Curiosity for places, people, cultures, food, histories. And specifically, a curiosity for the ways in which people in India encounter and consume ganja.

And over and over again, I've found that there's hardly any 'typical' user of cannabis in India. Its users include daily wage workers and corporate bankers, men and women and the nonbinary, city dwellers and beach bums, the young and the old, the healthy and the ill, the spiritual and the nonbelievers. In *Cannabis Indica,* Khagesh Gautam celebrated the wide spectrum of cannabis aficionados, as he wrote, 'Perhaps we might, in a "light-hearted" moment, note the incredibly secular potential of this plant that seems to promote world peace by simply existing for human consumption!'

Even as a controlled substance, the impact of cannabis on Indian society has been immense. So, my curiosity now leads me down another path, towards a wider view, an exploration of this plant's incredible impact on culture—ancient and contemporary—and the diversity of its experiences across the country.

Dum Maro Dum

'…Hum sabki parvah karein kyon?
Sabne hamara kiya kya…?'

A historical town in Uttar Pradesh, Barsana is believed to be the birthplace of Radha—the Hindu goddess who is an avatar of Goddess Lakshmi, and is described as the dearest of all consorts of Lord Krishna.* During the spring festival of Holi, the women of Barsana sit atop a hill by the Radha-Rani Temple, ready with matkas (pitchers) filled with water (or coloured water). Meanwhile, men arrive from the nearby village of Nandgaon, dressed in all-white as impersonators of Krishna. They chant 'Radha Rani Ki Jai!' and, as they rush towards the temple, the 'Radhas' of Barsana welcome the 'Krishnas' of Nandgaon with splashes of water and colour. The Krishnas hoot and holler at the Radhas, and later, the Radhas grab sticks to give a good-natured beating to the Krishnas. There is singing and dancing, a wild tamasha, a pluvial of every colour on the palette.

And the only thing flowing as freely as the colours is the bhang.

In Manipur, Holi takes the form of Yaoshang. A straw hut is set on fire on the full moon night in the Manipuri month Lamta (February–March) to kick off five days of festivities. Children go from home to home—Halloween style—offering blessings and receiving gifts in return. A moonlight dance is held around a circle. There's singing and dancing and an ejecta of colours. And yes, there's ganja.

---

*The stuff that our polyamorous gods get away with….

Holi in parts of Bihar is known as Phagunwa, where folk songs are sung and gujiya is served. There's an eruption of colours and dance, and sweet thandai—often spiked with bhang.

Thandai is a Holi favourite across many parts of India: the desi, cannabis-infused version of a White Russian cocktail. Whole milk, sugar, badam (almonds), elaichi (cardamom), a few more masalas, and maybe essence of rose, mango, whatever else, all topped off with some bhang paste. It takes a few hours for the ingredients to enter your bloodstream, for the nourishment to alter your brainwaves. It won't be a sudden switch that turns on the ananda, but a light dimmer that gradually turns reality into something hyperreal, until you land right in the middle of a dreamsphere, unsure how you even got there.

Similar creations of the cannabinoid cocktail are concocted across the country. Sometimes, the drink is known as siddhi, sometimes as ghota, and in some parts of South India, ramras or ram rasain.

There's the Shigmo festival in Goa. Colours and intoxication. Rang Panchami in Maharashtra. A burning pyre, colours, and yes, ganja. Dol Jatra in West Bengal, which features recitation of Rabindranath Tagore's poetry. And colours. And cannabis.

Then, there's Hola Mohalla, the three-day long Sikh spring festival celebrated in a similar spirit as Holi, with music, poetry, kirtan, colours, and displays of martial tactics like horsemanship and sword fighting. During this festival, some of the Sikhs of the warrior Nihang sect consume the Shaheedi Degh, a traditional drink made of almonds, black pepper, sugar, water, rose petals, cardamoms, and cannabis. The drink is said to help bring peace of mind and put the warriors in a meditative spirit. A less intoxicating form of bhang known as sukhnidhaan is offered at some gurdwaras as prasad.

Most Sikh teachings, however, assert that the founder of Sikhism Guru Nanak was against the use of cannabis (or any mind-altering substance).

Top: Waiting in my train compartment for another cup of chai.

Bottom: Parvati Valley in Himachal Pradesh, abundant in apples, hydroelectric projects, and charas.

Twilight hour at my campsite in Kheerganga.

Top: The oft-mysticized hamlet of Malana, home to the world famous strain of Malana Cream.

Bottom: A charming little hamlet—Kasol.

Top: Har ki Pauri, probably the most sacred spot in Haridwar, where it is believed a drop of amrit was dropped (or spilled) by Garuda.

Bottom: An ascetic lights his chillum for a relaxing afternoon smoke in the by-lanes of Haridwar.

Top: 'Each plant here in Uttarakhand's Urgam Valley is generously well-endowed, grown naturally with little or no human interference, with flowering tops of the female plants so rich with trichomes that one can hardly help but simply reach over and rub a little resin off.'

Bottom: The motherlode: At Uttarakhand's Urgam Valley, acres upon acres of the greenest, cleanest weed I have ever seen, over bugyals coruscating golden in reflection under the afternoon sun.

Giant shrubs of bhang—some 10-20 feet high—line the roadways around Urgam Valley.

Top: Jagdamba Prasad Maithani of AAGAAS Federation giving a lesson about cannabis cultivation sites around Uttarakhand's Chamoli district.

Bottom: Edible hemp seeds at Pipalkoti.

Top: In my jeep back to Dehradun, Ramu the goat is well-behaved and doesn't make a mess.

Bottom: Another train to another destination.

A tranquil lotus pond at an ayurvedasram near Cherpulassery, Kerala.

Top: Beachside at Fort Kochi.

Bottom: Alcohol prohibitions make bars like these a rare sight in many parts of Kerala.

Top: All I need in this life of sin is Odomos cream.

Bottom: Passing by tea estates on the bus to Munnar.

Top: Munnar: If there's one thing I think of when I think of the infant Jesus, it's tyre work.

Bottom: A town hall meeting for Bonda community members at Mudulipada village in Odisha.

Top: Women of the Bonda Adivasi community at the Bonda Ghat, Odisha.
Bottom: On the picturesque train journey to Araku.

Top: Sheelavathi.

Bottom: A view of Pushkar.

Top: The Wall (in Pushkar).

Bottom: A Sunday stroll around Kohima.

'I don't know how much time has passed before I realize that this is one of the greatest walks I've ever taken (Khonoma).'

The headquarters of Shanglen (Universal Friendship Organization) in the outskirts of Imphal. Behind the statues of Pakhangba and Kangla Sha is the cottage which houses the corpse of the organization's founder, R. K. Manisana.

A couple of Satjal members enjoy hits from their chillum at a shanglen in Imphal.

Late afternoon in Churachandpur.

Top: India Hemp Expo, New Delhi.

Bottom: Scenes from the first ever India Hemp Expo in New Delhi.

Top: The Tata Memorial Hospital in Mumbai.

Bottom: One of the many popular spots for lassi (and special lassi) in Varanasi.

The past and the present meet every day on the ghats of Varanasi.

Top: A view of the ghats by the Ganga River in Varanasi.

Bottom: 'This eternity becomes even easier to imagine around the oldest parts of Varanasi, where civilization has existed by the riverbanks for thousands of years.'

Varanasi is a city where the divine finds itself in comfortable confluence with the mundane.

There are no such restrictions in Shaivite Hinduism. Holi is particularly a hungama in Varanasi, the principal city of Shiva. As the festival signals the end of the winter thaw, spring is celebrated with refreshing cool, bhang-infused thandai. Hordes of men and women (but mostly men) hit the streets after the colourful celebrations of the morning, to sip some thandai, and spend the rest of the day in a blissful haze. There are other alternatives, too, like the daily dose of 'goli', a little round pill of bhang available at many neighbourhood paanwallahs.

It's all in the inexorable spirit of Shiva. In another tale of his many (stoned) adventures, the god went into a meditative state after the loss of his consort Sati. On the day before Holi, Parvati—the reincarnation of Sati—got a helping hand from Kamadeva—the god of love—to discharge a bhang-laced arrow at Shiva and shoot him out of his misery. The lovers are reunited, with bliss and love.

It's only natural then, that on Holi, lovers of cannabis and Shiva unite, too. Holi is often celebrated as a festival to make amends, leave behind old conflicts, start anew, and perhaps, even look past social and cultural divisions. It's the festival of celebrating *together,* as the heady waves of bhang wash over and refresh the tepid shores.

Some vaidyas believe that there are health reasons for bhang's close alliance with spring. Ayurveda speaks of three categories of 'dosha', meaning 'faults' or 'defects'. Some have the dosha of spring, known as 'Kapha'; the use of marijuana—Ayurveda experts say—can help prevent illnesses associated with this season.

It isn't just Holi, of course. Festivals like Shivratri are a major draw for those falling together in the Venn diagram of Shiva bhakts and cannabis. In their 1957 paper 'The Use of Cannabis Drugs in India,' I. C. Chopra and R. N. Chopra* cited examples of more such celebrations from the past:

---

*The Chopra Bros. return!

> In Bengal, for instance, the custom still persists among certain classes of offering a beverage prepared from the leaves of the cannabis plant to the various family members and to guests present on the last day of Durga Puja (Vijaya Dasmi) which is the biggest Hindu festival in that state. In Tarakeshwar temple in Bengal, ganja is used as an offering on the Shivratri... Less commonly, it is used in other religious festivals such as Trinath Puja, a religious ceremony observed also by certain Mohammedan sects in a slightly different form. In Puff (Odisha) one of the greatest places of Hindu pilgrimage in India, ganja and bhang are largely used by the attendants and worshippers of the god Jagannath.

Much like the spirit of the Indian Constitution, cannabis is secular, and particularly a component in the synthesis of cultures of the 'Ganga–Jamuna Tehzeeb' across many North Indian cities with large populations of both Hindus and Muslims. Chopra and Chopra write of 'takyas' or 'dehras' which serve as congregation points for 'cannabis addicts'.

Later, they continue:

> To certain sects of Mohammedans, the plant is an embodiment of the spirit of the prophet Khizer Elijah [Khidr], the patron saint of water ('Khizer' means 'green colour of the drink made from bhang'). Many Hindustani poets, especially Nasir, have immortalized bhang by eulogizing it in their poems. The drug is mentioned by some Mohammedan poets as 'warak-al-khiyal' or 'fancy's leaf'. In Persian literature it is known by various names such as 'joy-giver', 'sky flier', 'heavenly guide', 'poor man's heaven',* 'soother of grief', etc. The Mohammedan fakirs revere bhang as the 'giver of long life' and they consider that it frees them from worldly bonds,

*And who are you to deny a poor man his heaven?

> and induces communion with the divine spirit....
>
> In India taken as a whole it would appear that the smoking of charas was more prevalent among the Muslims, while the habitual use of ganja was more common among the Hindus. This, we consider, was mainly a question of availability, as charas was more easily available in the north, where the predominant population is Muslim, while ganja was available in the south, where the population is mostly Hindu. Bhang was and still is largely used by the Hindus and the Sikhs.

In a nation where much of the middle and upper classes tend to pigeonhole marijuana as a dangerous 'nasha' or an antisocial element, there exists, concurrently, a widespread, underground acceptance of the substance. These include strains of cannabis which you have already met in our voyage so far, from Malana Cream to the Sulfa of Uttarakhand, from Idukki Gold to Sheelavathi. There's also the sweet, enchanting Mysore Mango—clean and green, with a faint aroma of mangoes—cultivated in the hilly regions in Karnataka. There's the Shillong Mango, as refreshing as the cleansing rains of Meghalaya. There are strains of ganja indigenous in Manipur, West Bengal, and Assam. There's weed that grows in Punjab, Uttar Pradesh, Madhya Pradesh, and Tamil Nadu. There's the Nepali Mango available readily in New Delhi, allegedly imported from our neighbours up north.

'Mango' is a common catch-all for ganja, an enticing ode to the juicy summer fruit and the sweet fragrance of certain strains. It's also a convenient code word to provide buyers and sellers plausible deniability. Similarly, 'Cream' or 'Black' is the code for charas.

When spring turns to summer—the real mango season—you might even come across some bhang-infused ice cream. For those with a sweet tooth, there are bhang-laced laddoos. Bhang in your gajar ka halwa, in your sooji ka halwa, in your Christmas plum cake, in pakoras, in the ras of your roshogolla, in the pani of your pani-puri. Bhang in majoun, too, the confection enjoyed by Babur, the first Mughal emperor.

I guess what I'm trying to say with this long-winded preamble is that, across most of our gigantic, colourful country, you're going to have a tougher time avoiding cannabis than confronting it.

Born in the small village in the north-west frontier (bordering Afghanistan), my maternal grandmother, Raj Chawla—Nani—was just eight when in 1947 she was displaced along with millions of others during Partition. In the chaos of the train filled with refugees to India, Nani was separated from her family and had to spend time in an orphanage for several months, before she was finally reunited with her loved ones at a refugee colony in Faridabad.

In the summer of 1947, after nearly two hundred years of the East India Company and the British Raj, India was tantalizingly close to its dream of freedom, of independence from foreign domination. But the excitement of Independence was blotched by the horror of what was to come. The viceroy of India, Louis Mountbatten, declared that the nation would be splintered and lacerated; a creation of new borders that would give birth to two independent countries. The areas with majority Muslim populations in West Punjab and East Bengal would become Pakistan; the remaining, massive chunk of land populated mostly by a Hindu populace would be India. As the colonizers left, the violence turned inwards. Hindus, Muslims, and Sikhs massacred each other across the nation.

Like my mother's side, my parental great-grandparents were displaced by borders, too, leaving behind their home in Gujranwala.

They were lucky to survive. Millions died at the time of Partition. And for my ancestors, home was suddenly a foreign nation.

By the time I was born, many of those children of Partition

had become grandparents, and the *three* new nations (now including Bangladesh) found each other in an uneasy liaison: bonded in much of language, culture, traditions, history, sports, food, and religion, yet split by politics. As I grew older and learned about my family's history, I couldn't help but feel a sense of fernweh—as the Germans say—for places in Pakistan I have never seen, homesickness for the old alleyways of Gujranwala, nostalgia for the formidable mountains filling up the skyline across the Khyber region.

I've never had a chance to cross this border. When I began working on this quixotic, nationwide 'ganja project', the ubiquity of cannabis was the prime driver of my motivation to be on the road again, to explore parts of India I'd never seen before, and revisit familiar places with a new perspective. But the more I travelled, the more I saw the absurdity in my arbitrary limitation within the borders of the Indian republic—as arbitrary as the borders themselves, largely sketched out by foreign men who hadn't stepped foot on the subcontinent, pulling apart two arms of the same body to create new nations.

It is in the Khyber district—across the difficult terrain in the mountainous tracts close to the Pakistan–Afghan border—where one arrives in the grassy lands of the Tirah Valley, a small region that has gained cult status for producing some of the finest charas available on Earth. According to a popular legend, a supposed 'Sufi tourist' from the 'eastern part of India' wandered into Tirah in the late nineteenth century. This tourist brought with him the cannabis plant, and convinced the local tribesmen to grow it.

Sufism is a form of Islamic practice that focuses on mysticism and ascetism. Some Sufi Muslims are known to consume bhang in honour of the spirit of the saint Khidr, 'The Green One'. While it is considered to be khamr—an intoxicant—in Islam, Sufi tradition also attributes the rise of cannabis use to Qutb ad-Din Haydar, a twelfth century Persian saint. Of all the ways the Sufis have been known to traditionally consume hashish, one of the most popular methods is smoking through a hash pipe, which is called the nafir-e-vahdat—the trumpet of unity.

The Tirah Valley is now known for being 'the land of pure hashish', where it has been claimed that nearly a 100,000 people from local tribes make their living from the cultivation and trade of cannabis, producing over 100 tonnes of charas annually. The conditions here provide the perfect environment for the giant stalks of cannabis to grow: hot days, cool nights, and brief showers of rain all summer. Some farmers even employ the century-old technique of putting freshly prepared hash resin into a goatskin or a sheepskin, pickled and preserved, absorbing the oils that seep through. This method is supposed to enhance both the quality of the charas as well as its psychotropic effect on the user. Various charas melas (hash carnivals) are held across the valley every year, for buyers to sample and purchase the maal directly from local farmers*.

Much like the Malana Cream, the Tirah Valley charas—or its derivative—is smuggled all over the world, sold as 'Hindu Kush' or 'Pakistani Hash'.

Traversing the rugged mountain passes, across the Kush to the daunting Himalayan peaks that create natural walls of borders between our nations, one gets to Kashmir, past the snowy mountain passes and valleys and that imagined line of control.

As per landrace experts, much of the cannabis in the Kashmir Valley originates in the Pir Panjal ranges and by the Jhelum River basin. Farmers in the countryside here cultivate a type of charas known as 'challi' or 'garda'. There is also the story of man who brought an 'Ice-o-lator' to Kashmir, which is a method of separating the cannabis resin by submerging it in cold water. This man taught local farmers how to make 'ice hash' using the frigid Himalayan water, resulting in a rare form of charas now known as 'Kashmir Ice'.

---

*Recreational cannabis is illegal in Pakistan. In May 2024, the government set up a regulatory authority to manage and control the cultivation and trade of cannabis—counting on hemp to be an answer to ongoing economic woes.

Like its 'creamy' cousin in Parvati Valley, Kashmiri hash (and hash oil) has its own mystique among stoners in India. In recent years, various law-enforcement agencies have hit back at the mass cultivation in the region. The most aggressive of these drives was in the late 2000s and early 2010s, which revealed that 'lakhs of kanals' of land* was being used to cultivate cannabis in south and central Kashmir.

A little south of the valley is Jammu's CSIR-IIIM (Indian Institute of Integrative Medicine, a research institution under the Council of Scientific and Industrial Research). In 2020, this institute made history by signing a major agreement with a Canadian company for scientific research on the medical potential of cannabis. This agreement was the first foreign investment in Jammu and Kashmir since it became a union territory, after the controversial repeal of Article 370 in August 2019.

D. Srinivas Reddy, who took over as director of CSIR-IIIM in summer 2020, mentioned that the institute was in particular researching the use of cannabis for cancer pain relief, and looked forward to conducting human trials soon. The institute is currently conducting cannabis research on a one-acre protected space and climate-controlled glass houses at the Chatha Farm, about a dozen kilometres away from IIIM.

A review meeting of the Cannabis Research Project at this institute was held in June 2023, where the Minister of State for Science and Technology Jitendra Singh giddily spoke about the potential for medicinal marijuana, including medicine for neuropathies, cancer, and epilepsy. Singh predicted that this research could provide impetus for massive investments in the territory in the near future. The project's success could also reduce India's dependency on imported seeds and medicine.

These are exciting developments, particularly coming out of

*Eight kanals equals to about one acre.

territories close to the Kashmir Valley, which have long been mired with insurgency and armed occupation. Many parts of Kashmir continue to be hostile and disputed territory, and rarely have the politics of union-making considered the will of the Kashmiris themselves. Of late, the region has also faced an increase in the crisis of harder drug abuse; a 2023 report by the Parliamentary Standing Committee on Social Justice and Empowerment claimed that over 10 per cent of the population in Jammu and Kashmir were now abusing some form of drugs—including cannabis, opioids, sedatives, cocaine, and more. In recent years, there has been a disturbing rise of heroin abuse (in its many formulations) in the Kashmir Valley, including Brown Sugar, chitta, or nasally consumed varieties. In a Muslim-majority state where alcohol is considered haram, harder drugs have become the intoxicant of choice; while alcohol is forbidden by the Quran, there is no mention of narcotics like cannabis in the holy book, leaving its status open to interpretation. It has also been hypothesized by mental health experts that the history of Kashmir's militarized conditions and human rights violations have had a direct effect on the mental health of the valley's youth, leading many to seek an escape through drugs.

Beyond these snowcapped borderlands, cannabis has added its deep green shade across the subcontinent. Even more porous is our northern border with Nepal. Much like India, cannabis is the most common crop across several districts here, where the plant serves a variety of purposes: leaves and fruits for ganja and hash oil, seeds for cooking and medicine, stems for fibre. In the 1960s, Nepal licensed and taxed the sale of hashish across stores in Kathmandu and beyond, giving rise to what became known internationally as the 'Hippie Trail'. Western beatniks headed East, to explore the world, to explore themselves, across Turkey and Iran to Afghanistan, Pakistan, Nepal, and India. In his essay about the politics of cannabis in Nepal, the journalist Sean Williams writes: 'By 1972, cannabis was the second-largest industry in western Nepal, and an illicit market transformed cities and towns on the Indian border—Nepalganj, Biratnagar, Kanchanpur—into smugglers' paradises.'

Under pressure from the international community, Nepal enacted its own Narcotic Drugs (Control) Act in 1976, prohibiting the cultivation, production, preparation, purchasing, selling, distributing, exporting or importing, and any trafficking, storage, or consumption of cannabis. Decades later, the nation is beginning to reconsider this decision: in the summer of 2023, Nepal's government announced their plans to conduct a feasibility study for medicinal marijuana and a year later, the country's finance minister announced plans to legalize the cultivation of cannabis for medicinal purposes.

The illicit trade across the borders to Nepal continues for now; a few months after the announcement above, Uttar Pradesh police arrested four people and seized cannabis worth ₹3 crore sourced from Nepal, intended for distribution in north India. Over the course of a week in September 2023, authorities claimed making multiple busts of parcels arriving (via air routes) to Nepal from the United States, each carrying around a kilo of marijuana. Some of those parcels were labelled as children's toys or chocolates. The contraband was supposed to be smuggled across the border (via land) to India.

Meanwhile, off the southern tip in Sri Lanka, cannabis is legally sold in Ayurvedic shops and available to use for medicinal purposes. The country's tourism minister recently mentioned that with '22 varieties' of cannabis, Sri Lanka can become one of the world leaders in the industry. While it's not technically legal for recreational use, authorities are often lenient—like in India—when cannabis is consumed as part of the Hindu or Buddhist religious traditions.

All across South Asia, the variety of available maal is as diverse as the people of these places. And yet, much like the mother plant of cannabis, the people in these lands are bound together, plaited baskets sinewed with the sturdiest of hemp rope.

It was November 2008, and I had left home on a self-imposed exile. All I carried on me was a roomy hiking bag, in which I stuffed a change of clothes, two or three paperbacks, a diary, a few toiletries, a sleeping bag, an MP3 player, a thermos, and a towel.* My first step into the unknown was to Pushkar, the pilgrimage city in Rajasthan. Friends who had visited in the past recommended the town for its old markets, cafes catering to international travellers, the bathing ghats, the annual camel fair, and the famous Brahma Temple—dedicated to the Hindu god of creation.

I was also aware that Pushkar was a 'dry zone', like many other pilgrimage areas in India: no alcohol available, and no non-veg, either.** Almost any seasoned traveller around India knows that strict alcohol prohibitions are usually inversely proportional to a loose cultural acceptance of the gods' favourite intoxicant: cannabis. I'd learned this from experience in the dry zones of Varanasi, where bhang is far more readily available than booze.

In Pushkar, drifting tourists have been known to spend large amounts on Himalayan Cream; the weed from Chamba district, in particular, ends up all across northwest India, across Rajasthan, major cities in Punjab, and up to Jammu and Kashmir, too.

Rajasthan has its own strain, a cousin of the cannabis plants found in Punjab, which have now adapted to the hot conditions of the Thar Desert. Like the desert camels, these plants can survive long durations in the heat—persisting even as the mercury rises to 45–50 degrees Celsius (and beyond!) in the summers.

Elsewhere in Rajasthan, the persistence of cannabis has proven to be a conserver of history, too. It has been tradition for devotees of Shiva to offer food, flowers, and bhang to the Shivling at the Mahakaleshwar Jyotirlinga Temple in the ancient city of Ujjain. In 2017, an expert committee of archaeologists studying the tumescent

---

*I've read a lot of Douglas Adams.

**'No alcohol and no non-veg' in India usually means that both are probably available covertly at a steep mark-up.

idol discovered that the bhang may actually be preventing this ancient sandstone lingam from erosion, which would've otherwise been caused by the other floral and food offerings here that attract bacterial and fungal growth. The committee's report concluded that the bhang paste 'generally contains certain chemicals...that control biodegradation as they have anti-bacterial and anti-fungal properties.'

In this case, bhang—like the god Vishnu—plays the role of preserver.

Cannabis offerings at temples are hardly a rare phenomenon; similar to above, devotees in Chitrakoot, Madhya Pradesh, offer cannabis to a 400-year-old statue of the 'Lete huye Hanuman Ji' (reclining Hanuman) in a temple dedicated to the simian god as part of their worship rituals.

Back to Rajasthan. On my night bus from Jaipur to Pushkar—buttocks sore from the exposed metal of the bench I sat on, eyelids sagging after a tiresome day on the road—I felt, for the first time in my young life, truly unchained. I didn't know where I would be spending the night. *Get there and figure it out.*

Closer to Pushkar, I noticed a familiar design painted on the rocky hillside walls: the graphic of a human face screaming out in despair, in the foreground of tightly-packed white bricks. It was the album art from Pink Floyd's 1979 masterpiece *The Wall*, and I was looking at an advertisement for Pushkar's Pink Floyd Café. The restaurant/hotel was themed around one of my favourite bands, whose music and art had stimulated philosophically curious minds, as well as served as the companion soundtrack to many generations of weed smokers. In the absence of any places to lay my head that night, I decided to follow the signs to find this little haven of psychedelic rock in the city of Brahma.

When the bus stopped outside the entrance to Old Pushkar, I set off on foot with my backpack, wandering in the dark through the dusty, silent gullies of the town, following only *The Wall* signs painted on the walls. It got darker, quieter, past stone-cobbled paths, twisting and turning around crumbling old temples, past sleeping dogs too lethargic to greet a new stranger in town. Finally, I saw the small doorway to Pink Floyd, with the words 'Wish You Were Here' painted on the arch. The gate shutters were open, but there was no one awake in the reception area. I wandered into a dark lobby, walked up a flight of steps, and saw a single bed in the corridor, by an open window. Only the faintest rays of moonlight made it in from the window outside, bathing the night in deep purple.

It was perfect. The gods of rock had delivered.

There was a voice in my head, trying to squeak out louder to remind me that I had strolled in here uninvited. But I was high on a cocktail of exhilaration and exhaustion. I dropped my bag, kicked off my shoes, and rolled on to the bed. It didn't take me long to fall asleep.

At dawn, I awoke to the clanging ring of temple bells, cawing of crows, and stinging pinpricks of mosquitoes on my forearms.* I left the hotel before anyone else woke up.

I would return later that day and find a seat on the hotel's rooftop, from where much of Pushkar's unique topography is visible: the lake in the middle of town, encircled by fifty-two ghats; the old town that stretches out in a larger circular radius around these ghats; the vast swathes of desert surrounding this little oasis, and the many little hills that provide natural borders around this terrain.

All roads in Pushkar—more or less—lead to the Brahma Temple, one of the few temples in the world dedicated to this deity. Along with shops selling trinkets and gifts, and prayer offerings, and clothes and souvenirs, one could also easily stumble into a café or a tea stall offering bhang in its many forms: golis, smoothies, or special brownies.

---

*Sigh...

Soon, the desert would seem vaster than ever, the birds swooping across the ghat steps would sing the most mesmerizing tunes, the temple bells would ring in melodic symphony, the night view from Pink Floyd's rooftop would become enchanting—complete with a progressive rock anthem to really jet set me to the great gigs in the sky.

Towns like Pushkar, Varanasi, Manali, etc., are a natural draw for an eclectic variety of visitors: domestic tourists looking for a taste of spirituality, and international backpackers looking for a cheap avenue to find a slice of 'authentic' Indian culture. Spiritual centres like these exist in the comfortable sangam of doublethink towards cannabis: accepted with open arms for its divinity, rejected and blackmarked when used recreationally outside a strictly religious setting.

Another such mesmerizing destination is Virupapura Gadde, a small village located just across the Hampi River in Karnataka built around the Virupaksha Temple (another avatar of Shiva), which has earned the nickname of 'Hippie Island' for backpackers. The beaches of Gokarna in the same state provide a similar, welcoming feel for both travelling backpackers and Shiva bhakts visiting the Mahabaleshwar Temple. There's Kodaikanal (Tamil Nadu), Almora (Uttarakhand), Gangtok (Sikkim), or Jaisalmer (Rajasthan), where the famous Dr Bhang* shop—government authorized, of course—is immensely popular among travellers.

And of course, there's Goa, the beach state, which has become a centre for both nightlife and relaxing beach getaways, with easy (but stupidly expensive) access to a wide variety of drugs. In 2020, the BJP government in Goa had considered legalizing the cultivation of cannabis for medicinal purposes, but the plan was eventually dropped.** Cannabis remains a favourite of the reported

---

*Dr Bhang has the same medical qualifications as Dr Dre.

**Goa did give us the stoner-zombie-comedy *Go Goa Gone* in 2013, a true rarity in Indian cinema.

narcotics seized in the beach state: Goan police reported that 98 per cent of drugs confiscated from 2020–2022 were cannabis-based. On average, the anti-narcotics cell conducted three drug raids per week during this period. A wide diversity of international citizens that would rival any United Colors of Benetton poster were arrested by the anti-narcotics cell: Nigerians, Russians, Ugandans, Japanese, Belarusians, Dutch, Americans, Nepalese, Tanzanians, the English, Liberians, and of course, many domestic dealers, too.

A particularly popular backpacker destination is Rishikesh, in Uttarakhand. It's a major draw for domestic pilgrims as well as for international visitors who visit for its reputation for being the 'Yoga Capital of the World' (the town usually hosts an annual International Yoga Festival in the spring). Rishikesh was once home to the spiritual guru Maharishi Mahesh Yogi. In 1968, the world's most famous band—The Beatles—just happened to stop by to get a taste of the Maharishi's brand of transcendental meditation. This period also led to The Beatles composing some of the trippiest music* they ever made, during the peak of the British band's experimentation of mind-altering substances to achieve their definition of a higher consciousness: yoga, good vibes, spirituality, LSD, and some Himalayan Mary Jane.

There was some tension in this yogic paradise, and The Beatles would eventually accuse the Maharishi of inappropriate sexual advances towards the actress Mia Farrow and other women at the ashram, an experience that resulted in the song, 'Sexy Sadie'. Years later, the New Age speaker Deepak Chopra—a former disciple of the Maharishi—claimed that the Maharishi's eventual clash with The Beatles arose because 'they were smoking ganja and taking LSD'.

The Beatles Ashram (Chaurasi Kutia) still stands on the banks

---

*Leading eventually to the classic *The Beatles* (the White Album), but also to the worst song in The Beatles's entire oeuvre, George Harrison's 'Dehradun'.

of the Ganga in the outskirts of Rishikesh, a draw for fans of the Fab Four, and the countless who visit India to discover a form of new wave spirituality—sometimes aided by cannabis and other substances, too.

The late 60s were the height of the hippie counterculture movement in the West, one that would appropriate the 'mystical' practices of Eastern spirituality, and marry it with a spirit of freedom, protest, and the use of various psychotropic and psychedelic drugs. Soon, some of the countercultural energy would rotate back to the East, too.

Over fifty years later, the opening scene of the song 'Dum Maro Dum' from *Haré Rama Haré Krishna* is still one of the most glorious moments in Indian film history. The song awoke to a world that John Lennon proposed in 'Imagine'—released the same year—a world without borders and violence, a world of diversity and dreams.

The year is 1971. The camera zooms out to a clay chillum, in the hands of a shaggy-haired white man. He takes a puff from the pipe. Then, as if the 'hit' has evoked a higher musical power, Bhupinder Singh's psychedelic guitar riff kicks in. A chilling synth revs up in the background. Then, that quick-fire, head-nodding drumbeat. A groovy baseline. The chillum is passed from one white man to another. The camera zooms and moves, placing us at a large hippie congregation, featuring a diverse crowd of extras with long hair, clad in loose shirts and headbands. Some boast psychedelic prints on their shirts, some use the iconography of South Asian culture that The Beatles and Jimi Hendrix had borrowed in the late 60s, and some are in simple earthly whites—an ode to Mother Earth and Flower Power. Thick smoke hovers in the air. Eyes are glazed. A couple embrace in a passionate French kiss. Bottles of alcohol are passed around. Someone sits in a corner, mushing together a little more maal, perhaps to fill the next pipe.

And then, there she is: Zeenat Aman, the heart of this epicurean shindig. The young actress lip-syncs along to the first words of the song, sung in the playback by Asha Bhosle. A wisp of smoke exits out of her pursed lips. '*Dum maro dummmmmmm....*'

Take another hit.

Released nearly fifteen years before the NDPS Act, *Haré Rama Haré Krishna* brought the hippie movement of the time back to the culture that had inspired it. The film pitted Dev Anand—one of the biggest stars of his time—alongside the newcomer Aman, as the two portray siblings separated at childhood. Much of the film is based in Kathmandu, Nepal, where Anand's character (Prashant) goes in search for Aman's Jasbir (or 'Janice'). The main drama is held in the foreground of the international Haré Krishna Movement, with global smuggling rings and commentary on the impact of 'Western' culture on South Asian youth.

Dev Anand wrote, directed, and produced *Haré Rama Haré Krishna*, but it was the twenty-year-old Aman—in her breakthrough role as pot-smoking, heavy-drinking, broken-hearted hippie—who stole the show, winning the Filmfare Best Supporting Actress Award that year. The film is a sort of morality tale with an anti-drug message. But one look at Aman—clad in red, decorated with yellow marigolds, as she sings and sways with a sense of jouissance—and one could be forgiven for momentarily interpreting the moment as a celebration of youthful ananda.

Produced and composed by R. D. Burman, 'Dum Maro Dum' was the best-possible auditory substitute for a blissful marijuana high, a little disco, a little rock, and a lot of soul. Its intentions as a cannabis anthem couldn't be clearer, as the chorus goes:

Dum maro dum
Mit Jaaye gham
Bolo sub-aur-shyaam
Haré Krishna Haré Rama.

Take another hit
Erase all your sorrows.
Say it day and night
Praise to Krishna, praise to Rama.

Religion, here, isn't merely the root of recreational cannabis use—it's also the natural result of being stoned, of sorrows being erased. Take another hit, and say the names of your preferred almighties—in this case, both avatars of Vishnu.

Men and women continue to sway side to side as the song progresses, with more hits from the chillum, more smoke permeating the atmosphere. Then, Bhosale sings the track's most haunting lyrics, posed in the form of four rhetorical questions:

Duniya ne humko diya kya?
Duniya se hamne liya kya?
Hum sabki parvah karein kyon?
Sabne hamara kiya kya?

What did the world ever give to us?
What did we ever take from the world?
Why should we worry about anyone?
What has anyone ever done for us?

Masked by the upbeat production, the lyrics are a desperate, existential call for rebellion. A *fuck you* to the rest of the world. All that we need is to keep praising the gods—and the next hit.

Decades later, 'Dum Maro Dum' continues to have a cultural impact. The song has been sampled and covered by artists around the world.* The most direct homage came in the 2011 film *Dum Maaro Dum*, about a cop (Abhishek Bachchan) tasked to bring down the drug cartels in Goa (now, the 'dums' are for cocaine, not cannabis).

---

*Including the funky 'What's Happenin', by Method Man featuring Busta Rhymes. 'Dum Maro Dum' is also heard in the popular video game *Grand Theft Auto: Liberty City Stories*.

The film's song 'Mit Jaaye Gham (Dum Maaro Dum)' samples Burman's original, remixed as an 'item number' to a quicker, coked-up beat, with this generation's starlet Deepika Padukone swaying to the song on the screen.

Meanwhile back in the 70s, in the far corner of the world, the Indo-Caribbean diaspora was experimenting with mind-bending fusions of Indian folk, Bhojpuri, Caribbean calypso, soca, and Bollywood, altogether to create the 'chutney' genre. Several chutney songs were written as odes to ganja; the cultural affinity for cannabis, and the term 'ganja' itself, crossed the oceans with the Indian diaspora who were taken as indentured labourers by the British authorities to the Caribbean islands in the nineteenth and early twentieth centuries, settling across Trinidad, Jamaica, Guyana, Suriname, and more. Some of the popular chutney tracks of this time include 'Chilam Chilam' by Rasika Dindial and Ravi B., 'Marijuana' by Mookraj Sahadeo, and 'Ganjawala' by Ravi B and Karma the Band.*

In India, cannabis and cinema continued to have a casual, merry relationship. In the 1974 film *Aap Ki Kasam*, the characters played by Rajesh Khanna and Mumtaz visit a Shiva temple to pray for the birth of a child. Then, things take a turn for the wackiest possible outcome, as the two—under the influence of bhang—break into a memorable garden dance party around a bunch of other extras (presumably intoxicated) to the hit song, 'Jai Jai Shiv Shankar'. In the voice of Kishore Kumar, the song begins:

Hey Jai Jai Shiv Shankar
Kaanta lage na kankar
Ki pyaala tere naam ka piya

---

*A popular recent example of a chutney-inspired song is 'Hunter' from Anurag Kashyap's *Gangs of Wasseypur* (2012).

Victory to Shiva
Let neither thorn nor rock befall us
For I drink this goblet in your name.

In the name of love, or in the name of god? Either way, we know what the pyaala (goblet) is filled with.

In 1980, Amitabh Bachchan danced around to 'Rang Barse' from *Silsila*, after his character had a little shot of bhang. In 1985, R. D. Burman and Asha Bhosle—a magical pairing of producer and vocalist—reunited for another cannabis-infused track, 'Bhang Jamaye Rang Jara Sa', for the film *Shiva Ka Insaaf* (Shiva's Justice), starring Jackie Shroff as a desi swashbuckling Zorro. There's the film *Koyla* (1997), where Madhuri Dixit lip-syncs to the song, 'Bhang Ke Nashe Mein Kho Gaye Hum' (I'm lost in the intoxication of bhang) while inexplicably dancing on a hillside with a dozen children.

More recently, Ranbir Kapoor and Deepika Padukone danced to the track 'Balam Pichkari' from the film *Yeh Jawaani Hai Deewani* (2013). Somewhere in Parvati Valley, Padukone's character Naina—who had thus far been portrayed in the film as a stereotypically bookish and conservative girl—is now immersed in the intoxicating blend of love and bhang. She jumps carefree into the throes of a Holi celebration. She is now sexualized: glasses off, hair open, with gyrating hips on display. Sung by Shalmali Kholgade, the first verse goes:

Itna maza kyun aa raha hai?
Tune hawa mein bhang milaya?
Dugna nasha, kyun ho raha hai?
Aankhon se meetha tune khilaya?

Why am I having so much fun?
Have you mixed bhang in the air?
Why am I twice as intoxicated?
Did you feed me sweets with your eyes?

From Aman in *Haré Rama Haré Krishna* to Padukone in *Yeh Jawaani Hai Deewani*, there is a clear line of insinuation that ties cannabis with both religious festivity and a freedom of mind, an 'unlocking' of one's inhibitions which could be as much a spiritual experience as it is a romantic one.

In 'Dum Maro Dum', as Aman and her troupe of friends continue to sway along, the film's hero, Prashant (Dev Anand) soon enters the scene, wearing a lugubrious expression on his face. The psychedelic tune is replaced by the solemn hymn 'Dekho Toh Deewanon', a song imploring the congregation to change their ways, to read the scripture, and not take Rama's name in vain. It's a bucket of cold water over the hot-blooded carnival. The party is over.

But nothing could stop 'Dum Maro Dum' from becoming a youth anthem for the generation—and a song that continues to connect with every successive generation which feels alienated by society. *Duniya ne humko diya kya?*

It's bewildering to consider how much has changed in India's cultural zeitgeist—as represented by our mammoth movie industry—since the early 70s. And how much, perhaps, remains the same. While bhang continues to enjoy almost nonpartisan spiritual and social acceptance, the other preparations of the cannabis plant—ganja, charas—are illegal. Even as the portrayal of bhang in Indian cinema is excused as a fun, frolicsome celebration—festive in the name of Shiva—the use of ganja/charas is used as a political tool to villainize some of the biggest names in the same entertainment industry.

There's a thin line between spirituality and sin.

On 14 June 2020, thirty-four-year-old Sushant Singh Rajput, a rising Hindi film star, was found dead at his home in Bandra, Mumbai. Months later, his therapist would claim that Rajput suffered from depression and hypomania. On the day of his suicide,

Rajput had Googled information about 'schizophrenia', 'bipolar disorder', and 'painless death'.

What followed was one of the ugliest episodes of a trial by media, as, searching for a scapegoat, news channels dissected and speculated every aspect of the young man's life. Rajput's death would make the use of illegal drugs in the film industry a topic of daily national conversation. The NCB identified two men: Abbas Lakhani and Karan Arora—who allegedly had links to the actor—for holding on to 59 grams of ganja and 5 grams of 'a dark brown substance'. Then, Rajput's cook told investigators that he 'saw him smoke ganja' one time in 2018. There were WhatsApp conversations between a staff member of Rajput and Rajput's girlfriend, the actress Rhea Chakraborty. 'Hi, can you give Dipesh Rs 17,000 for 2 bags of weed? 1 for us & another for him & he will transfer it to us.' Another staff member of Rajput claimed, 'Before Sushant sir committed suicide, I rolled the marijuana cigarettes for him for three days which were kept in a cigarette case in a cupboard near staircase. After Sushant sir's suicide, I saw that the marijuana cigarettes box was empty.' Later reports suggested that Rajput's former talent manager Jaya Saha had arranged CBD oil for him and a few other actors (including Chakraborty). Then, there were allegations that Chakraborty was mixing 'drugs' (it was CBD oil) in Rajput's coffee or tea.

There are no clear answers for depression: a faulty mood regulation in one's brain, genetic vulnerability, or stressful life events, are all (indefinite) parts of the cause. The *Indian Journal of Psychiatry* did publish a report in 2017 on the pernicious effects of marijuana, claiming that, 'There is growing evidence that chronic and persistent use of heavy marijuana can cause long-term sequelae, especially to the developing brain. It predisposes people to anxiety, depression, and even psychosis.'

But marijuana doesn't impact everyone the same way, and many around the world use cannabis products—including CBD oil—for stress relief. In India, Rajput's death caused a spike of interest in

CBD and its stress-alleviating properties. Delzaad Deolaliwala, the chairperson of Pan India Medical Cannabis and Hemp Association (PIMCHA) told *The Print,* 'It was actually the two months that clocked in the highest sales for the industry in some manner because a lot of people started talking about CBD.'

Depression is a multi-layered, complex phenomenon, and not a crime that is easily solved by accusing a single perpetrator. No substance or shortcut will cure depression; there is always a longer route, through therapy, through lifestyle changes, through trying and failing and trying again.

And sometimes, that shortcut to bliss may cause one to stumble into their worst nightmares, a seemingly infinite fall deep into a dark abyss. A bad trip. Suddenly, you see yourself for the first time without the protective filters of your own delusions. This is the real you: your real skin and your real hair and the real shape of your nose and the real flab around your waist and the stench of real flesh and the creaking of real bones. You see how others finally see your inadequacies. You see yourself even as you're alone, your pathetic groans of constipation, your disgusting form convulsing as you masturbate. You cut through your own bullshit, the rules you created to convince yourself that your form of intelligence is intelligent, or the way you shifted the goalposts around your definition of morality to convince yourself of your own. You see the disguises you wear to boost your self-worth. You fall deeper into the abyss. The darkness gets darker. All you hear are the faintest whispers you'd hope to mute in your memories, the secrets you hold within, the lies you've told yourself. You hope to grit your teeth and clear your throat and scream the loudest scream you've ever screamed, but all the abyss hears is a faint whimper, a pinprick in the vacuum of space-time.

What is fun about this? Why would you ever try this again?

How could a handsome, young, successful, famous man kill himself? There were no clear answers in Rajput's case. The country wanted to find the villain who killed the hero. Trial by media turned into the court of the people. Marijuana was labelled as the cause of his depression, and Chakraborty—who allegedly provided him the weed—was held responsible for his death.

In the eye of the storm, Chakraborty was charged by the NCB for receiving and delivering marijuana to her late boyfriend, and arrested in September 2020 on the abetment of suicide charge, after being accused of wrongful restraint, wrongful confinement, theft, breach of trust, and more. Soon, more individuals from the film industry came under the scanner, including Deepika Padukone, Shraddha Kapoor, Arjun Rampal, etc. Nightly news* debates were filled with headlines like #BollywoodDarkSecrets, We All Hung Out with SSR (Sushant Singh Rajput), Sushant Conspiracy, Bollywood Drug Racket Explodes, etc. Hashtags followed on social media, asking for a boycott of the entire industry seemingly swimming deep in the throes of drugs. Matters got so out of hand that some top filmmakers filed a civil defamation suit against several news channels.

Chakraborty's supporters flagged it all as a witch hunt. A former chief at Mumbai's anti-narcotics cell said, 'A sadhu's chillum holds more marijuana than what she is being convicted of.'

It's rare for the NCB to even act upon such a relatively miniscule amount. In a recent interview, cannabis advocate Khagesh Gautam explained how, without any widely known clarity of what constitutes a 'small quantity' of ganja, the Indian police has often exercised its powers arbitrarily. 'Sometimes if they see a group of friends in a corner smoking a joint, they could arrest you or they could let you go,' Gautam said. 'There is no exact definition of what small amount is an arrestable offense!'

And there's no amount small enough for the big fish, with high-profile incidents including the Aryan Khan case and the overreaction to Rajput's alleged cannabis use and death. There have been other recent cases, too. In October 2020, stand-up comic Bharti Singh

*The word 'news' here is being used in the loosest possible sense.

and her husband Haarsh Limbachiyaa were arrested in Mumbai on the discovery of 86 grams of cannabis at their office and residence. Telugu film actress Hema was taken into custody in June 2024 after testing positive for (unspecified) drug consumption at a farmhouse rave party near Bengaluru, where the police confiscated hydro cannabis and various other illicit substances.

A few months after Sushant Singh Rajput's death, I had gotten in touch with the actor and podcaster Mantra Mugdh, who told me that he had begun to get calls from authorities warning him that his 'number is next'. 'I had known Sushant in his earlier days,' Mantra said. 'We had been in get-togethers where joints were being passed.'

Mantra, who doesn't shy away from admitting to marijuana use, once hosted a podcast titled 'Chai Chillum Charcha', which lasted only a few episodes, but featured discussions about India's legalization movement. In response to the growing fervour of negativity about the substance, Mantra penned an open letter to defend the plant, highlight its medicinal and joyous aspects, and criticize the government's archaic laws. 'Let me confirm this,' Mantra wrote, 'Drugs might be huge in Bollywood. But Cannabis urf Ganja is NOT a drug.'

When I spoke to Mantra, he said that he felt strongly about dispelling the caricature of the lazy, good-for-nothing stoner, the type of person that, he says, 'lies around all day'. 'I'm proof that, even after being in touch with cannabis for twenty years, I could be a successful man.'

Mantra is from Indore in Madhya Pradesh, and told me that he was very influenced by the Omkareshwar Mandir (a Shiva temple) not far from his hometown. It's here that, sitting with the 'babas', he found a connection with both spirituality and cannabis. 'That leaf, that plant—it has guided me with everything. People think that cannabis is only about "smoking up". But that is such a small percentage of its capability. It's so much more.'

'Just because something is illegal doesn't mean that it's right or wrong,' Mantra added. 'Slavery was also legal for hundreds of years. It was allowed to buy or sell a human being. It was fucking legal. And when it was to be abolished, there were wars. *Jung!* Then, for hundreds of years, homosexuality was a crime. People were hung and burnt alive for being homosexuals. And now, that has been decriminalized.'

'That's the same way I feel about cannabis,' Mantra continued. 'But, ek din aayega. Its day will come.'

Lekin kab aayega? As the mainstream media wages war against cannabis use, even the biggest film stars in Mumbai—from Shah Rukh Khan's son to those associated with Rajput—have realized that no amount of power gives access to complete security.

As someone from a (relatively) smaller North Indian city, every trip I took to Mumbai felt like a sensory overdose, an adjustment of expectations. It made me reimagine my idea of India, of comforts and discomforts, of civic services, of traffic, of commute. The city is, of course, the capital of the Hindi and Marathi film industries, home to the biggest names in showbiz—their pizzazz, their scandals. But it's so much more: it's a city of astonishing history, culture, and arts, extreme inequalities, ambitions delivered, and dreams devastated, struggle and excess, the intoxicating scent of the wide waters drifting inland from the Arabian Sea, the high-rising skyscrapers, the voices going hoarse at Dalal Street, the claustrophobic local trains, the long days and longer nights. It's everything I could've imagined—and then, it's a lot more.

In 2015, I visited Mumbai for a film project in the Nagpada area. My colleague and I stayed at a homestay near Haji Ali,* along with

*Near Christmas 2022, someone hacked into a roadside LED display board in Haji Ali, replacing the traffic instructions with the words 'Smoke Weed Every Day'. Word to Nate Dogg.

the homeowner, Rayyan. After each long day of work at Nagpada, we would return to Rayyan's apartment, to the common room usually clouded under a heavy layer of marijuana smoke. Rayyan told us stories about their past, their work, and most passionately, their weed.

It was through Rayyan that I first learned about the dark web, darknet markets, tumbled digital currencies, and how it all related to the massive underground drug industry. At the cost of a few thousand rupees, Rayyan was able to make an online order of cannabis from their laptop, and it would arrive a few weeks later—via snail mail—from somewhere in Europe. The weed would be grown and hybridized in professional labs and greenhouses, high in THC. It would be delivered to Rayyan's doorstep securely packed in an envelope, last touched by the hands of the friendly neighbourhood postwallah.

I was astounded.

As the years passed, I became more aware of the deep intricacies of the darknet marketplaces of drugs (and other contraband) imported into India. Another friend in Delhi told me of a dealer who once ordered psilocybin (magic) mushrooms from Mexico off the dark web, delivered by an agent who took an international flight with a special pouch stitched in the inside of his shirt.

This was a hidden world that first gained true international exposure with the 2013 arrest of Ross Ulbricht, the creator and operator of Silk Road. Silk Road was considered to be the world's first 'modern' darknet market, allowing users to buy or sell products and services anonymously with cryptocurrencies. Its downfall spawned a number of successors: Silk Road sequels, Agora, Black Market Reloaded, Sheep, DeepBay, Pandora, etc.

Most of these websites work (or worked) like Amazon, eBay, or Flipkart, with a thorough system for users to review other users and products, make returns, and offer bids in auctions. But you wouldn't be logging on to Silk Road only to buy copier paper or to replace your lost phone charger; here is a wild, wild world where almost any product or service is allegedly for sale, including weapons, stolen credit cards, sex workers, child pornography, assassins, and every kind of narcotic, delivered almost to any corner of the world.

In recent years, several major busts have exposed the true reach of darknet hubs. In the summer of 2022, German police shut down the German servers for Hydra, a Russian darknet marketplace, from where they seized bitcoin worth €23 million (over ₹200 crore). Hydra had around 19,000 registered vendors and 17 million customer accounts. This was a year after a German-led police sting took down DarkMarket, a similar marketplace with hundreds of thousands of users.

By now, India had produced our own answers to Ulbricht. In February 2020, the NCB arrested twenty-one-year-old Dipu Singh, the son of a retired Indian Army officer and a graduate of hotel management from Lucknow, who has been branded as India's first dark web narcotics vendor. Singh was known to send drugs by courier out of India around the world (under the guise of sexual stimulation medicine) and receive payment in cryptocurrency. The NCB has said that the use of the dark web to traffic drugs—using crypto—has increased dramatically since the turn of the 2020s.

The biggest fish (so far) in the Indian pond has been Raghunath Kumar. In June 2021, Kumar was arrested with LSD and sentenced to serve time at Karnataka's Bellary Prison. It was from behind prison bars—seated with his laptop and his phones—that Kumar created the country's biggest known digital drug racket.* Kumar, whose nicknames included 'LSD King', 'Guruji', or 'ShoppersStop', used bitcoin to buy drugs from the UK, US, Canada, Netherlands, and Poland, and then delivered them to customers in India disguised as herbal products. His operation used popular food/

*This does nothing to expel the stereotype of every Indian having the potential for being a tech genius.

product delivery services (like Zomato, Swiggy, and Amazon) to distribute the contraband. It was only when Kolkata's Foreign Post Office discovered forty-four unclaimed parcels, all with high-THC cannabis, that investigators found themselves chasing the LSD King's tail.

In her report for *The Print*, Bismee Taskin wrote:

> During the course of the investigation, the team recovered Rs 23 lakh, 25.8 kg of high-quality cannabis, 286 MDMA or Methylenedioxymethamphetamine tablets, 40 kg of heroin, 275 kg of charas, 3,449 LSD blots, 13 kg of psilocybin…and a cache of pills that would put a pharmacy to shame...
>
> Kumar's operation allegedly had a turnover of Rs 2 crore—all in cryptocurrencies—but the investigating agency couldn't recover the money.

In February 2022, twenty-two active members of Kumar's syndicate were arrested in simultaneous raids all around India: Gujarat, Maharashtra, Karnataka, Assam, Delhi NCR, Punjab, Jharkhand, West Bengal, Rajasthan, and Uttar Pradesh. These included a financial analyst who handled the finances in crypto and unified payments interface (UPI), the son of a high-ranking Indian Army officer, and a young fashion designer. Later that year, the Hyderabad Narcotics Enforcement Wing also busted a racket to catch two darknet drug kingpins in the city, who had made transactions of at least ₹30 lakh in cryptocurrency.

In Gujarat, the Ahmedabad Cyber Crime cell and the Customs department discovered cannabis and cocaine worth over ₹48 lakh concealed in children's toys and books in international courier packages, arriving on Indian shores from Canada, the US, and Thailand, with all transactions conducted through social media and the dark web.

Larger Indian metropolises have become a major market for contraband, as they are often the centres of a young, cosmopolitan population: workers in the tech industry, creative minds, students, etc. In Bengaluru, for example, the Mysore Mango is the 'local flavour', with ganja cultivation reported in regions like Chamarajanagar, Kodagu, Kolar, and Mysuru itself. But NCB officers say that most of the marijuana now sold in Bengaluru is smuggled in from the Andhra Pradesh–Odisha region, usually cultivated in the Adivasi regions further east.

In 2015, authorities in Bengaluru finally nabbed a woman known as Farida, the infamous 'Ganja Godmother', who had held a stronghold over the city's cannabis trade for over thirty years, often selling to students at the top medical/engineering colleges. The seventy-six-year-old had become the first woman in the state to be officially declared as a 'goonda' by the state of Karnataka. She has passed away since, but the Ganja Godmother's children are, allegedly, still active in the family business.

Street-level operatives who work for bosses like Farida are the heartbeat of every Indian urban centre, sourcing the maal from near and far, and always being a short call away from railway platforms, college campuses, or busy marketplaces.

A relatively new iteration of products now gaining popularity in the south of India are bhang chocolates, little homemade bars laced with cannabis. In July 2023, police in Karnataka's Mangaluru raided several shops after a rise in these 'special' chocolates being sold outside educational institutions in the city, often wrapped in colourful packets or in the guise of familiar chocolate brands to attract younger children. *News18* reported,

> Parents found that their children were constantly demanding a special chocolate named 'Bang' which was priced at Rs 20 per piece.
>
> Sudden behavioural changes in the children and the need to eat those chocolates at regular intervals raised a red flag. A group of parents then approached the Mangaluru Police which resulted in the raids and the recovery.

A similar discovery was made in Coimbatore (Tamil Nadu) earlier in 2023, where the police discovered widespread infiltration of chocolates and toffees blended with ganja available in many shops around the city. In Telangana, school students were reported to be behaving drowsy (or 'abnormally') at a local school after consuming Charminar Gold Munakka chocolates. Authorities discovered that each yellow-and-gold packet—available for just ₹10 to ₹30 rupees at cigarette and chai stalls—came stuffed with golis laced with bhang.

Many of these 'edibles' have been manufactured domestically; as mentioned earlier, however, stronger strains of ganja are arriving from abroad, too. In December 2022, the centre filed an affidavit to the Supreme Court of India, noting the rapidly rising trends of drugs being trafficked into the country through sea and air routes. The Directorate of Revenue Intelligence (DRI) reported that most of these drugs included cannabis, which is now legally available in many parts of the US. At the time of writing, the recreational use of cannabis had been legalized in twenty-four American states, three territories, and Washington D.C. A further eight states have decriminalized the use of the substance. An American federal survey reported that marijuana use reached an all-time high in 2021 among young adults (ages nineteen to thirty), nearly doubling over the past decade. Beyond the old-school smoking options, edibles high on THC have made consumption laughably convenient, avoiding any likelihood of being seen with a joint or a vape pen. These legally available products can be relatively easy to import across international borders, for anyone willing to take the risk.

(In 2019, India issued a ban on all e-cigarettes—but it has hardly stopped smokers from getting access to vapes from their foreign connections.)

The irony isn't lost on me: India is likely the most ganja-rich nation in the world, with hundreds of thousands of acres of natural cannabis growth, where ganja is found in two out of every three districts across the land, where forms of the plant are not only permissible, but celebrated. And yet, there are people in the same country who have to go through the trouble of *importing* marijuana?

It's preposterous, frankly. Unpatriotic.

There are many users like Rayyan who would rather click a few buttons online on a hidden, anonymous browser, rather than deal with the consequences of buying marijuana off the street in India, or face the potential of unregulated, contaminated weed. Plus, the imported maal—generous in THC—is simply way better.

Rayyan and I remained connected on social media, and almost seven years passed before I get in touch with her again. She still lives in the same apartment where I'd crashed years ago, still very much in love with cannabis. In 2022, however, Rayyan—who grew up in Dubai identifying as male in a conservative Muslim family—came out as transfeminine soon after she turned thirty. In a Zoom conversation a few months later, she spoke to me about her many intersecting lives: substance use, mental health, a confrontation with her identity, and the pedantic nitty-gritties of scoring weed off the darknet.

Rayyan is slim, with frizzy, curly hair. She wears bright red lipstick, and applies polish on her long nails as we speak across the screen, reminiscing about her early days of exploring digital currencies and darknet purchases soon after she had first moved to Mumbai from Dubai in the early 2010s. 'Back then, we had *Second Life* [the online multimedia platform], where the currency we used was the Linden Dollar,' Rayyan says. 'There were bitcoin exchanges in Mumbai, but they weren't anonymous: they required you to share your ID, PAN card, vagerah, vagerah. The currency came with your name on it. But I could purchase Linden Dollars from rupees,* and then convert those to Bitcoin. Nowadays, you can purchase Bitcoin on any exchange. There are tonnes of websites.

---

*As of June 2024, the value of one Linden Dollar was equal to about ₹0.26. $1 Bitcoin, ever-volatile, was worth almost ₹58 lakh.

You can literally just GPay someone and get it.'

The next step, after acquiring the cryptocurrency, would be to 'tumble' it to ensure further anonymity. 'Tumbling' means that the bitcoin is scrambled (or 'laundered') across the internet, so that one could end up using the currency associated with nearly anyone else in the world. Rayyan would only log into a marketplace through an open-source browser which enables anonymity by directing internet traffic through a worldwide overlay network, consisting of thousands of relays to conceal a user's location and internet activity.

(Current marketplaces for tumbling on the network include a great number of applications which live a short, Whac-A-Mole life, popping in and out of existence, straining to avoid the scanner of police authorities.)

As she speaks, Rayyan begins to prepare a joint on the table in front of her: first breaking and mixing the weed, twirling the rolling paper between her hands, and then, tap-tap-tapping, till its stuffed. Tight but not too tight—after all, the spliff needs some room to breathe.

'That's when the fun begins.' *Window shopping*, she says. The time to browse through the marketplace—like Silk Road and its progenies—reading about various vendors, seeing who delivers to India, discovering the feedback from other (anonymous) users, mulling over the price point, figuring out exactly which strain of weed she was in the mood for. 'There's so much choice. There were 75,000 listings just in the drugs section on Silk Road before Ulbricht was busted. For example, I remember purchasing some hash from Spain. But I wanted to test it first before getting a large amount. It was just half a gram at first, and it cost some ₹300 to ₹400. It arrived to me in the mail, pressed between the leaves of the layered paper of a postcard.'

In such a modern, twenty-first century procedure, the last leg of snail mail—via the postal system—may seem like a surprisingly archaic option. But the idea is that the large volume of deliveries (in the 2021 financial year, India Post, for instance, delivered over 4.8 billion mails), most of the stealthily disguised contraband will easily pass through. Couriers and other forms of professional delivery systems usually face a higher degree of scrutiny.

Once Rayyan confirmed her choice, the contraband—usually marijuana or magic mushrooms in her case—would arrive at her doorstep within a three-week period, just 'like the electricity bill, like that shit'.

And if, for whatever reason, the envelope or package is intercepted, and a policeman shows up to one's door with the narcotic, there is simply no way to prove that the customer actually made the transaction. 'My reaction, in that case, would be, "Oh no!"' she feigns an innocent voice. "Are you saying drugs are available online? What is going on?" That has to be my reaction. The burden is on them to prove I made the purchase—because anyone can put your name on the address and send you something. And they can't prove it, if I've properly covered my steps, which is: take the Bitcoin, tumble it, use a Tor network. If someone understands the technicality of how it all works, and the legal side, then it becomes very safe.'

'Very safe' should come with an asterisk; Indian authorities have smartened up to the shadowy world of contraband imported from the internet, and many bigger operations—which inevitably attract more attention—have been busted. In September 2023, for instance, police in Kolkata arrested two twenty-one-year-olds for possessing 851 grams of imported cannabis purchased off the dark web. That's a lot of weed—the average joint usually contains less than a gram of marijuana.*

Rayyan's joint is now ready, the paper rolled thin and long. She lights it with a lighter and lets wisps of smoke hover over her face.

---

*Yes, a couple of people actually wrote an academic research paper titled 'Bayesian inference for the distribution of grams of marijuana in a joint'.

'Is it OK that I'm smoking?' she asks, to which I can only offer a grinning response. 'Sure, of course.'

'When I started purchasing this way in 2013,' she says between puffs, 'it was still a novelty. But now, Bitcoin has been part of the pop culture conversation for so long. Everyone knows somebody who owns some Bitcoin. So, I feel like it's not considered a "complicated thing" any more, that only a "hacker" can manage. It's become a lot more user-friendly. A lot more widespread, and more people are buying drugs off the dark web in India.'

We're a long way away from Rayyan's past, her frequent online purchases, from the period in her life where she admits she turned often to substance abuse 'like an addict'. In 2021, during the time of her public transformation, she also began therapy, a process that she hints helped her confront her identity.

When I ask her if marijuana had a role in this transformation, she takes a long pause to think, then looks up to the ceiling to formulate her exact words.

'Personally, for me and my journey, [marijuana] has been a huge ally,' says Rayyan. 'I started smoking it during visits to India when I was fourteen—which also happens to be the same year that I started dating as a cis man. I started hanging out with girls, and started seeing girls.' This was the time, Rayyan now believes, that her depression first took seed, rooted in her gender dysphoria. 'I was starting to live something that was not me,' she says. 'And I started to mask that depression and anxiety with substances. As a closeted transperson, I was perceiving a difference in society. A lot of queer people—sexually queer, gender queer, doesn't matter—have addiction issues. They're perceiving themselves as different from people around them, who are socializing and having fun. They believe that, "Oh, well, if I drink, I might feel like everyone else. Or it might be easier to pretend." So, it's like a coping mechanism for them. It comes from trying to hide [oneself], trying to just feel "normal".'

For Rayyan, the coping mechanisms took shape in various forms. In Dubai, she drank alcohol and tried out nutmeg (jaiphal), a spice that can give a hallucinogenic high if ingested in large doses. But it was marijuana—which she smoked on her visits and eventual move to Mumbai—that allowed her to confront herself in a more honest way.

'I remember the earliest days of being stoned in Mumbai, and realizing that there is something about my gender. Something I had already thought about, but I was not ready—because of my family, my surroundings, and my environment at that time.'

Marijuana, she says, was a small part of how she grew to be more open and curious about queer and LGBT-friendly environments. Being a stoner, one is already partaking in a social taboo. I, too, have found that the subculture of weed smokers often tend to be more liberal-minded, more likely to challenge conformities, to be more empathetic to the perspective of others. When a high is shared, state of minds seem to be shared, too, brainstorms and confessions and jokes cross-pollinating each other, flowering top to flowering top.

Rayyan lights the end of the joint again. 'My first feelings of being queer happened to me when I was really stoned,' she says. 'Now, when I speak to my therapist about it, I realize that this makes so much sense—because you're more sensitive when you're stoned. I had different voices in my head, arguing with each other. But when you're stoned, you can reason with your voices, you can make bolder decisions...If you're someone who knew me personally, you'd see how marijuana helped me get through really difficult times without making me really lose my shit.'

Even with her major life changes, Rayyan has many of the same preoccupations of her past: her social circles, her work, her love for smoking up, and her ability to understand and reflect upon herself—including the tightrope she has walked to avoid addiction to harder substances.

'I am an addict,' she says. 'But it's just by the grace of god that I didn't go and abuse heroin and cocaine. I have stayed on psychotropics and psychedelics—that's my blessing. That's where my education, somewhere, was stuck to. But it doesn't stick for everyone.'

By its technical definition, addiction occurs when a person experiences changes in their brain or behaviour, as a result of a drug. As per the National Institute of Drug Abuse (NIDA), a US federal government research institute, 'It's possible to be *dependent* without being *addicted*,* so there aren't reliable statistics on marijuana addiction.' A report on *Healthline* clarifies that, when a human body is too accustomed to the regular boost of cannabinoids, the brain reduces its own production of endocannabinoid receptors, which can 'result in irritability, mood swings, sleep problems, cravings, restlessness, and lack of appetite for several weeks after stopping. *This is different than addiction*.'**

'Anything in large amount can be the cause of your death,' Rayyan says. 'If you wish to put an ethical lens on marijuana, then let's put that lens on alcohol, tobacco, your shopping habit, your ice-cream habit, social media, work, chasing money...There are so many "addictions".'

The slim, slow-burning joint which she holds between her fingers is now nearly over. So is our conversation.

Rayyan's words would continue to haunt me long after I've shut off the Zoom call and closed down my laptop, for days, months, years more. I dwell upon these addictions, these dependencies and longings, these coping mechanisms, these avenues of escape. Some of us are more successful at resisting the urge to form unhealthy habits, at reducing and removing the habits out of our lives. Some, however, may feel that they are immured by these dependencies, like a shraap they carry, cursed by nature or nurture. For some, the

---

*Emphases mine.

**Emphasis mine, again.

curse excuses the habit. For some, the lines between habit and curse get blurred, the colours intermix, until one dissolves into the other.

The high can help some see the world for the absurd thing it is.

I often think about my night at Pink Floyd Café in Pushkar. It was a time in my life free of the burdens of plans or directions, free of being answerable to anyone but myself. It was a time of pure escape, where I could drop into a new city for a few days, drift from place to place, and abscond again the next night, on another overnight train, on another journey where the only guarantee was anonymity. All I wished for was to witness the world without participating in it.

That longing returns to me all these years later, making me twitch, like a long-forgotten addiction.

Some freedoms are expressed as riotous celebrations: colours on Holi that allow a temporary disguise, a war-paint for times of peace, or a bonfire that burns away the thaw and tension of the winter, all topped off with a powerful bhang drink to make the reality of living—temporarily—a little more liveable. Some freedoms include a heady dose of religion, of spiritual mysticism, where the only escape is a journey to the imagined divine, a brief break from Maya, that painful cycle of our lives. Some freedoms are in music and in art, in food and in literature, in song and dance, in debauchery. In the comfort of a commune of other people: smoking, drinking, loving, being.

Nasha

'...It can feel like the present moment is all there is, an instinctive nowness free of the cargo of the past and the ventures of the future...'

In Homer's *Odyssey*, a storm sent by Zeus leads Odysseus and his men astray at sea, before their ship finally reaches the Land of the Lotus-eaters. After getting their fill of food and drink, Odysseus sends a few men to find the natives of this land. He narrates:

> they mingled among the natives, Lotus-eaters, Lotus-eaters
> who had no notion of killing my companions, not at all,
> they simply gave them the lotus to taste instead....
> Any crewman who ate the lotus, the honey-sweet fruit,
> lost all desire to send a message back, much less return,
> their only wish to linger there with the Lotus-eaters,
> grazing on lotus, all memory of the journey home
> dissolved forever. But I brought them back, back
> to the hollow ships, and streaming tears—I forced them,
> hauled them under the rowing benches, lashed them fast
> and shouted out commands to my other, steady comrades:
> 'Quick, no time to lose, embark in the racing ships!'—
> so none could eat the lotus, forget the voyage home.

It's a chilly, December day. I sit on the open rooftop of a two-storey building, soaking in as much of the afternoon sun as I can in a suburb outside New Delhi. Seated on a wooden cot opposite me is fifty-six-year-old Anita David, a former heroin addict, who now works to guide other men and women through their addictions at a rehabilitation centre in Ghaziabad's Tronica City. David wears a black puffer jacket and denim jeans. She holds a cigarette in her hand, and after she smokes it, she lights another one, and then another.

'Let me put it away for the photograph,' David points at the cigarette. She puts her hands in her jacket pockets and looks intently into the camera as I click the photos.

When I'm done, she quickly reaches into her pockets to light another cigarette.

'I do nothing now,' she says. 'No soft drugs, cannabis. Until four to five years ago, I would have a beer or occasional drinks on Christmas. But that also I gave up. I'm only into cigarettes now—nothing else.'

These Christmas parties are held annually on this same rooftop, evenings that provide some much-needed celebration for the few dozen patients who inhabit the rehab centre. Most of the men and women here are addicts of a substance colloquially known as 'Brown', short for 'Brown Sugar'. 'Pure' heroin—a semi-synthetic derivative of the drug morphine (found in opium)—is a white crystalline powder. But this inferior version of the drug (usually found in Southwest Asia) is seen in the form of brownish powder. Brown sugar (or smack) is often adulterated with a variety of other substances, including zinc oxide, chalk powder, or topical ointments. Some will smoke the brown like a joint; some will heat the powder on a piece of tin-foil and inhale the fumes; some will fill a syringe and inject the substance straight into their blood streams.

David consumed brown in a variety of ways, and did so for nearly twenty-three years. Now, she has been sober for over a decade, leaving behind the addictions that haunted her for most of her adult life.

The daughter of an ex-army man from Kerala, David was born

and brought up in New Delhi before tragedy first struck her family: at age twelve, she lost her mother. 'After that, I had my own way,' she says. 'My dad was not there to take care of me.'

A few years later, more heartbreak followed. By sixteen, David had met a young man whom she'd decided she would marry. But, while riding behind him on his motorcycle on a kaccha road around Delhi's Munikra locality, their bike zigzagged and crashed into a lamp post. David was in a coma for one and a half months. When she woke up and queried her gathered friends and relatives about her boyfriend, nobody responded.

He had died on the spot.

'I was totally lost,' David says. 'I didn't know what to do. After that, I started drinking. After drinking, I got into hash—charas, ganja. Then, LSD, whatever else I came across.'

'At last, I landed into brown.'

For years, researchers around the world have debated on whether marijuana is a 'gateway drug', i.e., the type of substance that will eventually lead the user to use even more dangerous drugs like cocaine or heroin. Significant research papers have argued that there is little evidence that marijuana use increases the risk of using other drugs. The 'gateway hypothesis' has since been debunked by a number of studies arguing that marijuana is not a reliable cause for harder illicit drug use, and its prohibition is 'unlikely to reduce illicit drug use'.

On the streets, however, there are numerous 'gateways' presented to every regular marijuana user, options that many find too enticing to pass away, pathways offering an exciting alternative down the roads not taken. In several interviews that I conduct with former or current heroin addicts, a common theme is the presence of drug peddlers who cajoled marijuana users with free samplers of brown sugar. Try a higher high. The freebies act as a mere bait, used to entrap young men and women, who flounder helplessly in the suffocating net of addiction.

This is exactly how Mustaqim Ansari, David's colleague and the director of the rehab centre at Tronica City, fell into the trap of heroin in the mid-1980s. 'The peddler told us to try the "English nasha",' says Ansari. 'They were passing out brown for free. They wanted us to keep returning for smack. And once we started on brown, we *had* to have it. When we took charas after that, it didn't feel as good.'

Addiction can also occur if the peddler sells cannabis spiked other synthetic substances, which is extremely prevalent in India.

In the days after the 1985 NDPS Act, the cost of all drugs on the street—like brown sugar—shot up exponentially, as police authorities began a strict clampdown on cultivation, smuggling, and possession across the country. In Delhi, users like Ansari and David turned to peddlers in areas such as Seelampur, where 'dens' emerged of users congregating to find a safe place of their own.

'We used brown for excitement, sexual pleasure,' David recalls her younger days in the city. 'But with cannabis, one simply sits in the corner, not interested in worldly matters. "To heck with the world," they say. Bhaad mein jaye!'

Nowadays, much of the city's illicit drug use is found across the Yamuna River in the Yamuna Bazar area (near the Kashmere Gate interstate bus hub). Delhi Police have also claimed that areas like Jama Masjid, Chhatarpur, Nizamuddin, and Majnu Ka Tila have become the 'hotspots' for narcotics peddlers. Delhi University's North Campus was also identified as a major hub for peddlers selling narcotics—mostly brown and cannabis—to students.

Recently, Sanjeev Bikhchandani, the co-founder of a reputed private university in Sonipat (near Delhi), raised his concerns on Twitter about possible drug abuse on campus, including an allegation that some students were receiving drugs via room delivery or drones. The tweet sparked a widespread conversation about drug use on Indian campuses. Not long after, a video went viral from a de-addiction campaign event held by local police at the Dr. B. R. Ambedkar National Law University in Sonipat. A student seated in the amphitheatre boldly said to the police spokesperson that ganja was easier to procure around campus than a toffee or a lollipop. If a first-or second-year student could easily trace the dealer, he asked, why couldn't the police?

For college students in Delhi, social media has also played a major role in expediating narcotics transactions. Say, a *hypothetical* young person—a college student, or an employee at a call centre, or a writer looking for direction—decides to pick up some ganja in the city. One must ideally have a trustworthy local reference, or cross paths with the right contact, someone who is perhaps already a stoner. Or maybe, one can get lucky and meet an acquaintance, or even a stranger, with a joint in their hands, perhaps at a house party, outside a bar, or near the campus chaiwallah. Once a bond of trust is established over the spittle of the shared spliff, one can hope to acquire the cipher to the puzzle for themselves: the peddler's number. Think of this number as a hotline rather than an individual person: customers will drop a message to a WhatsApp account operated by that shadowy source, and the customer's request will be circulated among a number of drug peddlers: some who may work under the same operative figurehead, or some who may be freelancers. One could ask for 'Mango' (ganja) or 'Cream' (charas). Some customers may request for harder drugs like 'White' (cocaine), 'Brown' (heroin), or 'X' (MDMA/ecstasy). Some dealers in the city may even offer more dangerous cocktails: there is Bazooka (a mixture of crack cocaine and marijuana), Atom Bomb (marijuana and heroin mix), or Pikachu (ecstasy and the hallucinogenic drug phencyclidine / Angel Dust). But our hypothetical protagonist isn't interested in that heavier stuff—they only desire what they consider to be nature's green gift. They drop their location to the WhatsApp number, and then receive a call from *another* number, that of the delivery agent. They will be given a time, and if your delivery-person is punctual,*

*Or as punctual as one can possibly be on Indian Standard Time.

they will arrive in a two-wheeler, and offer you a box of 'mango'. They will tell the customer that it's confirmed 'good maal'. There's no need for further niceties: the customer pays cash—or if they're feeling especially trustworthy, they pay by UPI on their phone-banking app—with a ₹500 fee for delivery. Both sides will ride away into the crowds, with our newly-loaded hero set to enjoy a great weekend for themselves.

Back in Tronica City, David and Ansari invite me for lunch, under a shaded part of the rooftop. Dal chawal. They have a handful of pet parrots in a cage besides the table where we eat. I'm told that the parrots have just begun mimicking human speech. All I hear, however, are their incessant squawks and chirps, a continuous *keet keet keet* making a lively ruckus over our otherwise hushed conversation.

David tells me that once she and her friends began dabbling with 'the hardest stuff'—heroin—then that is all they did. 'We gave up on charas and ganja. We didn't even get a high from it after that. But *this* [brown sugar] was energetic. There was a "kick" with it.'

The energy and fun of the early days, however, quickly descended into catastrophe for David. In the early 90s, she married a man—also a brown addict—and moved in with him into a shelter. She gave birth to twins, both of whom passed away in infancy. Then, a miscarriage followed. Then, she had a son, but her relationship with her unstable husband turned abusive, all the while as they juggled the financial and personal challenges of addiction.

'My husband began to torture me for money [for drugs], bash me up, harass me, force me into prostitution. He gave me a scar on my face.' She points at a gash above the side of her upper lip, like an uneven second philtrum.

And one day, the couple's bickering turned fatal. 'I had to protect my son and myself,' she says. 'We threw hands at each other, and in our fight, he fell off the balcony.' From the first floor of the building, he landed on a charpai. His head hit the charpai's corner post, and the impact forced his jaw down his own throat.

'He was safe for a week,' David says. 'But after that...'

After that, David leaves a moment for silence, adding a soft hush, *Shhhh*, over the sound of the parrots.

She spent three years behind bars. 'My son was still at the breastfeeding stage,' she says.

She attempted to quit her brown habit a number of times, including after conceiving each of her other children. 'But after I delivered, I got into the shit again. My life was like this.' After her jail time, she rehabbed, recovered, relapsed, and repeated. Withdrawal from brown can be an obstinate, violent affair, leading to insomnia, irritability, consternation, loss of appetite, and depression. She recalls that when she first attempted to go 'cold turkey' (to completely abstain from the substance), she couldn't eat food properly for a whole month. 'When we used to go into withdrawal, we used to jump around, we used to puke out,' she says. 'The puke would be pinkish, greenish colour.' Sometimes, the pills she was given for the detoxication process caused David even more pain.

It took decades before the cycle finally stopped, before David found herself clean for a sustained period. It was during the process of wellness and healing* that she met Ansari, and found herself working with him at the rehab centre.

Ansari, also in his fifties, is Delhi born and bred, too. He turned to alcohol and charas/ganja with his friends when he was a teenager. 'At one time, I was very worried, had some family problems. [My friends] told me to sit here and have two dums. I was like, wow, this is an amazing thing! Then, whenever I went to those friends, we repeated the same. There was less tension now. I started to feel better.'

---

*David tells me that 'wellness' and 'healing' are now the preferred nomenclature in the rehab world, to the more common term 'nasha mukti' (freedom from addiction).

Ansari was soon besotted, now seeking out only the higher high. 'I was an "all-rounder",' he says. 'Charas, afeem (opium), ganja, sharab (alcohol), injections, everything. I was a dustbin. Whatever's coming in, let it come. I had no wish to live at all. My attitude was, "If I have to die, I'll die. So what?"'

Behind a pair of thick-framed spectacles, Ansari has stern eyes, a full head of white hair, and a bushy white moustache to match. Seated with a straight back and folded arms, he gives the countenance of great pride and discipline, a present that seems a far cry from his chaotic past.

'Slowly, slowly, we went too deep in,' says Ansari. 'We needed money, and so all the addicts became criminals. Even people from good families began to steal. I'm from a middle-class family, so I had to start doing a lot of topibazi.' 'Topibazi' or 'topi pehnana' literally means 'to put a hat on someone', slang for swindling people. 'We didn't have money, so we began some small-time robberies. First, this drug ends your household and relationships. If the addict is married, he'll beat his wife. If he's not married, he'll beat his mother. But whatever happens, he needs the high.'

Ansari had become a street peddler too, selling small wares and shikanji drinks on the roadside. 'I had very few clothes, and no shoes on my feet.'

One of Ansari's early inspirations in his rehabilitation process was the actor Sanjay Dutt, who, Ansari professes, 'went from living in mansions to sitting with babas at railway stations and sleeping in the slums.' It was a downfall while facing an aggregation of other legal trouble, a long path before Dutt finally kicked his addictions. 'Yaar, I thought, if he can quit it, why can't I?' says Ansari. 'I had no aukaat (status) otherwise!'

It took twenty years of intense detoxification, of NA (Narcotics Anonymous) Meetings, of listening to the struggles of other addicts, and stories of those who had made it to the other side. By the time I meet him in late 2021, Ansari is close to completing twenty-two years since he left the 'nasha'. 'It had been so hard to re-join society,' says Ansari. 'To not relapse.'

Now, there are fifteen patients at the foundation where Ansari and David work. Many of these young men and women are from middle class or poor backgrounds from the Delhi NCR area. They spend their days participating in mindfulness and yoga sessions, seated in a circle of confessionals to inspire each other, cook and clean for themselves, and listen to the sound of the chattering parrots on the rooftop, all in a quiet suburb away from the hubbub of the city.

Heroin addicts usually require chemical intervention in their detox process, including anxiety reducing pills, and medicines like buprenorphine. But for those dependent on marijuana, there is no such chemical strategy. 'We try to help them with counselling,' says David. 'Encourage them to work. Motivate them, and tell them they could be capable, give them some responsibilities, try to keep them active, involve them in classes and sharing sessions.'

Despite the turmoil caused in much of her life due to brown, David surprises me with the disdain she holds specifically for frequent charas/ganja users. In them, she perceives what she considers to be the worst of all the sins: sloth.

'The ganja users... You could try and explain their tasks to them, but they don't understand anything. They can't think of anything but ganja. Of course, it's an addiction. They're so lazy that they never bother to have a bath. They're not interested in going anywhere. We [users of brown] could work. But they're not interested in work, because their habit is not expensive. They become addicts and shut their mind out. They can be very smart for their own small benefit. But they don't know anything beyond ganja. They think only of doing their jugaad for ganja.'

'What I've seen from charas and ganja users is that they're totally "shut",' David continues, 'they don't understand anything. Their memory is lost. Educate them, but they won't get it. Their mind is not active, their body is lazy. They are not interested in anything. They are in their own zone.'

Then, Ansari chimes in, too. 'Ganja doesn't seem that dangerous because it's cheap. You can get a lot of people high on a little bit of money. The main issue is that they don't want to work. They get an attitude of laziness.' Ansari loosens his deep voice, to mimic a stoner. '"I'll do it, maybe… I'll go there, maybe." Their thinking becomes, "Kamayegi duniya, khayenge hum (The world will earn, we will eat)". They prefer to become a fakir (ascetic) instead. They prefer to stay filthy. They get completely separated from the society. Bahut time hai!' he adds sarcastically, and then looks at an imaginary watch on his wrist. *There is so much time!*

From Ansari and David's perspective, heavy marijuana smokers are wandering aimlessly in their euphoria, gorging only on the magical 'lotus', unable to act or react, unable to leave, unable to remember. The threat of memory loss is particularly present in young, developing minds. In studies (conducted mostly on rats), researchers noted that exposure to THC at a younger age impacted some learning and memory tasks later in life. Other research on animals and humans has shown that marijuana exposure during the developmental years 'can cause long-term or possibly permanent adverse changes in the brain'.

THC alters an area of the brain responsible for memory formation, the hippocampus. This is one of the first regions of the brain to be damaged for those afflicted with Alzheimer's disease or other forms of dementia.

But it is here that the impact of cannabis twists and turns; research has also shown that the CBD and THC compounds of cannabis could be useful to treat and prevent forms of dementia, too—including Alzheimer's.*

Any frequent stoner will attest to shades of some memory

---

*A conclusion echoed by the Ayurvedic cannabis treatment I had explored in Kerala.

loss. Misplaced keys. A conversation that needs repeating. A film barely remembered. In the deepest labours of a high, it can feel like someone has clicked refresh in the memory banks, a defragmentation process of the hard drive that blows all thoughts down to its roots, and then builds it all up again, like Tetris bricks falling back into their space. It can feel like the present moment is all there is, an instinctive nowness free of the cargo of the past and the ventures of the future. Strong indica strains make one drowsy, to the point that even one's waking experiences feel dreamlike, or as if one is in a constant state of being a hollow shell, only sleep-walking through life. To the sober observer, the affected mind may seem docile, unambitious, satisfied to watch the world pass by.

Frequent cannabis use can form what feels like a cloud within one's head, making it seem more difficult than ever to be conscious of the firing neurotransmitters. The brain allows the doddery body to go into autopilot, fulfilling the basest needs without the motivation to formulate complex or dynamic thought. You may get your creative juices flowing, but for many, the creativity remains theoretical, celebrated in personal observations or in-jokes between friends. Hardly anything new is remembered. Hardly anything new is built.

Instead, present moments can be filled with intensely heightened sensory experiences: the twittering of a bird; the shadows made by a reading light; the embrace of a bucket of hot water, undulating down over naked, warm skin; a body pulsing with connected convulsions at the moment of orgasm.

It feels arduous to store any new information. You think of all that's present, and you overthink it. The balance shifts: new sensations are found; some memory is lost.

For some, this short-term memory loss is intentional, making it easier to bear the mistakes one has made, to delete feelings of regret, to ease the pangs of pain and loss, to let it all fade away into the recesses of one's mind. Some heavy users become a shell of themselves. Lotus-eaters refusing to board the ship back to Ithaca.

Certain research has shown that about one in ten adults who use marijuana suffer from a form of addiction known as Cannabis Use Disorder [CUD]. In a 2023 study by the *Addiction* journal that tracked around 60,000 Canadian participants, adults with CUD appeared to have about a 60 per cent higher risk of experiencing 'incident adverse cardiovascular disease events'.

Frequent use of marijuana can cause vicissitudes in the circuits of the brain, messing with our natural production of endocannabinoids. When this happens, the endocannabinoid system can only rely on the 'artificial' alien interference to produce a shot of bliss. Experiences that should naturally be joyful—the love of family and friends, interactions with nature and art, the rush of new adventures, the taste of your favourite foods, the euphoria of sex—may lose their usual spark. Now, a feeling of stress could replace the experience of the everyday world—unless accompanied by cannabis.

Regular marijuana smokers have shown impaired neural connectivity. Dependent users may furthermore suffer cannabis withdrawal symptoms when sober, including irritability, sleeping difficulties, and dysphoria.

At the rehab centre, I speak to many young men who grew up in poorer families in Delhi, and now have been admitted for their cannabis dependence. They have both been called derogatory terms like 'charsi' for being frequent pot smokers. For nineteen-year-old Dilshad and twenty-two-year-old Aahil,* their stories were tied with some common threads: both suffered the early pressure to provide financial stability for their families, both were caught in the lure of peer pressure, and both began with curiosity to try something new, a search for escape.

'After a few joints: I would just get lost in my own thoughts,' says Aahil, who sits bundled up behind a thick denim jacket, many

*Both names changed.

more layers of sweaters, and a scarf around his neck. 'I would overthink. I would worry about what I'll do, what I won't do. I wouldn't talk to anyone at home. I would just lie in my room all the time. I would think about my next joint. I would think about the songs playing on my mobile phone. But I never thought about work or business. I had left my studies because of this nasha.'

Both these young men started smoking weed in their mid-teens, but both were sagacious enough to avoid the temptations of brown sugar. Dilshad did it by promising himself a daily delay. 'I kept telling myself that "I'll try it tomorrow",' he says. 'And then tomorrow, and tomorrow, and tomorrow...until I never tried it.' Aahil, meanwhile, did try a few lines of smack, but he says that, he never developed a habit.

As I leave Tronica City that afternoon, I find it difficult to empathize with the harsh opinion that David and Ansari have expressed towards weed smokers. Most research around the world has pointed at marijuana not being a painful addiction in the way that heroin and other harder drugs seem to be. Sloth may be a sin, but I feel a sense of relief for Dishad and Aahil, who *only* suffer from sloth, instead of the gut-wrenching, life-ruining tryst with heroin that others have endured for decades, drowning in an ocean of addiction, gasping for breath, struggling to surface, drown, and resurface again.

I consider it incorrect to classify cannabis as an addiction in the same vein as the harder drugs. Many states around the world share this opinion, too: in 2020, at the UN Commission for National Drugs, India reportedly voted along with twenty-six other countries to remove cannabis from Schedule IV of the 1961 Single Convention on Narcotics Drugs, where it was listed alongside opioids like heroine.

Danger lurks, however, in the recreational use of stronger, chemically enhanced strains of weed abroad, which are leading to dire consequences, especially for young people. Experts in the United

States have found that, with unnaturally high THC levels in some of the cannabis products, an entire generation of experimenting teenagers are becoming highly dependent. (Some of these high-THC strains are referred to as 'skunk' as an ode to their strong odour.)

Regulations of THC concentration haven't kept up with the market, and thus, even the fiercest laboratory-formulated maal is now available wherever cannabis by-products have been legalized in the US. These include strains of cannabis cultivated using the sinsemilla technique that separates the female plant before it can be fertilized by the male, and thus have fewer seeds with a higher density of cannabinoids and terpenes. It's sticky, fragrant, easy to crumble, and drowning in THC.

Recent research by the University of Sydney discovered that in regions of the United States that had decriminalized or legalized marijuana, the rate of cannabis poisoning—which occurs when individuals ingest an overdose of weed—spiked up dramatically, including for children.

A *New York Times* report in 2022 noted that a method of inhaling highly-concentrated THC called dabbing had become increasingly popular with American teenagers. Many of the products have been made to look like 'juice boxes' to target the young. The percentage of high-school seniors in the US reporting marijuana use tripled from 2017 to 2019.

> In addition to uncontrollable vomiting and addiction, adolescents who frequently use high doses of cannabis may also experience psychosis that could possibly lead to a lifelong psychiatric disorder, an increased likelihood of developing depression and suicidal ideation, changes in brain anatomy and connectivity and poor memory.

The report further noted that in 1995, the average concentration of THC in cannabis samples seized by the Drug Enforcement Administration in the US was about 4 per cent. This average increased to 17 per cent by 2017. At the time of writing, many products had THC levels that exceeded over 95 per cent.*

Suicide ideation? Depression? Anti-marijuana crusaders will no doubt make the connection with Sushant Singh Rajput here, the actor who was allegedly suffering from a period of depression before his suicide. But, without speculating further upon Rajput's personal history of substance use, scientific research does signal that using higher doses of cannabis could lead to greater anxiety, paranoia, and psychosis. Clinically depressed patients could worsen their symptoms with frequent marijuana use.

This is not ananda at all. There is no bliss here. The high THC levels are the antithesis of ganja's earthly, organic qualities. In this form, the cannabis becomes merely another synthetic substance.

For younger, developing brains, consuming large amounts of the high-THC strains is akin to consuming too much processed food: sooner or later, the habit will mess with the natural biological ecosystem of our bodies. I imagine that a child's developing brain is like wet cement, lacking in the firm structure and composure that comes with age. They may not be able to confront the deep, painful introspection, or be comfortable with their own instincts when the brain does somersaults on THC. The bliss could turn to fear. Cannabis misuse could cast a permanent mark, a handprint etched on the wet cement forever.

Instead, it might be better when one has lived long enough to know and recognize their own selves better, to understand one's flaws, to trust oneself. At the risk of sounding like your darling parents: Dear Youths, just wait till you're old enough.

The two young men I meet in Tronica City—Dilshad and Aahil—had both begun heavy consumption of cannabis at a young age that coincided with a feeling of alienation from their families. One of David's and Ansari's fears for ganja/charas is its cheap access.

---

*Baap re baap.

In 2018, a Berlin-based data-driven media campaign outlet ABCD released in-depth data about marijuana use in 120 cities around the world. At $4.38 (around ₹360) per gram, Delhi fell among the ten cheapest cities in the world to buy marijuana (Tokyo is the most expensive). Consequently, Delhi fell third in ganja consumption in the world, following behind only New York City and Karachi.*

The ABCD data misses some important specificity, as only two Indian cities appear in the list (Delhi and Mumbai), which, I assume, serve as placeholders for many other nearby states and districts. In a more localized report released by India's Ministry of Social Justice and Empowerment in 2019, it was noted that the highest percentage of charas/ganja use is in Sikkim, followed by Nagaland, Odisha, Andhra Pradesh, and Delhi NCR. About 3.1 crore Indians (a little less than 3 per cent of the population) consume cannabis. The ministry also added that, 'Overall, just about 0.25% of Indians use cannabis in a dependent pattern.'

Four states from India's Northeast make up the top ten, making this region fertile ground for ganja consumers—as well as for the abuse of harder drugs like heroin, brown sugar, meth, and more.

The Northeastern states of Mizoram, Manipur, and Nagaland fall within what is often referred to as the alternative 'Golden Triangle', sharing their borders with Myanmar, Laos, and Thailand. The Indian Army has suggested that this is the main opium-producing region in Southeast Asia, and a major trade route for smuggling narcotics across the rest of India and around the world.

This is also my next destination.

The city centre in Dimapur is a crowded mess of traffic and dust. I learn early that the most efficient way to get around town is on the back of someone driving a two-wheeler taxi, a motorcycle

---

*Shoutout to our brethren across the border.

or a scooter that cuts through the narrow roads and the gaps in the traffic. Walls in town are painted with Proverbs, Psalms, and other verses from the Bible. Nagaland is one of India's three Christian-majority states, and the streets of Dimapur are filled with churches, Christian literature bookstores, and church-sponsored health centres. The long arm of the Baptist church has also led the movement for the awareness, counselling, and rehabilitation of those seeking help from addiction.

It's my first time anywhere in India's Northeast, beyond the narrow Siliguri Corridor (otherwise known as the 'Chicken's Neck') that connects eight states of this region to the rest of the country. This trip is another reminder of India's mind-bending diversity, in a country that is a hundred different countries, states nudging and shoving, embracing and spooning, to somehow make the complex jigsaw puzzle fit together.

Nagaland itself is packed with delightful diversity, too. The sixteen administrative districts of the state are inhabited by seventeen major tribes (and many more sub-tribes), each distinctively unique in character, dialects, and tradition. While Dimapur was the ancient capital of the Kachari, the district is now home to several more Naga tribes, migrants from nearby states, plus a growing population of Burmese, Tibetan, and other refugees.

On my first evening here, I meet an old friend for dinner. Cheeseburger. The yellow yolk of a fried egg oozes over the dark beef. Then, my friend suggests I try some of the Naga chilli pickle. It's a form of the ghost pepper popular in a number of Northeast states, known in Nagaland as raja mircha. I *tss-tss-tss* and wash it down with a drink. Then, I pack a few pickle jars to take home with me.

After my meal, I'm visited by a young man named Nokman,* a weed dealer, semi-pro guitarist, and a manager at a local shooting

*Name changed.

range. Nokman is dressed in a sharp, brown suit, with his hair neatly parted with hair gel. His young girlfriend, also dressed in a formal gown, is by his side. 'We've just come from a wedding programme,' he tells me.

Nokman is among the many in the nation operating in the margins of legal systems, who has benefited particularly from the gig economy to distribute cannabis and other substances. The impact of Covid was felt particularly by many like him who were laid off from their regular jobs, or forced to work part-time. When business slowed down at the shooting range, Nokman turned his attention towards delivery services. It is from Nokman that I learn that the most popular brand of ganja that passes through Nagaland is the Shillong Mango, grown across the lush forests of Meghalaya. It has a clean, fruity smell, with a lush, voluminous high that may remind one of the Sheelavathi. 'The Khasi people grow it really well,' Nokman says, referring to Meghalaya's majority ethnic population. Nagaland has its own brand, usually referred as Pfutsero, named after the high-altitude town around where it is cultivated. There are a several villages higher up in the mountains in Nagaland where the weed grows wild.

As cannabis use rises in Nagaland—particularly among the youth—there has been a counter-reaction by police and security forces to stifle the smuggling networks. In recent years, there have been stories of big busts every few months, including the arrest of five persons with marijuana worth ₹4 crore in Dimapur in 2021, in a joint operation by the local police and the Assam Rifles. The Rifles are a central paramilitary force responsible for border security and counter-insurgency in the Northeast, and have often had clashes with separatist groups and other citizens in the region. In April 2018, the Rifles and other departments destroyed several acres of marijuana being cultivated at the Intanki National Park in Peren.

Like most departments around the country, the Nagaland Police tend to send regular press releases of these busts, proudly proclaiming the amounts of illicit alcohol and drugs they've recovered and the people they've arrested.* For example, in a single week in January 2022, the Police arrested thirty-seven individuals in thirty-five different cases for a variety of contraband material, including hundreds of kilos of ganja, some heroin, opium, brown sugar, and thousands of Spasmo-Proxyvon capsules, an over-the-counter painkiller made of a synthesized opioid.

The raids also uncovered thousands of bottles of alcohol. Backed primarily by church groups, Nagaland is one of the handful of Indian states with complete alcohol prohibition, banning its sale and consumption since 1989. But prohibition has hardly stymied availability, as booze can be unofficially purchased at corner shops across all major towns and served at many restaurants. In smaller villages, drinking rice liquor is part of many indigenous cultures—sometimes beginning from childhood—for special ceremonies, as medicine, or to ease the stress after a long day of work in the fields.

The larger, unfortunate impact of prohibition has been the widespread abuse of counterfeit alcohol (adulterated by bootleggers with cheaper chemicals, including cleaning fluids, nail-polish remover, methanol, and more). Inevitably, this had led to a dependence and severe health issues.

For these reasons and more, activists have long been petitioning for the state government to overturn the prohibition.

In my conversations with friends and local journalists, I learn of another danger now trickling through the porous borders of Thailand and Laos that surround Nagaland. This (relatively) new substance comes in the form of a small tablet, available in a variety of colours—yellow, blue, and pink—a synthetic drug that looks like candy. An acquaintance who had tried it tells me that it had her pranging out for two straight days, unable to sleep. A mixture of

*There has been an amusing trend of many Indian police departments releasing photos of confiscated illicit items neatly arranged to spell out something meaningful about the case.

methamphetamine and caffeine, these tablets are called Yaba (which in Thai literally means, 'crazy medicine'). Some in Nagaland refer to it as 'The World Is Yours'.* Each pill cost around ₹250 in Manipur. In December 2022, Yaba tablets worth around ₹24 crore were seized from Moreh, Manipur's border town to Myanmar.

Nearby states like Tripura, Mizoram, and Meghalaya also share a border with Bangladesh. This border features a 3,200-kilometre fence, which is one of the longest international barriers in the world, and the source of large quantities of ganja and other drugs smuggled between the countries. In Mizoram, another state where liquor is prohibited, heroin has been described as the 'main killer' by an official in the state's Excise and Narcotics Department.

Meanwhile in Tripura, there has been a dramatic increase in busts in the past few years, as the state has become a popular corridor to move drugs between borders. After the Assam Rifles burned cannabis plantations worth ₹1.5 crore in the Sepahijala district in December 2023, Chief Minister Manik Saha admitted that the state now topped the list of illegal drug seizures and destructions in the Northeast. Approximately 28 lakh cannabis plants—its pronunciation slanted locally to 'ganza'—have reportedly been destroyed in Tripura in 2023, with the Assam Rifles leading the way in the narcotics counter-offensive, and hundreds of acres of forest land have been 'reclaimed' by the BSF and other agencies from illegal cultivation. Tripura is the third-smallest state in the country, but from 2022–2023, over a thousand individuals were arrested in drug smuggling cases. Earlier in the year, Union Home Minister Amit Shah presided over a conference on 'Drugs Trafficking and National Security', where he watched—via video conference—the destruction of drugs worth ₹9.5 crore (including over 5,000 kilos of ganja) in Tripura.

The busts have revealed many cases of extreme desperation and

---

*Shoutout to *Scarface* and Nas.

absurdity, too. In November 2023, Tripura police apprehended seven women at the Dharmanagar inter-state bus terminus with 12 kilos of cannabis taped to their bodies. The women were accompanied by six infants.

A month later, when members of the Tripura Police and Tripura State Rifles destroyed 60,000 cannabis plants in Mohanpur district, villagers blocked their path on their way back, demanding compensation for the farmers' losses. Tensions flared: the police conducted a lathi charge, while the villagers pelted stones and vandalized police vehicles. A handful of police personnel were left injured.

In South Tripura, police have begun experimenting with drones to identify and survey cannabis plantations in more remote, hilly regions. Drones and artificial intelligence software have come handy in such plantations in the far west of the nation, too: by late 2023, district police in Dahod, Gujarat, developed AI and machine learning systems to identify weed being illegally cultivated next to other crops and vegetables in a number of nearby villages. After locating the suspected areas, the police conducted raids that led to cannabis busts worth ₹1 crore.

(For every such action, there is an almost equal and opposite reaction. The *Times of India* reported that Maoists in Odisha asked local farmers to plant saplings of cannabis camouflaged between other trees and shrubs to confuse auto-detection from satellite imaging systems.)

In mid-2023, the Home Ministry shared reports of drug seizures across all Indian land and sea borders by the BSF which includes data of seizures by the Sashastra Seema Bal, Assam Rifles, the Indian Coast Guard, and special joint operations conducted with other agencies including state police forces, the NCB, and DRI from 2020–2023. The report particularly highlighted the porous borders for cannabis trafficking into India through the Bangladesh border, with the greatest amount of ganja/charas recovered in Tripura, West

Bengal, and Assam. Recent busts have also uncovered narcotics rings working in reverse, too, including a major racket where marijuana grown across the north of West Bengal was collected and smuggled for distribution in Bangladesh.

After a couple of days in Dimapur, I take a two-hour drive across a dry, mountainous highway to Kohima, the capital of Nagaland. Located on hills that peak up to 1,500 metres above sea level, this town is in parts serene, in parts cosmopolitan. It has historically been home to the Angami ethnic group.

I get into town on a Sunday to find the town centre completely abandoned, all shops shuttered, and hardly any individuals out on the street. The following morning, I meet a local journalist, Atono Tsükrü Kense, who stresses that people take their church day seriously: even those who are hardly believers.

Over the past few years, Kense has closely chronicled the cycle of drug smuggling, abuse, addiction, and rehabilitation in the state. From the perspective of the drug trade, she calls Nagaland the 'Bermuda Triangle', within the aforementioned Golden Triangle. 'Nagaland is surrounded by Assam on one side, Myanmar on one, and Manipur on the third. All the drugs that pass through, cross Nagaland.'

In Nagaland, Kense says that drug and alcohol abuse was at its height in the 1980s, along with an increase in insurgency. 'In those days, they didn't know what is counselling, what is rehabilitation,' says Kense, 'so, "The Underground" (the catch-all for Naga insurgency or militant groups) started to warn drug users and alcoholics. As a form of punishment, they would even parade them naked. Sometimes, they would hang a lock on the ears of addicts—like an earring—to brand them as a drug or an alcohol user.'

Slowly, the churches and the Naga Mothers' Association (NMA) began to raise some positive awareness, and helped to promote a new type of rehabilitation and counselling. 'The problem here is that we don't have official accurate data regarding the use of anything—it could be either cannabis, alcohol, other drugs. The church is the most influential group here, more than the government or any other organization. But, when you look critically, discrimination also starts [at the church]. Suppose I'm a drug addict, and I go to church for help. Rather than making me feel at home, it is the church members who may discriminate [against] me. So, the drug users and alcoholics didn't often feel comfortable at church.'

While the church is directly responsible for the Alcoholics Anonymous (AA) programmes, Kense feels that they should be doing more. 'Because mostly everyone here is a Christian. Whether I'm a good Christian or not, I go to church. Everybody does.'

Just days after I'd left Dimapur, a dozen tribal, church, and student organizations held a closed-door meeting to discuss the 1989 NLTP alcohol prohibition. An adviser to the excise department at the meeting stressed that, 'alcohol need not necessarily be viewed from the prism of religion and be left to personal choice.'

At the time of writing, however, prohibition continues in the state.

There is some ambiguity from readings of the Bible regarding cannabis use. In Genesis 1:29-30 (King James Version), it is written:

> And God said, Behold, I have given you every herb bearing seed, which is upon the face of all the earth, and every tree, in the which is the fruit of a tree yielding seed; to you it shall be for meat. And to every beast of the earth, and to every fowl of the air, and to everything that creepeth upon the earth, wherein there is life, I have given every green herb for meat: and it was so.

And in the New Testament's closing book, Revelation (22:2) says:

> In the midst of the street of it, and on either side of the river, was there the tree of life, which bare twelve manner of fruits, and yielded her fruit every month: and the leaves of the tree were for the healing of the nations.

There is no specificity here, of course; but some in the fringes have chosen to interpret the mentions of 'every green herb' and the leaves of the healing tree to mean references to healing herbs found in nature—such as cannabis.

The day after meeting Kense, I take a small taxi on a rocky, broken mountain road, up to the village of Khonoma. Even in the expansive list of terrible Indian roads I've experienced, this little stretch might be one of the worst. Then, it begins to rain, and the rain turns into a pouring thunderstorm. For the next hour, there's loose gravel, muddy puddles, and many precarious twists and turns on the highway, alleviated only by Border Roads Organisation (BRO) billboards plastered with puns and advice about safe driving.

But, by the time I arrive in Khonoma, the rain slows into a drizzle, and soon, gives way to an enchanting afternoon mist. Tucked between thick forests and grand steppes of paddy fields, Khonoma takes pride in calling itself the first 'green village' of Asia, where conservationists and village elders created protected areas to ban hunting and industrial logging to maintain the region's ecological balance. The jhum (or shifting) cultivation system is popular here, as the naturally grown alder trees are pollarded, cutting the tree tops to burn vegetation on land, before a new patch of land is used for the next cultivation cycle. Khonoma is also famed for the 1879 anti-colonial uprising, which is known as the 'last effort to remove the British invasion from the Naga Hills'.

Today, Khonoma is one of the most popular destinations in Nagaland for visitors hoping to experience a (manufactured-for-tourists) quaintness of Naga village life. And in my desperation to take a break from the rumble and dreck of civilization, this trip is exactly what I need. The afternoon walk around the village is shrouded in a silent mist, disturbed only occasionally with croaking roosters and trees shrugging off leftover raindrops. All around Khonoma, there are many more restless animals in their pens: grunting pigs and mooing cattle. Many of the homes here are made of wood, bamboo, or held together by large metal sheets. I walk a little bit further to the village centre, and to the biggest, grandest building around: the 125-year-old Baptist church. Then, a little further, is the only structure to match it: the local Catholic church.

I don't know how much time has passed before I realize that this is one of the greatest walks I've ever taken.

Today, I'm the only tourist in this village.

Whenever I get an opportunity to spend time away from the stress of urban civilization, I inevitably think about loss. The loss of silence around the country, around the world. As someone who frequents the Garhwal Himalayan region, I have hoped to be more aware of my natural surroundings, to at least have good intentions for conservation. But there's hardly a more addictive drug in the world than capitalism, and it's difficult for most of us to undo the comforts of what our civilization deems to be 'progress': better roads, bigger structures, everything electrified, everyone connected.

Inevitably, I begin to wonder what the trade-off would've looked like for me. Was it better for me to be raised in an urban(ish) setting, with access to a good education, with hyper-connectivity to the rest of the world? Or would it have been a better life to be raised far away from this so-called civilization, more in sync with the natural environment?

Could I even survive without the comforts of the modern age? I can't chop wood. I can't raise a pig and slaughter it when it's necessary. I have no skills of realizing harvest times and strategies. I can hardly build a bonfire, or hammer together logs to construct shelter for myself. My palms aren't coarse with the self-sufficiency that comes with manual work. The only thing I have to show of my labour is the back that grows sore after hours of sitting in front of a computer screen.

Ultimately, the potential of choosing an alternative life is a meaningless thought experiment, because without the background that I was nurtured in, I wouldn't even be in a position to have the time and privilege to contemplate these scenarios. I wouldn't be me—the person who fathoms the option of 'returning to nature'. I'm nothing but a tourist here, a visitor who will enjoy a few days in a comfortable village, pump a few rupees into the local economy. And then, leave.

The choice exists only because the choice has already been made.

There is a storm after sunset, followed by a cloudy, overcast night, followed by a brief power cut. I sit in the darkness, alone in a common lobby area of my homestay. There are no outside lights. The night's bonfires haven't yet been lit. This darkness is unlike any darkness I've ever known.

It takes some time before my eyes adjust, when I begin to see different shades of black within the blackness, until I'm able to identify the faintest glow in the absolute void to light my way.

Sometimes, that glow may not be a glow at all, but something in my imagination; not a light, but a memory of light.

I'm still feeling the nasha of this place the next morning, comparable to the bliss weed smokers experience after a night of particularly heavy stoning. It's as if the brain is still thanking us for the experience, allowing the residue of the previous night to provide a beautiful haunting for much of the following day.

This isn't the ugly nasha of paranoia, sloth, and depression; it's a glow of inner joy, a celebration of each scintilla of being alive. I feel the feathery wafts of mountain breeze, see the clear horizon appearing after the night's downpour, and watch farm animals grazing on grass, soaking in the morning sun, reminding me of my unlikely place in this highly unlikely planet, of the grand cosmic accidents that led to my existence. It's the 'pehla nasha' of Aamir Khan gallivanting across hillocks in *Jo Jeeta Wohi*

Sikander, basking in the bliss of love.*

On another isolated, hypnopompic walk around the village, I ruminate about a particular feature of cannabis that aids its users confront their own selves, often sparking unresolved inner conversations. The ananda can help one look deeper inwards, to deal with one's least appetizing ingredients.

But I also wonder why some heavy marijuana users—and addicts of harder drugs—are only able to find 'peace' by spending as much time as possible away from their sober selves. Most of us have a version of ourselves that we simultaneously desire and fear, a version that we can hardly expose to the rest of the world without the enhancement of other substances. Sometimes, the 'enhancer' is a stimulant that allows that hidden self—our personal Mr Hyde—to make an aggressive, active appearance. For a drunk person, 'Hyde' may try to choke Jekyll out of the picture completely.

For some, however, there could be a peaceable new creation, like the stoned curiosity of marijuana that allows for acceptance of both Jekyll and Hyde, a synthesis of our many selves—rather than a violent replacement.

As I leave Khonoma, I feel grateful to have rediscovered a sense of wonder in my travels. I find myself considering each day on its own merit, breaking out of the easy comforts of adulthood. Perhaps, the longing for ganja is a longing for nostalgia: not the nostalgia for actual memories of the past, but for the freedom with which one perceived the world as a child. The anandamide release allows the brain to be inquisitive and inspired. Senses are heightened, and each experience feels new and mind-blowing all over again.

When I considered my own marijuana use, I imagined that the substance's real gravity—it's facility to draw me back to it—consisted in its ability to convince me that I was a better person when I was stoned, that my life was sunnier, that I was no longer missing

*But don't remind Anjali (Ayesha Jhulka) how this song ends.

the trees for the forest, that—in the goal-oriented 'big picture' lifestyle—I was able to hone in on the specifics that made life so worth living. It made me better appreciate the taste of food, the magic of literature, the cinematography in my favourite films, the company of my closest friends, the thrill of an adventurous trip.

I often observe my daughter (a toddler when I'd begun working on this project) with a sense of envy, of how she must perceive the world in utter amazement, moment after moment. As I grow older, I yearn to be *moved* again. To exclaim, to have a true emotional response to the world, the type that requires a certain unlearning of perceived wisdoms, an emptying of the vessel, just so it can be refilled. I yearn to see the world as my daughter sees it: her amazement at the water swirling down the drain after I help her brush her teeth at the sink, her fascination for the changing seasons, the way she looks up at the night sky. Isn't it wild that the stars are up there all the time—day and night—but we only perceive them when the sun turns off its blinding light?

She makes me realize who I'm not any more. I see myself becoming a person that seizes and hides his emotions, as if they are contraband. I find myself more hurt by the admission of pain than the pain itself. I watch films and read books and listen to music in hope for small doses of stimulation. I meet people in a hope that they'll inspire me, but I hesitate to let them in. I yearn to feel more passion, more greed, more pity, more remorse, more nostalgia, more ambition.

Just fucking feel something.*

On cannabis, one can oscillate between being overtly self-conscious and completely carefree. Or, sometimes, one falls into the trap of focusing on one thing alone, which then becomes *the only thing*. A common stereotype of a stoned person is the 'munchies', as in, a heightened appetite that gets them to crave every snack

---

*This entire book might be an elaborate midlife crisis.

on Earth. Chips and cookies and aloo bhujia and paratha and rice and that spicy ghost chilli to eat and eat and eat again. Yes, cannabis is indeed known to enhance one's appetite, but the craving goes beyond it: it becomes an extension of that heightened focus, something that a stoned person must simply see to completion. It's the hours spent in a deep Wikipedia rabbit hole, reading about football pioneers from the 1880s or algae found in the Indian Ocean. It's sitting beside your child, meticulously teaching them to draw, forgetting the passage of time altogether as the two of you work on a birthday card for Mommy. It's getting lost in long passages of a novel, bingeing on TV shows, going on an arduous hike without realizing one's own physical limits.

My long walks around Khonoma take me to the 'Hobbit' themed homestay, to the churches, a small war memorial, and back to the only little cafe in town, where I drink a soothing 'pink'* tea. I feel no fatigue when I pack up again to take the cab down to Kohima, out of the mist of the village and back to the city.

I wake up early the next morning in Kohima to catch a shared Tata Sumo, a ten-seater SUV. The Sumo driver offers me and my five elderly co-passengers some Happy Dent chewing gum. Then, we're off on the hour-long trip to Khuzama, from where we change cars to get into another Sumo—this one with Manipur plates—to head to the 'Mao Gate', the border between Nagaland and Manipur. (This is also called the 'Jack Gate', a mispronunciation that I would later discover is meant to be 'Check Gate'.)

The Manipuri roads are a sharp upgrade to the bumpier paths on the Naga side. Within a few hours, the Sumo drops us at Senapati, the northernmost district of Manipur. I wait by a crowded city centre for my next ride—an inter-city bus—where I squeeze into my window seat.

---

*My editor suggests that it might have been Roselle tea, but I have no way of confirming this.

Now, I'm surrounded by the musical chatter of conversation in a new language. Another few hours will pass before I excuse myself through the crowds—with a backpack and my small rollie suitcase—and get off on the streets at the state's capital: Imphal.

It's through a common friend that I've been introduced to Thokchom 'Jimmy'. Jimmy is forty, and I know this because he tells me that he has come to see me on the morning of his fortieth birthday. 'Oh wow!' I respond, and get on my feet to give him a hug. His youthful eyes, however, make it seem otherwise. He also wears a black hoodie with the silhouette of a cannabis plant symbol, in front of a greenish print of a rising sun.

'I wore this specially to come see you,' he says with an excited smile.

Jimmy has worked as a freelance videographer, a stringer who has captured local footage for international networks like the BBC and Al-Jazeera in Imphal. But the project closest to his heart is a documentary that he hopes to make about Satjal, an organization from Manipur with approximately five or six lakh members around the state. Among their many tenets, members of the Satjal Academy are well-versed in indigenous forms of martial arts and have an adoring, ritualistic relationship with ganja.

I had only heard of the Satjal (full form: Meitei Huyen Langlon Sintam Shanglen) the night before meeting Jimmy. I was with a young man named Thotreiyo Keishingh—who goes by Aboy—a former heroin addict and now a proud connoisseur of the Manipur's local strain of marijuana. As we drove around Imphal and its outskirts in the evening, Aboy had pointed out of the car window to my right, towards a black flag next to a blimp of light on a hillock. He'd said that it was a campsite—or 'shanglen'—for the Satjal. 'They are...' Aboy had said, 'not a cult, actually... They have a different mindset. You can chill with them and have a smoke. Usually, they are the ones that supply the weed to everyone. They have big farms, and hectares of cultivation across the mountains here.'

'Are they like... Shaivites?' I'd asked him. 'Sadhus?'

'They're different. They don't worship a Hindu god, or the Christian god. They have their own particular god: known as Pakhangba, a dragon. Some of them take part in black magic. Some believe in reincarnation.'

A weed-smoking, martial-arts-practising, dragon-god-worshipping, secret-but-not-secret group that is allegedly, *not* a cult? Colour me intrigued.

There are over 250 Satjal shanglens around Manipur, and a few in nearby Assam, too. Each campsite is a mini-shrine to Pakhangba, equipped with space for a martial arts academy, and some room for members and visitors to gather, where they chat, smoke ganja, and share a moment of spiritual connection. The group was officially registered as a non-profit organization in 1984, working 'primarily in the domain of Art & Culture'.

The stereotypical Satjal member has long hair, a long beard, practices vegetarianism, abstains from alcohol, and—despite martial training—is a pacifist, inhaling hearty puffs from the chillum, lost in the mysteries of their personal cosmos. But Satjal members will tell you that there's much more to their overall philosophy. One of the group's main objectives is preserving the traditions of the Meitei, the majority ethnic group in Manipur. They have proudly contributed to a number of charitable, humanitarian, and ecologically-conscious efforts around the state. In 2003, with ambitions of greater expansion, the group changed their name to the Universal Friendship Organization. UFO.*

The UFO have made a grand case for universal brotherhood, and their members come from all walks of life: bankers, graphic designers, doctors, engineers, athletes, politicians. The banner on

---

*Yes!

their official Facebook page states:

> We are all covered by the same blue sky
> We are all living on this common planet earth
> We are all brothers from a common father
> We should not fight amongst us
> Hence, universe peace and love is better in such a precious span of life
> We stand still for the shake [sic] of this fatherland.

On his fortieth birthday, seated in the back garden of my homestay in Imphal, next to a small lotus pool and surrounded by a heavy cover of trees, Jimmy tells me that he has recently completed nine years as a UFO/Satjal member. And it was his love for smoking weed—which he had picked up in his younger days in Chennai and New Delhi—that first attracted him to the organization.

Jimmy speaks with a strong stutter, and adds a slight accent turning the 's' sound to 'sh' at the beginning of certain words. Each sentence begins with a loud, enthusiastic burst, only to trickle away and softly evaporate into the thin air. 'At first, I didn't know about Satjal, but I knew that they smoked [ganja], and that they are the protectors of our Meitei culture.' Jimmy, like over half of Manipur's population, is a Meitei, too, and like most Meitei, he was born into a family that follows a variation of Hindu spirituality.

The Meitei make up around two-thirds of Manipur's State Assembly, and thus dominate many of the motions that are passed regarding the lives of both Meitei and the minority tribal citizens. These decisions have included the government evicting tribals who live in forest areas in the state to bring the land (and its considerable natural resources, including cannabis farms) under the hand of the state. Disputes over land—and many more communal and political complications—have led to friction and protests within different communities in Manipur. A year after my visit, this friction would take a tragically violent turn.

In early 2022, however, there is little talk of politics when I sit with Jimmy in Imphal. His preoccupations are his arts, his spirituality, and the easy access to his favourite narcotic from the shanglens.

Jimmy had first visited a Satjal shanglen in 2011 with his cousin. 'I wanted to make a documentary about the organization. I was very afraid at my first time there, but everyone was very welcoming. They said, "Come, come", and my fear... gayab ho gaya tha,' he adds in Hindi. *It disappeared.*

As part of the commitment to the group, Jimmy would sweep and clean the camp ground and the indoor martial arts hall, bring food and groceries for the other members, and donate money. He showed up regularly to the camps. 'I was very involved, and so I gained membership quite soon.'

'A lot of [other] Manipuri people think that those in Satjal are crazy,' he adds. 'That they smoke, they have long hair, they do nothing. But when I went inside, I found a beautiful, nice system of hierarchy. From the outside they may seem dirty, but they are actually incredibly clean and tidy. You cannot even go inside without a bath or washing up properly first.'

Satjal's founder was R. K. Manisana, who was the son of a well-known martial artist, with the ambition of promoting Meitei culture and self-discipline through his interpretation of the Manipuri martial art of Thang Ta. Another member of Satjal, Kapil Arambam, has offered more detail about the group's preoccupations in distinguishing the Meitei identity as distinct from the rest of the Hindu community. 'Haana semba konna loiba', writes Arambam. 'We were created first and we will end the last. The UFO's universe is centred on the philosophies of the Meitei.'

'I'm a Meitei,' Jimmy tells me, 'and I didn't know the whole culture of Meitei myself. But when I smoke with the Satjal, I found that they were fucking knowledgeable about Meitei culture, and about the way of the world.'

Legend is that sometime in the 60s or 70s, Manisana set off on his motorbike to ride around Manipur, showing up to village after village with a bottle of whisky and his philosophies of spiritual combat. He gained a legion of followers in the rural regions in his travels. With time, the ethos of this young 'movement' evolved: alcohol was shunned and ganja—the more natural, earthly option—was adopted alongside the evolving practice of martial arts.

'We have two kinds of martial arts in Manipur,' says Jimmy. 'The one that the Satjal teaches is very deadly. There's no defence, only attack!' Fought with swords and spears, Thang Ta is a component of the Manipuri martial art Huyen Langlon, which also features the unarmed fighting style known as Sarit Sarak.

I'm fascinated by the juxtaposition, of an offensive physical action being balanced with the calm and relaxation that results from ganja smoking. Within the Satjal, there is a comfort of this paradox, seeking peace of mind even within a fighting body, all for a higher spiritual cause. I can't help but make the connection with the popular martial arts philosophies like Jeet Kune Do—associated with Bruce Lee—where meditative Buddhism, Taoism, and other forms of meditation are used to enhance combat.

As Manisana's influence grew in Manipur, Satjal's academies began to crop up around the state. Membership grew rapidly, as did the interest in Thang Ta. There are whispers that even Nongthombam Biren Singh—Manipur's chief minister at the time of my visit—is a member of Satjal. 'It's a rumour!' Jimmy laughs it off, covering his bases. 'Before [Biren Singh], there was another chief minister [in Satjal], too, who was known to smoke weed.'

Over the years, politicians have donated food, money, or made appearances at the group's annual 'Flag Raising' ceremonies. In December 2021, Biren Singh's wife Nongthombam Ongbi Hiyanu attended a UFO 'Rising Day' event as chief guest at the Koirengei shanglen.

'The politicians know it's a vote bank,' says Jimmy. 'And they fear Satjal.'

Many of these flag-raising ceremonies feature men dressed in matching militaristic black shirts, trousers, and berets. The Satjal Pakhangba flag is raised to march pasts and parade music. Jimmy has filmed a lot of footage about the organization, but is still mulling about the appropriate way to release it. There are some secrets in this 'not-cult' which, he knows, must be kept preserved. 'I could film everything... But they won't tell you the secret of Satjal—the deeper secret. There are many more things [about becoming a member].' A nervous laugh follows. 'They have a rule: that we'll keep some things private.'

He is happy, however, to discuss his ganja smoking habits, and that of his fellow members. Jimmy confirms to me what I have recently gleaned from conversations with other young people in Manipur: ganja is easily accessible around the state at a relatively low cost. Festivals such as Shivratri are celebrated with amalgamation of music, prayers, and cannabis. The UFO weed is considered by many to be the finest around. 'They grow and clean it themselves,' says Jimmy. 'It is very good weed. Smoking weed is normal for them. And smoking with Satjal is like a different experience. We welcome everyone to smoke.' But there's an age limit, he adds. No children.

'Any kind of person can join them,' he says. 'No religion matters, no black, brown, white, nothing. That's why they call it the Universal Friendship Organization.'

Despite the inclusive edicts of Satjal's smoker's circle, Jimmy is stumped when I ask him if female members of the organization are allowed to smoke ganja the way the men do. He hesitates, first saying that many Manipuri women simply choose not to smoke or drink;* and later, adds that perhaps Satjal wouldn't allow them to do so at the shanglen, even if they wished. The UFO is divided into

*Many in Manipur will claim that this is objectively untrue.

several 'battalions', each under the leadership of top-rung leaders of the organization. These include an all-woman battalion, too, and other battalions that are a mix of genders.

Later that morning, I hop on to the back of Jimmy's motorcycle and we ride across inner Imphal, from the gullies and dusty side streets, across the crowded main throughways. He takes me to a number of different UFO campsites which he frequents himself. I am given a warm welcome, invited to sit in the circle of smokers, and peek a glance at the Thang Ta training rooms. I see posters with the progressive tenets of the brotherhood—*We are all covered by the same blue sky*—but 'brotherhood', by its very literal definition, seems to exclude sisters. I don't see any women gathering to sit and smoke among the circle of men.

Most of the UFO camps are a small courtyard of space, perhaps smaller than a tennis court, within which rests a temple in honour of Manisana, an indoor space for martial arts, and, most prominently, a large idol of Pakhangba perched atop a round figure of the Earth.

As per legend, the Pakhangba is a shape-shifter, a human ancestor of one of the Meitei clans who now represents himself as a small dragon. This dragon has featured on the royal flags and coats and arms of Manipur. When I visited the citadel of the Kangla Fort—one of Imphal's most popular tourist sites—I also saw the two large sculptures in the shape of a hybrid lion-dragon creature, a form known as Kangla Sha.

Much of the other reading and interviews that I conduct about the Satjal also reveals a suspicion of modern technology and medicine, and a closer relationship with natural substances like cannabis. In many ways, Satjal has some cultural similarities with the Rastafarians. Like this religious/political movement that developed in Jamaica, UFO members have special communal gatherings (members are known to solemnize for a worship on full moon nights), have a meditative preoccupation with some forms of art (in Satjal's case, of Thang Ta), and a preference for traditional patriarchal roles. For the Satjal, cannabis and other herbs play a part in their natural, Aesculapian practices. This extends to inoculation, too; during Covid-19, Jimmy tells me that many of the members resisted taking the vaccine.

'But, if you do get vaccinated, they won't discriminate,' says Jimmy. 'They're not against anything. For example, their rule is not to drink and eat meat; but I drink a lot of whisky, and no one complains, because I do it elsewhere—not at the shanglen.'

When we arrive at the shanglen, I follow Jimmy around the Pakhangba idol. We take off our shoes and sit next to an elderly man, stationed next to small, faintly burning fire pit. The man has already lit his chillum, and after two hearty hits, hands it over to Jimmy. *Puff puff pass.* Jimmy expertly takes a couple of hits, too. Another young man joins our circle, dressed in tattered clothes with long hair, carrying a guitar in his hand. As they smoke, the guitarist begins to belt out a Meiteilon folk song. More men of all ages drift in and out. From a vendor outside the camp, Jimmy purchases some fruits and vegetables for the elders here. Then, he purchases some more to donate at our next stop.

There is a larger huddle of smoking men at the next shanglen. A small, stone bowl lies within the circle, containing ganja that has been broken, kneaded, and mixed into soft, pasty goo. One of the men expertly cleans a chillum, fills up the pipe with some of the goo, and lights it. There is a new face in the circle today, a younger man who has brought charas sourced from Himachal Pradesh. The rest of the men exclaim with joy; the black 'Cream' is a rare sight in these parts. The charas is then intermixed with the ganja goo to create a new hybrid flavour—a pan-Indian high—adding a wild hit of potency to the morning gathering.

There are certain rules and traditions in a smoker's circle like this one, and the Satjal members follow them to varying degrees: which hand a chillum must be held in, which hand it is passed on with, which hand receives it. There may be some concern if those hands are clean, if one has brushed their teeth and rinsed their mouth before the first puff. Only chillums here: joints or bongs are frowned upon. If the circle is big enough, a second chillum might begin to make its rounds, and then, maybe a third.

Morning turns over to afternoon. I'm back behind Jimmy on the motorcycle. The sun sends down relaxing waves of warmth, and the clamour of the marketplace peters away into a soft, harmless buzz.

My last stop that day is also the strangest. This is the headquarters of the UFO, a large campus at Langol, Lamphelpat, a suburb in West Imphal. Here lies the corpse of R. K. Manisana, the UFO's founder. The dead body is un-cremated, unburied, un-embalmed.

Manisana passed away at the age of seventy-two in February 2006. Before his death, however, the leader of the movement had predicted his own resurrection. A death certificate was issued by the hospital where he died; and yet, a week later, a top leader of the organization told a reporter that, 'The body is still warm and fresh and is not decomposing. Even his beard is growing. He is only taking rest and not dead.'

Thousands of UFO members held vigil for their 'ojha' (master) after his death, waiting for him to resurrect, like a mythological messiah.

They're still waiting.

Sixteen years have passed when I go to see Manisana's 'resting place' at Langol. The headquarters are in a quiet, serene area, at the foot of picturesque hills that encircle Imphal's outskirts. Statues of Pakhangba and Kangla Sha surround a flag-hoisting platform on the outside courtyard. Behind it lies a one-storey cottage with a long veranda. The white walls are losing their colour, and there are some cracks and chipped paint on the red veranda floor. But the cottage is otherwise in fine condition.

Jimmy and I walk up to the wooden doorway in the middle. There is a wooden Pakhangba portrait above the door frame, and a thin, wooden stick placed across the two handles on both sides of the door, as if to deny exit to anyone who attempts to open the doors from the *inside.*

Of course, I'm not permitted to step in.

Manisana's promised resurrection is a matter of some dispute within the Satjal organization; Jimmy, like many younger members of the community, doesn't subscribe to the idea.

'The body,' Jimmy says, 'is just lying there. On the bed.'

'How do they preserve it?' I ask.

'Nothing. They just cover it with a blanket.'

I take a hearty, long inhale at the door, expecting sixteen years of stench, of decomposition, of flesh-eating maggots, the larvae of flesh flies feasting on the decaying matter, of bacterial decay, disintegrated, lukewarm meat.

Out here in the veranda, however, I don't smell anything, except for the light, earthy scent of the wood, and the clean, suburban air. I'm told by caretakers later that the organization's elders have used agarbattis (incense sticks) in the room to cover the stench.

It is likely up to the topmost members of the organization to decide how long the UFO will wait for a miracle. For now, the corpse continues to lie behind that door, bolted and secured to avoid any unintended consequences if Manisana re-emerges someday, a stoned zombie. With the political and social influence enjoyed by the UFO, it seems to me that the state government is happy to leave the group (largely) unmolested, allowing them their traditions, the land where they've set up their camps, and the open secret of their heavy cannabis use.

In February 2020, the Manipur government even considered legalizing cannabis plantation. Chief Minister Biren Singh had told the state assembly that the legalization would be for industrial and medicinal purposes, and to earn potential tax revenue. But when I visit Imphal two years after this announcement closer to the state's assembly elections, Biren Singh has changed his tune with changing political expectations, saying that his 'primary duty' was to destroy the cultivation of 'various drugs like ganja'.

Biren Singh returned as chief minister after the BJP won the elections a month later.

There are large swathes of farm land around smaller districts of Manipur—like Churachandpur, Senapati, Ukhrul, and more—where cannabis has been cultivated since the 1970s. In the early 2000s, the International Fund for Agricultural Development had attempted to urge local farmers to grow crops like passion fruit and aloe vera, but their efforts were largely unsuccessful due to the ease of growing cannabis and its great potential profits.

Many of these plantations in Ukhrul and other districts are now, allegedly, under the protection of extremist groups. Some drug enforcement officials have even claimed that this is considered the 'best weed'* in India. Much of the Manipuri weed available in the market can dry out too quickly. Since the male and the female plants are cultivated close together, it results in a large quantity of seeds.

K. C. Verma, the former head of the NCB, recently shared a somewhat comical tale of a bungled drug operation from Manipur in the late 2000s. The bureau had been charged with destroying 'about five truckloads of ganja and substantial quantity of charas', which Verma decided to do by burning all the cannabis in an open, deserted hillside 30 kilometres outside Imphal.

> The ground was damp, and the moisture content of the cannabis was high. The ganja refused to catch fire... Even through my mask, I could smell the acrid smoke. With great difficulty, the local officer and others managed to get the drugs to burn evenly, but then it started to rain!
>
> ...
>
> Curious villagers came from near and far and stayed to inhale the smoke. Word spread to other areas, and soon more than a thousand men and women collected around

*People love to root for their home team.

> the burning heaps. The handful of NCB officials had a difficult time trying to keep the reluctant biomass burning, shooing away the villagers to prevent them from inhaling the smoke and chasing away some intrepid ones who tried to surreptitiously take away fistfuls of half-burnt ganja.
>
> …
>
> we were fortunate that no one from the media had reported the ignominious happenings. The local officer corrected me. 'Sir, a reporter had indeed come and declared that he would write a story about the botched destruction of drugs. But you can rest easy. I let him take away about 5 kg of ganja from the burning stacks. I know he won't be writing that story!'*

Nowadays, drug enforcement agencies have a bigger headache, an anxiety that perhaps even the finest Satjal weed can't alleviate. Hill areas such as Ukhrul district—often inhabited by Scheduled Tribes—are also hotspots of poppy plantation. Compared to cannabis, a fraction of poppy farmland can result in opium that is exponentially more lucrative for the farmers, and many are now happy to ditch ganja cultivation to make space. The porous border with Myanmar has also led to widespread smuggling of the drug into Manipur.

The Home Ministry reported that over 17,000 acres of poppy fields were destroyed in Manipur between 2018 and mid-2023. Many of these farms came under the control of the local Kuki tribe (and other hill tribes). The forced destruction of poppy and cannabis cultivation has played no small part in the tribes' resentment towards the state government, as has the state's declaration to evict the locals and declare many of the village areas as protected forest. These tensions would sow the seeds of protests, skirmishes, and large-scale ethnic violence in Manipur in 2023.

---

*I'm sure the reporter met *all* his deadlines that afternoon.

The abundance of poppy in the region has also led to a rampant addiction across the state. In 2009, an NGO called the Social Awareness and Service Organisation (SASO) estimated that there were around 34,500 injecting drug users in Manipur, an epidemic that has also led to widespread cases of HIV/AIDS. Manipur, with only about 0.2 per cent of India's total population, contributes to nearly 8 per cent of India's total HIV-positive cases. Of the female injecting drug users in India, 28.2 per cent are from Manipur, the highest in the country. In a state that is already facing growing insurgency, communal violence, unemployment, and inflation, the added curses of addiction and disease feels like a gross adulteration of the promise of life itself.

Jimmy tells me that he has suffered from heroin addiction in the past too, and has spent four years from the ages of seventeen to twenty-one in rehab. Cannabis, he says, was a helping hand to get off heroin; and in Satjal, he found a welcoming community which became an extended family.

We part ways. A month after this conversation, Jimmy will move with his family to the Delhi NCR region, for his new job teaching theatre at a high school. The documentary footage of Satjal still sits with him, terabytes of memory, waiting for the day he chooses to reveal it to the world.

The main city roadways of Imphal are clear by nightfall. The car I'm in takes a turn into the North AOC street, where I see a sudden world of vice. Young women hang out on the street corners, backs leaning against makeshift walls of large steel slabs. Young men sit on the pavement, scratching the inside of their forearms. Behind the slabs are some small rooms and dens, used for prostitution and drug use.

'People are shooting up, selling, and walking around,' says Aboy, my friendly local guide for the night. 'Police and army are nearby, but it's as if they ignore what's happening just around the corner.

'Lots of lives have been spoiled here.'

Aboy, who is in his early thirties, sits in the passenger seat up front, dressed in a black hoodie and a matching black bucket hat. He is of Naga descent, but grew up mostly between Imphal, and later, New Delhi. The car is being driven by Marinao Lekngayo, who is a decade or so older. Our destination is an orphanage in the Mantripukhri neighbourhood of Imphal, which houses orphans aged five to eighteen living with HIV/AIDS, many of whom have lost their parents to the disease. Lekngayo, who is living with HIV too, is a volunteer here: he and the children are all undergoing anti-retroviral therapy (ART), a treatment that consists of a combination of drugs that helps to supress HIV replication.

Lekngayo and Aboy are both recovering heroin addicts, and Aboy cites that he followed his late father as a role model. 'He was a guitarist, a smoker, a druggie,' says Aboy. 'They were a big group of friends who hung around Imphal, looking really cool. That's what I wanted, too... I belong to an addict family. My dad was addicted to heroin. My mom was also addicted to heroin.'

Aboy's own journey with substance abuse began with the misuse of prescription drugs when he was only a fifth-grader. Then came alcohol. Marijuana. Then, in 2008, he was introduced to heroin while studying in New Delhi. His mother died. Then, his father died of HIV. 'Then, I had too many freedoms,' says Aboy. His eyes well up.

Aboy's heroin use lasted for the better part of the next decade. He speaks with a juxtaposition of humour and pathos, and adds almost offhandedly that he'd tried committing suicide 'six or seven times' in the past by attempting to overdose on heroin and cocaine.

Eventually, he was able to rehab and recover, and nowadays, he says, he's mostly clean. 'No heroin, no alcohol, no pills, no LSD, no cocaine, no nothing. Only marijuana.'

In Manipur—like Nagaland—several drug rehab centres

are regulated or supported by the church or local NGOs. Aboy and Lekngayo both attended rehab with the help of the AA and church networks. But the aggressive criminalizing of hard drug users persists here too, often turning addicts like Aboy into social outcasts. It's an approach that favours punishment rather than rehabilitation.

An alternative solution to tackle drug abuse has been explored in Sikkim, the least populous and second smallest of all Indian states, sticking up almost like a proud thumbs-up above the rest of the Indian landmass around it. Struggling with a deluge of alcohol and drug abuse (particularly the illicit use of prescription pharmaceutical drugs) for decades, the state enacted the Sikkim Anti-Drugs Act (SADA) in 2006, taking a different approach from the national NDPS. Sikkim's model is based on deterrence, rather than a rush for punishment and imprisonment. SADA adopts a rehabilitative approach, treating consumers—caught with a small quantity of drugs—as different from peddlers, sellers, and manufacturers. The act also determines consistent volumes of different drugs, to correctly identify what constitutes a 'small quantity'. The Vidhi Centre for Legal Policy recently concluded that this approach 'enabled SADA to channelise Sikkim's healthcare services to the most vulnerable drug users'.

In 2018, SADA decriminalized illicit drug use, and set up (voluntary) provisions for detoxification and rehabilitation for addicts.

Like neighbouring Nagaland, alcohol is prohibited in Manipur; but also like Nagaland, it's relatively easy to purchase booze at restaurants and thinly-veiled corner shops. In September 2022, in response to the rise of dangerous unregulated liquor, Manipur's state cabinet partially lifted prohibition in the state.

Here in Manipur, Aboy says, many like him can consume marijuana openly—just like smoking a cigarette—without much fear of prosecution. 'Marijuana is a part of my life,' he says. 'It doesn't create any problems—it solves problems. When you're angry and you smoke up, it chills you.'

Lekngayo, who has mostly been quite on the wheel, cuts in, 'I've tried weed, but I don't like it. I don't like the kick.'

Aboy smiles, and then turns to me. 'Some people are allergic to weed. I feel very bad for them. They're missing something in their life!'

Later that night, the three of us sit for dinner at the orphanage, outdoors but under the cover of a large, straw canopy. The weather turns a little chilly and Lekngayo presents us each with a cup of honey-infused green tea. Dinner follows, featuring rice and spicy pork curry. This version of the ghost pepper is called umorok, and it's just as excellent as the varieties I've tried in Nagaland. We're joined by some of the young women who live at this orphanage, all of whom are familiar with Lekngayo.

As we sit together, scraping our plates clean, Aboy continues to share his impassionate enthusiasm for the local Manipuri ganja, sharing specifics of different strains he enjoys. For Aboy, this substance has brought great equilibrium to the chaos of his life: he tells me that the version of him I'm meeting today—friendly, social, calm—was hardly his personality for most of his life.

'I had serious anger and rage issues,' Aboy says. 'Weed didn't cure my anger issues, but it helped me control it. There are particular things in my life... for which, I have a reserved mentality. The timing of the things that happened to me, it makes me so bitter, that I can't let go of it. It's not revenge that I seek… It's just that my mind is *so soft* about that part of my life that it doesn't want to let go of it. Because I know if I let go, it will hurt me.'

Aboy, I know, is still hurting, still looking for a way back into the pace of 'acceptable' society. He tells me he spends most of his day taking care of his motorcycle. He is vague about how he makes a living, beyond some support from his family and the money from live streaming his gameplay of 'Mobile Legends', an online battle arena game where he earns around ₹1,500 per day. His evenings end with a spliff or two, and a sense of tranquillity that he has hardly ever enjoyed in his young life.

I spend my last couple of days in Manipur with an old friend, Solomon, whom I haven't seen in nearly twenty years. Solomon lives at Churachandpur, a district about two hours south of Imphal. We take a short drive in the evening to the serene lakes and hills in the outskirts of the city. Like many other parts of Manipur, there is a significant influence of Burmese culture here, particularly in the street side snacks, the Burmese tea, and some of the dialects and garments, too. It is relatively easy to cross over to Myanmar (Burma) from Manipur: the road border at Moreh is only a few hours' drive from Imphal, and several travellers and labourers cross over from the Myanmar side (Tamu) regularly in search of employment.

On the drive back from Churachandpur to Imphal, Solomon and I stop by the Loktak Lake, which is one of the largest freshwater lakes in South Asia, with a typical area of 287 square kilometres, featuring floating islands, a national park, protected animal species, and what seems like an infinity pool of deep, blue waters. The floating Keibul Lamjao National Park here also features a shanglen of the UFO, and is known to be a major draw for foreign nationals interested in immersing themselves in Thang Ta and other cultural practices of the Satjal.

Solomon and I take some pictures at the national park, from where we're able to see a vast, panoramic view of the lake behind us. It's a warm, breezy day, and the blue seems to stretch to the far horizons, all around us.

India's endlessness will never cease to amaze me. I could travel like this for years and still feel incomplete. There is always something new to digest and appreciate. And the past few weeks have given me a khazana of new memories: spending time with old friends, trying exciting new varieties of food, seeing my country from new perspectives. I've encountered many individuals on my way who have suffered a dependence on a variety of nashas: brown, Yaba, pills, weed. While I may soon return to my 'real life',* they will continue with no certain end to their travels. This isn't a brief excursion for them, but the slog of daily living.

I wonder why I have romanticized cannabis in such a way, a substance which, for some people, has ruined ambition, wrecked families, destroyed lives. Even if its impact as a gateway drug and an addictive substance is overblown, it can still be a vice that can fog the mind and stifle growth. Why choose a bliss supplement, when bliss is already found everywhere around us?

But I also wonder why cannabis is so often painted by these extreme colours of dread. Shouldn't we feel the same way about so many other human vices? Addictions to alcohol, gambling, tobacco, gaming, sugar? Addiction to our screens, to our jobs, to caffeine, to prescription drugs, to sex? Why not accept cannabis in moderation, like we do any of our other dependencies? Why not remove the stigma, stop harassing the disenfranchised communities caught in the web of production and sale, and relish the substance for its positive qualities?

I start to feel a sense of melancholy on my final day in Imphal. I have a last lunch with Solomon at a traditional Manipuri canteen and stroll through a little independent bookshop, before I'm dropped at the airport for my flight to New Delhi. I have no check-in luggage, but the officers at the security check station catch the pickle jars of chilli that I've been carrying with me. My bhut jolokia, my umorok. It won't go on board, they say. Do you want to check your bag?

In the rush of travel, I don't have too long to mull the decision. *No*, I say, and I hand the jars to them. The officers smile at each other, more than happy to inherit the gift.

I might order some online for myself. Or, someday, I'll just have to come back for more.

---

*Whatever that is.

Hempistan

'...our entire resolve is transitioning the image of cannabis from dope to hope...'

July is sticky season in Delhi. The weather is still hot, but now, clouds lie still over the Northern Plains, sometimes teasing a hint of rainfall, sometimes threatening it. The national capital becomes a national sauna. There's always an added layer of air pollution, PM 2.5 particles contaminating the atmosphere, seeping into our lungs. Sweat flows down our collective backs and sticks in the folds of our inner thighs. Between our eyebrows and down the sternum. Patches of sweat under our armpits and around the waist. We wait for the clouds to tear open. We wait for relief.

It was on one such July day in 2016 when Tathagata Satpathy, a former member of the Lok Sabha, attended the Lower House of the Parliament wearing the only garment that made sense in the stifling humidity of the capital: a loose-hanging, light kurta made of hemp fabric. 'Today's high', Satpathy later declared proudly on his Twitter account.

Ah, the humble, lovely kurta. Light, breathable, perfect for the high Celsius climates of the subcontinent. A tunic that is simple and affordable enough for the South Asian everyman and woman, a garb capable of being devastatingly fashionable under the right guidance, and a garment that is also aggressively embellished by our politicians. The kurta is equipollent, from the prime minister at his biggest campaign rallies to the local MLA invited to your inter-school badminton tournament. Right, centre, left, conservative, liberal, communist, progressive, whatever.

Satpathy, who was a member of the Biju Janata Dal (BJD) political party, is as progressive as they come, a rare species in a nation of politicians, who seems to be more concerned with challenges of the present than the imagined fictions of the past. A journalist by trade, Satpathy served as a Lok Sabha member for a decade and a half from Odisha's Dhenkanal constituency. In his time as an elected representative, he supported bills to decriminalize homosexuality, called for a repeal of pornography bans, spoke in favour of a uniform civil code (instead of laws based on various religions), opposed the construction of nuclear power plants, batted for net neutrality, and raised privacy concerns about the Aadhaar card project.

It was Satpathy's stand on cannabis that, briefly, made him a stoner viral sensation. In 2015, while serving his fourth term as MP, Satpathy held an 'Ask Me Anything' (AMA) session on Reddit. When queried about the BJD's stance on decriminalizing cannabis, Satpathy responded,

> While in college, I have smoked (and unlike Clinton have inhaled)* cannabis many a times. In villages of Orissa, many people openly smoke and, as their representative, I am not entitled to be judgmental.
>
> BTW cannabis, luckily, is legal in certain states in India, like Orissa. You can walk up to a government excise shop and buy your day's need.**

In an interview that followed, Satpathy confirmed that he had no regrets or remorse about smoking pot in his youth. 'I don't support the ban on cannabis consumption,' he said, and then added that there is an elitist bias in India that looks down upon cannabis smokers as compared to those that consume alcohol. Satpathy's

*A legendary use of parentheses.

**He means bhang.

stand was one of the rare times since the NDPS Act was conceived that an Indian lawmaker openly spoke about the decriminalization of cannabis—and particularly, did so without basing his conclusions on retrograde pseudo-sciences.

I read the quotes above over and over again to believe my eyes. An Indian politician admitting to smoking weed? Admitting to not being judgemental? *Is this even real life?*

So, I give him a call.

'I have not changed my stand [on cannabis],' Satpathy tells me over the phone from Odisha. 'It's a god-given, natural product, which needs to be made available for people. I don't think I will back down on this.'

In 2019, Satpathy retired from politics; now in his late sixties, he serves time as the editor of the Odisha-based newspapers *Dharitiri* and *OrissaPOST*. On social media, he continues to take strong political stances, often sharing memes and news reports from around the world that highlight his progressive sympathies.

These are the same sympathies that shade his opinion regarding the economy of cannabis, too. 'I don't approve of legalization,' says Satpathy, 'because it will mean that the big corporations will take thousands of acres and control the farming. I want decriminalization, so that the marginal, small farmer can grow the plant on site, on their fields, and sell a lot of it.'

For Satpathy, a ban on a naturally available product seems nonsensical. 'If you go to the Himalaya, Uttarakhand, Kashmir, it grows all over,' he says. 'This is a very, very hardy plant. It grows on the hillside. Nobody waters it, nobody puts manure. It recreates itself with its own seeds and becomes a jungle. It doesn't need much tending or care.

'Just because it was told to some government bureaucrat, who was stuck-up in the mid-80s, they criminalized it,' he continues. 'If they think everyone can become a ganja abuser—that's the height of stupidity. It has immense industrial and medicinal issues. Most people mistakenly think that it's only an intoxicant that you smoke, or drink in shape of bhang. That, of course, is a part of it. But even your cough syrup contains codeine, which is habit-forming. There are so many habit-forming drugs that are medically prescribed. If somebody wants to abuse a certain thing, they can do it any which way, including clandestinely, through the black market. So, why not bring [cannabis] overboard? Why not bring it on the table and certify the product?'

While steady progress has been made state by state, Satpathy believes that a larger overhaul is needed at the centre. His suggestion is that the government needs to set up a relevant parliamentary committee which is empowered to review and revisit the old NDPS Act, and remove cannabis from its ambit. A new central policy will eventually guide the states to liberalizing their own narcotics acts. From there, he hopes that other ministries (such as the Ministry of Agriculture and Farmers' Welfare) can take the necessary steps forward, including empowering farmers to learn and earn more.

Decriminalization, Satpathy asserts, will also help thwart the 'mafia operation' around the cultivation and trade of cannabis in his home state, Odisha, and across the border in Andhra Pradesh—including in regions that produce the dominant Sheelavathi strain, where many tribal communities are entangled in the tussle between Naxalites, security forces, and the mafia.

'See, if you criminalize rice, rice will go to the black market, too!' says Satpathy. 'They're making something wild illegal. What if some leaders say that, for creating "So-And-So Rashtra", you must not eat mango. Will you make mango illegal? So…if you bring [cannabis] upfront, the black market will collapse.'

'My suspicion is that the mafia is fuelling and paying off bureaucrats and politicians. They want to maintain status quo. Quote me on this.'

Satpathy may have been the most outspoken Indian politician on this issue, but I would soon discover that he is far from the only one. Several elected officials—on all sides of India's chaotic and fractured political spectrum—have hinted their support for liberalization of state or national cannabis laws. Even some members rabble-rousing in the houses of parliament find unity under the hot July sun, threaded together like the hemp in Satpathy's kurta.

A few months after Satpathy's 'high fashion' appearance, Dharamvir Gandhi—then a Lok Sabha MP from Punjab for the Aam Admi Party (AAP)—moved a private member's bill seeking to legalize cultivation, production, possession, transport, trade, and recreational use of cannabis in India. Gandhi's supporters included Romesh Bhattacharji, a former commissioner of the Central Bureau of Narcotics, and the late actor Vinod Khanna, who was a BJP MP. 'Soft drugs are part of the cultural history of India and does [sic] not lead to an abusive lifestyle or rise in crime,' Gandhi had said at the time. 'It was only used as a measure of "mauj-masti" (relaxation and enjoyment) by the common people.'

Like Satpathy, Gandhi shared concerns that the current NDPS Act had only helped aid the mafia and cartels to proliferate more harmful drugs (like cocaine and heroin).

In July 2017, Maneka Gandhi (not related to Dharamvir), a BJP leader who at the time was the Minister of Women and Child Development of India, showed support for the legalization of medical marijuana to combat the abuse of harder drugs, and for the benefit of cancer patients. A year later, the Congress party leader and wildly successful author Shashi Tharoor co-wrote an essay supporting the legalization of marijuana. Tharoor began his piece with a disclaimer, just in case any support for weed hurt his personal political ambitions: 'I have never tried a recreational drug in my life... I have never tasted bhang, even for Holi.'

'And yet,' adds Tharoor, 'I am convinced that legally regulating the production, supply, and use of cannabis in India will reduce the potential harms of the drug's use, put a dent in corruption and crime, and provide our country with an economic boost.'

In January 2022, Maharashtra MP Pratap Patil Chikhilar of the BJP—arguing against the sale of wine in supermarkets and walk-in stores—counterbalanced with his support of cannabis instead. 'The government thinks it will get more revenue by selling wine at such outlets, then it should also give permission for the cultivation of ganja.' Later that same year, BJP MLA Krishnamurti Bandhi in Chhattisgarh went a step further to promote cannabis as a better alternative than alcohol in regards to public safety. 'I had (been) told that somewhere alcohol is the reason for rape, murder and quarrel, but I asked (in the House): Tell me whether a person who consumes bhang has ever committed rape, murder and dacoity?'

Strong arguments, all.

Of course, one doesn't need to be a wise vidyan to conclude that politicians are gonna politic, that almost any statement (pro and against) cannabis will likely be boosted with some ulterior motive. And in India, where the average citizen is bombarded daily with much nonsense, I've had to clothe myself in an extra-insulated layer of scepticism in regards to any aggressive stance made by our public servants.

And wherever the words of kurta-clad men may come short, allow the principles of science and economy to pave the rest of the way.

But first, a little history: welcome to my bhangshala.

In the late fifteenth century, an Italian explorer named Christopher Columbus—funded by the monarchs of Spain—set out to sea, perhaps hoping to sail all the way to the shores of India. Instead, he stumbled into what the Europeans would call the 'New World' and end up changing the course of modern human history.

From lucrative start-ups to Instagram 'weedfluencers',* the hemp

*I apologize for introducing you to this term.

business loves to repeat a collection of their favourite Columbus facts. For instance, the sails and ropes on famous *Nina*, *Pinta*, and *Santa Maria*—the ships that Columbus sailed to the Americas—were made of hemp fibre. The ships were made watertight with the help of hemp filling the cracks between the planks. Columbus's men consumed hemp seeds on their long journey for nutrition. Columbus' 'kurta' (shirt) was made of hemp, too.

There are many more hemp-friendly anecdotes in common circulation. The first flag of the US was made by Betsy Ross from industrial hemp. The US Declaration of Independence is said to have been drafted on hemp paper. Abraham Lincoln used hemp seed oil for his household lamps. The 1941 Ford's Model T (the 'soybean car') used material made of hemp plastic. Painters like Vincent van Gogh, Rembrandt, and Thomas Gainsborough created several of their masterpieces on hemp canvases, using hemp-based paints. Even the word 'canvas' owes its etymology to 'cannabis'.*

Nowadays, the global market for hemp consists of tens of thousands of different products, including ropes, sails, banknotes, carpeting, home furnishings, nutrition, biofuel, paints, textiles, plastics, and construction material. South Africa's Cape Town opened the doors to the twelve-storey Hemp Hotel in June 2023, the world's tallest building made of industrial hemp.

Despite its already widespread use, many believe that we're still only scratching the surface of this disruptive industry. China is already far ahead of the race, investing to become a hemp superpower. Two Chinese provinces account for a whopping 70 per cent of all global hemp fibre production.

The hemp/cannabis/bhang plant is versatile, ubiquitous, and sturdy enough to survive the toughest conditions. And it's good for the Earth! Hemp products can be a natural alternative to plastic, reduce the use of agricultural pesticides, reduce the use of landfill,

---

*High art.

and more. Hemp plants breathe in four times more CO_2 than most trees. One acre of hemp can help clean 10 tonnes of carbon from the atmosphere.

Like some other wild weeds, the cannabis plant is also a 'hyperaccumulator', capable of absorbing the nastiest of pollutants in the atmosphere—heavy metals, pesticides, and petroleum, etc., while remaining stable itself. It is considered a strong candidate for phytoremediation (using plants to clean up contaminated environments); the cultivation of hemp has been useful in removing soil contaminants from agricultural land in Chernobyl (now in Ukraine) after the 1986 nuclear disaster. The US Department of Agriculture is sponsoring further research on how to bioengineer cannabis to absorb greater levels of toxins.

As countries like the United States, China, and more race ahead, India is stumbling somnambulant into the party, a step back for every two steps forward. Indian Standard Time. The good news is that cultivation of cannabis for medicinal and scientific purposes has been authorized in Uttarakhand. This was followed by Madhya Pradesh, Chhattisgarh, and Manipur. Himachal Pradesh has recently legalized controlled cultivation of the crop. Uttar Pradesh, Manipur, and Jammu & Kashmir have framed out policies for cannabis cultivation for R&D purposes.

The industry, however, is still in its nascent stage. The National Botanical Research Institute in Lucknow has developed some lines (varieties) of the desirable >0.3 per cent cannabis seed, but the institute's former director Saroj Barik suggested a little more patience when we spoke, to see if the lines remain stable over the next few generations. Among its many objectives, the NBRI hope to develop low-THC (high fibre) varieties for industrial use, high-THC and high-CBD varieties for medicinal purposes, standardize the agro-practices for *Cannabis sativa* cultivation, and further evaluate and characterize germplasm lines.

The central government continues to take tepid, cautious steps forward, promoting the potential of hemp while remaining careful of the possible political blowback of saying too much. In November 2018, the minister of state for the Prime Minister's Office Jitendra Singh attended a conference entitled 'Cannabis R&D in India: A Scientific, Medical & Legal Perspective', where he said, 'Since ancient times,* cannabis-based products like bhang have been a part of Indian culture, social customs and festivals. There is a very thin line between use, misuse and abuse of a substance, and it is our responsibility to draw that line, so that we do not throw the baby out with the bathwater.'

Over a Zoom call a few years later, Barik tells me that it's now time to start thinking about a national policy—beyond the state-to-state regulations—regarding agricultural cannabis.

'The time has come now that we think on that line,' Barik says. 'And we're not saying that there shouldn't be restrictions. The use of THC for non-medicinal purpose should be restricted... [The policy] has to be carefully drafted. We should re-look, revisit the existing Act, and amend it in such a way that misuse is restricted; and at the same time, we get the good things [from cannabis] for its medicinal and industrial purposes. Because the whole world is going down that route. If you see the global scenario, many countries have opened up, and many countries are now going ahead.

'That's why, we say that it's the future crop, particularly when you talk about climate change, when traditional crops are failing.'

Barik pauses, and then adds, almost with a dash of admiration. 'Smart crops, these are... These are our own plants. *Indica.* If we don't catch up, the world will go ahead, and we'll be left behind. So, it's time to re-look at our policy, and revise our policy.'

At the time of writing, India's contribution to the global hemp market stands around 0.0002 per cent. That's a frighteningly small share for a country with about 17 per cent of the world's population.

---

*Indian politicians absolutely *love* the 'since ancient times' argument.

This, despite India also becoming a major manufacturing hub for a certain enhancer of the weed-smoking experience. Since the late 2010s, over a dozen units have been established around New Delhi by the company Hara, who are the world's largest manufacturer of cones—empty, pre-rolled joint papers with a filter tip. Hara employs over 4,000 individuals in India and produces over 1.2 billion cones a year for the biggest cone brands in the world, controlling about 30 per cent of the global market.

Barik is correct: the world is, indeed, racing ahead. By early 2023, medical use of cannabis had been legalized to various degrees in close to fifty nations around the world, including Argentina, Australia, Brazil, Canada, Denmark, Georgia, Germany, Israel, Italy, the Netherlands, Spain, Sri Lanka, and the United States. In 2013, Uruguay became a pioneer of the marijuana industry after President Jose Mujica signed the legislation to make them the first nation on Earth to legalize recreational cannabis. South Africa, Mexico, Malta, Georgia, Canada, and most recently, Brazil, have followed suit. In a suburb of Johannesburg in South Africa, hundreds of students have been taught the intricacies of growing the plant in a first-of-its-kind educational institution, in preparation for the upcoming economic boom in the hemp economy.

Canada's economy has been absolutely revolutionized by cannabis.* An early 2022 report confirmed that since recreational use was legalized in the country in October 2018, cannabis had already contributed 43.5 billion CAD (that's about 2.7 trillion rupees) to Canada's GDP through labour income, tax revenue, and more. Along with nations like China, France, Germany, England, Australia,** and the Netherlands, Canada is at the forefront of hemp

---

*Before you ask, no, 'Canada' doesn't owe its etymology to cannabis. And that ganja-looking symbol on the Canadian flag is a maple leaf, no matter how much your second-cousin from Vancouver might claim otherwise.

**Australia has also become the first country in the world to permit the use of psychedelic mushrooms and MDMA (ecstasy) for the treatment of mental health

cultivation, with about 20,000 hectares of land dedicated to hemp food production. A number of cannabis and hemp product start-ups in India are supported by investors from Canada, hoping that their experience in the industry will give them an upper hand in the potential Indian market.

Many countries are customizing the model for their own culture and conditions. In Georgia, only consumption is legal, not cultivation or sale for recreational purposes. In Germany, after experimenting with a preliminary plan, the health minister announced a scaled-back legalization policy in April 2023, allowing adult residents to join non-profit 'cannabis clubs' with a maximum of 500 members each,* who may grow a limited amount of cannabis for the members' personal consumption. In late 2023, Japan—one of the strictest nations in terms of its anti-drugs policies—passed a major bill in their House of Councillors to legalize cannabis-based medicine. Around the same time, the parliament of Ukraine voted to legalize medical marijuana after the war against Russia 'left thousands of people with post-traumatic stress disorder that many believe could be eased by the drug'.

The most dramatic recent change in policy has come in Thailand. The credit for originally introducing ganja to Thailand and other Southeast Asian nations is usually attributed to Indians who shared the plant with this region, among other reverent cultural exports. The Thai kancha, Cambodian kânhcha, Lao kan xa, and Vietnamese cân xa all have a familiar ring, don't they? Until recently, Thailand had scheduled cannabis as a class-5 narcotic, with strict punishments for offenders who consumed, possessed, or sold the drug. But in June 2022, the Thai Food and Drug Administration went ahead and made some weed history, removing all parts of the cannabis plant from this classification, making Thailand the first Asian nation to allow sales, cultivation,

conditions, including post-traumatic stress disorder, depression, anxiety, etc.

*Ganja gymkhanas.

possession, and recreational use of the substance. Health Minister Anutin Charnvirakul announced on Facebook that the government would even distribute one million free cannabis plants across the country to allow people to grow pot at home like 'household crops'. This was a politically savvy move for Charnvirakul, who ran for the prime minister's seat a few months later on the promise of further liberalization of marijuana laws. On election day, Charnvirakul arrived to vote in a marijuana-print shirt.

The swift decriminalization in Thailand had some limitations. Sale was prohibited to minors, pregnant and breastfeeding women, and smoking cannabis—like smoking tobacco—was prohibited in public areas. But the country—which already credits much of its GDP to the tourism and service sector—hoped to become a destination for recreational and medicinal marijuana tourism. Dispensaries lined up many areas in Bangkok, offering everything from joint-rolling workshops, cannabis tea, and stoned yoga classes. Organizations in the country have since launched competitions like the 'Ganja Cup' to reward the best cultivated weed. There were contests for the 'fastest joint roller' that had participants lining up to crush, crumble, and roll the quickest spliff for a cash prize.

The liberalization and accessibility of marijuana in Thailand soon carried its pungent waft to India, too. When six alleged traffickers were arrested for distributing a variety of marijuana strains and MDMA crystals to students in Delhi NCR in late 2023, investigators uncovered an intricate journey that transported the maal from Thai jungles to Manipur, Nagaland, and then to the capital on trains, buses, private vehicles, often distributed through delivery apps.

Thailand's high, however, wouldn't last long: After assuming office in August 2023, the country's new prime minister Srettha Thavinsin voiced his opposition to the recreational use of cannabis, and despite the boom of the cannabis economy, the conservative coalition government pushed for the laws to be updated again.

Thailand is an anomaly in Asia, where many other nations

continue to practise ruthless narcotics laws. In countries like the UAE, Malaysia, and the Philippines, marijuana possession could lead to long term (or even life) imprisonment, fines, canings, lashings, and execution. Despite their ambitions for hemp supremacy, China reserves some of its most severe punishment for narcotics possession and use—including cannabis.

In 2017, Indian-origin man Tangaraju Suppiah was convicted of abetting the trafficking of around 1 kilo of cannabis into Singapore. Suppiah allegedly coordinated the import of cannabis, but never came into contact with the product himself. This might be a low-level offence in many states around the world, but in Singapore, Suppiah was sentenced to death. Voices of concern were raised globally, from Amnesty International, United Nations, and even British billionaire Richard Branson—an advocate against the death penalty—who criticized Singapore for targeting those on the 'lower rungs of the illicit drug supply chain', and argued that the country's draconian laws do little to deter actual drug-related crime.

None of it mattered. Singapore executed Suppiah by hanging on 27 April 2023. He was forty-six. This was Singapore's twelfth execution in just over a year, all for drug offences.

Singaporean authorities have argued that the death penalty is indeed a deterrent against drugs. Activists, however, vehemently disagree. Transformative Justice Collective, an activist group in Singapore, said, 'It is just illogical to know that countries nearby are enjoying cannabis in food and beverages, and using it for its medical benefits, while our country is executing people for the very same substance.'

It is the very same substance that is driving the eyes of the world on Uruguay, a country slightly larger than Andhra Pradesh, whose developing economy serves as real time experiments of the tantalizing future of the various legal uses of hemp/cannabis: industrial, medicinal, recreational. It would also serve as a model for how legalization and decriminalization can influence crime rates, and the burden on their criminal justice system.

In August 2021, the Borgen Project analysed the impact of full legalization in Uruguay, concluding that the decision had led to a large decrease in overall drug trafficking:

> Uruguay's marijuana model aims to create conditions where marijuana use isn't rampant. It's affordable, procedural and normalized... For countries looking to cut down on black market sales, incarceration rates and drug trafficking, Uruguay's experiment shows interesting signs of social and economic wellbeing. The decision to legalize marijuana in Uruguay boosted the economy and stands poised to improve the lives of citizens.

Meanwhile in Canada, a survey of 2,000 medical cannabis patients revealed a reduction in alcohol use. Following these results, the International Journal of Drug Policy concluded

> Since alcohol is the most prevalent recreational substance in North America, and its use results in significant rates of criminality, morbidity and mortality, these findings may result in improved health outcomes for medical cannabis patients, as well as overall improvements in public health and safety.

Maybe other countries are starting to listen—even if it's in small doses. In many cases, it helps to earn political brownie points, too. In the United States, President Joe Biden pardoned thousands of people convicted of marijuana possession under the federal law. The pardons cleared everyone who was convicted on the simple possession charge. 'The federal government currently classifies marijuana as a Schedule 1 substance,' Biden said, 'the same as heroin and LSD and more serious than fentanyl. It makes no sense.'* Biden's perspective was affirmed by the US

*Biden will face an independent challenger in the 2024 presidential elections: the

Justice Department in May 2024, which proposed that marijuana be rescheduled at a federal level from a Schedule I drug (a list that includes drugs like heroin, LSD, etc.) to Schedule III, a classification that acknowledges the substance's medical benefits. This may lead to legal changes for cannabis in more American states. As expected, cannabis stocks skyrocketed almost instantly after the DOJ's proposal.

Annual cannabis sales in the US are expected to hit $31.8 billion in 2023, and are projected to cross the $50 billion mark by the end of 2028. In 2022, Americans spent far more on legal marijuana products than they did on opioid medications, chocolate, and craft beer. An estimated 55 million Americans—roughly one-fifth of the nation's adult population—used cannabis in 2022. A national survey published by the *Addiction* journal in 2024 reported that, for the first time, the number of Americans using cannabis daily or near daily now exceeds those who drink alcohol.

Five and a half centuries ago, Christopher Columbus sailed with some hemp on his ships across the Pacific. Now, the US is the leading importer of hemp products from around the world.

The rise of recreational cannabis use has also been inversely proportional to the fall of tobacco. The population of American cigarette smokers fell from 35 per cent in 2001 to 11 per cent by 2022, with many consumers choosing cannabis or other smoke-free products. Perhaps this is the reason why the Altria Group—one of the world's largest tobacco companies—began pivoting to cannabis. Formerly known as Philip Morris Companies, Altria in 2018 spent $1.8 billion for a 45 per cent stake in the Cronos Group, a major multinational cannabis firm based in Canada. Since then, Altria has spent its considerable resources to lobby for cannabis-friendly laws in the US Congress—the same way tobacco companies had

rapper Afroman (real name Joseph Edgar Foreman), who is running on a platform to fully legalize cannabis. I hope the campaign trail spawns a patriotic sequel to 'Because I Got High', one of the most beloved weed songs ever recorded.

done for decades prior. Altria has also acquired patented marijuana vaporizers, like the vaping device company Juul.

As private entrepreneurship grows, not everyone in the United States is happy about the government's increased interest and interference in the industry. In a 2022 cover story, *Forbes* argued that the United States had botched the legalization process of cannabis due to 'overregulation, overtaxation, and state-by-state inconsistencies... the biggest no-brainer in the history of capitalism—legalizing the world's most popular illicit drug—is turning into a massive market failure.' The high taxes and regulations have made it expensive for many small businesses to legally sell recreational cannabis, and thus ensuring that the illegal sales of the product remain high.

I have also heard the faint hum of this anxiety rumbling in the interviews I conducted with cannabis activists in India. It's a sense that their expertise and passion is being misused by the powerful hands of Big Business, Big Government, Big Brothers. That the little green plant—which is almost celebrated as a divine gift—is becoming only a means to greener pockets.

Much of the industry worldwide is still in the process of trial and error. There is no perfect formula yet for India to adopt (it will never be 'perfect'), and certainly, nothing that can be merely stencilled over our unique social, cultural, and economic conditions. If the weed industry is in its adolescence in the United States, it's merely a toddler in India, teething its way through early bites, discovering which parts taste good and which bits to spit out in disgust.

There are innumerable hidden players in the ganja life cycle: the farmers cutting and gathering the crop, the transporters moving it across the state, the peddlers selling it on the street, and even the mafia bosses atop the chain of command. But their profits begin to seem relatively miniscule as the long arms of industry step into the fray, eager to turn sticky green into shiny gold.

Deep in the valleys in the Uttarakhand, I had felt a certain sense of peace wading through the giant shoots of bhang in the farms. Clear blue skies, gorgeous Himalayan peaks, clean air, and a serene silence of (relative) solitude. I allowed the plants to rustle past my palms, each touch a longing whisper under the lazy, afternoon sun.

But today, I'm not in those verdant valleys any more. The gentle rustles of the farms have been replaced by the sound of feet stomping on a red, carpeted floor. Visitors scurry from stall to stall in an air-conditioned banquet hall. The cannabis is still here, but now, it has completed a metamorphosis into 'acceptable' new forms: topical massage ointments, lip balms, hemp energy drinks, seed oils, CBD oils, fibre composite products, and anti-anxiety tablets for your pet.*

Now, I'm in the convention hall of a luxury hotel in Shahdara, in an area populated with relatively new construction projects close to the banks of the Yamuna in New Delhi. This space is hosting the first ever India Hemp Expo, a gathering to showcase a wide variety of hemp-related products and services. Companies like BOHECO, Svadhisthan, Neet, Savikalpa, Indian Hempire, and more are present. Representatives from smaller start-ups offer elevator pitches in search of interest and investors. Everything here is legal: the NDPS Act recognizes cannabis as a source of biomass, fibre, and oil, and the Government of India encourages the research and cultivation of cannabis with low-THC content.

The Hemp Expo is the brainchild of Indianvaidyas, the largest network of Ayurvedic physicians in the country, who claim to have registered over 50,000 Ayurveda doctors, students, and clinics in just the first two years of their inception. Founded by Piyush Juneja, Indianvaidyas also offer training sessions for aspiring Ayurveda practitioners, including courses in the use of cannabis-

*I'm the associated human of a particularly over-hyper Lhasa Apso—Bilbo Baggins—who could probably use a heavy dose of CBD anxiety medicine. Calm down Bilbo!!

based medicine. Their associated platform, Hempvaidyas, highlights physicians that specialize in conditions including infertility, thyroid disorders, polycystic ovarian disease, and spine and joint disorders, with the assistance of hemp-based medicine. Juneja is a practitioner of medical cannabis himself; on 20 April 2023 (Happy 4/20 Day!), he launched his book *Medical Cannabis A to Z,* calling it 'India's first book on medical cannabis'.

Since this first event, the Expo hit the road around India, hosting bigger iterations in Mumbai and Bengaluru in 2023 and 2024 respectively. Juneja is the driving force behind the show, and it should be no surprise that it is the language of Ayurveda that is helping him and other physicians navigate past the taboos associated with the plant, offering a path of least resistance, setting a peaceful sangam between the hemp plant and the hemp industry.

In the US, political lobbying has often played a larger role than medical research to quicken the process of decriminalization and legalization. There is potential for the same to happen in India, where politics is often belly wrapped under a cover of Ayurveda. The expo in Delhi is inaugurated by an elected Rajya Sabha Member of Parliament—Anil Agarwal of the BJP—adding a surreal feel of legitimacy to an industry that often finds itself skipping across the boundary lines of legality. Several more representatives of India's ruling national party show up as guests of honour over the next two days. The organizers hold a number of technical sessions, including lectures on the uses of industrial hemp, and discussions on the cultivation, manufacturing, extraction, and legal aspects of cannabis. At the end of the two-day event, awards are given out for categories like 'Hemp Company of the Year' and 'Entrepreneur of the Year'. As I walk through the halls of this fair, it feels a little odd to hear delegates speaking about cannabis without fear: not just in its low-THC or hemp forms, but as weed smoked for the purpose of pure bliss. There seems to be a happy understanding between the worlds of recreational marijuana and industrial hemp.

I catch an infectious whiff of that positive energy in Khagesh Gautam*, author of *Cannabis Indica.* Dressed in a sharp, grey suit, Gautam—who is in his early forties—greets me with an effusive smile when I tell him about my project. We sit in a sunlit lobby behind the main expo floor, where he casually drops a few F-bombs in reference to the cobweb of Indian narcotic legalities, and offers the best weed recommendations in the United States ('Go to Colorado,' he suggests).

It was Gautam's time abroad that shaded some of his own perception towards the plant: after briefly practising in both the Supreme Court and the Chandigarh High Court, Gautam attended the Colombia Law School in New York City, where he graduated as a Stone Scholar. He has taught in Beijing and in Hawaii. Now, as an associate law professor at a private university in Sonipat, Haryana, one of the courses he teaches is entitled 'Cannabis Decriminalization in India', which encourages students to question what he considers the 'illiberal acts' of the NDPS.

Gautam lists the three main arguments in his book, which speak for the *potential* of cannabis, rather than its *perception* in India:

'One,' he says. 'From a legal perspective, we could decriminalize small quantities of possession—say around 2 ounces, about 50 grams—so that people aren't put in jail unnecessarily. This will also take care of the issue of policemen who arrest people in bullshit cases. We don't want to create bad cops.

'Two: from the public policy perspective, we want to go for full legalization.

'And three: The Parliament's claim to criminalize cannabis is doubtful.' Gautam espouses on this idea further in his text, arguing that the original NDPS Act which criminalized cannabis in 1985 was based on ignorance about the plant, as well as misinformation that clubbed it together with opium.

---

*Who has already been quoted in this book multiple times.

'Weed is *already* widely available in India,' Gautam says. 'Legalizing it won't change much in that. It will just help tax and quality control it.' He suggests that there should be a union law ministry to 'aid and advice' the governor or president about the post-decriminalization scenario. Decriminalization, he writes, 'is the penance that we as a nation, through our state, will need to do, for unjustly incarcerating thousands of our own citizens, pre and post-conviction, for trading in a healing herb that has been a part of our culture, tradition, and even ancient medicine.' Specifically, Gautam feels that the ministry's work should include cataloguing prisoners convicted in the NDPS Act for small offences, and in drafting a model legislation to legally regulate the cannabis industry. The revenue generated from decriminalization (and eventual legalization), he argues, should be 'sufficient to offset the expenses of running this ministry'.

For Gautam, full legalization of the substance is the only rational eventuality.

'But,' I ask him, 'If it makes so much sense...why is it still illegal?'

'My hypothesis is ignorance,' he says. 'We don't know our own culture.'

Flanked by the scaffolding of industrial demand and scientific research, this culture is present all around me at the Hemp Expo. But I know that this is only a protected bubble, enclosed under a cloud of joyful smoke, in a nation that is often as magnetically repelled to the same plant that attracts it. Many start-ups and corporations in the industry continue to be concerned with this malaise of ignorance. The 'notorious' reputation of cannabis precedes itself: the stereotyped images of stoners wasting away their days, the sight of holy men unconcerned with hygiene, intemperate young people partying in a state of debauchery, the fear-mongering of 'reefer madness' that leads weed users down an uncontrollable spiral of drug addiction. Dismantling this reputation will be the crucial first step before the endgame, like a careful crumbling and cleaning of the maal before it is truly ready to be rolled into a succulent, fat joint.

On the video call, Yash Kotak sits in the conference room of his office in front of a large canvas print. The print is an image of colourful space nebulae, and between it all, the universal symbol for ganja:* a leaf with seven well-separated leaflets, standing in perfect symmetry, radiant from the halo of a bright star behind it.

It's almost cosmic.

Kotak is in his thirties, with neatly combed hair, a clean, trimmed beard across his svelte cheeks, and wearing a dark blue shepherd's check shirt. He's the chief marketing officer of BOHECO, a company he cofounded in 2013 with six other young men, who all met while studying at the H. R. College of Commerce and Economics in Mumbai in the late 2000s. At the time, the seven young men had institutionalized a rural solar electrification project, a project that took them on long road trips to small villages across the country. 'We realized that almost everything changed every hundred kilometres,' Kotak says. 'Language, culture, people, food. But one thing that was constant was cannabis. It was growing wildly. Legend has it that wherever the river Ganga flows, you will always find cannabis on its banks. We just kept on seeing it.'

With BOHECO, Kotak and co envisioned a company that could be a culvert for the flowing river of ganja, carrying it across to new destinations. One of the moments Kotak vividly recalls during his trips was when the group stopped for a meal at a small dhaba in Uttarakhand. On the menu, besides the usual dal-roti-sabzi options, they discovered a special bhang-inspired list of items: Bhang chutney, bhang pakora, or the regular food salted with bhang. At first, Kotak

*As always, this symbol reminds of the adidas 'Trefoil' logo. Or the cover of Dr. Dre's *2001*.

thought that these dishes were infused with high-THC cannabis, as if they were intoxicating bhang edibles (none of the original co-founders were 'passionate stoners' at this time, he says). But Kotak soon realized that this 'bhang' came from the (non-psychoactive) hemp seeds used to prepare the food. The method of preparation, Kotak discovered, had been passed on for generations as a cultural delicacy in these parts.

'We were glad to see the promise of cannabis,' says Kotak. 'But we saw that it was mainly being used for subsistence purposes: for ropes to tie cattle, for juttis (traditional footwear), jackets... Not from a commercial point of view.'

At this time, there was no blueprint for industrial hemp in India. Kotak and his co-founders knew that they would have to speak to tons of people to align the entire ecosystem: including research scientists, farmers, policymakers, industry partners, and consumers. Unlike the cannabis plant, the business of legal hemp wouldn't merely cultivate itself: it would be a gradual, mammoth, uphill climb.

'We said to each other: "Guys, we're not here looking to start a new company. We're looking at starting a whole new industry."'

In the decade that has passed since BOHECO's inception, the company—and the industry—has taken several important strides ahead. In 2017, with a focus on studying the medical benefits of cannabis, BOHECO raised a seed round of ₹6.25 crore from high-profile investors that included Ratan Tata (chairman emeritus of Tata Sons) and Rajan Anandan (then Google India's marketing director). Apart from their partnership with CSIR–NBRI for medical research in Lucknow, BOHECO has opened cannabis health and wellness stores in Bengaluru and Delhi. Some of their most popular CBD products have included items for arthritis and joint pain. BOHECO has also launched several associated brands that incorporate hemp products, including hemp seed, oil, clothing, fabrics, textiles, and beauty/wellness products such as shampoos, soaps, body oils, and pet care.

I saw one of BOHECO's pop-up stalls for their brand B Label at a festival in Mumbai, which was attracting attention with a sign-twirler outside holding up the message, 'Bhang Ke Kapde' in the Devanagari script. *Bhang Clothes*. These kapde included kurtas like the one Satpathy had worn to Parliament. In many instances, hemp-made clothes can be the perfect substitute for cotton. The water footprint (WF) of industrial hemp is less than a third of cotton, and a hemp T-shirt can save hundreds of litres of water compared to one made of cotton. The future is bright: some reports suggest that the 'bhang ke kapde' market is estimated to grow at a compound annual rate of 27.1 per cent in the coming decade—almost ten times that of cotton.

Many other start-ups around the country have found a relatively safe space by introducing Ayurveda in a blend with medicinal cannabis. Some have launched wellness centres in Bhubaneswar, Bengaluru, and Mumbai that sell cannabis-based tablets and oils prescribed by Ayurvedic vaidyas. In Chennai's Chetpet locality, a company opened what they refer to as 'India's first integrative healing clinic' which combines 'functional medicine, Ayurveda, acupuncture, and medical cannabis'. Their patients come looking for treatments for arthritis, diabetes, nausea, and aches. Some bring their terminally ill pets to help ease the painful last years of their lives.

Industry insiders are predicting that many more such wellness centres which use legal cannabis-based products will open their shutters over the next few years. Over a hundred companies investing in hemp or its by-products were launched in India by the early 2020s. Wellness start-ups featuring cannabis-based products have begun to appear in mainstream television shows like *Shark Tank India*, where representatives have attempted their best to dispel the negative stereotypes associated with the substance, and convince investors of the plant's immense economic potential. In a special televised report, CNBC-TV18 projected that there could be 500 companies working in industries related to hemp in India by 2027.

Patanjali Ayurved—a private, multinational conglomerate founded by the godbusinessmen Acharya Balkrishna and Baba Ramdev—has been one of the most aggressive advocates for the cannabis economy. Manufacturers of Ayurvedic medicine, cosmetics, personal care, food products, and more, Patanjali has been valued at around ₹40,000 crores. Ramdev's elaborate performance as a spiritual leader has helped with the company's rapid growth.

In a 2018 interview, Balkrishna, the company's CEO, said that Patanjali is 'looking at various formulations' for the medical purposes of cannabis. 'We should ponder over the benefits and positive uses of the cannabis plant.' Balkrishna said. 'By criminalizing marijuana, we are denying a full-fledged business opportunity to our people.'*

Another major step for the industry was taken in November 2021, when the Food Safety and Standards Authority of India (FSSAI)—a government statutory body established under the Ministry of Health and Family Welfare—announced revolutionary new regulations for hemp as a food source, stating 'The hemp seed, hemp seed oil and hemp seed flour shall be sold as food or used as an ingredient in a food for sale subject to conforming standards.' Hemp seeds are said to be high in protein, enriched with essential amino-acids that are not naturally produced by our bodies.

Not long after this decision, hemp-based restaurants began to pop-up around the country, including a café in Pune that offers 'bhang sandwich, hemp smoothies, and hemp biscuits'. BOHECO opened a hemp cloud kitchen in Mumbai, with burgers, pizzas, pastas, etc., infused with hemp oil, seeds, and flour.

No, eating this food will *not* get you high.

The scenes that Kotak and his co-founders had experienced at that dhaba in Uttarakhand are now being recreated, with a legal

*Patanjali has been mired in a whirlpool of controversies, from violations of the Land Reform Act, accusations of sketchy research, and poor product quality. In February 2024, nearly four months after the Supreme Court directed Patanjali to withdraw 'misleading' ads, it imposed a temporary ban on the company's advertisements.

stamp of approval (and a considerably more upmarket menu) at their own establishment. It's as if India's lawmakers are playing catch up with our own learned cultural knowledge and traditions. With the FSSAI's new regulations, some have predicted that hemp could become the country's new 'superfood'.

Even with all this progress being made, Kotak admits that his organization—along with many others in this space—are facing concerns with the 'perception battle', i.e., the 'ignorance' that Gautam had alluded to about the potential of cannabis in India.

'Everyone has that myopic view attached to it, that it's a "drug",' says Kotak. 'In our mission, the first thing is to educate—because for people to learn about something, they have to unlearn, and relearn. Learn what [cannabis] is. Learn what it's not. And this education has to be bespoke: what appeals to the consumer is very different from what appeals to a doctor, a policymaker, or a scientist. For example, when it comes to a new batch of bureaucrats that are looking to work in the narcotics department, we want to educate them about this other side of cannabis, too. We want to help the enforcers see everything; but right now, these enforcers are walking with blinders on. They read the word "cannabis", and they react to it.'

Kotak believes that it wouldn't be prudent to take the global concept of industrial hemp and apply it to India. 'It's not a plug-and-play thing. You have to contextualize it for our country, to our ecosystem, to our people. We are on this constant education and awareness drive. Cannabis has been a huge part of Indian culture. The plant is older than some religions, it's older than democracy as a concept. It has seen everything. Hemp *entered* the West; it was not a native crop. But its origins are here. So, we knew that a certain approach where we blindly copied and pasted whatever Canada or other countries were doing won't work.'

A blind 'copy-paste' wouldn't be compatible anyways, due to India's strict restrictions, including the requirement that allows cultivation of only low-THC (<0.3 per cent) plants. For now, as scientists still pour in their efforts to develop the low-THC seed, BOHECO and others have to settle for the 'collection model' for their raw material (the bhang plant) rather than a cultivation model. Much of the bhang distributed is unrefined, filled with seeds, sticks, and other forms of dirt, and sorting it can be an expensive process. The cannabis collected is mostly the plant that grows wild, or has been captured and confiscated from smugglers, which the Excise Department then sells in bulk to hemp corporations.

'The *entire* industry,' Kotak says, 'is based on a collection model, and not a cultivation model.' This includes the legal CBD in anxiety medicine, the seeds in a hemp-burger, or the bhang thandai available at shops in Jaisalmer and Varanasi. 'The same bhang that the local shops use to make thandai, we use to make dawai (medicine).'

Under the regulation of the Ministry of Ayush, the raw material is sold and distributed in the form that it is found, with no recognition or segregation based on THC, CBD, etc. It comes as Ayurveda would recognize it: as simply, *vijaya.*

BOHECO pays an annual fee to renew their collection licence, and pay for the raw material for every batch. The average cost in the early 2020s was about ₹400 to ₹500 for 1 kilo of cannabis leaves, about the price of a paperback. (A kilo of good quality ganja would likely cost a thousand times that amount on the street in the metros.) The government has collection programmes across the country from different states, and the collected cannabis is put together in a central warehouse. 'Which leads to batch-to-batch variation, quality issues, and whatnot,' says Kotak. 'Also, when you get bags from the government, there is so much kachra (dirt) in it, which we have to filter and clean out.

'It's extremely tough to have a consistency. In my last season, for instance, we got a large high-THC batch, so most of our products then will have high-THC, because we use full spectrum extracts. There's no batch report or buyer's report. Whatever you get, you work with it. You can't go and say, "Mere ko high-THC nahi chahiye, exchange kar ke do" (I don't want high-THC, please exchange it). That doesn't work.'

Kotak also adds that there is no transparency in the supply chain. 'There is no industry report. You're working with a lot of known unknowns, and unknown unknowns. It's an unorganized industry. [During] the year there is the Kumbh Mela happening, there is a massive shortage of supply—and the price goes up.'

BOHECO's eventual pursuit is to get into the space of organized cultivation, which is why they have been investing in seed breeding and other aspects of agriculture. In the last cultivation cycle in 2022, BOHECO were able to cultivate cannabis with less than 0.3 per cent THC on a small plot in Bageshwar, Uttarakhand. This was a major milestone for industrial hemp in India—and Kotak says that BOHECO plan to extend the cultivation area for the next cycle.

These are positive steps. For now, the lack of large-scale, organized cultivation remains the big gap in India's aspirations as a hemp producing (and exporting) nation.

Currently, the miniscule market share of hemp that India legally produces is hardly planned growth; instead, it's amassed from vast swathes of ganja that grows naturally—if it isn't destroyed in extravagant bonfires by overzealous police authorities.

The whole approach is a tragic waste of potential, a swift, daily atrophy of the profits that could be made with planned cultivation. I believe that the country has the potential to be among the world leaders in this industry. Uttarakhand alone has more natural hemp than all of Canada.

'We're ten to twelve years late compared to the rest of the world,' says Kotak. 'They're using *our* plant to create jobs, to develop opportunities, for *their* own people. And we're still playing this catching-up game, doubting the credibility of the plant. (Cannabis) really has a lot to offer. And I'm not saying it—the science is saying it!'

Kotak stresses that change will come when India's government and lawmakers stop looking at cannabis as a problem, and instead, as a solution.

'Now, our entire resolve is transitioning the image of cannabis from dope to hope. It does not have to take a Sushant Singh Rajput or an Aryan Khan to take a substance, for people to take a more serious look at it. There is so much under the garb, even for recreational users. What are they consuming? People have no idea! It is all ditch weed, adulterated materials, and people don't know the difference. There is a report [by Prohibition Partners] that showcases that there are 38 million active users in this country. In my view, that number is *a lot* more.'

'It's already touted to be a trillion-dollar super crop,' Kotak adds. 'It's an Indian plant, and it has all the credibility and science attached to it. I'm not sure what we're waiting for.'

On a pleasant, December day in Bengaluru, about a dozen young men and women gathered at the city's Freedom Park for the first-ever march of the Great Legalisation Movement India (GLM India). They carried posters that had wide a spectrum of messages written on them, including 'Fight Cancer with Cannabis', 'If Nature is Illegal, Freedom Doesn't Exist', and 'Make India Great Again'*. The march was an accumulation of several years of grassroots awareness work that had already been set in motion by GLM, which included medical cannabis conferences around the country and a growing social media presence.

GLM India was launched as a non-profit organization in 2014 to advocate for the legalization of cannabis. A native of Bengaluru, the organization's founder Viki Vaurora was only twenty-two when the first seeds of GLM India were sowed. Donning a full beard and dreadlocks, Vaurora entered the world of activism with the full

*Forever cringe-worthy.

bombast of youth: he helped organize major conferences around the country, led marches and youth movements, produced a web series to help increase awareness about cannabis, sent petitions to various branches of the government, and claimed to have found medicinal marijuana treatments for terminal conditions. A 2015 GLM conference featured Rick Simpson, the Canadian engineer and cannabis advocate who developed the Rick Simpson Oil (RSO), a cannabis extract that he claimed could be used as a treatment for cancer. (Simpson has alleged that he treated his own skin cancer with RSO in the mid-2000s.)

From the time I began to research the recent history of pro-legalization activism in India, Vaurora was one of my obvious first targets. But, despite multiple efforts, he declined my requests for an interview, or suspended the plans indefinitely. Even when we made plans to meet in Delhi, there were no specifics. Nothing materialized in the low-resolution hope for the future. Uncertainty principal in full effect: I could know of this energy and his momentum, but never glean his exact location in space-time. In a WhatsApp conversation, a representative claiming to be from Vaourora Foundation told me that Viki has gone 'into complete silence, and he chose to be undisturbed'*.

With Vaurora's absence hanging like a spectre, I continued to discover more about the work conducted by him and his foundation. Among its missions, GLM hope to 're-legalize' cannabis in India, hope to protect Indian ecology, revive this crucial component in our ancient system of health care, and, most ambitiously, 'eradicate human suffering, unemployment, poverty and diseases'.

In 2017, Vaurora wrote an open letter to the prime minister and members of the parliament urging them to legalize cannabis/hemp for medicinal and large-scale industrial use. Furthermore, a petition by GLM India challenging the prohibition and criminalization of

*Vaurora emerged from this silence in 2024 when he announced a GLM tour under the title 'Cannabis Legalisation So far and What Next for India', to be held almost like the year's Lok Sabha election cycle, over a two-month period (February to April) across nearly a dozen cities in the country.

cannabis in India reached the Delhi High Court in 2019.

I find Vaurora in remnants of his past, in the many YouTube videos he has uploaded in recent years. In one of them entitled, 'Liberate2020 (01) – Reality of the World by Viki Vaurora', he sits in a dark room, dimly lit by the glow of the computer screen where he is recording. As he talks, the video shows stock images of environmental degradation, with quick flashes of the cannabis symbol, as if to hypnotize me with the mystique of this great, ancient plant. Vaurora's dreadlocks are tied up in a bun, his delivery is sombre and intense. 'It's a strange situation on planet Earth where we humans have removed our only solution to our poisoned health, our toxic industries, and our chained consciousness,' he says. 'All of this can be solved from one plant.*'

One of Vaurora's most intriguing arguments is that he considers it a human right to perform the act of 'alleviating one's consciousness through cannabis'. Denying cannabis, he argues, is like denying the 'sampradaya' (which means tradition or sect in the Vedic convention) that is associated with ancient Hinduism.

Without offering adequate proof in his video, Vaurora declares a long list of ailments that cannabis can allegedly cure: cancers, HIV/AIDS, tuberculosis, cardiovascular diseases, mental disorders, metabolic disorders, immuno-stimulation, rejuvenation of all the vital parts of the body, anti-ageing. He criticizes the modern health care systems and Big Pharma, which he claims have replaced our natural health solutions. He profusely quotes the late American cannabis rights activist Jack Herer, the author of the popular text, *The Emperor Wears No Clothes*. He argues that cannabis has played a crucial role in the lives of creative minds: of artists, musicians, and performers. And writers, too.

In a TEDx talk in Bengaluru in 2015, Vaurora claimed that he made a version of Rick Simpson's cannabis oil extract in India, and

*No awards for guessing which plant.

administered it to a woman who had been on her deathbed with an advanced stage of stomach cancer. He claimed that the woman was 'cancer free' within three months.

Cancer free?

I don't believe it.

There comes that itch again, that little discomfort I inevitably feel every time a discussion about cannabis ventures into the shakier grounds outside the borders of science. It's the same itch that crawls across my skin when I hear of 'miracle' cures. When other proponents of cannabis use the crutches of mysticism, religion, and ancient texts to support their theories, when I'm told that the plant is a 'victor' because Shiva loved it, or because it was uttered by some scholars a few thousand years ago. Cannabis in India often hides behind the disguise of Ayurveda, which is often a disguise for religion, which is often a disguise for nationalism. I'm reminded of the members of Satjal rejecting vaccines, of unproven cancer treatment oils, of healing through quantum energies, conspiracy, paranoia, prosecutions, scandals.

In matters of health and wellness, it has been nearly impossible to avoid the murmurs of competition between the Indian and the foreign way. Between Ayurveda and 'allopathy'. Between thousands of years of our cultural and scholarly knowledge against the 'Western' perspective, one that often lacks the language to translate our homegrown ways of surviving. And thriving.

Any debate about cannabis and its links to Indian history often walks a tightrope. Casting any doubt upon our country's indigenous systems of knowledge and healthcare could earn one accusations of pandering to foreign cultures, of suffering from a colonial hangover. It can be interpreted as disrespect of our native religions, of the tiranga flag itself. But, like an adulterated tola of charas, the knowledge I seek has come tainted from a variety of agendas: industrial, spiritual, political, personal, economic. Can you blame me for being a little bit cynical?

Personally, I've found my solace in the reliability of proven science: in the scientific method of systematic observation, research, hypothesis, tests, analysis, leading to the next cycle of counter hypotheses and syntheses, over and over. Humans are a young species, perhaps still ignorant of most of the truths of our existence. Once, we used mechanical orreries to model the solar system; now we use super telescopes to paint the clearest pictures of the early universe. We don't have a completed path to those universal truths, but science—in its meticulous close examination of every hypothesis—challenges us to accept nothing lesser than the objective brutality of cold, hard facts.

And yet, one may reasonably wonder: even if the science isn't subjective, the people behind it might be. Practitioners of alternate healthcare systems have questioned if evidence-based medicine or oncological treatments are the conclusive answer. The numbers can't lie, but maybe, the approach does? From an even more conspiratorial perspective, how does one trust all the scientific research, if the big, bad world of Big Pharma and other competing industries of legal psychoactive substances (alcohol, tobacco, etc.) are colluding to suppress the mainstream resurrection of cannabis, afraid that its industrial and medical benefits may present a cheaper, better, and more readily-available solution to so many of our quandaries on Earth: mental, physical, economic, environmental. Why pop a paracetamol when you can try CBD? Why suffer the pain of chemotherapy without cannabis oil?

It's certainly something to ponder.

So, I continue to ponder. Is there truth to the claims of cannabis as a 'miracle' drug? Or is it a mere placebo: subtracting pain, adding joy, offering hope? Are the substance's medical boons limited to palliative care? Or can it help treat our maladies—including cancer, one of the most ruthless serial killers that humanity has ever known?

Can it make life less painful? Can it make it last longer?

Amrit

'... What to do now, with all the life that's still left to be lived...?'

Amit Vaidya was twenty-seven, working in New York City, when he fell sick. A loss of appetite, trouble swallowing food, and a constant feeling of tiredness, as if he could barely bear the weight of the day.

A diagnosis revealed gastric adenocarcinoma. Stomach cancer.

He was given six months to live.

This was around the year 2006. I speak to him in December 2022. Six months became sixteen years, and a twenty-something young man recently lived to see his forties.

Born to Indian immigrants in the United States, Vaidya (not an Ayurvedic vaidya—the surname in Sanskrit translates to 'scholar' or 'physician') was suddenly facing the end of days after his diagnosis. The nausea got worse. He took all the traditional treatment paths, but his condition hardly improved. The forecast looked grim.

Vaidya turned to a doctor for Chinese acupuncture, who, along with Chinese herbs, recommended him to try some cannabis for the pain. 'I thought this was strange,' Vaidya says. 'I had never smoked in my life, and I rarely drank, just on social occasions.' Growing up with mild asthma, he wasn't comfortable smoking marijuana, but he was happy to try it in edible form, which helped Vaidya regain some of his appetite, too.

'Hey! I felt hungry again,' he recalls. 'I wanted to eat!'

Vaidya explains that everything used to taste 'like sawdust', a side-effect of the chemotherapy which heightens the toxicity in the system. In chemo, powerful drugs are used to kill the fast-growing cancerous cells in the body. The side effects of this strong chemical treatment could be nausea, fatigue, fever, a loss of appetite, and a bitter, metallic tang on the tongue. 'There are some things that I can still no longer eat, since the past fifteen years—the taste has forever been ruined for me.' At the time of his chemo, Vaidya's taste buds only accepted sugary, sweet items. So, brownies or cookies laced with cannabis proved to be a winning ingredient.

Cannabis is also known to be helpful for nausea and dealing with what some cancer patients refer to as 'chemo brain', a side effect of the chemotherapy that could lead to sleep problems, headaches, or that dense feeling of 'brain fog'. Surveys have revealed that anywhere between 25 to 40 per cent of all cancer patients in the US are using cannabis for additional relief. However, medical cannabis in all forms can be expensive, and is not covered by most health insurance providers.

Long before medicinal marijuana was allowed in New York, Vaidya had friends who were able to score some for him. 'My friends would say, "Oh my god, Amit, we're finally gonna get you stoned! We're even willing to partake in this with you. We got you, man!" There was this camaraderie to it that I had only witnessed from afar before: whether it was my high school friends who would go out and smoke cigarettes, or my college friends who would go to a party and get drunk. I was always within their sphere, and we had a connection, but I could never really engage in *that* part... So, there was a joy in not being judged, by partaking in it with others. Everyone else is letting their guard down at the same time you are.'

The comfort of cannabis and camaraderie, however, was a mere distraction, an occasional ray of sunlight under a torrential thunderstorm. Adenocarcinoma is the most common type of stomach cancer. Its exact cause isn't yet known, but risk factors could include a long-term H. pylori infection, weight issues, inherited cancerous conditions, or excess consumption of processed meat, alcohol, or tobacco. The cancer starts in the glands that line the inside of the organs, and then spreads rapidly, harming healthy tissues. It's a fierce inside job betraying the body. The cancer becomes metastatic, stomach to liver to lungs, a raging internal forest fire, now causing new malignant growths away from its primary site.

Then, to compound Vaidya's seesaw of health between recovery and remission, his mother was diagnosed with grade three brain tumour. He had already lost his father at a young age.

'At that point, I was starting to question the legitimacy and illegitimacy of everything that I was doing,' Vaidya says, 'from the food I was eating, the medication that I was taking, to the lifestyle that I had.'

His mother passed away. Alone and sick, Vaidya felt that he had entered what would be his 'last chapter'. His health deteriorated rapidly; he had no other immediate family in the United States.

This was when Vaidya decided to come to the nation that his parents had once left behind: India. He tells me that this was his own version of *Swades*, a man's return to the homeland in the face of tragedy, in reference to the 2004 Shah Rukh Khan film. Vaidya had given up on curative treatments to focus only on the palliative, hoping to face the inevitable abyss as comfortably as he possibly could. 'I thought I was going to die. Both my parents passed away in the US despite being from India. I had this romanticized, Bollywood notion that I will come to India and die.

'It was very poetic.'

This vision of a 'poetic' death would bring Vaidya to Gujarat for the first time, the region where many of his family traced their roots. Here, following the advice of an aunt, Vaidya ended up at an Ayurvedic hospital in Valsad, to take a shot at the Panchagavya treatment plan which uses a mixture of cow dung, urine, milk, curd, and ghee.

This is a moment, Dear Reader, for us to again break down this pesky fourth wall that separates us. Before you hear the rest of the story, do heed a word of caution. There is no peer-reviewed or scientifically-confirmed basis for cow therapy. Despite rare examples, there is simply not enough sufficient proof that gobar is a treatment for cancer. I may swish a miraculous, full-court basketball shot one time, but that doesn't exactly make me Steph Curry.*

Vaidya, however, *did* hit that rarefied, full-court, miracle shot. After some time at this hospital, he moved to live in a gaushala in Karnataka for two years. Cow therapy was coupled with a drastic change of diet and lifestyle. And the cancer subsided, to a point of recovery. To life—all over again.

Vaidya wrote about his journey in the 2015 memoir *Holy Cancer: How a Cow Saved My Life.* Since then, he has spent much of his time around India, living and working in Mumbai, Delhi, Hyderabad, or heading to the peaceful environs at a small island off the coast of Kochi in Kerala. His memoir and survival story led him to health advocacy and an NGO to help guide others down their path to wellness.

He had survived.

But survival is one thing. What to do now, with all the life that's still left to be lived? 'Oh shit,' he says, 'I had spent my years planning to die. And now I realize, oh god, I may have more time now! I no longer knew who I was, where I come from, what I believe in. Everything had changed. And that's when the anxiety comes in, when, all of a sudden, you have to start from square one again. You have to make a lot of tough decisions on your own.

'I had spent two or three years literally thinking that I was gonna die, living a day-to-day life, and I remembered how my attitude in those days actually gave me a second life. So, I know about the power of positive thinking. And I know about the flip side of it as well.'

Living in Delhi, the lifestyle began to take a toll on his physical health. There was a new pain now, and a form of neuropathy which

*I know my basketball-loving brethren were waiting for a shoutout.

made it difficult for him to sometimes complete simple tasks like picking up a glass of water. There was pain in his back, his arms, and severe migraines. (In a vast survey of cancer survivors in the United States, over one-third reported suffering from chronic pain.) 'Anytime there is a stomach ache, or a cough or a fever, or Covid happens, you're immunocompromised. You have fifteen other things that make you more susceptible to anything. So, a stomach ache isn't just a stomach ache. A blood number comes back, and I'm told, "This number is higher, or your white blood cell count is low." So, I can't rule out this could be a reoccurrence, this could be lymphoma.' To Vaidya, every new discomfort felt like a red flag, a warning sign that the cancer had returned. Even when death wasn't lurking around the corner, it continued to haunt him, fogging his mind with its heavy vapours.

Vaidya turned to cannabis in the face of the physical stresses of this 'second life' and the anxieties for his new future. He had moved away from all modern treatments altogether. Instead of painkilling OTC pills, he would try CBD or cannabis oil.

He began to find joy in consuming food again. *Pet puja.* There is some greater good in the 'munchies' associated with a weed high: studies have found that cannabis can help cancer patients regain their appetites and sense of taste. Vaidya's solution for the nausea he felt around his favourite dishes was to return to the pain-killing of nature's homegrown solutions. 'I had access to good pot,' he says. 'When I was in Kerala, I was already making all my own food in my garden, which was like medicine for me. Why can't I incorporate [cannabis] as a proactive measure? The only way I can consume pav bhaji now, is if I have it with cannabis-infused butter!' More savoury dishes followed to satiate his appetite. He began to incorporate hemp products into his life in a variety of ways: hemp seed oils, hemp teas, hemp T-shirts, and hemp trousers.

With time came perspective, and Vaidya was able to realize that the physical stress of his fight with cancer had forced him into a sense of self-delusion, where he had ignored much of his mental anxiety, while the biology of his body screamed out louder for help.

'I think, at the time... I didn't see the level to which my mental health was being affected,' Vaidya says. 'I had blinders on for a number of years as a patient. Whatever I'm physically going through, I decided that my mind has to be sharp and focused. And only with time, as the physical pain reduced, I was able to then have the clarity to realize, "Oh shit! I've been going through a lot of stuff mentally as well." Cannabis... alleviated much of my physical pain, and then it calmed my mind down enough to assess what was going on with my mental health.'

'I believe in cannabis' power. I believe in its ability. I believe in its curative elements. But I don't believe it to be *the* cure. Saying that is as much of a sham as anyone telling me that the chemo drug is a cure.' Similarly, cow therapy wasn't a 'cure' for Vaidya, either, but what he would call a 'positive curative element'.

Vaidya stresses that there is no single such answer to the hundreds of different ways in which a person could be suffering. 'We need to give people options, instead of making [cannabis] the end all. You have to talk about these things proactively, preventively. Especially in a country where preventative medication—and even the conversation of preventive health—is so minimal. It's important to have dialogue... You don't just wanna be talking about it when shit hits the fan.

'From my doctors in New York, I'm literally the only person with Stage 1 gastric adenocarcinoma that they know that's still alive from 2007. From the hospital that I was in Gujarat, I'm the only patient that they know has survived since I was there in 2012. Everyone has a different path. Everyone has a different journey. Everyone has a different cancer.'

Vaidya, like many other cancer survivors, refuses to believe that his journey with the disease is over. Even when feeling copacetic, he still lives scan to scan. A month after we speak, he returns for another pet scan. He will undergo these scans every three months; then, once every six months; and then, once a year; each test follows an agonizing wait, a nervous click on an attachment, a concerning follow-up call.

'I've never in my journey used the words "cancer free",' Vaidya says. 'I will say, "I do not have active cancer in my body." But if I say I was "cured", then I would stop caring for my health.'

Health specialists will consider a patient to be in complete remission if all signs and symptoms of cancer disappear. Some doctors may consider a patient 'cured' if the patient remains in complete remission for over five years. Yet, it's possible for some cancer cells to remain in one's body, even many years after their treatment.

'I have yet to meet a person who has been "cured" of cancer from strictly cannabis,' Vaidya adds. 'But then again, I've yet to meet anyone who has been "cured" of cancer from *anything*, including any drug, or any medication. Science has made great strides... But technically, it's still cancer. [Science] is now making cancer a disease that you would die of, into a disease that you live with.'

Since his recovery, Vaidya has spent his years forging close connections with other cancer patients in India and learning about their respective journeys. He has encountered patients and caregivers who were able to procure high-THC cannabis oil, and he has observed how the treatment benefitted some of them.

'I'm not someone who took high doses of cannabis oil on a regular basis for pain management,' he says. 'But I know a number of patients who have. I know from the patient's perspective, and I know it from the caregiver's perspective, that when you're looking for solutions, [cannabis] is a much better place to start with, rather than to end at.' In India, he says, the vast amount of people who explored medicinal cannabis do so much later in their treatment process.

'Now... if I wanna take [cannabis] because I wanna have joy

in my life, if I wanna have it because I'm depressed, if I wanna have it because I have cancer, if I wanna have it for whatever the fuck I want it for... It's so easy to grow yourself, and it's so easy to cultivate. There's absolutely zero reason or logic in my head for it to be considered a controlled substance. Not anywhere in the world, but especially, *especially* in India, where there is such a core belief in the power of plant-based medicine. Medical cannabis should be legal, legal, legal! It should also be administered in hospitals. It should also be reintegrated into Ayurvedic medicine. And as far as recreational use: there's no reason for that to also be controlled.'

Now that Vaidya has his feet firmly planted across the continents—in both the pardes and the swades—he compares the cultural osmosis of cannabis to that of yoga. An inherently Indian discipline, yoga was exported and capitalized by Western economies, before it was reclaimed by India in a mainstream way. The same fate could lie ahead for our homegrown ganja: it has already made strides abroad; now, the hope is that its impact will boomerang to spread the seeds of acceptance back in India.

In an ideal world, ganja would be one of India's great legal exports. It's a lucrative raw material, of course; but it can also be a marker of our cultural soft power, like yoga*, Bollywood, and butter chicken. The cannabis plant and our millennia-old cultural practices with bhang/ganja are tied directly to the exploration of meditation, spirituality, and that Nirvanic, mind-altering bliss. It's a truly 'Made in India' innovation, and has been so for thousands of years.

And yet, we're stuck in conflicting minds, further slowed by the faulty engineering of our slow bureaucracy. It was India's desire to appease the West that turned this indigenous, cultural touchstone into a taboo and a crime. And now, as scientific research from the West self-corrects its biases and eases its laws, India is failing to catch

*In recent years, a new trend of 'Ganja Yoga' has also begun in the West, which is exactly what it sounds like: getting a little high, practising a little pranayama.

up, more comfortable in the conservative safety of prohibitions, instead of plunging ahead towards revolutionary change.

'We have to look back to look forward,' Vaidya says. 'I think the joy of cannabis is that it's reconnecting us to Mother Earth. I always look at it as simple as that. The more natural the source is, the more I'm in control of my destiny.'

I agree with Vaidya's instinct to favour the gifts of nature, in forming a symbiotic relationship with the plants that have evolved alongside our species on this planet. The quick pace of human progress has untethered us from nature, and to each other, too. This progress is only further dividing us, making us think we're better than everyone else, better than nature itself.

Yet, I remain sceptical of the assumption that all of us can *truly* make the responsible decision regarding our personal destinies. Doctors spend years gaining expertise and experience in their particular fields of medicine, just like any specialists in any profession: singers and their vocal cords, I.T. professionals and their coding languages, bankers and interests rates, writers and our words. We trust the experts with their life's work, just like we expect them to trust us with ours.

In India, as a rising number of patients are looking to procure high-THC cannabis oils, one must be wary of the lack of standardizations, censure, or even recognition of these substances. Without quality control and peer review, the medicines could have unpredictable results: maybe that mysterious 'oil' heals you, or harms you, or is a mere dud, firing blanks into your system.

'Personally, I have only ever consumed cannabis at levels where it didn't cloud my judgement to a level that I was impaired,' says Vaidya. 'But a lot of patients who I've worked with, who have been exclusively on cannabis oil, are compromised mentally as a result, in terms of day-to-day cognitive abilities. For someone who is working and supporting a family, it's a very hard choice to make. Who is going to pick up that slack? It can impair your cognitive functions.

There is nothing wrong with that—it's only temporary. But at the same time, are you willing to go through that?'

Vaidya tells me about a friend of his, whose fifteen-year-old daughter was put through the rigour of cancer and its associated treatments. With little relief from other options, the friend turned to cannabis-based treatment for his child.

I've been on video call for Vaidya for almost an hour at this point, listening to him as he shares the complicated intricacies of his life, a life thoroughly haunted by death. Despite this, however, his voice had remained stable, as if he'd clearly practised each thought, recited each twist and turn of his journey. However, now as he speaks about his friend's daughter, it's the first time that I hear Vaidya stumble over his words. His voice is suddenly weightless. 'There were improvements. And then, there was a complication. And then, she passed away, at the age of sixteen.'

I gulp.

'Like, you know...' says Vaidya. '[My friend] didn't stop believing in cannabis. We can't offer that here... especially in India, where so many people are diagnosed late. Stage 3, Stage 4. It's a very different situation. The body is, sort of, degenerating at a quick pace. You have to...'

Vaidya lets his voice trail away. The unsaid is left unsaid.

Much of the mythology of cannabis as a medicinal herb stems back to the story of the Great Churning—Samudra Manthana—a colossal episode in mythology that wrestled with grand theological themes of good and evil, health and illness, joy and sorrow, death and immortality. An episode mentioned in scriptures including Bhagavad Purana, Vishnu Purana, and the Mahabharata, the Samudra Manthana begins as the devas seek the help of their foes, the asuras to churn the Kshira Sagara* and find amrit, the nectar of immortality. The mountain Mandara is submerged in the ocean to be used as a churning rod, while the snake god Vasuki is roped around the peak, held on each end by the devas and asuras. Then, the battling divine fellows follow the same principal that Indian households have mastered for centuries to churn a pot of curd, by using a rope to twirl a stick back and forth on its axis, until the aggressive rotations finally produce unctuous lumps of fat. Butter.

Fourteen ratnas rise in forms of gifts and boons from the waters of the Kshira Sagara, including a cow that grants wishes, a seven-headed horse, a tree of wine, a goddess to marry Vishnu, and even the moon itself. Finally, there comes the man of the cosmic hour: Dhanvantari, the physician god, an avatar of Vishnu, a doctor who could treat and heal the gods themselves. He emerges ordained with garlands and ornaments, holding on to that magical pot of immortal nectar—amrit—in two of his four hands. Devas and Asuras clash in more divine battles for Dhanvantari's pot.

This legend exalts Dhanvantari as the Hindu god of health and medicine, the great deity of the Ayurvedic practice. Many believers will chant the Dhanvantri mantra 108 times when they or their loved ones are facing a serious health condition:**

> Om Namo Bhagavate Vasudevaaya Dhanvantaraye Amrita-kalasha
> HastaayaSarva-amaya Vinashaaya Trailokya Naathaya
> Dhanvantri Maha-vishnave Namaha.

There are a number of such mantras, pleas to the Doctor God to restore good health, to be removed of fear and disease. By its very

---

*The name reminds of the great, milky mithai store in Varanasi: Ksheer Sagar. Now, I'm craving their rasmalai.

**Perhaps the most sacred number in Hindu spirituality, evoked in a variety of interpretations. In the Ayurvedic context, 108 refers to the marma points in the human body/soul that preserve what some call the human 'life force energy'.

definition, mortal life ends, but some Hindus believe that a little splash of immortality from Dhanvantari's amrit might help extend it a little.*

Real amrit, however, remains elusive; thus, the principles of Ayurveda often strive for the next best thing. If death can't be defeated, it could at least be delayed. In following Dhanvantari and the scholars in the scriptures, Ayurvedic health practice makes use of several indigenously available plants and herbs: cumin, gotu kola (pennywort), mucuna, ashwagandha (Indian ginseng), brahmi (water hyssop), and more. One of the most common Indian herbs is neem, a tree native to the subcontinent, producing products that are used as pest repellents, shampoo, and as an antioxidant. Neem is sometimes referred to as sarva roga nivarini, Sanskrit for 'the cure for all ailments'.

Similarly, Ayurveda also recognizes cannabis as a medicinal plant, and records over 200 classical cannabis-based formulations. Bhang shows up repeatedly in the recipes for Ayurvedic mixtures, as a remedy for a variety of common issues including digestive and stomach illnesses, headaches, insomnia, muscle and joint pains, and whooping coughs. In their 1957 paper, Chopra and Chopra also noted the cultural use of bhang in veterinary medicine in India (as a remedy for intestinal worms and for its aphrodisiac properties), for treating some STDs, dysuria, or as a poultice to apply on wounds and sores. In parts of the Himalaya, there has been a custom of planting ganja at the burial site of a killed cobra; the resulting plant is believed to be a super-healer.**

In a 2018 study conducted on patients undergoing treatment

---

*In James Cameron's film *Avatar: The Way of Water* (2022), scientists discover a yellowish 'neurocrine' liquid in the glands of the tulkun, a massive and hyper-intelligent marine species on the planet Pandora. This liquid is believed to stop human ageing, and becomes the most valuable resource on the planet. The scientists name the substance Amrita.

**I humbly request you to refrain from trying dead cobra weed at home.

at the Tata Memorial Hospital in Mumbai, the Central Council For Research in Ayurvedic Sciences (CCRAS), concluded that cannabis can also help to alleviate symptoms after chemotherapy, including severe pain, nausea, loss of appetite, anxiety, etc—just what Amit Vaidya had experienced after his recovery.

The Tata Memorial Hospital (TMH) in Mumbai is one of the foremost government-funded institutions in India for cancer research and treatment, where Indian scientists and doctors are conducting the most detailed studies of the various medicinal potentials of cannabis—particularly in treating 'the Big C'. Just two days prior to the CCRAS study, the Council of Scientific & Industrial Research's Indian Institute of Integrative Medicine (CSIR-IIIM) announced that they would be developing three drugs from cannabis to treat patients of cancer, epilepsy, and sickle-cell anaemia. The IIIM in Jammu cultivated cannabis for research in its campus on a one-acre plot to formulate the derivative compounds. The TMH planned to conduct clinical trials of the medication upon twenty-five cancer patients in Mumbai.

'The drugs would be "natural" instead of "synthetic",' said Rajendra Badwe, the director of TMH, during an interaction with the media in 2018. 'We are also trying to see whether the way the whole human being becomes complacent under the influence of cannabinoids—the feeling of elation, the feeling that everything is comfortable—translates into a cell. While we're treating cancer, whether it is by surgery, radiation, or chemotherapy, can we put the tumour into complacency?' Badwe added the trials will be likely offered to patients with lung or pancreatic cancers, which have relatively low survival rates. Researchers at TMH announced that they will also begin trials to test the impact of cannabis to reduce the risk of cancer metastasis, i.e., the spread of cancerous cells from one part of the body to another.

In early 2023, researchers at the National Institute of Ayurveda in Jaipur (Rajasthan) conducted human trials on the efficacy of using cannabis for sandhivata (osteoarthrosis) and vicharchika (eczema). In both cases, the vijaya oil (the institute preferred to use the Ayurvedic term, rather than 'cannabis') gave positive results, reducing the pain and symptoms of the ailments. The medicine for these tests were provided by BOHECO, who are also involved in tests for the viability of cannabis (or vijaya, whatever) for sleep conditions, chronic pain, cancer-based pain, and digestion.

In many countries, marijuana-based products—based on both sativa and indica strains—are already being prescribed by practitioners of modern medicine. Our bodies engender its own cannabinoids—endocannabinoids—which are present across our organs and tissues: our muscles, our cellular systems, our brains. The endocannabinoid system assists several complex actions in our immune system, nervous system, and other organs, helping to create a balance in our bodies, known as homeostasis. This balance can help regulate and control a number of our functions, effecting appetite, sleep cycles, memory, inflammation, and our pain receptors.* It has been called a 'bridge' between the body and the mind. As humans age, we make fewer natural cannabinoids, thus leading to a deficiency in that homeostasis; experts in the United States have explored the benefits of cannabis in helping restore that balance for elder patients who may be suffering from an assortment of health issues.

While it may serve as a copula to strengthen the bonds of our cannabinoid receptors, cannabis interacts with so many different systems in the body that doctors have found it hard to target any specific ailments. Like in the great story from the Mahabharata, cannabis acts like Dronacharya's young archery disciples (excluding Arjuna) aiming for the eye of a wooden bird. It sees everything: the eye, the bird, the branches, the trees. It can't be trained—like Arjuna—to see the eye of the bird alone.

Research in the United States and elsewhere has suggested some positive outcomes for the benefits of both THC and CBD

*Our species isn't extra special, by the way: all animals have endocannabinoid systems.

compounds found in cannabis, including nausea, pain, epilepsy, glaucoma, AIDS wasting syndrome, seizures, Amyotrophic lateral sclerosis (ALS), Multiple sclerosis (MS), Crohn's disease, Alzheimer's, and more. Depending on the state, patients in the US can qualify for medical marijuana if they meet certain requirements for the above conditions. The US Food and Drug Administration (FDA) has approved of various cannabinoids like cannabidiol and dronabinol—available in the form of pills, powders, liquid, dried leaves, etc.,—for a number of these conditions.

In May 2023, a cannabidiol-based product was approved in India for the first time, to be manufactured in Hyderabad and Visakhapatnam by a pharmaceuticals company. The medication will be developed as an oral solution for use in neurological disorders.

The medicinal potential of cannabis made news during the Covid-19 pandemic. The virus became the biggest khalnayak of health emergencies, leading to immunity breakdowns, organ failures, deaths, an over-burden on our healthcare systems, and a resulting shutdown of movement and economy. In a frantic hunt for solutions—a daub of amrit to prolong mortality—a number of studies were conducted on mice and men to test the efficacy of CBD compounds in the face of the virus. These studies suggested that CBD can block SARS-CoV-2—the strain of coronavirus—at both early and later stages of infection.*

(During the pandemic, a mix of Covid anxiety and isolation resulted in the skyrocketing of recreational cannabis use in the US: in 2020, legal marijuana sales increased by 120 per cent).

With these ever-growing lists of boons, you may wonder why there is any debate about medicinal marijuana at all. Why don't we

*Paradoxically, a 2024 new study by researchers at Washington University School of Medicine in St. Louis linked cannabis to an increased risk of serious illness for those with Covid-19. See: Tamara Schneider, 'Cannabis use tied to increased risk of severe COVID-19', Medicine.Wustl.edu, 21 June 2024, <https://medicine.wustl.edu/news/cannabis-use-tied-to-increased-risk-of-severe-covid-19/>.

have the option to purchase pre-rolled joints at the cost of a new toothbrush from the chemist down the road?* Unfortunately, these curative qualities are only one side of the story: healthcare specialists around the world are still generally wary about prescribing cannabis as this magical cure-all due to side effects and other related health concerns that might accompany frequent marijuana use. A 2024 study funded by the National Heart, Lung, and Blood Institute [NHLBI] found that the daily use of cannabis was associated with a 25 per cent increased likelihood of heart attack and 42 per cent increased likelihood of stroke when compared to non-use of the substance. Some studies have theorized that medical marijuana could lead to impaired memory and concentration, slower reaction time, hallucinations and mental illnesses, and the increased risk of heart attack and stroke. A 2020 report in the *Cureus* journal concluded that the THC in cannabis, can 'be the main culprit causing psychosis and schizophrenia in the at-risk population'. Men aged between fifteen and forty-nine may be at the highest risk of schizophrenia as related to cannabis use disorder.

Remember, the property of the cannabis as a hyperaccumulator, a plant that absorbs the heavy metals from the atmosphere? The environment may benefit, but in the life cycle of a plant, the user pays the price: recently, researchers discovered statistically higher levels of heavy metals like lead and cadmium in the blood and urine of regular marijuana consumers. Cadmium, in particular, has been linked to kidney and lung disease.

Marijuana use can have an impact on fertility, including a decrease in sperm count and delay in ovulation. Research published by the *Canadian Medical Association Journal* (CMAJ) suggests that, 'For most couples, smoking marijuana does not affect their ability to conceive, but for couples with subfertility or infertility, it could be a contributing factor.'

---

*Aaah, one can dream.

With more studies—including the ones being conducted in India—the benefits and side effects of cannabis will become clearer. In India, our large population and the great natural availability of the plant could potentially provide a vast sample size of patients.

And the stakes are high. A report by the Indian Council of Medical Research has predicted that the number of Indians suffering from cancer is projected to rise to 29.8 million by 2025—up from 26.7 million in 2021—including cancers of the lungs, breast, oesophagus, mouth, and stomach. (Oncologists have theorized that the increased consumption of food with preservatives may be a contributing factor to this rapid rise.)

Varun Rungta, the general secretary of Pan India Medical Cannabis and Hemp Association (PIMCHA), believes that India is also suffering from 'a massive disease burden', listing issues of arthritis, chronic pain, insomnia, etc. 'To combat these new-age forms of mental and physical fatigue,' Rungta writes, 'Medical cannabis has been found effective through a mix of clinical research and anecdotal evidence in regulated markets globally.' Rungta has further suggested that part of PIMCHA's plan over the coming years is to push for reclassification of high-CBD/low-THC medicine as a non-narcotic.

So, can cannabis really be a solution to this burden of diseases? In 2020, Dr Pankaj Chaturvedi—the deputy director of TMH's centre for cancer epidemiology—along with other senior doctors, published a report in the *Indian Journal of Palliative Care*, where they settled for a more conservative conclusion, resisting any recommendations for legalization of the product's medicinal use. 'It would be prudent to wait for studies which prove beyond doubt the advantages of marijuana over the existing drugs and also outweigh its side effects and addiction potential.'

The concept of palliative care, in general, is relatively new to India, gaining widespread use only around the time of the NDPS Act in the mid-1980s. The Act made it difficult to obtain morphine because of the ban on opium. It took amendments by various state governments to make exceptions for the use of morphine in dealing with pains induced by cancer treatments, surgery, etc. A 2008 study estimated that less than 3 per cent of India's cancer patients have access to adequate pain relief, and 'many states in India have no medical facilities that dispense morphine'.

Could an aggressive, nationwide push towards cannabis help relieve the burden on these medical facilities—and thus, relieve the pain and burden on the patients themselves? There may be a fear of side effects and dependency with cannabis, but these worries are miniscule in comparison to the larger threats of opioid-based abuse—medicines that many patients have access to worldwide.

A system already sits in place. A trusted medical professional writes a prescription* for their patient, along with a recommended dosage. The pharmacist is trusted to only sell a supply of the prescribed medication, and no more than the amount prescribed. The patient is trusted to consume only the recommended quantity of the medicine, to ensure that they treat their illnesses and their symptoms, and not trip out, or worse, overdose.

Of course, this is an imperfect arrangement. Some doctors overprescribe, some pharmacists oversell, some patients overuse. The line between medicinal drug and narcotic drug is thinner than the wafery paper used to roll your joints. Some of my classmates in school found an addictive high in the misuse of common products like Corex cough syrups** or Spasmo-Proxyvon capsules, which they were able to purchase off the counter from indifferent local chemists.

Sometimes, medical professionals can be the culprit themselves. Analysis by *ProPublica* in the United States, for instance, has concluded that doctors are often given financial benefits by pharmaceutical companies to overprescribe their drugs to patients.

---

*In terrible handwriting.

**Pfizer Inc.'s India unit stopped selling Corex in 2016, after it was banned by regulators for posing a risk to humans.

Opioid abuse and dependence are major crises in the US, so much so that *anyone* who is prescribed *any* opioid is now considered at risk for addiction. Meanwhile, healthcare providers in American states which have medical cannabis programmes have reported to prescribing fewer opioid pain medications.

In India, there is no formal system to monitor antibiotic use, leaving room for overprescription, overuse, and the sale of unapproved medicines at our local chemists.

Humanity is defined by its mortality; but, it's also human nature to strive for survival; if not of self, then of the species, to prolong life, delay death, to chase Dhanvantari's magical pot as desperately as the devas and asuras did. It's no surprise, then, that health has been commodified to such a gross degree, until the business of medicine teeters on the edge of exploitation: the price of medicines and vaccines, the cost of hospitalizations, the unfulfilled promises of our public healthcare systems.

Despite its flaws, however, most of us have chosen to accept the infrastructure of the 'modern' medical industry. Why not trust the prescription of cannabis within a similar arrangement, too?

A part of me imagines that the plant could become a grand disrupter, a viable alternative option to the healthcare economy that has been corrupted by the machinations of commercialism. But, another part of me quickly abandons this notion. The global market for medical marijuana is expected to cross $50 billion by 2027—the same machinations have *already* conquered this ancient plant.

While these global economic estimates use inexact market research to make their forecasts, the numbers can hardly predict how the industry could change if India—the home of cannabis and of a billion-something people—truly plunges with a spectacular dupki into the game.

For now, Indian companies are working on the margins of legality, limiting their products to high-CBD (and low-THC) medicine as they wait for favourable research and legal reforms.

Many companies currently offering cannabis medicine make sure to wear their Vedic/Ayurvedic inspirations on their sleeves: whether it's on the posters outside their stalls at the Hemp Expo or on the front pages of their websites. Savikalpa Sciences, for example, describes its products as 'ayurvedic inspired cannabis medicine', where you can purchase—with Ayurvedic prescription—CBD medicine for 'calm', 'pain', and 'balance' in various flavours: cinnamon/vanilla, orange/spearmint, and tulsi/turmeric: their offerings read like the menu card at a swanky tea shop.

During a telephonic conversation, Savikalpa's CEO Raghav Priyadarshi tells me that he has worked closely with a handful of cancer patients who have accessed cannabis-based medicines at various stages of illness and recovery. He believes that too many patients turn to cannabis only after they have exhausted all other options. 'The good thing is that, in India, there is a very prevalent history of cannabis,' says Priyadarshi. 'But in our country, I can't clinically tell a patient to go smoke a joint. There are patients who are suffering, the nanis and dadis of the world, people who may have never smoked.... We want a positive outcome—but we don't want them to get inebriated and maybe hurt themselves.' While Savikalpa expected the early adopters of cannabis medicine to be younger Indians, the most enthusiastic were the elderly—many of those nanis and dadis—who are probably more accustomed to seeing formulations of this 'dawai' used to tend to minor illnesses and injuries from their childhood, long before the Narcotics Act.

In terms of modern medication, India is the world's top supplier of generic pharmaceuticals, and its pharma industry is the third largest in the world. Priyadarshi has argued that the onus is then on the pharma industry to undertake the research to 'establish cannabinoids as therapeutic agents'. In a recent article, Priyadarshi wrote that, 'India has the necessary ecosystem—scientists, clinicians, researchers, a large drug manufacturing ecosystem and very large patient population—to really catapult the Indian life-sciences industry, and in particular cannabinoid therapeutics firms into global leaders.'

But before the forces of industry can attempt that catapult, they must wait for healthcare experts to confirm and approve their observations, to turn medical research into legislative action.

All roads paving the path of medicinal cannabis in India lead me a hospital in Mumbai, to the scientists and clinicians at the forefront of the research that could revolutionize Indian healthcare—and perhaps, even save a few lives.

Mumbai greets me again into its familiar arms, like an encounter with an old habit, like riding a bicycle again, like picking up the PlayStation controller after a long period to play my favourite game,* like that first hit of weed after years of abstinence, a billow of bliss straight up into the cranium. In the city of maximalism and excess, I find joy in the smaller familiarities: clothes drying on the steel grilles outside the colonial-style windows; a ride in a kaali-peeli taxi**, windows drawn down to breathe in the thick seaside air; basketballs grimy with dust as they bounce on the outdoor courts at Nagpada; or juicy chicken shawarma near the Colaba promenade. And like any major metropolis on Earth, Mumbai is a city of vice, too: of drinking addas, dance bars, gambling dens, and red-light districts. Access to cannabis is easy and efficient—but, much like the city's real estate, every little packet of charas—called 'kala sona' (black gold) in local slang—is exponentially more expensive for a considerably smaller amount.

To those of us from smaller cities, Mumbai is an electric shock to the heart, a defibrillator that pulls me into its manic, unforgiving pace. I feel like I'm almost always on the run, taxis to local trains,

---

*2K

**Which will, alas, soon be extinct.

autorickshaws and on foot, earning the value of each minute, each appointment.

It's another frantic Monday afternoon, between appointments and surgeries, when Dr Pankaj Chaturvedi finds a window of time to see me at the Tata Memorial Hospital in Parel. Dressed in all-blue scrubs, he peels off his surgical gloves, sits down beside me, and then calls upon a peon to bring us a couple of beverages. Black tea for him, a regular masala chai for me.* I take a sip and add half a teaspoon of sugar.

Now in his late fifties, Chaturvedi has worked at TMH for over twenty years, where, besides being the deputy director of the Centre of Cancer Epidemiology, he is a professor and surgeon in the Department of Head and Neck Surgery. Chaturvedi's main area of research and study during much of this time has been the prevention and early detection of oral cancer in India. In a country where chewing tobacco (areca nut, paan) is a major cause of oral cancers, Chaturvedi has been part of several public health initiatives to combat this epidemic; some of these initiatives also extended to focus on alcohol misuse.

A lifetime of treating and advocating against these common, legal substances have shaded Chaturvedi's opinions on the legality of cannabis, too. Not long after the TMH declared their plans to develop cannabis-based drugs and begin conducting human trials, Chaturvedi and his team authored a paper entitled 'Review of Medicinal Use of Cannabis Derivatives and the Societal Impact of Legalization', a collation of already existing literature from around the world, looking at marijuana's benefits regarding a plethora of different diseases and conditions. Regarding the potential use of cannabis in treating cancers, the paper declared:

> There is some evidence in literature that Cannabis has antitumor properties and prolongs life... Few investigational

---

*Chai diplomacy is undefeated.

> studies have been conducted on various tumors such as gliomas, lymphomas, prostate cancer, breast cancer, lung cancer, skin cancer, and pancreatic cancer... Cannabis has been shown to be effective when used in combination with other anticancer drugs. This has particularly been seen in pancreatic cancers and gliomas. Thus, the evidence for the anticancer effect of Cannabis does exist, but it is exploratory and evolving.

The paper states that cannabis could be a cause of cancers and diseases, too. Some of the carcinogens present in tobacco are also present in marijuana smoke, thus increasing the threat of 'transient ischemic attacks, stroke, myocardial infarctions, and Cannabis arteritis'.

The most pertinent sentence in the report, however, is also one of the simplest: 'Till date, no death due to marijuana poisoning has been reported.'*

Ganja/bhang is certainly not halahala, the poison created during the Great Churning. It certainly is the great antidote to some poisons, cooling down pains and anxieties like it did Shiva's throat. Now, the cancer research could help to prove if it can be a form of amrit, too.

'For everyone, cancer is *the* disease,' Chaturvedi tells me. 'And if you can find a solution for *the* disease, it works like...' Chaturvedi stops speaking, leaving room for silence, the air heavy in the density of the obvious, of the *do I really need to spell it out for you?*

In his Pulitzer Prize-winning book, Indian-born oncologist Siddhartha Mukherjee called cancer the 'Emperor of All Maladies', which has haunted humanity for thousands of years. Chaturvedi says that he considers cannabis just an extension of the research and curiosity of scientists to find any weapon to confront this peerless 'emperor'. And cannabis is the latest astra against cancer in this millennia-long war.

---

*

Despite human trials for cannabis-based medicines in TMH being announced in late 2018, it took approximately four years for the process to gain any traction. 'They're just starting now,' says Chaturvedi. 'One year of regulatory approvals... Oh my god! Because of the NDPS Act, we had a long, torturous process... Bahut suffer kiya (We suffered a lot).'

'I'm open [to cannabis],' he adds. 'I want my cancer patients to really live long, and not suffer. For that, we'll conduct whatever research that may be needed. We have found that in our literature review that there is a potential that the [cancer] drugs might be more effective if they are given concurrently with cannabis products.'

Health news often makes for unsubtle, clickbait headlines. It's common to see conflicting advice on our feeds every other day. A regular glass of wine is somehow both a lifesaver and a life-destroyer. Are two cups of coffee a day too many, or just right? Strenuous exercise could heal your heart, and strenuous exercise could weaken your immune system. The Covid-19 vaccines, in particular, spawned an entire industry of WhatsApp epidemiologists. There exists a treacherous amount of misleading information out there regarding cannabis, too: its boons may be exaggerated by those in the business of medical and recreational marijuana; its dangers are overblown by those who only see it as an entrapping nasha. Browsing online, the average consumer can be trapped in a bubble of half-baked pseudo-facts, with the influencing hands of politics and industry presenting their respective sides of the issue without the necessary nuance.

So, when we meet at the hospital in Mumbai, Chaturvedi speaks in a calculated manner, careful of each word he tells me—and of the possible implications of his perspective in regards to India's future public health decisions. He seems wary of how any instruction either pro- or anti-cannabis could be misinterpreted, or lead to extremes.

'What has happened over a period of time, especially in the US, is that there were a lot of people who were incarcerated because of marijuana,' Chaturvedi says. 'Because of that, the government thought it was much easier to legalize it, rather than keep it prohibited, which leads to huge amounts of expenditure. And when you want to legalize... the only logic is that there is a medical use [for the plant]. The medical use became a reason why it was legalized; but ultimately, the purpose was recreational.

'To date, we all know that the majority of the marijuana [in the world] is being used for recreational use, and only a small portion is being used medically. It's a huge market. And once there is a huge market, then the industry comes in. Once industry comes in, then advertisements come in... And because of that, something that was traditional, something that was already there in our society… Suddenly, it's a *brand*. And when there's a brand, the consumption goes up.'

Chaturvedi's fear, he says, is that irresponsible promotion will make the substance a health menace, like tobacco and alcohol. Citing the examples of many famous Bollywood superstars who openly promote paan masala brands, he said that he feared that celebrity endorsements could begin for ganja, too. 'Filmfare will be sponsored by ganja companies*,' Chaturvedi said. 'So, recreational use is something we have to be very conscious of, in a country where the regulation of such products is a problem.'

I argue that substances like alcohol and tobacco are already well-regulated: every cigarette packet contains warnings and graphics of the dangers of tobacco, and alcohol companies have to advertise under the guise of soda waters or music CDs. Couldn't this be the future for the cannabis industry too, I ask, where it's legal, but with strict regulations for advertising and sale?

'For me, everything is equally important,' Chaturvedi responds. 'A road traffic accident is as important as pollution, or sanitation issues, or homicide, or suicide, or whatever. For me, every life

---

*To be fair, this might be the only way I would be persuaded to watch the Filmfare awards.

matters. If tobacco has been a historical mistake that our great grandfathers did by legalizing it, we have to learn from our mistakes. And do not commit similar mistakes in the future, under the disguise that if 'Yeh ho raha hai, toh yeh justified hai'. One wrong cannot be justification for another wrong.

'There *has* to be a strong justification,' he adds, '[to argue] that in India, there is an unmet need of people depressed, people having lot of anxiety, they need a break, and for that, I want to introduce [cannabis].'

I find myself agreeing with Chaturvedi's premise that the legalization of alcohol and tobacco shouldn't be justification for 'another wrong'—cannabis. But this argument unhesitatingly assumes that cannabis is a *wrong*, despite all the evidence concluding that it's a relatively safer substance for most adults. Furthermore, there are many who would argue that cannabis is a naturally available product, one that grows with the same freedoms like so many other herbs and plants available for common 'rogas' and diseases: cumin, brahmi, mucuna, neem, etc. Cannabis activists have said that the citizen should have a right to seek a path to natural healing, to pluck off the plants they've used for thousands of years without the arm of the government blocking their way.

Chaturvedi fears that allowing a new product like cannabis will exacerbate the stress of our healthcare systems, which are already strained under a bazaar of ongoing crises. According to the Global Adult Tobacco Survey India of 2016–17, there are nearly 27 crore people—almost one of every three adults—who use tobacco in our country, in the form of smokeless products like khaini, gutka, areca nut, or smoking it through cigarettes, bidis, and hookahs.

'It's a disaster,' says Chaturvedi. '13.5 lakh people are dying every year because of tobacco. It is *such* a problem. And alcohol is the number two problem. So... given this picture, if there is a push for legalization of cannabis in India...' He thinks for a moment, before asking me, 'I don't know if you've been to Varanasi or not?'

I smile. 'I'm from Varanasi.'

'I'm also from Varanasi,' he says.

'Arre, wow! That's amazing.' I clap my hands and immediately expect some hometown camaraderie, based on that code of conduct that all of us Banarasi bhaiyas and behenjis reserve for each other.

The abuse of vices like paan, gutka, bhang et al. is prevalent and widespread in Varanasi. Chaturvedi assumes—correctly—that he doesn't have to explain any further. Our shared hometown, one of the most populated cities in India's most populous state, serves as an important representative sample for the country's larger struggles with tobacco and the cancers that it's infamously responsible for. 'In Varanasi, we made a population-based cancer registry—for the first time in India,' he says. 'We found that there was a huge burden of cancer. The number one cancer in men, and number three or four cancer in women, is mouth cancer. And that is because of chewing tobacco. So, that means that the population is already struggling with a noxious substance. And there's an entire generation of youth eating paan and gutka. If I add one more addiction (cannabis), then we are going to have a public health disorder.

'Now, in cancer care, if cannabis was such a "holy grail", then in Varanasi, where [bhang] has been there in use for so many years, we shouldn't have [cancer]... But, there are gall bladder cancers, mouth cancers... If you go to our hospital, next time when you go to your homeplace, just visit the hospital. It's flooded with people.'

For now, Chaturvedi's conclusion is that the proven medicinal property of cannabis is restricted to three conditions: chronic pain, forms of epilepsy, and anxiety disorders. For anything else, he says that, 'There is no great evidence of the use of cannabis over and above the existing medication. There is some medication already available where cannabis is supposed to work. I should have a strong reason to change my current practice to cannabis. For that, I need good evidence.' He feels the same way about palliative medicine, too, for which he doesn't see a strong enough justification for cannabis to replace the available opioids.

There are some doctors in the US who share Chaturvedi's apprehensions: regarding the efficacy of medical marijuana, experts have suggested that there simply isn't a large enough research sample size to properly diagnose health hazards related with the plant. Cannabis has many carcinogens and toxins also found in tobacco, and thus, some suspect that the substance could be unsafe if abused.

There are two main potentials, then, that Chaturvedi and his team are studying regarding cannabis and cancer. The first: can the substance improve the outcome of cancer? As in, if someone has a survival rate of 20 per cent over the next five years, can it be extended to 50 per cent? Can cannabis and its derivatives reduce the chance of cancer metastasis?

And the second: can cannabis help in the quality of life of cancer patients, especially if they're dealing with the rigours of chemotherapy and other forms of radiotherapies? Can it help take better care of anxiety and pain, compared to the existing drugs?

I ask Chaturvedi if the societal disapprobation against cannabis would impact how the results of the various studies at TMH would be interpreted.

'Well, cannabis is already being used. My daughter… My children….' Chaturvedi pauses and smiles without finishing this line of thought. 'I know,' he continues, 'in all the [college] campuses, it's common. So let us accept it. There has to be a more organized societal way of informing our children what is good or bad for them, so that they are able to make an informed choice. I have a very simple logic. Are you married?'

'I *am* married,' I say, with a surprised smile.

'Whatever you might think, whatever you might preach. One litmus test is there,' he says. 'Everything is right what you want your son to do it, or your daughter to do it.* Don't have double

*I chuckle at the assumption that marriage automatically equals children. Or that

standards. "I will have alcohol, but I don't want my kids to have it… I will do ABCDEF, but I don't want my kids to do it." As long as you feel that your children should indulge into all these things, please go ahead. What happens is that in the pursuit of freedom of expression, creativity.... We forget that tomorrow, it may affect our own children....'

Our time is nearly done. I get up to shake his hand.

'These are the areas of research for which we are working with an open mind,' says Chaturvedi. 'With respect for "Ayush", and great respect to thousands of years of knowledge that we have inherited.'

'In India, we have to *always* say that,' I respond with a laugh. 'There's always that pressure of history in our country, isn't it?'

'Ek bahut simple si baat yeh hai...' Chaturvedi says in Hindi, softening his voice, as if he's speaking in a conspiratorial tone. 'Wapis main uss bacche kaa keh raha hoon. Mera bachha jab bimaar parta hai na, toh main usko haldi pila ke uski khasi theek nahi karta hoon. (There's one simple thing. I will return to our kids. If my child falls ill, then I'm not going to treat their cough by just serving turmeric.) If my parents fall ill, my kid falls ill, so what will I do?'

'Haan, haan,' I nod on my way out.

'You were expecting something different from this conversation, weren't you?'

I laugh again, and I assure him, 'No, no. Not at all!' I tell him that, I, too, have to try and keep an open mind.

What I definitely didn't expect from that conversation, however, was to be left thinking about myself as a parent. Till my early thirties, I had enjoyed the freedom to be stubborn, to set my ethos and values, to live by a personal code of morality, my own truths. But when that burden of parenthood hits, the codes crumble, and absolute truths become flexible. When my daughter falls ill, there

---

children are only a by-product of marriage.

is no greater value left than her health.*

Yes, thousands of years of Indian medical history tells me that cannabinoid medicine has worth, that sometimes, it makes sense to trust the natural option rather than lab-made medicines. Recent scientific studies have only supported these age-old hypotheses. I find myself being open to the option of cannabis—when legalized**—to provide respite for the multifarious ailments it has clinically proven to be advantageous for: pains, anxieties, nausea, appetite, and other symptoms and diseases. Medical marijuana has the faculty to bind and boost our endocannabinoid systems. It could be a positive curative element, too. It could bless our lives with a zephyr of bliss before that inevitable, permanent shutdown.

As for recreational use: let's revisit that when you turn eighteen, OK beti?

Growing up in Varanasi, I've always felt that Death was just another familiar presence that flickered in the gullies and colonies. In some households, it became a regular guest, smashing through the shutters, climbing through the windows. Its reminders are everywhere: grey ashes floating over the dark waters of the Ganga, skiffs laden with mourners and the clay urns of their departed, processions of men marching with their beloved deceased, carried over their shoulders. At the cremation ghats, hundreds of bodies are burned every day, adding black fumes of the dead into the city's thick oxygen, so the living may breathe in tiny whiffs of our own mortality.

My first memory of death was my grandfather's. Amrit Lal 'Ishrat' Madhok, a name that beckoned both the amrit of immortality and the ishrat of bliss. I only remember my dada in the briefest flickers of memory: the sound of his deep voice reciting

---

*Bas, ho gaya: I sound just like my parents now.

**Hey, I would never break the law.

a ghazal; the way he leaned on his walking stick, staggering to share the weight on his good foot; the way he petted Badal and Bijli, his beloved, lethargic Labradors.

And I remember the sight of him bedridden, the slight stench of ammonia and dust in his bedroom, the vapour of death.

Any death reminds me of the inevitability of *all* death, and the longer time that passes, the more these former lives are reduced to the fading recesses of memory. I think often about how I will remember my own parents: their physical presence, their achievements, their goals, the way they raised their eyebrows before sharing a juicy morsel of gossip at the dinner table, the boisterous sound of their laughter, the scent of their shoulders and hair, the way I snuggled myself into the warm fit of their bosoms. Their totality is soon reduced to these flashes, mere blimps of complex lives.

One Thursday evening, I sit beside my daughter in our living room, laptop on my thighs, legs reclined over the wooden table, eyeballs reflecting the glow of the screen. I realize that this very evening could be the blimp by which she remembers *me* forever, how she'll access the last remnants of my existence. Perhaps this is the biggest reminder I need to be in the very present—here and now—remain creative and curious, so that any given Thursday could be as moving as it's mundane.

Amrit Lal was a blimp, too, but he was one of *my* blimps. He had lived a fairly remarkable life. In Varanasi, he was a professor and a poet, a husband and father of three, a lover of sher-o-shayari, and of his mushairas, and of drink, and of hunting expeditions. He was one of the many artistic personalities that added to the colourful mosaic of the city.

But I hardly experienced that colour. Ishrat was diagnosed with a tumour in his brain in the late 1980s. It would soon turn malignant. Cancer. He was hospitalized in Varanasi, in New Delhi, back in Varanasi again. He died in 1989, at fifty-eight. I could only witness the final couplets of his life-long ghazal.

In my youngest technicoloured memories, I remember the morning when I saw his body for the last time—lifeless—lying on a wooden funeral bed by our main gate, eyelids shut, nose and ears stuffed with cotton, a garland of flowers around his neck, a white chaddar wrapped around his body, before it was to be transported to the shamshaan (cremation) ghat. An advantage of living—and dying—in Varanasi is that, for Hindus, the ideal place to say the final rites is just a short drive away. It's a privilege not afforded to families who often travel hundreds and thousands of kilometres around the world to reach the banks of the river, by the Manikarnika or Harishchandra ghats. In its last lap, Amrit Lal's body was carried on foot through the narrow, stone-paved gullies, the plank lying on the shoulders of my father, my uncles, and the other adult men in the family, as they chanted, 'Ram naam satya hai'. Ram's name is the truth.

In an existence where all mortal life is fleeting, this maudlin chorus is a reminder—perhaps even an instruction—to evoke these gods, characters enriched with amrit who are destined to live forever.

I was a few months shy of five at the time, about the same age my daughter is as I draft these words today. I was too young to accompany the grown-ups to see the burning cremation pyres, but I did hear their chants as they left home, building up a hypnotic rhythm, a musical soundtrack to fill up the silences we were left behind with.

Growing older, I heard that soundtrack more often. I saw dozens of those burning pyres on the banks of the river. I smelled the fumes of the dead, heard the crackle of sweltering logs over the recitation of the last hymns, saw the sandal paste rubbed over dead bodies, the ghee and rice sprinkled over the burning pyre, the whole overblown bandobast.

As a child, these rituals held no spiritual meaning for me: they were merely a way to indicate the passage of time—as many religious ceremonies seem to be across the world. Some of these ceremonies are festivals held to celebrate the changing seasons, or to mark days of the week where the planets aligned to the favour of certain gods, or life milestones anointed with elaborate baptisms and christenings, or the sights and shapes of the moon that decide when one fasts or feasts, or to pay obeisance to the celestial bodies that mark the months and years flipping by on our calendars.

With time, these rituals have begun to feel even more futile to me: rules decided by the priestly class of each community on Earth to keep the order of things, to keep us distracted and occupied, filling up the brief flickers of mortality with a schedule, a task to complete, a deity to prostrate in front of, a chant that provides the rhythm for forward movement, laded with the mortal remains of our loved ones for a final farewell.

For, if there was nothing to chant, we would be left with only nothingness: a realization of the cruel, cold vastness of the universe, millions of light years of vacuous dark space, and a frightening silent reminder that once we're gone, we're gone forever.

Despite this infinite silence that awaits us all—believers and non-believers, the faithful and the faithless—we continue to live in the face of this grand absurdity. We fight to survive through the pains and the heartbreaks to see another day, to make the best of the little time we have as conscious animals. In a vast, green field of ganja, most of us hope to be a seed that eventually grows to its full potential, that glows under a warm summer sun, blooms to fluorescence under the relief of rain, until it rots to its death, or is consumed and extinguished in a final shot of bliss.

Until recently, I only thought about my grandfather in selfish terms; as in, what did he mean to *me,* specifically? What do *I* share with my ancestor? How did his life and legacy shape my father's, and thus, my own?

But now, my father is older than my grandfather had ever been. Now, I'm closer in age to that body lying on the funeral pyre, than the young child who last saw him alive. Now, I imagine the pain of Amrit Lal's last days: the headaches, the weakness, the loss of coordination, the quick disintegration of bodily functions, the cloud of overpowering medicine, the nausea, the vomit, a sudden loss of weight, the skin sagging under his arms, the quick spread of disease, difficulty swallowing, paler skin, heavier eyelids, a marathon in each breath… the heart races, a spasm, bile and urine, the lungs stop, the heart stops, the brain stops.

My grandfather died a few years after the NDPS Act. There was no amrit to save him, but I wish there had been some ishrat—some herbal ananda—to make his final years a little more comfortable.

For months now, I have also been haunted by the story of Abdullah,* the hydrophobia patient in Bengal in the mid-nineteenth century, whose case was recorded by Irish physician William O'Shaughnessy as he conducted landmark clinical trials on medicinal cannabis. While O'Shaughnessy couldn't save Abdullah's life with cannabis, he did note that, with the help of the medicine, 'the awful malady was stripped of its horrors'.

'…Next to cure,' wrote O'Shaughnessy, 'the physician will perhaps esteem the means which enable him "to strew the path to the tomb with flowers."'

The only predetermined path is that to the tomb; or to the burning ghats, garlanded by flowers, and accompanied by the chants—*Ram naam satya hai*—a posthumous reminder of mortality.

Perhaps, we may hope to be strewn with the flowers while we can still smell them.

The memories of my grandfather take me back to Varanasi. And then, I go back on the path myself, to the city of death, the city of Shiva, the city where the consumption of bhang isn't just a traditional institution—it's an intricate part of how many live their lives.

This journey could end nowhere else but back home.

---

*Mentioned in the 'Idukki Gold' chapter.

Forest of Bliss

'...A ringing that carries you across history, until you fall right back into your present self...'

One of the most famous songs from the 1978 film *Don* features the megastar Amitabh Bachchan—at the peak of his powers—celebrating the magic of Varanasi's popular export: the Banarasi paan. Vijay, played by Bachchan, dances along to Kishore Kumar's words, 'Khaike paan banaras vala, khul jaaye band akal ka tala. (Eating Banarasi paan can unlock closed minds.)'*

The song immortalized the local paan industry, and popularized the city's attitude of 'mauj-masti'—pure fun!—to a national audience. The song begins with Vijay pouring a drink for himself—or, perhaps, for his gathered friends—as he sings under the influence in the local Bhojpuri dialect: '*Arre bhang ka rang jama ho chakachak, phir lo paan chabaye* (Once the colour of bhang properly sets in, then chew on some paan)'. His needs are simple. He is the self-anointed '*Chhora Ganga kinare vala* (Just a dude from the Ganga's riverbanks)'.

Banarasis—the residents of Varanasi—will often speak of mauj-masti, a celebration of epicurean delights, of finding time for rest and relaxation. It's an easygoing attitude that operates as a mask—or a form of self-respite—to face the sobering stresses of life: academic pressure, unemployment, poverty, hunger, and violence. In some cases, the attitude can slip into a state of laziness, lethargy, procrastination, or fatalism. In her article, 'The Night before Bhor Ārti: Play and Banarasipan in the Ramnagar Ramlila,' Bhargav

**Don* also stars Zeenat Aman.

Rani describes 'Banarasipan' (the personality traits of quintessential Banarasis) as:

> …a characteristic set of cultural practices—like the love for bahri alangs, paan, bhang/ganja, thandai (a drink of almonds and coagulated milk), a tongue-in-cheek disdain for material pursuits, and a general ease and comfort at unperturbedly whiling away long hours of leisure in relative indolence and nonchalance.

In Hindu belief, being born in Varanasi is truly a stroke of divine luck: all that you need now to break that endless cycle of human reincarnation and pain is to merely die here. Then, liberation awaits you. Moksha, nirvana, a union with the Brahma—the supreme being—and eternal bliss. Some Banarasis tend to see the cosmically bigger picture, where this life is just the final chapter in a long string of little lives. Why take up any stress, now, when that eternal release is just around the corner? It's common for some Banarasis—and especially those who work at the crematoria—to say that, 'Sab ke sab ko ghum phir ke yahin aana hai (After all the travels, everyone eventually ends up back here).'

Varanasi has many names. The main moniker is derived from the description of the old city's limits between the rivers Varuna and Assi, two tributaries of the Ganga. 'Banaras' (which was anglicized to 'Benares' by the British) refers to the readymade (bana) ras or 'juice' of life: the food, the spirituality, the arts, the fun.* 'Kashi' refers to the Sanskrit phrase that means 'City of Light', a nod to spiritual enlightenment.

Varanasi is also called Anandavan, the 'Forest of Bliss'. It might be hard to imagine now, in a town jostling for space between concrete structures, gasping for breath in the heavy flow of traffic—a half-

---

*Some claim that the word 'Banaras' is a colloquial twist on the pronunciation of Varanasi.

baked explosion of the industrial revolution—but some believe that there was a time, pre-civilization, when the city was covered with woodlands and lakes, a serenity cherished by Shiva and Parvati, a natural 'high' to spark their anandamides, too.*

Perhaps this is part of the reason why the city has yet another alias: Avimukteshwara, the place never forsook by Shiva. Shiva is primarily known as the 'destroyer' in the Hindu holy trinity, but is also regarded as the 'Adiyogi': the god of meditation, asceticism, and the arts. A famous local anecdote goes, 'Kashi ke pathar pathar Shiv Shankar (Shiva is in each stone/pebble of Kashi).'** Shaivites and other Banarasis often adopt their favourite deity's habits, too: deep meditation, sravanam, devotional song and dance, and the generous consumption of cannabis. Like the Banarasi paan mentioned in *Don,* bhang can also open a 'band akal ka taala': the external (exo) cannabinoid sources act as a duplicate key, fitting the inner configurations of the brain's padlock, and successfully breaking in with a flurry of creativity and joy.

It is common to see mostly naked ascetics sitting by the ghat steps or roaming the old town, a loaded chillum in hand, a cloud of smoke billowing around them, a kanthi mala necklace around their necks. Some of the ascetics include the Aghoris, who are Shaivites that often subvert and ablate the barriers of caste norms, like purity, untouchability, etc. They are known for alternative and tantric prayer ceremonies, ignoring religious dietary rules, and consuming ganja: chillums passed hands to hand, lip to lip, person to person.

With each puff, the mind expands in a burst of inspiration. THC passes through the lungs or the stomach and into the bloodstream,

---

***Forest of Bliss* was the title of a 1986 ethnographic documentary by Robert Gardner, focusing on everyday life in Varanasi: priests, cremation workers, the sounds of each passing day, dogs by the ghat-side, and the river itself.

**There is no greater text about Varanasi's spiritual history and sacred geography than Diana L. Eck's *Banaras: City of Light* (1992). I have returned to it often, and can never recommend it enough.

and the chemical spreads across the body. The anandamide release tricks the brain into a brief sense of omniscience: as if you are you and you are beyond yourself, too; as if you are here but you could be everywhere, if you so choose. It's the high that double underlines the philosophical notion of atman, of god being a part of everything—including ourselves. It's a feeling that seems to prepare one for divinity, for the moksha that awaits your demise.

The term 'ananda' isn't just the bliss of being alive; the Sanskrit meaning of the phrase extends to a sort of timeless, *absolute* bliss, a celebration of the end of the cycle of rebirths, the bliss of enlightenment. In Eastern philosophies, it's the ultimate goal of each being. The *Encyclopedia of Religion* (published by Thomas Gale) adds that, 'Those who renounce the fruits of their actions and submit themselves completely to the divine will, arrive at the final termination of the cyclical life process (Saṃsāra) to enjoy eternal bliss (Ānanda) in perfect union with the godhead.'

Devotees believe that the potential of bliss and enlightenment pre-exists in all living beings, just waiting to be unlocked and experienced. This is the ananda that served as an inspiration for our endocannabinoids, the system of self-reward within our natural biology. Our neurotransmitters—or some external psychoactive help—can trick us into imagining a little rendezvous with eternity.

This eternity becomes even easier to imagine around the oldest parts of Varanasi, where civilization has existed by the riverbanks for thousands of years, where wandering through the gullies can feel like travelling in a wormhole of time, seeing all of history exist on the same dimensional plane.

One evening in the spring of 2008, my friends and I hired a small row boat. As the sun slowly set in a distance, the boatwallah manning the oars took us on a ride on the Ganga by the ghats for a few hours.

I was in my early twenties at the time. I had recently begun working in Varanasi as a local correspondent for a national newspaper, and part of my assignment had included covering stories of cultural and historical interest. Whenever friends visited from out of town, I would become the de-facto tour guide, adding a little spice to the usual rote repetition of history.

These boat rides were extra special because there are few individuals better versed in the city's local knowledge and history than the boatwallahs of the Manjhi community. The captain of our particular vessel was a Scheherazade on the skiff, capable of narrating historical events with the urgent energy of any contemporary drama, as if he was proudly passing on an ancient heirloom of stories.

We saw the Ganga Aarti at the Dashashwamedh Ghat, a crowded ceremony of fire and sound, performed each evening in homage to the river goddess. We waded past the shamshaan ghat—Manikarnika—where bodies of the recently dead lay on fiery cremation pyres, flesh and bones disintegrating into ash and smoke. We saw temples and mosques, old homes, abandoned forts, and many, many stepwells that descended from the banks down to the river.

The sun had completely set, and we were shrouded in the dark. 8 p.m., maybe 8.30. It was quiet. There were no other boats in sight, and the ghats—a few hundred feet away—were asleep. We had found a rare moment of seclusion on the river under the comforting chaadar of night. There was this earthy, fishy smell to the Ganga. These waters are notoriously polluted by the discharge of sewage water, industrial dyes, and the waste of humans and animals. But in the dark, everything around us was shaded with the same, unassuming blackness. She was opaque to us—the Ganga—trapping her fortunes and her filth far below the surface.

From our distance, I could hardly see anyone on shore under the sparse yellow lights of the ghats. A few men walked home. A few people sat cross-legged on raised platforms. Cows roamed astray.

Street dogs enjoyed their slumber under the night sky.

But then, as our boat passed by the Mansarovar Ghat, we saw the most peculiar sight. On the sands touching the water, there was a dancing figure: a white woman, dressed in a Rajasthani-style black lehenga-choli, swaying with aggressive, wild movements to nothing but the silence of this sleepy night. Her bare feet slapped hard against the sand. She spun and she pranced, an ecstatic form of ghoomar. There was no sound except for the slow splashes of our boat. She was all alone.

And then, our boatwallah rowed away. We wondered if we had seen a ghost.

The next day, I reached out to people who lived nearby, and they confirmed that the apparition was very much real. That a 'foreign' woman came to dance by the banks of the Ganga after sunset every night, a première danseuse of the ghats, moving in silence as a fast-paced raga played in her own mind. She didn't speak to anyone, and would leave after an hour or so, just as mysteriously as she had arrived.

My journalistic curiosity kicked in, and just a few nights later, I found myself at the Mansarovar Ghat, all alone, with a ballpoint pen and a notepad stuffed in the front pocket of my shirt. I came on foot this time, taking the labyrinthine route through the gullies. When the path opened to the riverside, I saw her: the white woman in her lehenga, dancing alone on the sand and dry mud, facing the dark river. I took a seat on the stone steps a few feet away from her and watched in silence.

She was in her late thirties, perhaps. From my distance, I could see that she wore a pair of earphones, likely listening to the beats providing rhythm for her movement. But all I saw was a haunting, silent swing. She spun her hands above herself to form mudras and then sliced the air with the sharp cuts of her forearm. She trotted and kicked her legs, stretched, and jumped, each time landing on her bare feet.

A half hour passed before she finally stopped, unplugged her earphones, and looked up at me. I waved to say *Hi,* and she came over to sit beside me on the steps.

I introduced myself—in English. 'I saw you dancing here a few days ago. I was wondering if we could speak.' I told her that I had worked on several culture pieces about the city, and asked if she'd be willing to share her story with me for an article.

'Of course!' she smiled. She told me her name, and then thanked me for not interrupting her dance. I asked about the music she was listening to from the iPod* tied around her waist, and she played me a few seconds of psytrance. She was here every night, she said, and her dance was her own version of the Ganga Aarti, an obeisance to this grand river, and more specifically—she said—to the goddess Ganga herself. 'It's how I heal my broken heart,' she said. American accent.

She told me that she'd moved to India almost a year ago, soon after the death of her mother. Her father had passed away earlier. She quit her job and toured around the country, before finding herself in Goa, where she lived for a long stretch of time and forged new relationships. Then, she travelled with a significant other to Varanasi, before that relationship came to an acrimonious end. He left her.**

The encounter of this new grief left her further disillusioned. She decided to stay. She found a small, rented room close to the ghat, spent her days learning Hindi and Hindustani classical music, and her evening at the banks of the river.

At a length of over 2,500 kilometres, the Ganga is the longest river in India, snaking its way down from the Himalayan peaks. In Varanasi, the river briefly changes directions, moving upstream, before twirling around again, eventually heading further southeast, until it discharges into the Bay of Bengal. This woman was streaming through life too, a slow rush towards that eventual discharge, with a

*Dear children, the iPod was like your phone on permanent airplane mode. And it was glorious.

**I promise she was *not* the author of *Eat Pray Love.*

brief meander in my hometown where she would steal a rendezvous with Ganga, dancing under the stars to the river goddess.

She told me that now, she danced to forget, to let go of past hurt and trauma. The river, the breeze, and the living history of the ghats energized her, and she transformed that energy into dance. This dance was a form of meditation, a trance that she churned within herself, a physical movement that cleansed her emotional debris: the people she'd loved, the people she'd lost, and the person she encountered within herself.

She was a disciple of the Ganga now, adopting a little bit of the sacred river, twirling her form to match the water currents.

She had been here for over four months, discovering her own ananda in Varanasi.

Finally, I had to ask the unavoidable. How was she affording this life?

She told me that she had inherited a large sum of money—some tens of thousands of dollars—after the death of her parents. And even before the rupee's sharp tumble in the past decade, those dollars could go a long way in India on a frugal budget.

A share of purchased bliss; time and freedom that only money can buy.

I would wonder, later: in the flow of her riverside meditations, did she meditate upon this privilege, too? Did she realize her rare position to enjoy an indefinite stay in India, without the pressure to make a living, to compete? Did she not notice how the rest of the city succumbed under the stress of survival: bunkars working overtime by the handlooms, daily-wage labourers fighting to be picked for the day's construction sites, teachers exhausted by the burden of overfilled classrooms, the mounting stress of rent, electricity bills, water bills, school fees, old taxes, new taxes, inflation, the cost of giving birth, the cost of hospitalizations, the cost of death? It was like drowning deep in the river, struggling to swim under the dense fluid pressure.

Did she understand it?

Do I?

Haven't I been the same, a traveller without a destination, wandering alone around Khonoma, finding a bed in Pushkar, or sharing conversations on the train to Kochi, moving place to place as per my whim?

In pursuit of my ananda and mauj, haven't I tried to skip over the sobering strains of the world, too?

Over fifteen years have passed since, and the memory of that night returns to me. It's a reminder of the way that I, too, have merely drifted in the breeze. Even as I floated away, I always knew that help was near. I could dive deep into the river, swim upstream or downstream, but I always knew that a boat was by my side, a respite for every time I needed a lifebuoy.

A few days after meeting her, I wrote a story about the woman. I don't know if she ever saw the published article in the paper, but she wasn't at the Mansarovar Ghat the next time I passed by.

For the following weeks, readers and friends asked me often about her. They'd all enjoyed the story, and in turn, I was proud of my work.

And yet, I never saw the woman again. I wondered if I had snatched away the little haven of peace she had enjoyed every evening. Perhaps she regretted consenting to share her story. Or, perhaps, this wasn't about me at all; she was a drifter who needed to drift away: upstream to the far end of the ghats, across the river to the sands on the other side, away to a different town, maybe a different country, or maybe even back home.

In the month of Shravan—which falls during the monsoons in the Hindu calendar—millions of Shiva devotees undertake what is called the Kanwar Yatra, a pilgrimage that takes them to the hotspots of Shiva worship around the country: Haridwar, Gangotri, Sultanganj, Devgarh, Meerut, and of course, Varanasi. In July/

August every year, these Kanwarias are seen on their great journey across the Gangetic belt. The crowds are made up of mostly men (including younger boys) all clad in saffron gear with Shiva insignia, and carrying decorated bamboo poles known as kanwars on which they tie small earthen pots. While many hitch a ride on the way, the entire journey should ideally be walked barefoot, letting the soft bottoms of their feet feel the path: the bitumen or concrete of the highways, dust and mud, heat, moisture, sharp rocks, slippery pebbles, crawling creatures, the smooth marble floor at a temple, the wet stone steps down to the water.

Varanasi gets particularly crowded during Shravan each year, with hundreds of thousands of devotees streaming into town, filling up ashrams and queuing up outside the major Shiva temples—including Kashi Vishwanath, which recently received a glitzy renovation and was inaugurated by the prime minister in a high-profile blend of politics and spirituality.

But the main goal of the Kanwarias is to reach up to the riverbanks. Like many other aspects of Hindu customs and mythology, the Kanwar Yatra is also related to that great Samudra Manthana—the churning of the milky ocean. Before the amrit came the halahala, the deadly poison that Shiva had to swallow whole to save the rest of the cosmos. According to the legends, it was the consumption of bhang that brought Shiva some relief. But he would need an offering of Ganga water to cleanse his body of the poison altogether. Kanwarias have since marked the Kanwar Yatra as a favour back to the god: they travel from far and wide to get to the banks of the Ganga and collect the (supposedly) holy water in their earthen pots. Devotees believe that the river's water has regenerative and healing properties; they return home after the long season of journeying to pour the water upon a Shivling, to continue providing him an antidote for the poison.

It won't surprise you to hear that bhang/cannabis is linked to this entire process. Kanwarias plunge headfirst into full-Shiva roleplay during this journey, adopting a temporary ascetic lifestyle, singing and celebrating on their way. Many will consume bhang to keep their spirits high over the hundreds of kilometres of ultra-marathon walking.

Nowadays, there are even Kanwaria party anthems in Bhojpuri, Hindi, Rajasthani, etc., recorded and released for the devotees every few years in time for the long journeys, including titles like, 'Lagata Kanwariya Bhang Khaile Ba (Looks like the Kanwaria has consumed some bhang)', 'Bhangiya Ke Pisai Na Hoyi (The Bhang Hasn't Been Ground)', or 'Bhang Mein Talli Ho Raha Soo (Getting Wasted on Bhang)'.*

There is another traditional hymn among Shaivites that is the spiritual anthem of each monsoon journey, a verse that goes:

Gang, Bhang, Dono Behen Hai,
Rehti Shivji Ki Sang.
Charan Karne Ki Gang Hai,
Bhajan Karne Ki Bhang.

The Gang(a) and Bhang are sisters.
They live with Shiva
We chant praises with the Gang(a)
We sing bhajans with the Bhang

The praise-singing and cannabis-inspired meditations provide a sense of fun and frolic to the Kanwarias, some ananda once the heat of the North Indian summers subsides with the respite of rain. The Kanwar Yatra is almost like an ancient music festival: where a group of superfans gather for long journeys, camping out in fields across the country, singing and dancing, consuming a whole lot of narcotics, and cheering on their rockstar god.

As many of you may have already experienced, however, this 'Shaivite Coachella' can sometimes become a menace, too. In the

*I'm not sure if I should recommend a deep dive into the Kanwaria music video genre.

past, some locals have clashed with aggressive pilgrims. There have been traffic concerns in gridlocked Indian towns and some instances of violence and vandalism, including stone pelting and a lathi charge, during major clashes in Khandwa, Madhya Pradesh, in 2023.*

And still, the troupes march on; the great monsoon expedition has continued annually, for centuries.

In Varanasi, one doesn't necessarily need to wait for Shravan, or Holi, or Shivratri, or any such special occasion. Bhang and Shiva go hand in hand with the daily lifestyle of many Banarasis. The signboards are omnipresent across the old city: 'Sarkari Bhang Ki Dukan'—Government-approved Bhang Shop—often coupled with a portrait of Shiva or a Shivling. Varanasi is also popular for its akharas, a sort of academy of the physical arts, where pehelwans (wrestlers, bodybuilders, and other martial artists) congregate for kasrat (exercise) and competition. It is well known that the pehelwans will have a daily glass of bhang—mixed with fresh cow milk—to aid their focus and concentration for the long day of practice ahead.

Public fairs and festivals of the past and present Varanasi—like the Bhor Aarti during the Ramlila performances or the Burva Mangal Mela—have historically involved the preparation and use of bhang by local attendees. Close to the Holi festival, some Shiva devotees in Varanasi also celebrate 'Masaan Holi' or 'Chita Bhasma Holi' at the Manikarnika ghat. Here, along with the usual shower of colours, some even smear themselves in ashes of the recently dead as a symbolic gesture to embrace Shiva's role as the god of continuity between life, death, and the afterlife. There's dancing, devotional music on the loudspeakers, and no shortage of bhang.

When the *real* Holi hits a few days later, the whole city becomes a party zone. During my most recent visit, neighbours on both sides of my parents' home began to blast techno-bhakti tracks from as

*In the 2024 Shravan season, a major controversy erupted as dhaba owners on the Kanwaria path in Uttar Pradesh were coerced to display their names to discriminate between Hindu and Muslim shops.

early as 6 a.m. on Holi morning, while men congregated on the street to dance, drink bhang, and wash each other in a rainbow of colours. By afternoon, the celebrations finally quietened down, and the city becomes as ghostly as I've ever seen it. 'Everyone who drank too much bhang is now taking a nap,' my mother tells me.

There is no shortage of chai and paan shops across town, which often sell bhang golis—sometimes sprinkled with pepper or sweetened with sugar—to go as an appetizer alongside the afternoon chai. Yoghurt-based thandai drinks and lassis are sold in many older neighbourhoods of Varanasi, too, where one doesn't have to strive too hard to find the option spiked with cannabis: it will usually be labelled as 'Special' Thandai, and will be more expensive than the rest of the non-narcotic beverages.

One can simply walk into one of these hole-in-the-wall establishments, find a seat, and watch the expert mixologist operate. This bhang is extracted by crushing dried cannabis leaves with mortar and pestle, and water is added to make it into a pasty goo. Some people add black pepper to this goo, which could help lighten the strong smell and taste of wild grass from the bhang paste. This paste is strained through a piece of cloth to produce the final residue. It's stirred into your drink of choice—milk, chai, thandai, whatever—before the final concoction is ready, cheaper than the milkshake from any fast-food restaurant down at the mall. Sometimes it's sweet, sometimes it's salty. Sometimes it's icy, too. Since Varanasi is a major draw for foreign visitors, several tourist-friendly lassi joints can be discovered by anyone wandering through the narrow alleyways, offering a variety of flavours (coconut, banana, chocolate, dry fruits, etc.) mixed with bhang.

Like any edible form of cannabis, the 'high' isn't instant; instead, the THC works slowly into your system, stomach to bloodstream to brain. It could take an hour, sometimes more, while you wander through the gullies of this urban forest of bliss, sipping chai, eating samosas, sitting by the ghats, watching the river, listening to the sound of the temple bells, until you realize that each ring seems to last longer than the last, till the sound reverberates across your skin, until you realize you've been sitting in the same spot staring into the nothingness of the Ganga for what seems like hours, lost in the steady rush of the water, trapped in deep meditation. The world is a different place when you stand up: the steps you remembered down to the ghats seem infinitely high, the structures on each ghat glow under mesmerizing new colours in reflection of the setting sun. and the sound of the electric motors on the boats seem to throb across the breadth of the river, straight into your nervous system.

Time breaks down, so that what you once experienced as a seamless flow now feels like a tiny quantum packet. You begin to see the next packet before the present one concludes, almost predicting the immediate future. You finally understand that you may have no free will at all, that each step forward on the cobbled-stone lanes was a step you were always meant to take. You taste the sugary ras of the gulab jamun before it hits your tongue; you hear a conversation before it's said out loud; your limbs guide your ecstatic dance by the riverside, before your brain can choose for yourself. You're just a passenger, and your vessel is merely passing through the alleys of time. Through the gullies, you imagine yourself lost in the wormhole of time in this immortal city. You see scholars reciting scripture, you see holy men checking their Instagram accounts, you hear the chugging machinery of handlooms, you smell the incense sticks that have been burning around ancient idols, you wade across people and monkeys and dogs and cattle, you have conversations that haunt you all evening, and conversations you'll never remember again. You stop for a chai, you see human bodies burning on pyres, you hear the plucking of a sitar, you see the sun set, and you hear the temple bells again: a ringing that carries you across history, until you fall right back into your present self.

I make a brief visit to see my family in Varanasi. I'd recently told my parents about this ongoing project, and like many people, they hardly understood the properties and legalities associated with cannabis: the differences between bhang, charas, ganja, hemp, and how the plant is distinctly different from the harder, addictive drugs that it is often clubbed with. My research helped them—I think—ponder about some of these nuances; they may not completely agree with me, but my father would soon follow his own curiosity, ask me follow-up questions about how the 'high' feels, and begin to send me news alerts about cannabis dispensaries lining the streets of Bangkok.

After a few days in the comforts of home, I bid my parents farewell. My train seat on the forward journey is still on a long waiting list, so I decide to cancel my plans and make a U-turn. I leave the station to catch a shared autorickshaw to take me back to the riverside. I check myself into a small guest house near Meer Ghat. It's October; the climate is cool and pleasant. From the balcony, I keep my eyes on the Ganga, some 40 feet below the stone balustrade.

My family has always lived within a five-to-ten-minute drive away from the river. But, even with the ghats in proximity, my life has hardly been comparable to most of the permanent dwellers of the old city. My grandfather was an academic; my father spent a decade working with the Indian Administrative Service, before moving into the private sector. *My* Varanasi was mostly the Varanasi of convent schools, office buildings, press conferences, local academics, basketball courts, movie theatres, and shopping markets.

Still, I would end up by the riverside almost every week: to see the sunrise from Tulsi Ghat, take long walks across the ghats parallel to the river, go on boat rides with friends (including the large 'banjara' boats), explore the Chet Singh Qila, pass by the crematoria, stop for cheese pizza at Assi, or merely sit alone on the steps, somewhere quiet, letting the sight of the river lull me into deep contemplation.

It is only as an adult that I decide to reattune myself, to see my hometown from the curious eyes of an outsider. I pretend now that I'm a tourist, too, visiting this city for the first time, ready to succumb to its charms—like that woman I'd seen by the Mansarovar Ghat years ago, dancing to the tune of her own, private freedom.

In the past, I had found myself getting annoyed at the way some tourists exoticized my hometown, enamoured by places I had found mundane. But, a little change in perspective makes me into that kind of traveller, too. Over the past year of travelling for this book—from Kerala and Andhra to Manipur and Himachal—I realize that I haven't broken any new ground for anyone but myself. And yet, every new experience feels special. In some ways, there is value in experiencing a place with the energy of that 'annoying' tourist, too, of never losing one's sense of wonder.

I spend the next few days in intimate proximity to the river, letting the toxic waters brush past my hand. I feel the intense heat of the burning cremation pyres, as the final remains of these human vessels are ravaged by the fires. I consume the delights that these gullies offer, and it doesn't take long for me to harmonize with the rhythm of the city. I walk from gullie to gullie, day and night, without purpose or direction, ending up wherever the paths lead me. Some gullies open back to the river, some take me to the main motorable roads, to the chaos and traffic of city life. Some gullies are dead ends, a path that ends at a brick wall. I turn around and find a new direction to be lost in.

On another day, I shut myself indoors. I plug in my earphones and let the music warm up my insides, like the first sip of hot chai on a cold morning. I imagine that my banal observations are pearls of revolutionary new wisdom. I watch afternoon turn into evening from my bed. The lights are off, and the curtains are drawn shut, but little beams of sunlight still creep in from the windows, giving an eerie feeling of a total solar eclipse. It's a halo that seems to bless the dark room. The sunset feels like a personal reward for me, and me alone. I tell myself that this is the most beautiful thing I have ever seen. I hold up my camera phone to photograph the moment. *Click, click, click.* Small doses of visual enlightenment. It won't matter if the photos don't make sense tomorrow morning.

The ringing begins at sunset. It's the Ganga Aarti again, the mass worship of the river, as thousands of priests, devotees, and tourists congregate at the Dashashwamedh Ghat. The bells pick up volume and tempo, cymbals crash off-beat, motorboats gargle, and the powerful blow of conch shells rises in crescendo. It's an orchestra that attempts to tear apart our earthly limitations, too, to reach up to the stars, to create a racket all the way to imagined heavens.

If you find just the right spot, equidistant between the ghat and the mosque, you'll hear some more magic. The evening maghrib commences, the muezzin calls the namaz from the mosque's minaret, as the sun is given a formal goodnight by the confluence of the two religions. In recent years, the Banarasi air has become polluted with the smog of religious tensions. Spiritual chauvinism has been used to exhibit a muscular force of the majority community. In turn, the lives, livelihoods, and cultural identities of Muslims and other minorities have come under threat.

At this twilight hour, however, the aarti and namaz blend into an enchanting alap. You can close your eyes and celebrate the thriving cultural fusion, the Ganga–Jamuna Tehzeeb that gives all Banarasis a particularly distinct personality, a personality beyond religion and other partitions. The sound is an evocative snippet of humanity clearing its throat, announcing its spiritual presence. Varanasi is one of the most religious cities in the world, a sangam of Hindus, Muslims, Buddhists, Sikhs, Christians, Kabirpanthis, Ravidasis, Theosophists, and more, a city where gods and prophets haunt every corner, where all of fate is attributed to higher powers, where spirituality isn't a choice, but a state of being.

But not for me. Even under the tsunami of spiritual, I have remained unaffected by the pull of any specific faith, until I rejected the idea of religious faith altogether. I perceive the divine as mere placebo for answers till the real answers are discovered. Each society crafted a god in their own image; how is one fiction any truer than the other? I believe that morality can exist independently in itself, without the need of strict religious frameworks, or the awards and punishments offered in the afterlife.

But, in places like my hometown, it is these religious frameworks that have been part of the normalization and acceptance of cannabis. The plant has been part of our scriptural history and consumed by devotees for millennia. In 2023, when the Odisha government banned the use of bhang at Shiva temples and shrines ahead of the Kanwar Yatra to 'curb health hazards', the decision faced an angry opposition, asking the government not to interfere in religious matters. Recipes found in ancient scriptures have allowed our indigenous medicinal systems to consume, experiment, and innovate with the use of 'vijaya'. Great epic stories of Shiva and other celestial beings have given bhang a special exception in the inchoate NDPS Act. In a country where farmers, drug mules, and casual users of the drug are scapegoated and arrested, religion allows a cheat code to produce, transport, possess, and consume cannabis in its many forms—just as long as one gives the necessary tribute to the fictional deities.

(India is not the only country where religion has worked in favour of marijuana. A report by the US Department of State recognized how proposals for decriminalization in Caribbean nations like Barbados, Antigua and Barbuda, Saint Lucia, Dominica, Guyana, and Bahamas have been aided by a push of local Rastafarian communities.)

Cannabis, however, is much older than any religion. For almost the entire history of agriculture, our species has been in a close relationship with the plant. With thousands of years of experience, we have found how this plant can heal us, how it can ease our way of living, how it can delight us. It was only in reverence to its natural positive qualities, that—without understanding the science behind the chemical reactions—we elevated its status to something divine, too, something that provides respite in times of pain, something that can aid the process of deep meditation, something that subtracts the immediate sensory emotions—maya or illusion of this world—and helps to spark the creative imagination of something greater. A taste of the immortal atman itself.

But just like secular humanism—which believes in the capacity for ethics without gods—I feel that boons of cannabis can be celebrated without the interference of religion. India has constitutionally been a secular nation since our independence in 1947: a separation of religion from state, where, ideally, constitutional decisions *should* be made independently of religion, where religious laws *should* remain in the personal domain.

The word 'should', however, is doing a lot of heavy lifting here. In reality, matters of state and faith regularly taint each other, often for political gain, often to violent ends. The unconstitutional marriage of politics and faith was fully consummated at the inauguration of India's expanded new parliament complex in May 2023, as the prime minister led dozens of priests and godmen in the performance of Brahmanical rituals inside the halls of government.

There are few places in the country that witness the daily collision of religion and politics like Varanasi. The city has always been a prominent centre of religious knowledge, but its prominence has also made it an easy target for that religious fervour to be attacked or exploited. Some leaders raze down temples, some use them for votes.

Bhang has it easy in Varanasi—and in many other parts of India. The laws of the land are bent and refracted to match religious sentiments. The rest of the plant? Not so much.

Here's what I think.

Even if there were no great Vedic bhang prescriptions to make soma or grand stories of Shiva tripping through the forest of bliss, the cannabis plant, in itself, should be enough. It's a resilient, natural product which has been used and enjoyed by our species for tens of thousands of years, available damn near everywhere in our country. It makes too much sense for the cultural practices of many Indians. It's too great a natural resource to waste, while a lucrative, profitable industry awaits—particularly for the agrarian economy, with the potential of revolutionizing the livelihood of our farmers. It's a cheaper industrial alternative to the dominant crops, and it's better for the environment, as the Earth heads towards climate catastrophe. This plant is available as a medicinal option to relieve pain, dispel some diseases, and maybe even save some lives. For nations like India, it's too expensive to enact strict narcotics laws concerning cannabis, arresting and imprisoning individuals under the NDPS Act, disrupting lives over a common crop.

Of course, as it is further commercialized, we must ensure strict standards of manufacturing practice, and any medicinal use should be properly tested and licensed before it is prescribed.

Few people in the country have played a more active, on-ground role in advocating for those victimized by harsh NDPS laws than Tripti Tandon. Tandon is a Delhi-based advocate who specializes in drug policy, whose clients have included the most vulnerable individuals in the life-cycle of India's illicit drug trades: truck drivers, couriers, small business owners, etc. Often, these couriers would be assigned to complete high-risk, high-value deliveries in return for a measly sum. During a phone interview, Tandon tells me of a truck driver who had been arrested when transporting a large amount of ganja in Tamil Nadu, usually valued in these parts at over ₹10,000 per kilo, while only earning ₹17 per kilo himself. 'That small an amount!' she exclaims. 'This image that we have that the drug mafia makes a lot of money—it's not really true, especially on the lowest rung. Given the economic situation in the country, (especially) after Covid, we saw lots of people who had small-time jobs or small businesses—they crashed. Many of these people began acting as drug couriers. And ganja is the most ubiquitous.'

Tandon tells me that, in her ideal view, 'It doesn't make sense to send people to jail for cannabis use. And for those who grow and sell cannabis, I don't think they deserve ten to twenty years in prison. A more rational, practical view is needed, since (the plant) is less harmful than other substances... The poorer sections of society, who even in the small level of growing, transporting, or couriering cannabis suffer the most.'

Tandon is encouraged by states like Uttarakhand and Himachal Pradesh that, in recent years, have begun to explore legal cultivation of cannabis. These regions, she believes, will do a great service to dispel doomsday scenarios which fear that progressive cannabis policies will inevitably lead to 'uncontrollable, widespread abuse', and instead, show that the plant can be beneficial to farmers, entrepreneurs, doctors, and more.

'For centuries, we've had a socially-regulated use of cannabis in parts of the country,' says Tandon. 'We should go back and see how it was done at that time. We should learn from how it was then.'

I think often of the Sikkim Anti Drugs Act (SADA), which amended the NDPS Act, and essentially, focused on the rehabilitation and recovery of drug users, instead of treating them like criminals. As several Indian states consider legalization of industrial hemp, the rest of the country can also learn how Sikkim has implemented the first steps of decriminalizing cannabis. In 2021, the Ministry of Social Justice and Empowerment had the same ideas, too, recommending an improvement to the NDPS Act that decriminalizes possession of small quantities of drugs for personal consumption, and to treat drug consumers like 'victims, not culprits'.

The policies will continue to evolve, and may even complete a drastic metamorphosis between the day I finish writing these words and the day you pick up the book to read them. As further medical research continues to prove the plant's healing powers, there will come a time when it will simply be too difficult to deny both high-and low-THC strains of cannabis.

And what if the high-THC maal gets people high? Sometimes I wonder if the reputation of weed as a provider of ishrat—joy—has hurt its chance of legalization and acceptance. *How could something be useful if it makes people so happy?*

I believe that cannabis should be decriminalized—and eventually, legalized—even *in spite* of all the benefits above: medicinal, industrial, environmental, religious, and social. All it needs to be is itself, a source of ananda.

As we've seen from many other states across the world, this process may be a treacherous, ugly road. There will be aggressive pushback, political and moral debates, and the risk of abuse (including by minors). The rights of farmers will have to be protected from the biggest conglomerates. There will be the greedy hands of industry turning this natural resource into a contested commodity, and the greedy hands of the government placing regulatory and tax hurdles to complicate the process. It's inevitable that an underground criminal structure will be replaced by an overground one.

But, on balance, decriminalizing cannabis will only restore the natural order and repair mistakes of the past. No, it's not a completely 'safe' substance: neither is the sugar in your tea, or the ghee on your rotis, or the petroleum you burn in your vehicles, or the screens that you fix your eyes on. We don't need permission from gods and the scriptures to enjoy the many things that sprinkle our lives with these little bursts of happiness. The same should hold true for cannabis, too. Responsible, regulated, and controlled use of ganja is hardly worse than so many of our other human vices. In many cases, it's better.

Present tense.

I'm in the final stages of completing this project. Only the long 'roach' of reviews and edits remain, when I receive news from some friends in Manipur. My visit the previous year had been one of the most memorable time from my journey. But in the summer of 2023 mayhem and violence descended upon the region. Tensions had been simmering for decades between Manipur's majority Meitei population and its tribal minorities, conflicts over land, reservations, identity, and other social divisions. But now, the pressure cooker has finally burst, with widespread arson, ethnic riots, and killings across the state. The violence began in Churachandpur—where I had spent several days with my friend Solomon—and then quickly escalated to Imphal and elsewhere. The Manipur government issued 'shoot at sight' orders. The army and other armed forces created buffer zones on the state's hillside, including many that surround the illegal poppy and cannabis plantations. Curfews emptied the streets. Hospitals ran short of supplies and the transportation of essential medicine—including medication for HIV patients—was disrupted for patients in the hills outside of Imphal. Tens of thousands of paramilitary forces were sent to the state to 'restore' order. Over the next ten months, nearly 200 people were killed, hundreds more injured, over 60,000 displaced from their homes, and approximately 400 churches were damaged or destroyed. There were cases of looting, vandalism, and rape, including a harrowing video from the Kangpokpi district that went viral in July, shuddering the soul of the nation.

The internet shutdowns force Solomon to leave the state, so he could continue working online. He moved with his family to Aizawl in Mizoram, and then to Kalimpong in West Bengal. Aboy spent most of the year in Delhi before returning to Manipur in mid-December. For him, the holiday season is always a pleasant time with the family, but Aboy texts me about the continuing violence in Manipur. 'I don't think it will end soon... I don't think there will be any Christmas this year.'

I find myself checking in regularly; travel has helped ignite an urgent sense of empathy, to a part of the country that had once felt so distant from the India I had grown up in, challenging my ethnocentrism. In its tremendous diversity, India can sometimes feel like a canvas overpopulated with a chaotic mishmash of colours and designs. And yet, with the right perspective, this mishmash produces a visionary piece of art, where the strokes of colour complement each other to form a masterpiece.

It was in discovering the country's wide breadth where I found the greatest source of my ananda: in the individuals whose lives moved me, the wide variety of places so different from my own, the relaxing sound of a long-distance train chugging across the countryside, a hymn to accompany my passage forward. It is what the heady high of cannabis has in common with wanderlust: one finds bliss in living in the present moment, always peering at the world with curious eyes, hoping to understand, hoping to create. Nothing is more important than the experience of this very instant—on the road, or in your head. Perhaps this is why it's called a *trip*.

I wish that the plant can be as free as it makes us feel.

My daughter and I take a walk at night, far above Mussoorie, both insulated on a biting cold night under heavy jackets, beanies, and gloves. We stare up at the night sky. A vivid black canvas, populated with a prismatic array of stars. Suddenly, I realize how close the full moon feels, this object orbiting around us in space, primal and alive, held together by the tug and pull of gravity. My daughter acknowledges it in both English and Hindi. 'Moon. Chanda Mama.'

Following her lead, I find myself looking at its full majesty. *It's right there*, I realize. A rock balanced in the nothingness of space. Much like the rock we're stranded on.

The moon is blindingly white, and the craters on its surface are clearer than ever. It watches us as we watch it. I feel like I could rise on my tiptoes and flick the giant lunar surface with my outstretched fingers, and then stretch further up until my nails scrape against the thin lining of nirvana itself, before I fall back down, a universe restructured, a life re-examined.

Acknowledgements

I owe gratitude to Aienla Ozukum for flagging off this book's journey. It was she who first planted the seed of a book that tells the story of ganja in India. Aienla and Kanika Praharaj—my editors at Aleph Book Company—filtered out some good maal from an abundance of dirt weed. I'm grateful to both.

I'm thankful to my agent Kanishka Gupta for his continuous support and encouragement through the writing process.

There is a long list of people who offered me their time, patience, advice, and hospitality through the course of this project, including Priya Mishra, J. P. Maithani, P. M. S. Raveendranath, Jishnu Raveendranath, Sumit Bhattarjee, Akshay Sahoo, U. Radha Krishna, Rayyan, Anita David, Mustaqim Ansari, Atono Tsükrü Kense, Thokchom 'Jimmy', Marinao Lekngayo, Thotreiyo Keishingh (Aboy), Solomon Pudaite, Khagesh Gautam, Yash Kotak, Amit Vaidya, and Pankaj Chaturvedi.

I wouldn't be doing this without the unflinching support of my family. You have kept me anchored even as I drifted away; your patience and your understanding have allowed me to be me.

Notes

CHAPTER 1: THE SEED

1 **scientists have discovered that, within the first:** 'What are marijuana's effects on other aspects of physical health?', National Institute on Drug Abuse, 13 April 2021.

3 **The main psychoactive ingredient in cannabis:** Terence Ng, Vikas Gupta, Maureen C. Keshock, 'Tetrahydrocannabinol (THC)', National Library of Medicine, 12 November 2023.

3 **THC's successful coup of our system is based on:** 'How does marijuana produce its effects?', National Institute on Drug Abuse, 13 April 2021.

3 **(ANA), which is a fatty acid neurotransmitter found:** Deane Alban, 'Anandamide: Bliss Molecule for Happiness & Mental Balance', BeBrainFit.com, 16 January 2023, <https://bebrainfit.com/anandamide/>.

3 **It was the Israeli organic chemist Raphael Mechoulam:** 'Raphael Mechoulam and the history of cannabis research', *Epigraph*, Vol. 21, No. 1, 2019.

3 **anandamide takes its moniker from the Sanskrit:** Joseph Billions, 'What is Anandamide and How Does It Relate to THC and CBD?', *Cannabis.net*, 19 July 2021, <https://cannabis.net/blog/medical/what-is-anandamide-and-how-does-it-relate-to-thc-and-cbd>.

3 **It is an endogenous ligand:** M. Scherma, P. Masia, V. Satta, W. Fratta, et al., 'Brain activity of anandamide: a rewarding bliss?', *Acta Pharmacologica Sinica*, Vol. 40, No. 3, 26 July 2018.

3 **ANA participates in our endocannabinoid system:** Ibid.

3 **It takes over our neurotransmitters:** Ibid.

4 **Marijuana, in its common recreational form:** 'What is legal and illegal about weed in India? A look at the NDPS Act of 1985', *News Minute*, 23 September 2020.

4 **However, it is permissible to consume bhang:** Ibid.

4 **Former Narcotics Commissioner Romesh:** Sonali Acharjee, 'Should India make Cannabis legal?', *India Today*, 28 September 2020.

CHAPTER 2: MALANA CREAM

7 **Charas is a cannabis concentrate:** Jared Leighty, 'What is charas and how do you make it?', Weedmaps.com, 12 April 2021, <https://weedmaps.com/learn/

products-and-how-to-consume/charas#is-charas-legal-in-india>.

7 **Some estimate that this village:** Shailesh Menon, 'All the highs and lows on marijuana', *Economic Times*, 13 December 2020.

12 **the THC in cannabis mimics the anandamide:** Max Sargent, 'Understanding Anandamide and Its Relationship to THC and CBD', *RoyalQueenSeeds.com*, 5 July 2021, <https://www.royalqueenseeds.com/blog-what-is-anandamide-and-what-role-does-it-play-in-our-bodies-n507>.

13 **The United Nations estimate that:** 'World Drug Report 2023', United Nations Publication, 2023, p. 12.

13 **According to the World Health Organization:** 'Alcohol, Drugs and Addictive Behaviours Unit', World Health Organization.

13 **In 1985, a significant national decision:** 'THE NARCOTIC DRUGS AND PSYCHOTROPIC SUBSTANCES ACT, 1985', Department of Revenue, Government of India.

13 **In recent years, the central government:** Vijaita Singh, 'Centre intensifies crackdown with aim to make India drug-free by 2047', *The Hindu*, 22 April 2023.

13 **The government has claimed to have arrested:** Ibid.

15 **He couldn't be found for a few thousand:** 'Kheerganga Trek', HimalayanHikers.in, <https://www.himalayanhikers.in/kheerganga-trek/>.

15 **The mythologies are ripe with stories of Shiva:** Danielle Preiss, 'Shiva Is A God Who Likes Marijuana — And So Do Many Of His Followers', National Public Radio, 7 March 2016.

17 **There are thousands of acres of land in:** 'For this Himachal village, banned cannabis is its source of livelihood', *India Today*, 4 December 2016.

17 **It has been a recipient of the Cannabis Cup:** P. Krishna Gopinath, 'Malana: The valley of cannabis', *The Hindu*, 10 June 2018.

17 **It has been referred to as 'the charas piece:** Rohit Bhattacharya, 'When It Comes To Getting High Try Best Weed Of India', ScoopWhoop.com, 1 March 2018, <https://www.scoopwhoop.com/reads/kinds-of-maal-in-india/>.

18 **The reason to stay a little delinked:** Romesh Bhattacharji, 'View From the Ground: Heading for the Hills; Cannabis in Malana', Global Drug Policy Observatory, 23 April 2015.

18 **In 2023, there were finally signs of a thaw:** Abhinav Vashisht, 'Kullu: Malana residents seek ropeway connectivity', *The Tribune*, 19 June 2023.

19 **Jamlu is the regional name of Jamadagni:** Anand Parameswaran, 'Malana, The Magic – Of ancient Sages, Myths, Alexander & Malana Cream', Beyonder.Travel, 18 May 2020, <https://beyonder.travel/india/himalayas/malana-the-myths-and-malana-cream/>.

19 **Even to this day, a village priest in Malana:** Neeraj D., 'Malana: Fagli Festival', *Mysterious Himachal*, 5 March 2020, <https://mysterioushimachal.wordpress.

com/tag/jamlu-devta/>; Romesh Bhattacharji, 'View From the Ground: Heading for the Hills; Cannabis in Malana', Global Drug Policy Observatory, 23 April 2015.

19 **Around August every year, Malanis:** Carly Clarke, 'Jamadagni's Temple: The Real Full Moon Festival', PhotoAwards.com, 15–20 August 2014.

19 **'The men in the village drink alcohol**: Ibid.

20 **A thousand-some years after the scriptures:** Rohit Mullick, 'Malana: Does Himachal's Malana Have a Greek Connection?', *Times of India*, 3 January 2023.

20 **In interviews with locals in 2018:** Gopinath, 'Malana: The valley of cannabis'.

20 **Gopinath writes, 'Malanis tell the story of Glenu':** Ibid.

21 **Other journalists have claimed:** Adhiraj Bose, 'Goonj | Marijuana Documentary | Naseeruddin Shah', YouTube.com, 2 April 2013, <https://youtu.be/AJ5349w1sOA?si=BQbqfLCrSvAzR7wI>.

21 **In 1985, the Indian Parliament enacted:** 'THE NARCOTIC DRUGS AND PSYCHOTROPIC SUBSTANCES ACT, 1985', Department of Revenue, Government of India.

21 **In Section 2 of the NDPS Act, cannabis:** Ibid.

21 **More recently, the Supreme Court:** 'Selling ganja seeds not banned under NDPS Act: Supreme Court', *Times of India*, 28 April 2023.

22 **Outside the Act, the legislations of:** 'The Juvenile Justice (Care and Protection of Children) Act, 2000', IndianKanoon.org, 20 November 1989.

22 **A 2019 survey published by the Government:** 'Magnitude of Substance Use in India', Ministry of Social Justice and Empowerment, Government of India, 2019, p. 2.

22 **In late 2022, Mathura police alleged:** Vedika Sud, 'Rats blamed for eating 500 kilograms of cannabis stored by Indian police', *CNN*, 25 November 2022.

24 **It has been claimed that the THC content:** Tirthankar Bose, 'Malana Cream: 05 Facts Which You Don't Know', *Medium.com*, 30 December 2017, <https://medium.com/the-poor-nomad/malana-cream-f231bc36146c>.

26 **The Chabad House in Kasol was opened:** 'About Us: Chabad Kasol', IndiaKosherTravel.com, <https://www.indiakoshertravel.com/Chabad_Kasol>.

27 **It is also estimated that charas worth nearly:** Gaurav Bisht, 'Committee on legalising cannabis in Himachal to submit report within a month', *Hindustan Times*, 16 June 2023.

27 **But much of the charas in distribution in:** Arman Khan, 'Inside the Disastrous Network of Spiked Weed in India', Vice.com, 1 July 2022.

27 **or a prescription sedative called:** Neha Singhal, Naveed Mehmood Ahmad, 'Case for Decriminalising Cannabis Use in India', *VidhiLegalPolicy.in*, 20 August 2020, <https://vidhilegalpolicy.in/blog/case-for-decriminalising-cannabis-use-in-india/>.

28 Some of these adulterations: Arman Khan, 'Inside the Disastrous Network of Spiked Weed in India'.

28 While cafes as far as the Netherlands: Giles Tremlett, 'Ketama Gold puts Morocco top of Europe's cannabis league', *The Guardian*, 27 May 2003.

29 According to some police reports, nearly: Vishal Gulati, 'Increased surety may help fight drugs menace in Himachal: Officials', DaijiWorld.com, 18 March 2020, <https://www.daijiworld.com/news/newsDisplay?newsID=685759>.

28 In response to nuisance caused by the excessive: Giulia Heyward, 'Amsterdam will ban cannabis outdoors in its red-light district', National Public Radio, 10 February 2023.

29 Officials have claimed through seizures: Bhanu P. Lohumi, '"Chitta" reaching Himachal via Punjab more lethal', *The Tribune*, 14 April 2022.

29 In Punjab, which has been hit harder: Anju Agnihotri Chaba, 'Agri experts, farmers bat for cannabis cultivation: "will curb dependence on chitta"', *Indian Express*, 11 October 2022.

29 In his case for cannabis decriminalization: Khagesh Gautam, *Cannabis Indica: Perception Vs Potential*, India: OakBridge Publishing Pvt. Limited, 4 March 2022.

29 It is an industry, Gautam writes: Ibid.

30 In November 2021, the former chief minister: Gagandeep Singh Dhillon, 'Explained: Why is Himachal Pradesh planning to legalise cannabis cultivation?', *Indian Express*, 16 March 2021.

30 BJP minister Ramesh Chand Dhawala—formerly: 'Will consider a policy for controlled cultivation of hemp: Himachal CM', *Indian Express*, 6 March 2021.

30 Thakur's successor as HP's chief minister: 'Himachal hemp is of premium quality; will grow cannabis for medical purposes: CM Sukhvinder Sukhu', *Economic Times*, 13 December 2023.

30 In the summer of 2023, the Himachal: 'Drive against cannabis, opium in Kangra', *Times of India*, 23 May 2023.

30 Around the same time, however: Press Trust of India, 'Himachal Pradesh Government To Form Panel To Explore Possibility Of Legalising Hemp Cultivation', *Outlook India*, 18 April 2023.

30 A group led by the Himachal's Revenue: 'Negi in Dehradun to study cannabis farming', *The Tribune*, 20 May 2023.

30 In a report submitted to the state's chief: Pratibha Chauhan, 'Panel clears hemp farming, Himachal Pradesh eyes Rs 500 crore fiscal "high"', *The Tribune*, 22 September 2023.

31 In September 2023, Negi announced that the: 'Policy for Hemp cultivation soon in Himachal: Minister', *The Pioneer*, 2 September 2023.

31 Cheering on this decision, the BJP MLA from: Rohit Mullick, 'Himachal eyes pot of gold under grass', *Times of India*, 1 October 2023.

31 **Shimla-based advocate Deven Khanna:** Ibid.

31 **Around 4,000 kilos of charas:** Ibid.

31 **Manikaran valley—the same region:** Anand Bodh, 'Himachal Pradesh police detect illegal cannabis cultivation; arrest 34', *Times of India*, 12 October 2023.

31 **Matters had got so out of control that:** Gaurav Bisht, '"Deity orders" closure of joints, guest houses at Malana village famous for hash', *Hindustan Times*, 11 July 2017.

32 **During the Covid-19 pandemic, Malana:** Suresh Sharma, 'Malana isolates itself from world, keeps coronavirus out of village', *Times of India*, 18 May 2021.

32 **has described herself as 'Asia's first female:** Radio City Talks, 'Hempvati aka Priya Mishra | India's Only Female Certified Cannabis Activist | Bhang and Ayurveda', YouTube.com, 20 January 2023, <https://youtu.be/pbrtqp-H598?si=5__CaDaZ6CRWBvJq>.

33 **The 2013 documentary *Goonj—The Empty Call*:** Bose, 'Goonj | Marijuana Documentary | Naseeruddin Shah'.

34 **Until a few years ago, Haneesh Katnawer:** 'From face masks to designer clothes, startup turns hemp into prized ingredient', *Economic Times*, 29 January 2023; Haneesh Katnawer, 'Introducing Hemp Slap Hut - India's first Wattle and Daub Hut with a Workshop Model', *HimalayanHemp.in*, 31 January 2022, <https://www.himalayanhemp.in/post/introducing-hemp-slap-hut-india-s-first-wattle-and-daub-hut-with-a-workshop-model>.

39 **The plant that has gained notoriety:** Preiss, 'Shiva Is A God Who Likes Marijuana — And So Do Many Of His Followers'.

CHAPTER 3: VIJAYA

43 **Reports claimed that over 2.5 lakh lost:** Amit Bhattacharya, 'India's Covid toll in 2nd wave tops 2.5 lakh, 1 lakh more deaths than in 1st wave', *Times of India*, 14 July 2021.

43 **but it is widely accepted that the:** Soutik Biswas, 'Why India's real Covid toll may never be known', *BBC*, 5 May 2022.

43 **Kabristans and graveyards fell short of space:** Geeta Pandey, 'Covid-19: India's holiest river is swollen with bodies', *BBC*, 19 May 2021.

43 **And it was at the precipice of this incoming:** Sandeep Rawat, '9.1 million thronged Mahakumbh despite Covid-19 surge: Govt data', *Hindustan Times*, 30 April 2021.

44 **Two weeks into the fair, more than 2,000:** 'Over 2,000 Covid-19 cases detected at Haridwar Kumbh Mela in past 5 days', *Mint*, 15 April 2021.

44 **It was when India's healthcare infrastructure:** Neetu Chandra Sharma, 'Keep Kumbh mela "symbolic" from now on, says PM; event already a super spreader', *Mint*, 17 April 2021.

47 **One of the attempts to cool this burning:** Sonali Pimputkar, 'Maha Shivratri: Lord Shiva's connection with bhaang decoded!', *Free Press Journal*, 30 May 2019, <https://www.freepressjournal.in/cmcm/maha-shivratri-lord-shivas-connection-with-bhaang-decoded>.

47 **a special jari booti, a herbal:** Stefanie Staelens, 'The Bhang Lassi Is How Hindus Drink Themselves High for Shiva', Vice.com, 11 March 2015.

47 **One version of the story claims that the spilled:** G. A. Grierson, *Report of the Indian Hemp Drugs Commission, 1894-1895*, Vol. 3, p. 246.

47 **In his 1893–94 paper 'On References to the Hemp Plant':** Ibid.

47 **He wandered into a field, and—exhausted:** 'Holi 2022: The reason why Bhang is consumed on Holi', *Times of India*, 16 March 2022.

48 **Cannabis became his favourite little avocation:** Theodore M. Godlaski, 'Shiva, Lord of Bhang', *Substance Use & Misuse*, 2012, Vol. 47, No. 10, pp. 1067–72.

48 **In his 'Note on the Religion of Hemp' as part:** James M. Campbell, 'Note on the Religion of Hemp', in G. A. Grierson's *Report of the Indian Hemp Drugs Commission, 1894-1895*, Vol. 3, p. 252.

49 **In my hometown Varanasi, a city:** Barbara Grizzuti Harrison, 'Shiva's Holy City', *New York Times*, 16 May 1993.

49 **Some fast on the day, some meditate:** 'Stoners and the sacred: Cannabis will always be popular in India thanks to Maha Shivaratri', ScientificInquirer.com, 3 June 2022, <https://scientificinquirer.com/2022/06/03/stoners-and-the-sacred-cannabis-will-always-be-popular-in-india-thanks-to-maha-shivaratri/>.

49 **American psychiatrist Timmen L. Cermak:** Timmen L. Cermak, 'Lord Shiva and Cannabis: Destroyer and Creator', PsychologyToday.com, 6 December 2023, <https://www.psychologytoday.com/us/blog/healing-from-addiction/202312/lord-shiva-and-cannabis-destroyer-and-creator-0>.

50 **As popular mythologist Devdutt Pattanaik has:** Devdutt Pattanaik, 'Doesn't Shiva take drugs?', *Devdutt.com*, 15 June 2016, < https://devdutt.com/doesnaet-shiva-take-drugs/>.

50 **It is traditional for the Balarama statue:** Sourish Bhattacharyya, 'Bhang-On! How India Romances Cannabis', *FirstPost.com*, 18 March 2019.

50 **The Sikh Nihangs refer to cannabis:** Michael Edwin Hawley, Pashaura Singh (eds.), *Re-imagining South Asian Religions: Essays in Honour of Professors Harold G. Coward and Ronald W. Neufeldt*, Netherlands: Brill, 2013, p. 34.

51 **The 1894 Indian Hemp Drugs Commission's:** William Mackworth Young, *Marijuana: Report of the Indian Hemp Drugs Commission, 1893-1894*, United States: Thos, Jefferson Publishing Company, 1969.

51 **In Tantric Buddhism, the *Mahakala Tantra*:** R. C. Parker and Lux, 'Psychoactive Plants in Tantric Buddhism: Cannabis and Datura Use in Indo-Tibetan Esoteric Buddhism', *Erowid Extracts*, June 2008, pp. 6–11.

51 **One of those scriptures is the Atharva Veda:** Joshua J. Mark, 'The Vedas', World History Encyclopedia, 9 June 2020.

51 **Sometimes called the 'Veda of magical:** Gene R. Thursby, Sushil Mittal, *The Hindu World*, United Kingdom: Routledge, 2004.

52 **In Hymn 6 of the Atharva Veda:** Ralph Thomas Hotchkin Griffith (ed.), *The Hymns of the Atharva-veda*, India: E.J. Lazarus, 1895.

52 **The Sanskrit word 'भङ्ग' above was:** Ibid.

52 **Soma, here, is crowned as the ruler of:** Vamadeva Shastri, 'The Secret of the Soma Plant', Vedanet.com, 13 June 2016, <https://www.vedanet.com/the-secret-of-the-soma-plant/>.

53 **Soma would later be popularized in English:** Evan Romano, 'Soma in Brave New World Has Been Talked About Since 1932', MensHealth.com, 15 July 2020, <https://www.menshealth.com/entertainment/a33322972/what-is-soma-brave-new-world-peacock/>.

53 **Some Sanskrit dictionaries have defined vijaya:** 'Vijaya', WisdomLib.org, <https://www.wisdomlib.org/definition/vijaya>.

53 **In a 2021 essay arguing for the legalization:** Ashwin Sanghi, 'India's cannabis law is nonsensical, it's time for "Big Bhang" reform', *The Print*, 15 November 2021.

53 **In February 2017, Gujarat became one of:** 'Gujarat further tightens prohibition', *Times of India*, 23 February 2017.

54 **With the Vedas and victory in mind, law student:** 'Petition in court seeking to legalise cannabis for medical use dismissed', *The Hindu*, 27 July 2019.

54 **Estimates say more than a million people died:** Priya Satia, 'Stanford scholar explains the history of India's partition, its ongoing effects today', Stanford Report, 8 March 2019.

CHAPTER 4: BIG BHANG THEORY

63 **In 2016, Uttarakhand became the first Indian:** G. Seetharaman, 'Hemp cultivation: Uttarakhand's plan to hand out licences to grow the plant is a welcome step for farmers' livelihood', *Economic Times*, 20 December 2015.

63 **The new law in Uttarakhand is extremely:** Ibid.

64 **The '0.3' number is borrowed from the:** 'THCa + Understanding the 2018 Farm Bill: A Comprehensive Guide', CallmeTHCA.com, 21 April 2024, <https://callmethca.com/thca-understanding-the-2018-farm-bill-a-comprehensive-guide/>.

64 **Uttarakhand was officially formed in 2000:** 'State Profile', Government of Uttarakhand, <https://uk.gov.in/pages/state-profile>.

66 **The Chamoli district is also part of the:** Jonathon Amos, 'Chamoli disaster: "It hit the valley floor like 15 atomic bombs"', *BBC*, 13 June 2021.

66 **For over a decade, their chairman/founder:** 'Alakhnanda Ghaati Shilpi

Federation', Fao.org, <https://www.fao.org/mountain-partnership/members/members-detail/en/c/173047/>.

67 In the spring of 1999, Pipalkoti and: I. Sarkar, A. K. Pachauri, M. Israil, 'On the damage caused by the Chamoli earthquake of 29 March, 1999', *Journal of Asian Earth Sciences*, Vol. 19, No. 1 and 2, February 2021, pp. 129–134.

69 Hemp is particularly successful in sequestering: HempSaveEarth, 'Hemp: The Single Best Solution for Worldwide Carbon Sequestration', *Medium.com,* 11 December 2021, <https://medium.com/@hempsaveearth/hemp-the-single-best-solution-for-worldwide-carbon-sequestration-ff8573ba5f37>.

70 The Indian Industrial Hemp Association (IIHA): 'IIHA gets licence to grow industrial hemp in Uttarakhand', BusinessStandard.com, 10 July 2018, <https://www.business-standard.com/article/pti-stories/iiha-gets-licence-to-grow-industrial-hemp-in-uttarakhand-118071000871_1.html>.

71 Since the cannabis crop is not registered: 'Horticulture', Department of Agriculture and Farmers Welfare, <https://agriwelfare.gov.in/en/Hirticulture>.

72 Hundreds (some say thousands) of villages: Neelam Pandey, 'How Uttarakhand's pretty hill hamlets with blue skies & rolling greens became ghost villages', *The Print*, 10 February 2022.

73 According to the Department of Revenue: Sarthak Modi, 'What is the punishment for possession of marijuana?', *iPleaders.in*, 22 December 2017, <https://blog.ipleaders.in/punishment-possession-marijuana/>.

74 Cannabis is a genus of flowering plants in: 'History of Cannabis / Marijuana', TonyDasgostino.co.uk, <https://tonydagostino.co.uk/history-of-cannabis/>.

74 And within these forms of cannabis lie: Ethan B. Russo, *Cannabis and Cannabinoids: Pharmacology, Toxicology, and Therapeutic Potential*, United Kingdom: Taylor & Francis, 2013, p. 28.

74 THC is the 'psychoactive' compound: 'History of cannabis', Lambert Initiative for Cannabinoid Therapeutics, University of Sydney, <https://www.sydney.edu.au/lambert/medicinal-cannabis/history-of-cannabis.html>.

74 CBD, the other primary extract of the plant: Nuna Alberts, 'What Is CBD Oil? Uses, Benefits, Side Effects, and More', EverydayHealth.com, 14 November 2022, <https://www.everydayhealth.com/marijuana/cbd-oil/>.

74 When THC levels are low enough, one finds: Phoebe Nicholson, 'Is Hemp The Crop Of The Future?', YourDaye.com, 24 January 2020, <https://www.yourdaye.com/vitals/sustainability/is-hemp-the-crop-of-the-future/>.

75 In 1753, the Swedish botanist, zoologist: Carl Linnaeus, *Species Plantarum*, United Kingdom: Ray Society, 1753.

75 In this text, Linnaeus classified the 'Cannabis sativa L.': Ibid.

75 A couple years later, French evolutionary biologist: John White, 'Cannabis Indica', CNBSJournal.com.

75 **'*Cannabis ruderalis* Janisch' was identified in 1924:** Darrell Carrington, 'Cannabis 101: History & Terminology: Are These Products Right for Me?', *American Bar Association*, 23 June 2021.

75 **Sativa is usually found in hotter drier climates:** Kimberly Holland, 'Sativa vs. Indica: What to Expect Across Cannabis Types and Strains', Healthline.com, 22 March 2021, <https://www.healthline.com/health/sativa-vs-indica>.

75 **Indica is South Asia's gift to the world:** Ibid.

75 **Some believe that the 'purest' version of Indica:** 'Hindu Kush', Encyclopaedia Iranica, <https://www.iranicaonline.org/articles/hindu-kush>.

75 **To cultivators, 'indica' generally means a shorter:** Rachel Reiff Ellis, 'Indica vs. Sativa: What's the Difference?', WebMD.com, 17 April 2024, <https://www.webmd.com/mental-health/addiction/indica-vs-sativa-whats-the-difference>.

75 **Despite its resonance with our country:** Todd Mccormick, 'Ditch the Old Terminology (An Indica / Sativa Response)', HighTimes.com, 12 May 2023, <https://hightimes.com/weirdos/ditch-the-old-terminology-an-indica-sativa-response/>.

77 **In the 1800s, Nawab Saadat Ali Khan II of Awadh:** 'History of CSIR-National Botanical Research Institute (CSIR-NBRI)', CSIR-National Botanical Research Institute (CSIR-NBRI).

79 **The jumpstart to NBRI's cannabis R&D:** Shashwati Shankar, 'The high point is medical cannabis may come to your backyard soon', *Economic Times*, 2 January 2017.

80 **Meanwhile, on the other side of the globe, a bill:** 'Another bill to raise U.S. THC limit to 1.0% introduced in Congress', HempToday.net, 8 February 2022, <https://hemptoday.net/another-bill-to-raise-u-s-thc-limit-to-1-0-introduced-in-congress/#google_vignette>.

80 **In September 2022, Costa Rica implemented this:** '"Simple" Costa Rican hemp rules set THC limit at 1.0%, make licenses widely available', HempToday.net, 15 September 2022, <https://hemptoday.net/simple-costa-rican-hemp-rules-set-thc-limit-at-1-0-make-licenses-widely-available/>.

80 **There was a ray of hope by the end of the 2022:** Shivani Azad, 'Uttarakhand becomes 1st state to grow "industrial cannabis"', *Times of India*, 22 September 2022.

87 **There are many more varieties of ganja:** 'North India: The Cannabis Sanctuary', IndianLandraceExchange.com, 14 February 2019, <https://indianlandraceexchange.com/indianlandraceexchange/north-india-the-cannabis-sanctuary/>.

87 **The Indian Landrace Exchange describes some of:** Ibid.

88 **In October 2023, police in Maharashtra's:** Shishir Arya, 'Cops seize 20 quintal ganja growing in Ytl cotton, tur fields', *Times of India*, 5 October 2023.

88 Weeks after the police crackdown in Ghonsara: Shishir Arya, 'In Maharashtra's cotton bowl, debt-ridden farmers want nod to grow "ganja"', *Times of India*, 2 December 2023.

89 In a 2019 study, a research team from the: Chrissy Sexton, 'Origins of cannabis traced back 28 million years to the Tibetan Plateau', Earth.com, 12 January 2019, <https://www.earth.com/news/origins-cannabis-tibetan-plateau/>.

89 A 2021 study concluded that humans first: Guangpeng Ren, Xu Zhang, Ying Li, Kate Rideout, et al., 'Large-scale whole-genome resequencing unravels the domestication history of Cannabis sativa', *Science Advances*, Vol. 7, No. 29, 16 July 2021.

89 This latest revelation counters the long-held: Agata Blaszczak-Boxe, 'Marijuana's History: How One Plant Spread Through the World', LiveScience.com, 18 October 2014, <https://www.livescience.com/48337-marijuana-history-how-cannabis-travelled-world.html>.

89 Wherever it was first 'born', cannabis is considered: E. L. Abel, *Marihuana: The First Twelve Thousand Years*, Netherlands: Springer US, 1980.

89 Archaeological evidence for the burning of cannabis: Mary Barna Bridgeman, Daniel T. Abazia, 'Medicinal Cannabis: History, Pharmacology, And Implications for the Acute Care Setting', *P & T : A Peer-reviewed Journal for Formulary Management*, Vol. 42, No. 3, pp. 180–188.

89 The first documented use of cannabis may be attributed: Jaroslav Nemec, *Highlights in Medicolegal Relations*, United States: Department of Health, Education, and Welfare, Public Health Service, National Institutes of Health, National Library of Medicine, 1976.

89 Egyptian historical texts like the Ebers Papyrus: Shadia Mohammad Abdel-Aziz, Abhinav Aeron, Tarek Kahil, 'Health Benefits and Possible Risks of Herbal Medicine', *Microbes in Food and Health*, New Delhi: Springer International Publishing, March 2016.

89 Around the fifth century BCE the Greek historian: James L. Butrica, 'The Medical Use of Cannabis Among the Greeks and Romans', *Journal of Cannabis Therapeutics*, Vol. 2, No. 2, 17 October 2008, pp. 51–70.

90 The cultivation and consumption of cannabis: Barney Warf, 'High Points: An Historical Geography of Cannabis', *Geographic Review*, Vol. 104, No. 4, 25 September 2014, pp. 414–438.

90 One of the most revealing discoveries was made: Matthew Taub, 'The Ancient Pots That Hint at Cannabis's Early Use as a Drug', *The Atlantic*, 12 June 2019.

90 In his wide-ranging 1980 text Marihuana: E. L. Abel, *Marihuana: The First Twelve Thousand Years*.

90 In circa fifth century: Joshua J. Mark, 'Siddhartha Gautama', World History Encyclopedia, 23 September 2020.

90 **In the text *Lalitavistara Sutra* (possibly third century CE):** Chris Bennett, 'Buddha's One Hemp Seed A Day Diet', CannabisCulture.com, 7 August 2016, <https://www.cannabisculture.com/content/2016/08/07/buddhas-one-hemp-seed-a-day-diet/>.

91 **In Mahayana Buddhism, the Buddha is also depicted:** Ibid.

91 **By the eighth century CE, the Sanskrit-language medical:** G. A. Grierson, *Report of the Indian Hemp Drugs Commission, 1894-1895*, Vol. 3, p. 246.

91 **Cannabis has also been named in Indian texts like:** M. Singh, M. M. Sardesai, 'Cannabis Sativa (Cannabaceae) in Ancient Clay Plaster of Ellora Caves, India', *Current Science*, Vol. 110, No. 5, 2016, pp. 884–891.

91 **In the last sections of the Baburnama—the memoirs:** Robert Irwin, 'The Original Mogul', *New York Times*, 7 January 1996.

91 **Known as 'Modern Society's Oldest Edible', majun:** Herbert Fuego, 'How to Make Majoun, Modern Civilization's Oldest Edible', Westword.com, 16 August 2019, <https://www.westword.com/marijuana/how-to-make-majoun-modern-civilizations-oldest-marijuana-edible-11449805>.

91 **In the *Storia Do Mogor*, a seventeenth/eighteenth:** Niccolao Manucci, *Storia Do Mogor; Or, Mogul India 1653-1708 (Vol. 1)*, India: Alpha Editions, 2020.

92 **There is a popular account that involves:** 'India's cannabis law is nonsensical, it's time for 'Big Bhang' reform', *The Print*, 15 November 2021.

92 **In a 1957 report produced for United Nations:** I. C. Chopra, R. N. Chopra, 'The Use of Cannabis Drugs in India', United Nations Office on Drugs and Crime, 1 January 1957, pp. 4–29.

93 **Now, it can be found growing naturally:** Alexis Wnuk, 'How humans brought cannabis to every corner of the globe', NewScientist.com, 8 September 2023, <https://www.newscientist.com/article/2391228-how-humans-brought-cannabis-to-every-corner-of-the-globe/>.

94 **Surrounded by two rivers, environmentalists:** Tara Subramaniam, Vedika Sud, 'A hairline crack became a 3-foot chasm. That's when he knew they had to leave', *CNN*, 15 January 2023.

94 **In September 2022—around the same time:** Gaurav Talwar, 'A hairline crack became a 3-foot chasm. That's when he knew they had to leave', *Times of India*, 17 September 2022.

94 **Environmental experts blamed the construction of the:** Raju Sajwan, 'Joshimath won't be saved unless NTPC's project is shelved: Expert's dire warning', DowntoEarth.org, 6 January 2023, <https://www.downtoearth.org.in/news/natural-disasters/joshimath-won-t-be-saved-unless-ntpc-s-project-is-shelved-expert-s-dire-warning-86997>.

94 **By January 2023, parts of the city were declared:** 'Joshimath areas categorised as "high danger, danger, general"', *Economic Times*, 10 January 2023.

94 hundreds of families were evacuated, abandoning their homes: NDTV, 'Hundreds Evacuated From Danger Zones In "Sinking" Joshimath | The News', YouTube.com, 9 January 2023, <https://www.youtube.com/watch?v=2iENR5JklMc>.

94 Over a hundred families were given temporary shelters: 'Joshimath: Govt approves Pipalkoti site for first phase of rehabilitation', *Hindustan Times*, 18 Janaury 2023.

95 Scientists have said that the stretch of highway: 'Exposure Of Highway Stretch In Uttarakhand To Landslides Likely To Increase: Study', *Outlook India*, 17 January 2023.

CHAPTER 5: IDUKKI GOLD

99 India even has an entire government ministry: 'About the Ministry', आयुष मंत्रालय, भारत सरकार, <main.ayush.gov.in/about-the-ministry/>.

100 In February 2022, the management of the: 'Poonthottam Ayurvedasram', Poonthottam Ayurvedasram, <www.poonthottam.info/ayurcann.html>.

102 Drugs are often seized entering the state: Arjun Raghunath, 'Kerala: A transit point of narcotics', *Deccan Herald*, 3 October 2021.

102 In Tamil Nadu, the district of Nagapattinam: S. Vijay Kumar, 'State of Tamil Nadu vs ganja', *The Hindu*, 2 July 2023.

102 Through 2023, the Sri Lankan Navy seized: 'A large consignment of narcotics and 343 persons engaged in illegal activities brought to justice as a result of naval operations in 2023', news.navy.lk, <https://news.navy.lk/operation-news/2024/01/03/202401031100/>.

102 In January 2022, Kerala police seized: 'Kerala police seize over 460 kg ganja from Thrissur's Perambra village, arrest three persons', *New Indian Express*, 31 January 2022.

103 Over the years, the state's 'war on drugs': 'Kerala youth plant ganja on World Environment Day, Excise Dept not amused', TheNewsMinute.com, 7 June 2021.

103 Sometime around 1,500 years ago, rulers: Mark Cartwright, 'Ellora Caves', World History Encyclopedia, 8 March 2016.

104 The temples at Ellora are such an: HISTORY, 'Ancient Aliens: The Ellora Caves (Season 12) | Exclusive | History', YouTube.com, 13 December 2019, <https://www.youtube.com/watch?v=DYrHQfft07M>.

104 The first known use of the term ganja: 'ganja', Merriam-Webster Dictionary, <https://www.merriam-webster.com/dictionary/ganja?utm_campaign=sd&utm_medium=serp&utm_source=jsonld>.

104 By 1798, the East India Company: E. L. Abel, 'The Indian Hemp Drug Debate', *Marihuana: The First Twelve Thousand Years*, 1980, p. 78.

105 There were costly licences for farmers: Abhinav Srinivasan, 'It's High Time that India Reclaimed Its Ganja', SciencetheWire.in, 31 October 2020, <https://science.thewire.in/the-sciences/oshaughnessy-cannabis-ganja-mahal-lunatic-asylums-ndps-act/>.

105 'Peace!' said he, 'no brawls: it is: Philip Meadows Taylor, *Confessions of a Thug*, United Kingdom: Oxford University Press, 1986.

105 That man was William Brooke O'Shaughnessy: Abhinav Srinivasan, 'It's High Time that India Reclaimed Its Ganja', SciencetheWire.in, 31 October 2020, <https://science.thewire.in/the-sciences/oshaughnessy-cannabis-ganja-mahal-lunatic-asylums-ndps-act/>.

106 After years of research and clinical trials in Bengal: W. B. O'Shaughnessy, *On the Preparations of the Indian Hemp or Gunjah (Cannabis Indica)*, October 1839.

106 O'Shaughnessy recommended cannabis as: Sujaan Mukherjee, 'W. B. O'Shaughnessy and the Introduction of Cannabis to Modern Western Medicine', PublicDomainReview.org, 19 April 2017, <https://publicdomainreview.org/essay/w-b-o-shaughnessy-and-the-introduction-of-cannabis-to-modern-western-medicine/>.

106 '[T]he gunjah consumed in Bengal is chiefly': O'Shaughnessy, *On the Preparations of the Indian Hemp or Gunjah (Cannabis Indica)*.

107 'Its synonymes [sic] are 'bijoya,' 'ujoya': Ibid.

107 'The preceding cases constitute an abstract of my': Ibid.

107 More than 100 follow-up articles were published: Lester Grinspoon, James B. Bakalar, 'Marihuana as Medicine: A Plea for Reconsideration', *JAMA*, Vol. 273, No. 23, 1995.

108 including one by John Russel Reynolds: John Russel Reynolds, 'On the Therapeautical Uses and Toxic Effects of Cannabis Indica', *The Lancet*, Vol. 135, No. 3473, 22 March 1890, pp. 637–638.

108 O'Shaughnessy passionately detailed Abdullah's: O'Shaughnessy, *On the Preparations of the Indian Hemp or Gunjah (Cannabis Indica)*, p. 39.

108 '[I]t seems evident that at least one advantage': Ibid.

108 By the 1800s, the 'drug of the century': Sean Blanchard, Matthew J. Atha, 'A sociopolitical history of cannabis and the British Empire 1840–1928', Indian Hemp Drug Commission Report.

109 In 1842, China signed the Treaty of Nanjing: 'Treaty Of Nanjing (Nanking), 1842', USC US-China Institute, <https://china.usc.edu/treaty-nanjing-nanking-1842>.

109 the British were 'enabling the longest: Thomas Manuel, *Opium Inc.*, India: HarperCollins India, 2021.

109 Historian Utathya Chattopadhyaya recently: Ayesha Munawar, 'Cannabis Fueled a Revolt in British-Ruled India', UCSB Humanities and Fine Arts.

110 Since the earliest days of civilization: CPRG India, 'Legalization of Cannabis: The Next Big Question of Civil Liberties in India', YouTube.com, 21 July 2021, <https://www.youtube.com/watch?v=pYGe_O_gA_Y>.

110 But, by the 1870s, the colonizers shared: Khagesh Gautam, *Cannabis Indica: Perception Vs Potential.*

110 In an 1872 survey, a colonial administrator: Abhinav Srinivasan, 'It's High Time that India Reclaimed Its Ganja', SciencetheWire.in, 31 October 2020, <https://science.thewire.in/the-sciences/oshaughnessy-cannabis-ganja-mahal-lunatic-asylums-ndps-act/>.

111 where I finally meet Jishnu Raveendranath, and his: 'Our Story', Poonthottam Ayurvedasram, <https://www.poonthottam.info/ourstory.html>.

113 Studies have shown that the molecular: T. Cassano, R. Villani, L. Pace, A. Carbone, et al., 'From Cannabis sativa to Cannabidiol: Promising Therapeutic Candidate for the Treatment of Neurodegenerative Diseases', *Frontiers in Pharmacology*, Vol. 11, No. 124, 2020.

114 Ayurveda specialists have noted that the: Biljana Dušić, 'Cannabis from the perspective of Indian Traditional Medicine, Ayurveda', *International Institute for Cannaboids*, 2 June 2017.

114 Fresh leaf juice (bhang) is also used to treat dandruff: Ibid.

114 Researchers of modern medicine have: E. B. Russo, 'Cannabis and epilepsy: An ancient treatment returns to the fore', *Epilepsy & Behavior : E&B*, Vol. 70, Part B, 2017, pp. 292–297; C. W. Webb, S. M. Webb, 'Therapeutic benefits of cannabis: a patient survey', *Hawai'i Journal of Medicine and Public Health : A Journal of Asia Pacific Medicine & Public Health*, Vol. 73, No. 4, 2017, pp 109–111.

114 In 2018, the US Food and Drug Administration: 'FDA Approves First Drug Comprised of an Active Ingredient Derived from Marijuana to Treat Rare, Severe Forms of Epilepsy', US Food and Drug Administration, 25 June 2018.

115 And in early January 2024, an Indian: Somrita Ghosh, 'Cannabis-based drug launched to treat epilepsy in children', *The Mint*, 10 January 2024.

116 Another cannabis-focused healthcare: 'HempStreet join hands with Amrita School of Ayurveda to conduct clinical trials on Menstrual cramps', HealthWorld.com, 17 October 2022, <https://health.economictimes.indiatimes.com/news/industry/hempstreet-join-hands-with-amrita-school-of-ayurveda-to-conduct-clinical-trials-on-menstrual-cramps/94917453>.

117 But, every road to regulation features a couple: Abhinav Srinivasan, 'It's High Time that India Reclaimed Its Ganja', SciencetheWire.in, 31 October 2020, <https://science.thewire.in/health/oshaughnessy-cannabis-ganja-mahal-lunatic-asylums-ndps-act/>.

118 'ascertain whether, and in what form': William Mackworth Young, *Report of the Indian Drugs Hemp Commission, 1893–1894*, India: Superintendent of

Government Printing, 1894.

118 In an essay analyzing the work of historian: Sebastiaan Broere, 'Indian Hemp Drugs Commission', *UCLA Social Sciences MANAS*, <https://southasia.ucla.edu/history-politics/colonial-epistemologies/indian-hemp-drugs-commission/>.

118 Cases of alleged insanity—from asylums in: Abhinav Srinivasan, 'It's High Time that India Reclaimed Its Ganja', ScienctheWire.in, 31 October 2020, <https://science.thewire.in/health/oshaughnessy-cannabis-ganja-mahal-lunatic-asylums-ndps-act/>.

118 'Insanity,' writes Broere, 'came to be understood': Sebastiaan Broere, 'Indian Hemp Drugs Commission', *UCLA Social Sciences MANAS*, <https://southasia.ucla.edu/history-politics/colonial-epistemologies/indian-hemp-drugs-commission/>.

119 The commission's findings, however, would disappoint: Indian Hemp Drugs Commission, *Answers Received to Selected Questions*, Calcutta: Office of the Superintendent of Government Printing, 1895.

119 'deprive the very poorest of the population': Ibid.

120 In the US, closely following the hysteria of: 'Did You Know... Marijuana Was Once a Legal Cross-Border Import?', *U. S. Customs and Border Protection*, 20 December 2019.

120 Indian hemp was called a 'Billion Dollar Crop' by: *Popular Mechanics Magazine*, Vol. 70, Minnesota: Popular Mechanics Company, 1938.

121 A compromise was reached: India promised: Gabriel G. Nahas, Henry Clay Flak (eds.), *Drug Abuse in the Modern World: A Perspective for the Eighties*, 1 January 1981.

121 In his book *Cannabis Indica: Perception vs. Potential*: Khagesh Gautam, *Cannabis Indica: Perception Vs Potential.*

121 The bill passed in both houses of Parliament: Narcotics Control Bureau, 'THE NARCOTIC DRUGS AND PSYCHOTROPIC SUBSTANCES, ACT, 1985'.

125 The solution to this issue—i.e., the: Llyod Lee, 'Mosquitoes are most attracted to a chemical compound present in butter, cheeses and yogurts. Their deterrents can be a chemical found in plants, including cannabis', BusinessInsider.in, 20 May 2023, <https://www.businessinsider.in/science/news/mosquitoes-are-most-attracted-to-a-chemical-compound-present-in-butter-cheeses-and-yogurts-their-deterrents-can-be-a-chemical-found-in-plants-including-cannabis-/articleshow/100372119.cms>.

127 The first tea estate is believed to have been: Giji K. Raman, 'A brief history of tea industry in Munnar', *The Hindu*, 21 January 2019.

127 Today, there are more than fifty tea estates: Vijeesh, '100 year Lockhart Tea Factory Munnar', Munnar.holiday, <https://www.munnar.holiday/munnartourism/lockhart-tea-museum-factory-munnar/>.

127 **Journalist Bobins Abraham, in interviewing some:** Bobins Abraham, 'Asia's Best Marijuana Is Grown In India And Its In Kerala. Here's The Full Story Of Idukki Gold', IndiaTimes.com, 24 January 2017, <https://www.indiatimes.com/news/india/idukki-gold-the-legendary-indian-marijuana-that-you-may-never-get-your-hands-on-264249.html>.

127 **In 2023, twenty-eight-year-old Akhil:** Shaju Philip, 'Meet the Kerala Sahitya Akademi winner who drives an excavator by day', *Indian Express*, 22 July 2023.

129 **A 2012 study for the *Psychopharmacology*:** R. Andres Sewell, Ashley Schnakenberg, Jacqueline Elander, Rajiv Radhakrishnan, et al., 'Acute effects of THC on time perception in frequent and infrequent cannabis users', *Psychopharmacology*, Vol. 226, 2012, pp. 401–413.

131 **Similar claims have been made in Tamil Nadu:** S. Vijay Kumar, 'State of Tamil Nadu vs ganja', *The Hindu*, 2 July 2023.

132 **It wouldn't stay good for too long: two months:** 'Info leak to extremist outfits: Mobiles of three cops taken for inspection', *Times of India*, 19 May 2022.

132 **A few months later, the accused officers would:** '3 officers transferred for leaking information from Munnar police station to terror outfits', English.Mathrybhumi.com, 22 July 2022, <https://english.mathrubhumi.com/news/kerala/leaking-information-from-police-station-3-officers-under-scanner-transferred-to-different-districts-1.7717753>.

133 **In January 2024, fourteen members of a police:** 'Kerala forest personnel rescue lost police team from wilderness', *Deccan Herald*, 31 January 2024.

134 **In 2011, nearly 30,000 marijuana plants were:** 'War on Drugs: Nearly 30, 000 Marijuana plants destroyed in Tripura', NorthEastLiveTV.com, 12 December 2021, <https://northeastlivetv.com/topnews/war-on-drugs-nearly-30000-marijuana-plants-destroyed-in-tripura/>.

134 **Most dramatically, in early 2022, in the biggest:** 'Andhra Pradesh: Ganja worth Rs 500 cr burnt by police in Visakhapatnam-WATCH', TimesNowNews.com, 12 February 2022, <https://www.timesnownews.com/mirror-now/in-focus/article/andhra-pradesh-ganja-worth-rs-500-cr-burnt-by-police-in-visakhapatnam-watch/858254>.

135 **Kerala has consistently been one of the:** Nikhil Rampal, 'UP, Bihar at bottom of India's justice league', *India Today*, 1 April 2022.

135 **In May 2023, a joint investigation by the:** 'Nearly 2,500 kg of methamphetamine worth around Rs 12,000 crore seized by NCB, Navy in Indian waters', English.MathruBhumi.com, 13 May 2023, <https://english.mathrubhumi.com/news/kerala/nearly-2-500-kg-of-methamphetamine-worth-around-rs-12-000-crore-seized-by-ncb-navy-in-indian-waters-1.8555205>.

136 **Kerala was once known to have the country's:** Poonam Binayak, 'What You Need to Know About Kerala's Love Affair with Alcohol', TheCultureTrip.com, 3

February 2021, <https://theculturetrip.com/asia/india/articles/what-you-need-to-know-about-keralas-love-affair-with-alcohol>.

CHAPTER 6: SHEELAVATHI

141 The Upper Bondas—with a population: Akshay Kumar Sahoo, 'What is COVID? ask Bonda tribals of Malkangiri', *Deccan Chronicle*, 24 September 2020.

141 The BDA is a government programme launched to: 'Particularly Vulnerable Tribal Groups PVTGs in Odisha', CrackItToday.com, 16 May 2021, <https://crackittoday.com/current-affairs/particularly-vulnerable-tribal-groups-pvtgs-in-odisha/>.

143 In 2021, nearly half of the cannabis-based drugs: India in Pixels (@india.in.pixels), Instagram, 22 May 2023, <https://www.instagram.com/p/CsiXfO9NE8H/>.

145 In January 2023, the city was declared the: 'Visakhapatnam declared new capital of Andhra Pradesh, know the state's 3 capital plan', *Economic Times*, 31 January 2023.

146 By the end of 2023, the Vizag city police: Nalla Babu, 'Vizag key transit point for ganja smugglers', *Times of India*, 1 January 2024.

147 In 2009, former prime minister Manmohan: Rahi Gaikwad, 'Manmohan: naxalism the greatest internal threat', *The Hindu*, 11 October 2009.

148 Sahoo is an experienced journalist: 'Bonda tribals seek milk, not sattu for kids', OrissaPost.com, 8 October 2021, < https://www.orissapost.com/bonda-tribals-seek-milk-not-sattu-for-kids/>.

150 We pass another bend on the highway, near: 'Maoists target anti-Naxal force, kill 11 jawans in Orissa', *NDTV*, 4 April 2010.

151 In 2012, a day before the then-minister of: 'Maoists strike ahead of Jairam's visit', *New Indian Express*, 3 June 2012.

151 More recently, in the nearby forests around: '23 Maoists killed in encounter in Odishass Malkangiris, Business-Standard.com, 24 October 2016, <https://www.business-standard.com/article/news-ani/23-maoists-killed-in-encounter-in-odisha-s-malkangiri-116102400366_1.html>.

153 on 3 October 2021, a few hundred individuals: 'Lakhimpur Kheri violence: What happened on October 3 and what do we know so far?', *Newslaundry*, 11 October 2021, <https://www.newslaundry.com/2021/ 10/11/lakhimpur-kheri-violence-what-happened-on-october-3-and-what-do-we-know-so-far>.

153 Pedestrians were run over by the first: Kris Thomas, 'A Politician's Convoy Ran Into Protesters. Nine People Have Died Since', Vice.com, 4 October 2021, <https://www.vice.com/en/article/qj873m/farmers-protest-lakhimpur-india>.

154 It was, indeed, that same fateful Sunday—3 October: Tarini Mehta, 'Aryan Khan drugs case: Complete story of arrest of SRK's son in Mumbai cruise ship drugs case', *India Today*, 2 November 2021.

154 Eight individuals were detained that day: Ibid.

154 a number of charges including: Section 8(c): Ibid.

155 There were also some past WhatsApp chats: Arvind Ojha Saurabh Vaktania, 'Ananya Panday agreed to arrange "ganja" for Aryan. When asked by NCB, said "was joking"', *India Today*, 22 October 2021.

156 Now, an independent witness alleged that Sameer: 'Witness Prabhakar Sail stands by extortion allegation in Aryan Khan drugs case', *The Tribune*, 26 October 2021.

156 Saner minds soon prevailed, as Khan was finally: Tarini Mehta, 'Aryan Khan drugs case: Complete story of arrest of SRK's son in Mumbai cruise ship drugs case', *India Today*, 2 November 2021.

156 Six months later, the NCB dropped all charges: Deeptiman Tiwary, Sadaf Modak, Jayprakash S. Naidu, 'Narcotics Bureau admits no evidence: Aryan Khan cleared', *Indian Express*, 28 May 2022.

156 Since 2017, the NCB, the Coast Guard, the: Mahesh Langa, 'Heroin worth ₹1,500 crore seized at Kandla port in Gujarat', *The Hindu*, 21 April 2022.

156 Just a few weeks before Khan's arrest: Appaji Reddem, 'Mundra Port drug seizure | Big haul, small fish and a dead end', *The Hindu*, 20 November 2021.

157 This followed the seizure of heroin worth ₹1,500: Mahesh Langa, 'Heroin worth ₹1,500 crore seized at Kandla port in Gujarat', *The Hindu*, 21 April 2022.

157 I assume that the cargo seized is only a small: 'Maharashtra: Over 250 kg of hashish washed up on Ratnagiri beaches in 6 days, seized', *Mid-Day*, 21 August 2023.

157 They found over 3,000 kilos of: Taniya Dutta, 'India seizes 3,300kg of narcotics off Gujarat coast', TheNationalNews.com, 28 February 2024, <https://www.thenationalnews.com/world/asia/2024/02/28/methamphetamine-cannabis-india-narcotis/>.

157 In 2021, the DRI reported the seizure of a: 'Bihar, Nagaland, UP top in seizure of ganja: DRI report', *Indian Express*, 7 December 2021.

157 In 2020—the first year of the Covid-19: Sai Krishna Muthyanolla, 'Data: Quantity of Drugs Seized Increased in Last Few Years, Factly.in, 29 August 2023, <https://factly.in/data-quantity-of-drugs-seized-increased-in-last-few-years/>.

158 In a moment of refreshing yet sad honesty: Sonali Acharjee, 'Should India make Cannabis legal?', *India Today*, 28 September 2020.

158 A 2020 study in Mumbai by the Vidhi Centre: Neha Singhal, Naveed Mehmood Ahmad, 'Case for Decriminalising Cannabis Use in India', *VidhiLegalPolicy.in*.

159 In his 2020 paper, 'Racism and Its Effect on: R. Solomon, 'Racism and Its Effect on Cannabis Research', *Cannabis and Cannabinoid Research*, Vol. 5, No. 1, 2020, pp. 2–5.

159 'Marihuana is a short cut to the insane asylum': Ibid.

159 The word 'marijuana' itself originated: Rebecca Rivas, 'Why some people believe "marijuana" is a racist word, and why it doesn't offend me', MissouriIndependent.com, 2 May 2023, <https://missouriindependent.com/2023/05/02/why-some-people-believe-marijuana-is-a-racist-word-and-why-it-doesnt-offend-me/>.

160 'There are 100,000 total marijuana smokers in': R. Solomon, 'Racism and Its Effect on Cannabis Research', pp. 2–5.

160 The trailer of *Reefer Madness* leaves: thecoolidge, 'Reefer Madness | Original Trailer | Coolidge Corner Theatre', YouTube.com, 14 October 2019, <https://www.youtube.com/watch?v=yXtumnTN6zg>.

160 Reefer Madness is hilariously terrible: Louis J. Gasnier, *Reefer Madness*, 1936, 1 hr 6 mins.

160 A year after its original release, the 1937: U. S. Treasury Department, 'THE MARIHUANA TAX ACT OF 1937', DrugLibrary.org, <https://www.druglibrary.org/schaffer/hemp/taxact/mjtaxact.htm>.

161 It was only after the 1969 US Supreme Court: Richard D. Pullman, 'Leary v. United States: Marijuana Tax Act - Self-Incrimination', *SMU Law Review*, Vol. 23, No. 5, January 1969.

161 The decriminalization of marijuana in the: M. B. Bridgeman, D. T. Abazia, 'Medicinal Cannabis: History, Pharmacology, And Implications for the Acute Care Setting', *P & T : A Peer-reviewed Journal for Formulary Management*, Vol. 42, No. 3, 2017, pp. 180–188.

161 Since then, usually following along partisan: Elliott Davis Jr., Claire Hansen, Horus Alas, 'Where Is Marijuana Legal? A Guide to Marijuana Legalization', USNews.com, 30 April 2024, <https://www.usnews.com/news/best-states/articles/where-is-marijuana-legal-a-guide-to-marijuana-legalization>.

161 The criminalization of marijuana continues to: 'Highest to Lowest - Prison Population Total', PrisonStudies.org, <https://www.prisonstudies.org/highest-to-lowest/prison-population-total?field_region_taxonomy_tid=All>.

161 In both public and private prisons in the US: Paul Barach, 'Private Prisons and Marijuana', *PotGuide.com*, 20 July 2021, <https://potguide.com/blog/article/private-prisons-marijuana/>.

161 According to the American Civil Liberties Union: 'New ACLU Report: Despite Marijuana Legalization Black People Still Almost Four Times More Likely to Get Arrested', *ACLU*, 20 April 2020.

161 Data from the Justice Department revealed: Lee Fang, 'The Real Reason Pot Is Still Illegal', TheNation.com, 2 July 2014, <https://www.thenation.com/article/archive/anti-pot-lobbys-big-bankroll/>.

162 And then, there is perhaps the biggest: 'Pharmaceuticals - United States',

Statista.com, <https://www.statista.com/outlook/hmo/pharmaceuticals/united-states>.

162 It is no surprise then that pharma lobbyists: LZ Granderson, 'Column: Big Pharma won't be happy about marijuana cutting into its profits', *LA Times*, 20 April 2022.

162 In 2017, the US Department of Health: Dan Merica, 'Trump declares opioid epidemic a national public health emergency', *CNN*, 26 October 2017.

162 In 2021, synthetic opioids were reportedly: 'Drug Overdose Deaths in the U.S. Top 100,000 Annually', National Center for Health Statistics, 17 November 2021.

162 Shockingly, fentanyl overdose is now: 'DEA Administrator on Record Fentanyl Overdose Deaths', GetSmartAboutDrugs.org, <https://www.getsmartaboutdrugs.gov/media/dea-administrator-record-fentanyl-overdose-deaths#:~:text=LAST%20UPDATED%3A,100%20times%20stronger%20than%20morphine.>.

162 In April 2022, the MORE Act: Rebecca Shabad, 'House passes landmark marijuana legalization bill', *CNBC*, 1 April 2022.

163 In Chicago, India-born Annu Khot: Ishani Duttagupta, 'Meet Annu Khot, an Indian woman who runs a cannabis venture in Chicago', *Times of India*, 27 August 2023.

164 'Thank God. Could you imagine someone': 'Americans React To Brittney Griner Returning Home From Russia', TheOnion.com, <https://www.theonion.com/americans-react-to-brittney-griner-returning-home-from-1849871523/slides/4>.

164 On a February afternoon in 2022: The Print, 'From first seeds sown by traders to tribals' cash crop: How Andhra Pradesh became a "ganja hub"', YouTube.com, 15 February 2022, <https://www.youtube.com/watch?v=YHOS--BjwTU>.

164 The scenes were repeated in the NTR district: ANI, X, 25 December 2022, <https://x.com/ANI/status/1607043350468915200>.

164 The intention, according to state police: Siva G., '81% of cannabis seized in Alluri district came from Malkangiri and Koraput', *Times of India*, 2 January 2024.

164 The state's chief minister Y. S. Jagan Mohan: '1.93 lakh kg of ganja seized in five AP districts, destroyed', *The New Indian Express*, 25 December 2022.

165 According to some sources, nearly 150 villages: Prem Udayabhanu/Ullas Ilankath, 'Psychedelic "Idukki Gold", made in Andhra & Orissa | Video', Onmanorama.com, 27 July 2016, <https://www.onmanorama.com/news/kerala/ganja-trail-idukki-gold-andhra-orissa.html>.

165 In one particularly dramatic drug bust in: 'Massive Cannabis Bust in Guwahati: Two Arrested with 2640kg of Ganja', SentinelAssam.com, 11 October 2023, <https://www.sentinelassam.com/north-east-india-news/assam-news/massive-

cannabis-bust-in-guwahati-two-arrested-with-2640kg-of-ganja-670723 >.

165 In Siliguri, West Bengal, four individuals were: Rajesh Saha, '4 Smuggling Drugs in Coffin from Tripura to Bihar Arrested', *India Today*, 30 May 2023.

165 Of late, smugglers in this region have begun to: Nalla Babu, 'Ganja smugglers now move from road route to waterways in AOB', *Times of India*, 11 August 2023.

165 Many cross the river under the cover of night: Pinto Deepak, 'Marijuana smugglers avoid highways, tolls in bid to evade cops', *Deccan Chronicle*, 12 September 2023.

165 In a creative twist, a number of individuals: Hemendar Sharma, 'Cops arrest 4 more for transporting ganja using Amazon services', *India Today*, 23 November 2021.

165 In another major smuggling racket: 'Women operators of northeast-based narcotics racket nabbed in Bengal', DaijiWorld.com, 29 December 2023, <https://www.daijiworld.com/news/newsDisplay?newsID=1153610>.

165 The cat-and-mouse game in the nation's: Neeshita Nyayapati, 'Sai Dharam Tej to play a cannabis peddler in Gaanja Shankar', *Times of India*, 16 October 2023.

166 In the first three months of Operation: Ashish Pandey, 'Operation Parivartan: Andhra Pradesh police cracks down on cannabis cultivation', *India Today*, 10 February 2022.

166 Meanwhile in nearby Hyderabad, the: Nikhila Henry, X, 28 October 2021, <https://x.com/NikhilaHenry/status>.

166 By 2024 New Year's Eve, the Telangana: 'Telangana police to use drug detection kits this New Year: How it works', *News Minute*, 29 December 2023.

166 The secretary of the Joint Action Committee: Nalla Babu, 'Price of Sheelavathi variety touches new high after crackdown pushes up demand', *Times of India*, 27 November 2021.

166 On one single day in September 2021: Satyasundar Barik, 'Over 3 tonnes of ganja seized on single day in Odisha', *The Hindu*, 21 September 2011.

167 A few months later, local police: 'Odisha: PVTG Bonda villages come under ganja cultivation', *The Statesman*, 15 November 2021.

167 Malkangiri is among eight districts in Odisha: Ibid.

167 Police are said to receive satellite: 'Cops, NCB plan to rein in drug mafia', *Times of India*, 2 June 2023.

167 Controversy erupted in early August 2023: Debabrata Mohanty, 'Mob sets fire to police station in Odisha accusing cops of cannabis smuggling', *Hindustan Times*, 5 August 2023.

167 Dozens of police platoons were dispatched: Fareha Naaz, 'Odisha cannabis case: Section 144 imposed after violent mob sets fire to Kandhamal district's police station', *Mint*, 6 August 2023.

167 Villagers in Malkangiri have staged protests: Satyasundar Barik, '"We will give up ganja cultivation if MSP is guaranteed for agriculture produce," say Odisha villagers', *The Hindu*, 23 November 2021.

167 The district administration offered schemes: Ibid.

167 Demand for Sheelavathi across the country: 'Expensive high: Ganja prices touch an all-time high in India', Newsmeter.in, 24 December 2022, <https://newsmeter.in/regional/andhra-pradesh/expensive-high-ganja-prices-touch-an-all-time-high-in-india-705480>.

167 Nationwide, out of the 23 lakh kilos of: Nalla Babu, 'Andhra Pradesh's Sheelavathi smokes out Himachal Pradesh's Malana Cream, in new high', *Times of India*, 6 February 2024.

168 The name Sheelavathi is borrowed from: B. Vijayakumar, 'Sheelavathi (1967)', *The Hindu*, 28 August 2011.

169 The first recorded ganja arrest in this region: Sumit Bhattacharjee, 'War against weed in Visakha Agency', *The Hindu*, 22 December 2021.

170 An acre is estimated to yield about a tonne of: Sumit Bhattacharjee, 'Extremism and ganja a heady cocktail in Visakha Agency', *The Hindu*, 10 November 2021.

170 Bhattacharjee and others have hypothesized: Dr G. Shreekumar Menon, 'Opinion | "Sheelavathi" Takes India By Storm', News18.com, 1 March 2024, <https://www.news18.com/opinion/opinion-sheelavathi-takes-india-by-storm-8798810.html>.

171 The 'encounters' reached fever pitch: 'Andhra: Two TDP leaders, including an MLA, shot dead by Naxals', Business-Standard.com, 23 September 2018, <https://www.business-standard.com/article/news-ani/andhra-two-tdp-leaders-including-an-mla-shot-dead-by-naxals-118092300471_1.html>.

171 Parts of the Araku Valley were known to be: Ashish Pandey, 'Andhra MLA, ex-MLA shot dead in Maoist attack', *India Today*, 23 September 2018.

171 Haragopal, who passed away in October 2021: 'Maoist Akkiraju Haragopal dies due to ill-health in Chhattisgarh', *Telangana Today*, 14 October 2021.

171 Protestors in Araku and Dumbriguda burned: 'Visakhapatnam: Angry locals set fire to police station', *Deccan Chronicle*, 24 September 2018.

171 A few weeks later, Maoists released a statement: Sumit Bhattacharjee, 'Maoists own up killing of Kidari, Soma', *The Hindu*, 3 November 2018.

172 It takes a small industrial set-up: Prem Udayabhanu/Ullas Ilankath, 'Psychedelic "Idukki Gold", made in Andhra & Orissa | Video', Onmanorama.com, 27 July 2016, <https://www.onmanorama.com/news/kerala/ganja-trail-idukki-gold-andhra-orissa.html>.

172 In a major haul in May 2023, Bengaluru police: 'Bengaluru police seize illegal drugs worth Rs 6.61 crore in 2 major hauls', *Indian Express*, 11 May 2023.

172 A few months later, a similar haul of hash oil: '2 from Madurai held with hash oil worth Rs 2 crore in Bandra', *Indian Express*, 8 December 2023.

174 I depart early in the morning from the: 'Narcotics Sniffer Dogs Smell Out Ganja at Vizag Railway Station', *Deccan Chronicle*, 6 September 2023.

181 'Perhaps we might, in a "light-hearted" moment': Khagesh Gautam, *Cannabis Indica: Perception Vs Potential*, p. 76.

CHAPTER 7: DUM MAARO DUM

183 A historical town in Uttar Pradesh: A historical town in Uttar Pradesh, Barsana is: The Editors of Encyclopaedia Britannica, 'Radha', Britannica.com, 24 June 2023, <https://www.britannica.com/topic/Radha-Hindu-mythology>.

183 During the spring festival of Holi: Nidhan Singh, 'Barsana Bhog', *TheChakkar.com*, 23 June 2023, <https://www.thechakkar.com/home/barsanabhog>.

184 Sometimes, the drink is known as siddhi: Chopra and Chopra, 'The Use of the Cannabis Drugs in India'.

184 During this festival, some of the Sikhs: Ajit Singh, 'What is Shaheedi Degh', *FrontlinePunjabiYouth.com*, 12 November 2007, <https://frontlinepunjabiyouth.blogspot.com/2007/11/what-is-shaheedi-degh.html>.

184 The drink is said to help bring peace: Amrit Singh, 'Shaheedi Degh in Sikh History', AmritWorld.com, 12 August 2018, <https://www.amritworld.com/main/?p=82#sthash.agD98t5F.dpbs>.

184 Most Sikh teachings, however, assert: W. H. McLeod, *Sikhs and Sikhism: comprising Guru Nanak and the Sikh Religion, Early Sikh Tradition, The Evolution of the Sikh Community, and Who Is a Sikh?*, India: OUP India, 2004.

185 In another tale of his many (stoned): Zinia Bhargava, 'Bhang and Holi: What's the Story?', *Condé Nast Traveller*, 28 March 2021.

185 Some have the dosha of spring, known: Dr Anjali Sharma, 'An Ayurvedic Perspective on Marijuana', VandeAyurshilpi.com, 14 January 2021, <https://www.vandeayurshilpi.com/post/an-ayurvedic-perspective-on-marijuana>.

185 'In Bengal, for instance, the custom': Chopra and Chopra, 'The Use of the Cannabis Drugs in India'.

186 'To certain sects of Mohammedans': Ibid.

189 According to a popular legend: Tim Craig, 'In the land of towering pot plants, Pakistani farmers brace for a buzz kill', *The Washington Post*, 22 September 2015.

190 The Tirah Valley is now known for being: Ibid.

190 Some farmers even employ the century-old: Abubakar Siddique, 'Pakistan's Goat-Grown Hashish', Radio Free Europe/Radio Liberty, 2 June 2012.

190 Various charas melas (hash carnivals): Indian Landrace Exchage [irrazinig], 'The Hashish carnival or the "Charas Mela"...', Instagram, 15 August 2023, <https://www.instagram.com/reel/Cv-QuJKNSCH/?igshid=MTc4MmM1YmI2Ng%3D%3D>.

190 As per landrace experts, much of the cannabis: 'North India: The Cannabis Sanctuary', Indian Landrace Exchange, 14 February 2019, <https://indianlandraceexchange.com/indianlandraceexchange/north-india-the-cannabis-sanctuary/>.

190 This man taught local farmers how: 'Kashmir Ice - Dark Hash - Purchased from Bluebird | BushDoc Review', SmokersGuide.com, 20 November 2005, <https://www.smokersguide.com/hashweed/407/kashmir_ice.html#.Y_Fpd3bMK3B>.

191 The most aggressive of these drives was: Iftikhar Gilani, 'Cannabis and poppy are Kashmir's new cash crops', DNAIndia.com, 28 June 2011.

191 This agreement was the first foreign: 'First-Ever Cannabis Medicine Project Coming up in Jammu: Jitendra Singh | Council of Scientific & Industrial Research | CSIR | GoI.', Council of Scientific and Industrial Research, 2022.

191 D. Srinivas Reddy, who took over as: Tingmin Koe, 'India's national research institute boss on plans for CBD and cancer pain research', NutraIngredients-Asia.com, 27 July 2022, <https://www.nutraingredients-asia.com/Article/2022/07/27/India-s-national-research-institute-boss-on-plans-for-CBD-and-cancer-pain-research#>.

191 A review meeting of the Cannabis Research Project: 'Union Minister Dr Jitendra Singh says, India's first Cannabis Research Project will be set up in Jammu with Canadian collaboration', Press Information Bureau, 2 March 2023.

192 Of late, the region has also faced an increase: Fayaz Wani, 'Over 10 per cent of J&K's population are drug abusers: Report', *New Indian Express*, 5 August 2023.

192 In recent years, there has been a disturbing rise: Arrsh Kumar, 'Drug Abuse in Kashmir: A Generation Lost', RisingKashmir.com, 28 October 2023, <https://risingkashmir.com/drug-abuse-in-kashmir-a-generation-lost>.

192 In a Muslim-majority state where alcohol is: Maziyar Ghiabi et. al, 'Islam and Cannabis: Legalisation and Religious Debate in Iran.', *The International Journal on Drug Policy*, Vol. 56, 1 June 2018, pp. 121–127.

192 It has also been hypothesized by mental health: Mukhtar Khan, 'AP photos of Kashmir's mental health clinics show the invisible scars of decades of conflict', APNews.com, 2 September 2023.

192 Much like India, cannabis is the most common: Roshan Maharjan, Prasiit Sthapit, 'Red Is the Colour of Spring', *The Caravan*, 30 September 2021.

192 'By 1972, cannabis was the second-largest industry in': Sean Williams, 'Purple Haze: Cannabis Returns to Kathmandu', *Harper's Magazine*, October 2023.

193 Under pressure from the international: Vera Rubin (ed.), *Cannabis and Culture,* Germany: De Gruyter, 3 June 2011.

193 Decades later, the nation is beginning: Anup Ojha, Timothy Aryal, '"Highly anticipated": Activists stoked as government announces feasibility study plan for medicinal marijuana', *The Kathmadhu Post*, June 2023.

193 The illicit trade across the borders: Mohd. Dilshad, 'UP police busts international drug racket, four held', *Times of India*, 15 September 2023.

193 Over the course of a week in September 2023: Arun Bam, 'How American marijuana is entering India via Nepal?', MyRepublica.NagarikNetwork.com, 18 September 2023, <https://myrepublica.nagariknetwork.com/news/american-marijuana-enters-nepal-via-postal-parcels/?categoryId=81>.

193 The country's tourism minister recently: IANS, 'SL eyes cannabis cultivation to come out of economic crisis', Investing.com, 2 August 2023, < https://in.investing.com/news/sl-eyes-cannabis-cultivation-to-come-out-of-economic-crisis-3750917>.

194 In Pushkar, drifting tourists have been: 'Crackdown on cannabis mafia in Kullu, 34 arrested', *The Tribune*, 13 October 2023.

194 Rajasthan has its own strain, a cousin of: 'North India: The Cannabis Sanctuary', Indian Landrace Exchange, 14 February 2019, <https://indianlandraceexchange.com/indianlandraceexchange/north-india-the-cannabis-sanctuary/>.

194 In 2017, an expert committee of archaeologists: Neeraj Santoshi, 'Bhang preserving Mahakal Jyotirlingam from erosion, says ASI report', *Hindustan Times*, 5 October 2017.

195 Cannabis offerings at temples are hardly a: Dhirendra Shukla, 'Unique Rituals at Chitrakoot's Hanuman Temple: The Intriguing Tradition of Cannabis Offerings', News18.com, 27 June 2023, <https://www.news18.com/india/unique-rituals-at-chitrakoots-hanuman-temple-the-intriguing-tradition-of-cannabis-offerings-8190571.html>.

197 In 2020, the BJP government in Goa: Gerard de Souza, 'Goa govt considering legalising cannabis cultivation, opposition sees red', *Hindustan Times*, 30 December 2020.

197 Cannabis remains a favourite of the: Murari Shetye, 'From '20-22, 98% drugs seized in state were cannabis based', *Times of India*, 15 Deceber 2023.

198 Years later, the New Age speaker: 'Maharishi Mahesh Yogi hated the Beatles smoking pot in his ashram', OneIndia.com, 6 February 2008, <https://www.oneindia.com/2008/02/06/maharishi-mahesh-yogi-hated-beatles-smoking-pot-ashram-1202285760.html>.

204 Months later, his therapist would claim that: 'Sushant Singh Rajput's therapist: "He was suffering from depression and hypomania, Rhea Chakraborty his strongest support"', *Hindustan Times*, 2 August 2020.

205 The NCB identified two men: Abbas Lakhani: Kaveree Bamzai, 'Showbiz and Narcotics: A Bad Trip', *Open Magazine*, 8 October 2021.

205 Then, Rajput's cook told investigators that he: Mukesh Singh Sengar, '"Saw Him Smoke Ganja," Says Sushant Singh Rajput's Cook To Investigators', *NDTV*, 6 September 2020.

205 'Before Sushant sir committed suicide': 'Mumbai: Sushant Singh Rajput's death opened a can of cannabis', *Free Press Journal*, 4 October 2021, <https://www.freepressjournal.in/mumbai/mumbai-sushant-singh-rajputs-death-opened-a-can-of-cannabis>.

205 Later reports suggested that Rajput's former: 'Sushant Singh Rajput case: Jaya Saha confesses to ED that she suggested CBD oil for the late actor's depression', *Times of India*, 28 August 2020.

205 Then, there were allegations that Chakraborty: IANS, 'Sushant Singh Rajput Case: Was Rhea Chakraborty mixing CBD oil in the late actor's drinks at someone's behest?', Bollywood Life, 27 August 2020.

205 There are no clear answers for depression: 'What causes depression?', *Harvard Health Publishing*, 10 January 2020.

205 The *Indian Journal of Psychiatry* did publish: Aniruddh P. Behere, Prakash B. Behere, et. al, 'Cannabis: Does it have a medicinal value?', *Indian Journal of Psychiatry*, Vol. 59, No. 3, Jul–Sep 2017, pp. 262–263.

205 In India, Rajput's death caused a spike: Mohana Basu, 'Dope to hope—India is seeing unprecedented boom in CBD. With AYUSH blessing', *The Print*, 28 June 2023.

207 In the eye of the storm, Chakraborty: Sonam Saigal, 'Rhea Chakraborty delivered marijuana to Sushant: NCB', *The Hindu*, 13 July 2022.

207 arrested in September 2020 on the abetment: 'Rhea Chakraborty was kept in special cell in 2020, danced with inmates on last day', *India Today*, 19 October 2022.

207 Soon, more individuals from the: 'Bollywood drugs nexus: NCB grills Arjun Rampal for second time', *New Indian Express*, 21 December 2020.

207 Matters got so out of hand that some top: '"Irresponsible reporting": Top Bollywood production houses move court against Republic TV, Times Now', *Scroll.in*, 12 October 2020.

207 'A sadhu's chillum holds more marijuana': Sonali Acharjee, 'Should India make Cannabis legal?', *India Today*, 28 September 2020.

207 In a recent interview, cannabis advocate: CPRG India, 'Legalization of Cannabis: The Next Big Question of Civil Liberties in India', YouTube.com, 3 August 2021, <https://www.youtube.com/watch?v=pYGe_O_gA_Y&t=2s>.

207 There have been other recent cases, too: 'Narcotics Control Bureau arrests comedian Bharti Singh in drug case', *The Hindu*, 21 November 2020.

208 In response to the growing fervour of negativity: Mantra Mugha, Facebook, 26 November 2020, <https://www.facebook.com/mantra.mugdh/posts/pfbid087NCqsyv2Q5S8bbF9QNx7Py95kgNc7hGQQ1VsP7r4VHtLUHcfpKbG7nC7fDxS4k3l>.

210 But you wouldn't be logging on to Silk Road: James Ball, 'Silk Road: the online drug marketplace that officials seem powerless to stop', *The Guardian*, 22 March 2013.

211 assassins, and every kind of narcotic: Amrutha Gayathri, 'From marijuana to LSD, now illegal drugs delivered on your doorstep', IBTimes.com, 6 November 2011.

211 In recent years, several major busts: 'Germany closes Russian darknet market Hydra', DW.com, 4 May 2022, <https://www.dw.com/en/germany-closes-russian-darknet-market-hydra/a-61362417>.

211 In February 2020, the NCB arrested: Bismee Taskin, 'Karnataka's "LSD King" ran a Bitcoin drug racket like no other. And he used Telegram, Zomato', *The Print*, 15 November 2022.

211 The NCB has said that the use: Vijaita Singh, 'Centre intensifies crackdown with aim to make India drug-free by 2047', *The Hindu*, 23 April 2023.

211 The biggest fish (so far) in the Indian: Bismee Taskin, 'Karnataka's "LSD King" ran a Bitcoin drug racket like no other. And he used Telegram, Zomato', *The Print*, 15 November 2022.

212 'During the course of the investigation, the team': Ibid.

212 In February 2022, twenty-two: Ravi Jalhotra, 'NCB constable, financial analyst, Army officer's son among 22 held in pan India drug trafficking case', ANINews.com, 13 February 2022, <https://www.aninews.in/news/national/general-news/ncb-constable-financial-analyst-army-officers-son-among-22-held-in-pan-india-drug-trafficking-case20220213103545/>.

212 Later that year, the Hyderabad Narcotics Enforcement: 'Dark Web-Based Drug Racket Busted In Hyderabad, Crypto Used For Payment', *NDTV*, 2 September 2022.

212 In Gujarat, the Ahmedabad Cyber Crime: 'Drugs Worth ⊠ 48 Lakh Found Concealed In Toys, Books Packages In Gujarat', *NDTV*, 30 September 2023.

213 In Bengaluru, for example, the Mysore: Shweta Singh, Pragya L. Krupa, 'College students dial M for marijuana', *Deccan Chronicle*, 26 July 2018.

213 But NCB officers say that most of the: '"Grass" is not greener, cleaner in Garden City', *New Indian Express*, 12 October 2017.

213 The seventy-six-year-old had become: 'Ganja Dealer Farida Arrested, Proclaimed State's First-ever Woman Goonda', Manglorean.com, 21 March 2015, <https://www.mangalorean.com/ganja-dealer-farida-arrested-proclaimed-states-first-ever-woman-goonda/>.

213 In July 2023, police in Karnataka's: Neha Kidwai, 'Future Up In Smoke? Shop Owners Sell Ganja-Laced Chocolates To Children', *NDTV*, 10 August 2023.

213 Parents found that their children were: Rohit Swamy, 'No Kidding: From Ganja-Laced Sweets to MDMA & Ecstasy, Bengaluru's Drug Web Sets Sights on Children | Exclusive', News18.com, 12 August 2023.

214 A similar discovery was made in Coimbatore: Wilson Thomas, 'Coimbatore police intensify drive against "ganja chocolates" as samples confirm cannabis presence', *The Hindu*, 6 February 2023.

214 In Telangana, school students were: Ankita Sengupta, 'Ganja chocolates: 10 things to know about the highly addictive marijuana sweets', MoneyControl.com, 31 January 2014, <https://www.moneycontrol.com/news/trends/ganja-chocolates-10-things-to-know-about-highly-addictive-and-illegal-marijuana-sweets-12161281.html>.

214 In December 2022, the centre filed: Abraham Thomas, 'Drugs legalised in US finding way into India, Centre tells SC', *Hindustan Times*, 20 December 2022.

214 An American federal survey reported: 'Marijuana and hallucinogen use among young adults reached all-time high in 2021', National Institutes of Health, 22 August 2022.

214 In 2019, India issued a ban on all: O. Dyer, 'India bans e-cigarettes by executive order', *BMJ (Clinical research ed.)*, September 2019, p. 366.

215 In 2022, however, Rayyan—who: Laxmi Mohan Kumar, '"Now I'm Finally Home": Rayyan Monkey Talks On Positive Representation, Mental Health, & Queers Of Indian History', TheLogicalIndian.com, 23 August 2022, <https://thelogicalindian.com/lgbtq/rayyan-monkey-the-queer-activist-creating-more-positive-representation-37099>.

217 in the 2021 financial year, India Post: 'Number of mails delivered by India Post from financial year 2016 to 2022, by type (in millions)', Statista.com, <https://www.statista.com/statistics/1287273/india-post-number-of-mail-delivered-by-type/>.

217 In September 2023, for instance: Shiv Sahay Singh, 'Two arrested for sourcing narcotics over dark web in Kolkata', *The Hindu*, 9 September 2023.

217 the average joint usually contains: Michele W. Berger, 'New Penn Research Shows Average Joint Contains Much Less Marijuana Than Thought', *Penn Today*, 8 July 2016.

220 'It's possible to be *dependent* without being *addicted*': 'Is marijuana addictive?', National Insitutute on Drug Abuse, June 2015.

220 A report on *Healthline* clarifies that: Kimberley Holland, 'A Quick Take on Cannabis and Its Effects', Healthline.com, 22 June 2023, <https://www.healthline.com/health/what-is-cannabis>.

CHAPTER 8: NASHA

222 'they mingled among the natives': Homer, H. Rieu (ed.), *The Odyssey (Penguin Classics)*, London: Penguin Books, 2003.

223 Brown sugar (or smack) is often adulterated: 'Brown Sugar Addiction - Treatment, Symptoms and Causes', Lybrate.com, 24 June 2023, <https://www.

lybrate.com/topic/treatment-for-brown-sugar-addiction>.

224 Significant research papers have: 'Cannabis and Other Drugs', *Cannabis and Public Health*, 15 February 2024.

224 The 'gateway hypothesis' has: Cody Jorgensen, Jessica Wells, 'Is marijuana really a gateway drug? A nationally representative test of the marijuana gateway hypothesis using a propensity score matching designCannabis and Other Drugs', *Journal of Experimental Criminology*, Vol. 18, 6 April 2021, pp. 497–514.

225 Delhi University's North Campus: Karn Pratap Singh, 'Delhi plagued by 64 drug hot spots, says task force', *Hindustan Times*, 1 May 2023.

225 Recently, Sanjeev Bikhchandani: Sanjeev Beekhchandani, X, 7 September 2023, <https://x.com/sbikh/status/1699829193784324310>.

225 The tweet sparked a widespread: Leher Kala, 'To be young & high', *Indian Express*, 17 September 2023.

225 Not long after, a video went viral from a: Lavkesh Singh, '"Ganja is as easy as getting toffee or lollipop": Student's bold revelation video goes viral', *Times of India*, 8 March 2024.

226 Think of this number as a hotline rather: Samridhi Tewari, 'Drug cases on the rise, peddlers target college students', *The Hindu*, 30 January 2024.

226 Some dealers in the city may even offer: Anvit Srivastava, 'Karachi, atom bomb, Bazooka, Pikachu: These are street lingo for drug cocktails', *Hindustan Times*, 4 June 2018.

231 THC alters an area of the brain: Bruno Dubois, Harald Hampel, Howard Feldman, Paul Aisen, et. al, 'Preclinical Alzheimer's disease: Definition, natural history, and diagnostic criteria', *Alzheimer's Dement*, Vol. 12, No. 3, March 2016.

231 But it is here that the impact of cannabis: S. H. Kim, J. W. Yang, K. H. Kim, J. U. Kim, et al., 'A Review on Studies of Marijuana for Alzheimer's Disease - Focusing on CBD, THC', *Journal of Pharmacopuncture*, Vol. 22, No. 4, 2019, pp. 225–230.

232 Certain research has shown that about one: Keri Wiginton, 'Marijuana Addiction and Abuse', WebMD.com, 12 October 2023, <https://www.webmd.com/mental-health/addiction/ss/slideshow-marijuana-abuse-addiction>.

233 In a 2023 study by the *Addiction* journal: Josh Hathway, Denise Adams, et. al, 'Cannabis use disorder and adverse cardiovascular outcomes: A population-based retrospective cohort analysis of adults from Alberta, Canada', *Addiction*, Vol. 119, No. 1, January 2024, pp. 137–148.

233 Regular marijuana smokers have shown: A. Malik, K. S. Fatehi, N. N. Menon, P. Chaturvedi, et al., 'Review of Medicinal Use of Cannabis Derivatives and the Societal Impact of Legalization', *Indian Journal of Palliative Care*, Vol. 26, No. 3, 2020, pp. 369–380.

234 Many states around the world share this: Devirupa Mitra, 'India Votes to Remove Some Controls on Cannabis in UN Treaty', ScienceTheWire.in, 4 December 2020, <https://science.thewire.in/external-affairs/south-asia/india-votes-to-remove-some-controls-on-cannabis-in-un-treaty/>.

235 Recent research by the University of: Paurush Omar, 'Why are cannabis poisoning cases on a rise in United States? Research from University of Sydney reveals', *Hindustan Times*, 27 July 2023.

235 A *New York Times* report in 2022 noted: Christina Canon, 'Psychosis, Addiction, Chronic Vomiting: As Weed Becomes More Potent, Teens Are Getting Sick', *New York Times*, 23 June 2022.

235 In addition to uncontrollable vomiting and addiction: Ibid.

236 Clinically depressed patients could worsen: 'Marijuana', Mayo Clinic, 10 August 2023.

236 For younger, developing brains: 'What you need to know about cannabis use and teens', *Cannabis and Public Health,* 15 February 2024.

236 In 2018, a Berlin-based data-driven: 'This Is How Much Weed Costs in 120 Cities Across the World', Vice.com, 30 January 2018.

237 In a more localized report released: 'Three crore Indians use cannabis; ganja in Northeast, bhang elsewhere', *Indian Express*, 25 February 2019.

237 Four states from India's Northeast: Anupam Rohit, 'The drug menace in Northeast India', *Arunachal Times*, 24 January 2023.

237 The Indian Army has suggested that: Deutsche Welle, 'Myanmar's civil war drives up drug production', *Indian Express*, 6 June 2024.

239 As cannabis use rises in Nagaland—particularly: Atono Tsükrü Kense, 'Nagaland: Use of cannabis among youngsters on the rise', *Morung Express*, 6 February 2020.

239 In recent years, there have been stories of: 'Nagaland: 5 arrested with marijuana worth Rs 4 crore', EastMojo.com, 12 September 2021, <https://www.eastmojo.com/nagaland/2021/09/12/nagaland-5-arrested-with-marijuana-worth-rs-4-crore/>.

239 In April 2018, the Rifles and other departments: 'AR, Police destroy marijuana cultivation in Intangki forest', *Morung Express*, 11 April 2018.

240 For example, in a single week in January 2022: 'Nagaland Police arrests 37 persons in various cases', NagalandPage.com, 2 February 2022, <https://nagalandpage.com/nagaland-police-arrests-37-persons-in-various-cases/>.

240 Nagaland is one of the handful of: Joel Rodrigues, 'Welcome to the dry state: Dealing with alcohol prohibition in Nagaland', *Hyphen Journal*, 2020.

240 The larger, unfortunate impact of: Tokato K. Sumi, 'The perturbed impact of counterfeit alcohol in Nagaland', *Nagaland Post*, 30 November 2020, <https://nagalandpost.com/index.php/2020/11/30/the-perturbed-impact-of-counterfeit-alcohol-in-nagaland/>.

241 In December 2022, Yaba tablets: Arman Khan, 'World Is Yours: How a Cheap

Synthetic Drug Is Ravaging India's Northeast', Vice.com, 31 May 2023.

241 In Mizoram, another state where: 'Drug abuse claims 68 lives in 11 months in Mizoram', *The Hindu*, 2 December 2023.

241 After the Assam Rifles burned: 'Assam Rifles burns away illegal cannabis plantations worth Rs 1.5 crore in Tripura', RepublicWorld.com, 15 December 2023, <https://www.republicworld.com/india/general-news/assam-rifles-burns-away-illegal-cannabis-plantations-worth-rs-15-crore-in-tripura>.

241 Chief Minister Manik Saha admitted: '4 Tripura cops injured in attack after cannabis plantation destroyed in West Tripura', NorthEastLiveTV.com, 15 December 2023, <https://northeastlivetv.com/topnews/4-tripura-cops-injured-in-attack-after-cannabis-plantation-destroyed-in-west-tripura/#:~:text=However%2C%20incumbent%20Tripura%20Chief%20-Minister,illegal%20drug%20seizure%20and%20destruction.>.

241 Approximately 28 lakh cannabis: Debraj Deb, '5 cops injured, police vehicles damaged in clash after cannabis plantation destruction in West Tripura', *Indian Express*, 14 December 2023.

241 Earlier in the year, Union Home: Tanmoy Chakraborty, 'Tripura: Drugs worth Rs 9.5 crore destroyed in state', IndiaTodayNE.in, 17 July 2023, <https://www.indiatodayne.in/tripura/story/tripura-drugs-worth-rs-95-crore-destroyed-in-state-616220-2023-07-17>.

241 In November 2023, Tripura police: Abhishek Dey, 'Seven women along with six infants held with cannabis in Dharmanagar', TripuraChronicle.in, 6 November 2023, <https://tripurachronicle.in/local-news/seven-women-along-with-six-infants-held-with-cannabis-in-dharmanagar/>.

242 A month later, when members of: 'Seven women along with six infants held with cannabis in Dharmanagar', United News of India, 15 December 2023.

242 Tensions flared: the police conducted: Priyanka Deb Barman, 'Tripura cops who destroyed 60,000 cannabis plants attacked; 5 hurt: Official', *Hindustan Times*, 14 December 2023.

242 In South Tripura, police have begun: Biswendu Bhattacharjee, '2 cannabis smugglers from MP get 15-yr RI', *Times of India*, 2 September 2023.

242 by late 2023, district police in Dahod: 'Dahod police busts cannabis plantation with the aid of AI and Drones', DeshGujarat.com, 23 November 2023, <https://deshgujarat.com/2023/11/23/dahod-police-busts-cannabis-plantation-with-the-aid-of-ai-and-drones/#google_vignette>.

242 For every such action, there is an almost: Debabrata Mohapatra, '"Maoists grow ganja among other plants to avoid sats"', *Times of India*, 22 January 2024.

242 In mid-2023, the Home Ministry: 'DRUGS SEIZED BY BSF', Ministry of Home Affairs, 9 August 2023.

242 Recent busts have also uncovered narcotics: 'Bengal Police bust racket selling marijuana in Bangladesh', DaijiWorld.com, 17 September 2023, <https://www.daijiworld.com/news/newsDisplay?newsID=1121363>.

244 An adviser to the excise department: Imkong Walling, '"Need not view alcohol from the prism of religion"', *Morung Express*, 29 May 2022.

245 Khonoma is also famed for the 1879: 'Showdown between people of Khonoma village and British authorities, 1879', Indian Culture.gov.in.

252 They have proudly contributed to: Phanjoubam Chingkheinganba, 'UFO providing humanitarian services contrary to popular belief', E-Pao.net, 8 October, 2015, <https://e-pao.net/epSubPageExtractor.asp?src=leisure.Essays.UFO_providing_humanitarian_services_contrary_to_popular_belief_By_Phanjoubam_Chingkheinganba>.

253 'We are all covered by the same blue sky': 'Universal Friendship organisation', Facebook, <https://www.facebook.com/people/Universal-friendship-organisation/100063902319992/>.

253 Jimmy, like over half of Manipur's: Khomdon Singh Lisam, *Encyclopaedia of Manipur*, Vol. 1, India: Kalpaz Publications, 1 January 2011.

253 Disputes over land—and many: Patricia Mukhim, 'Patricia Mukhim writes on Manipur conflict: Meiteis and the Kukis and Nagas have to learn to co-exist and resolve differences amicably', *Indian Express,* 8 May 2023.

254 Another member of Satjal, Kapil Arambam: Kapil Arambam, 'UFO Sightings in Manipur', *KapilArambam.BlogSpot.com*, 27 September 2012, <https://kapilarambam.blogspot.com/2012/09/ufo-sightings-in-manipur.html>.

255 In December 2021, Biren Singh's: 'Satjal Academy holds 22nd Rising Day', *Imphal Free Press*, 10 December 2021.

259 A death certificate was issued by: Khelen Thokchom, 'Rest in peace for miracle - Disciples of Manipur NGO chief await resurrection', *The Telegraph*, 10 February 2006.

260 In February 2020, the Manipur: Sobhapati Samom, 'Manipur government considering legalising cannabis plantation', *Hindustan Times*, 22 February 2020.

260 But when I visit Imphal two years: 'Manipur Assembly Elections: BJP will secure at least 40 seats, says CM Biren Singh', *The Fress Press Journal*, 31 January 2022.

261 In the early 2000s, the International: Patricia Mukhim, 'Patricia Mukhim writes on Manipur conflict: Meiteis and the Kukis and Nagas have to learn to co-exist and resolve differences amicably', *Indian Express*, 8 May 2023.

261 Many of these plantations in Ukhrul: Rahul Karmakar, 'Cannabis high for Manipur's start-up dream', *The Hindu*, 23 September 2019.

261 K. C. Verma, the former head of: K. C. Verma, 'The bungled drug operation', *The Tribune*, 12 January 2023.

262 The porous border with Myanmar: Iboyaima Laithangbam, 'Drug running continues unabated in Manipur', *Frontline*, 15 February 2023.

262 The Home Ministry reported that over: Bharti Jain, 'Over 17,000 acres of Manipur's opium poppy fields destroyed since 2018: MHA', *Times of India*, 2 August 2023.

262 The forced destruction of poppy and: Dhiren A. Sadokpam, 'Looking at Manipur's Ethnic Violence From the Perspective of Drug Trade and National Security', *The Wire*, 30 May 2023.

262 as has the state's declaration to evict: 'Declaration of village land as protected forest areas in the hill district of Manipur triggers statewide protests', LandConflictWatch.org, 18 April 2023, <https://www.landconflictwatch.org/conflicts/declaration-of-village-land-as-protected-forest-areas-in-the-hill-district-of-manipur-triggers-statewide-protests>.

263 In 2009, an NGO called the Social: Sanjenbam Jugeshwor Singh, 'Menace Of Alcoholism & Drug Abuse In Manipur', *The Frontier Manipur*, 23 April 2022.

263 Manipur, with only about 0.2 per cent: A. L. Sharma, T. R. Singh, L. S. Singh, 'Understanding of HIV/AIDS in the international border area, Manipur: Northeast India', *Epidemiology and Infection*, Vol. 147, No. 113, 2019.

263 Of the female injecting drug users in: Sindhuja Parthasarty, 'GenderAnd Development: The highs and lows of women drug users in Manipur', *Indian Express*, 19 December 2017.

265 Struggling with a deluge of alcohol: Neha Singhal, Naveed Mehmood Ahman, 'Sikkim's Alternative Model to Tackle Drug Abuse: An Analysis of the Sikkim Anti-Drugs Act, 2006', *VidhiLegalPolicy.in*.

265 The Vidhi Centre for Legal Policy: Ibid.

265 In 2018, SADA decriminalized illicit: Ibid.

265 In September 2022, in response to: Sobhapati Samon, 'Manipur cabinet partially lifts prohibition of liquor in state', *Hindustan Times*, 21 September 2022.

267 the Loktak Lake, which is one of the: Devlin Leishangthem, Sangeeta Angom, Syd Ainul Hussain, Chongpi Tuboi, et. al, 'Socioeconomic considerations in conserving wetlands of northeastern India: A case study of Loktak Lake, Manipur', *ResearchGate.net*, 2021, <https://www.researchgate.net/figure/Location-map-of-Loktak-Lake-Manipur-India_fig1_303817911>.

CHAPTER 9: HEMPISTAN

269 It was on one such July day in 2016: Tathagata Satpathy, X, 20 July 2016, <https://x.com/SatpathyLive/status>.

270 In 2015, while serving his fourth term as: tathagatasatpathy, 'Hello /r/India, I am Tathagata Satpathy. Member of Parliament, Chief Whip of BJD, Editor of Dharitri & Orissa POST. AMA!', Reddit.com, 11 March 2015, <https://www.reddit.com/r/india/comments/2z493l/hello_rindia_i_am_tathagata_satpathy_member_of/?rdt=37824>.

270 In an interview that followed, Satpathy: Deeptiman Tiwary, 'Cannabis ban is elitist. It should go: Tathagata Satpathy', *Times of India*, 29 March 2015.

271 In 2019, Satpathy retired from politics: Nistula Hebbar, 'Satpathy quits active politics', *The Hindu*, 5 March 2019.

273 A few months after Satpathy's: Debayan Roy, 'Legal Marijuana in India? Punjab Lawmaker Dharamvir Gandhi Set to Move Parliament', *News18.com*, 2 November 2016, <https://www.news18.com/news/india/legal-marijuana-in-india-punjab-mp-to-move-parliament-1307450.html>.

273 In July 2017, Maneka Gandhi: 'Maneka Gandhi suggests legalising marijuana for medical purposes', *Indian Express*, 30 July 2017.

273 A year later, the Congress party leader: Shashi Tharoor, Avinash Tharoor, 'High time India, the land of bhang, legalises marijuana', *The Print*, 18 October 2018.

274 In January 2022, Maharashtra MP: 'Maharashtra government should allow cultivation of cannabis: BJP MP Pratap Patil Chikhilar', *The New Indian Express*, 31 January 2022.

274 Later that same year, BJP MLA: 'Encourage Use Of Bhang, Cannabis As Alternative To Liquor To Prevent Crime: Chhattisgarh BJP MLA', *Outlook India*, 25 July 2022.

274 From lucrative start-ups to Instagram: 'Columbus and cannabis', HashMuseum.com, <https://hashmuseum.com/en/collection/hemp-shipping/columbus-and-cannabis/>.

275 The first flag of the US was made: Garrett Bruno, 'Hemp Flag to Fly Over Capitol on Fourth of July', *ABC News*, 4 July 2013.

275 The US Declaration of Independence: Sean Gormal, '"The Declaration of Independence was written on paper made out of hemp."', Politifact.com, 7 Noveber 2016, <https://www.politifact.com/factchecks/2016/nov/07/kai-degner/kai-degners-falsely-says-declaration-independence-/>.

275 Abraham Lincoln used hemp: 'WHAT IS INDUSTRIAL HEMP?', Virginia Cooperative Extension, <https://www.ext.vsu.edu/industrial-hemp-overview#:~:text=Abraham%20Lincoln%20also%20used%20hemp,%2C%20shoes%2C%20clothes%20and%20more.>.

275 The 1941 Ford's Model T: Dipayan Dutta, 'Forget Electric Cars! Henry Ford's Cannabis car was made from Hemp: 10xStronger than steel, 100% green!', *Financial Express*, 17 November 2018.

275 Painters like Vincent van Gogh: 'For centuries painters such as Van Gogh, Rembrandt and Gainsborough created their classic works on hemp canvases using hemp based paints', *HempClothingAustralia.com*, <https://www.hempclothingaustralia.com/blog/21>.

275 Even the word 'canvas' owes its: 'canvas (n.)', Etymonline.com, <https://www.etymonline.com/word/canvas>.

275 Nowadays, the global market for hemp: 'HEMP', CASIR - National Botanical Research Institute, < https://nbri.res.in/cannabis/>.

275 South Africa's Cape Town opened: 'World's tallest hemp hotel set to open in June in South Africa', AfricaNews.com, 8 May 2023, <https://www.africanews.com/2023/05/03/worlds-tallest-hemp-hotel-set-to-open-in-june-in-south-africa/>.

275 Two Chinese provinces account for: 'How Is China Poised to Be a Hemp Fiber Superpower?', NewFrontirData.com, 27 May 2021, <https://newfrontierdata.com/cannabis-insights/how-is-china-poised-to-be-a-hemp-fiber-superpower/>.

275 The hemp/cannabis/bhang plant is: Andy Kerr, 'The Environmental Benefits of Using Industrial Hemp', AndyKerr.net, <https://www.andykerr.net/hemp-environmental-benefits/>.

276 Hemp plants breathe in four times: Henry Braham, 'Why hemp is good for the planet', PebbleMag.com, 26 October 2021, <https://pebblemag.com/hemp-carbon-sequestration/#:~:text=Hemp%20plants%20breathe%20in%20four,year's%20carbon%20from%20two%20cars.>.

276 Like some other wild weeds, the cannabis plant: M. Girdhar, N. R. Sharma, H. Rehman, A. Kumar, et. al, 'Comparative assessment for hyperaccumulatory and phytoremediation capability of three wild weeds', *3 Biotech*, Vol. 4, No. 6, 2014, pp. 579–589.

276 It is considered a strong candidate for: D. F. Placido, C. C. Lee, 'Potential of Industrial Hemp for Phytoremediation of Heavy Metals', *Plants (Basel, Switzerland)*, Vol. 11, No. 5, 2022, p. 595.

276 The US Department of Agriculture is: Sandee LaMotte, 'Marijuana users have more heavy metals in their bodies', *CNN*, 31 August 2023.

277 'Since ancient times, cannabis-based': Isha Arora, 'Is it right to outrightly ban cannabis cultivation?', *Financial Express*, 5 May 2019.

277 At the time of writing, India's contribution: 'GVR Report cover Industrial Hemp Market Size, Share & Trends Report Industrial Hemp Market Size, Share & Trends Analysis Report By Application (Animal Care, Textiles, Food & Beverages), By Product (Seeds, Fiber, Shivs), By Region (North America, Asia Pacific), And Segment Forecasts, 2024 - 2030', Market Analysis Report, <https://www.grandviewresearch.com/industry-analysis/industrial-hemp-market>.

278 In 2013, Uruguay became a pioneer: Simon Maybin, 'Uruguay: The world's marijuana pioneer', *BBC*, 4 May 2019.

278 In a suburb of Johannesburg in: 'Cannabis academy bets on South Africa pot revolution', *Forbes India*, 26 June 2023.

278 An early 2022 report confirmed that: 'Cannabis has added $43.5B to Canada's economy since legalization: report', GlobalNews.ca, 1 February 2022, <https://globalnews.ca/news/8585983/cannabis-canada-economy-legalization-report/#:~:text=Cannabis%20has%20added%20%2443.5B%20to%20

Canada's%20economy%20since%20legalization%3A%20report,-By%20Staff%20The&text=A%20new%20report%20says%20cannabis,was%20legalized%20in%20October%202018>.

278 Australia has also become the first country: Rich Haridy, 'Australia to prescribe MDMA and psilocybin for PTSD and depression in world first', Nature.com, 30 June 2023, <https://www.nature.com/articles/d41586-023-02093-8>.

279 In Germany, after experimenting with a: Louis Westendarp, Peter Wilke, Gabriel Rinaldi, 'Germany scales back cannabis legalization plans to focus on home cultivation', Politico.eu, 12 April 2023, <https://www.politico.eu/article/germany-focuses-on-home-cultivation-in-reduced-cannabis-legalization-plans-lauterbach-25-grams-thc-cem-ozdemir/#:~:text=In%20addition%2C%20possession%20of%20up,be%20restricted%20to%20specific%20areas.>.

279 In late 2023, Japan—one of the strictest: 'Japan to legalise cannabis-based medicines', *Times of India*, 7 December 2023.

279 Around the same time, the parliament: 'Ukraine lawmakers vote to legalize medical marijuana and help ease stress from the war with Russia', APNews.com, 21 December 2023, <https://apnews.com/article/russia-ukraine-war-medical-marijuana-aa6e3f71159e0726c68836bc7ccafd07>.

279 The credit for originally introducing ganja: Vera Rubin (ed.), *Cannabis and Culture,* Germany: De Gruyter, 3 June 2011.

279 But in June 2022, the Thai Food: Pongkwan Yimsaard, Kathryn E. Lancaster, Annette H. Sohn, 'Potential impact of Thailand's cannabis policy on the health of young adults: current status and future landscape', *The Lancet*, Vol. 10, 23 January 2023.

280 Health Minister Anutin Charnvirakul: Heather Chen, 'Thailand to give away one million free cannabis plants to households, minister says', *CNN*, 11 May 2022.

280 On election day, Charnvirakul arrived: 'Thailand PM candidate casts vote in marijuana-print shirt', *Times of India*, 14 May 2023.

280 But the country—which already credits: 'Share of tourism contribution to the Gross Domestic Product (GDP) value in Thailand from 2017 to 2020', Statista.com, 25 September 2023, <https://www.statista.com/statistics/1143467/thailand-share-of-tourism-to-gdp/>.

280 Dispensaries lined up many areas: Mike Ives, 'Weed Is Now Legal in Thailand. How Long Will the High Times Last?", *New York Times*, 10 November 2022.

280 There were contests for the 'fastest joint': WION, 'Thai man rolls the fastest to win the joint rolling competition in Phuket I WION Originals', YouTube.com, 28 March 2023, <https://www.youtube.com/watch?v=b3hgIfKV8GM>.

280 After assuming office in August 2023: 'Thai PM: "I don't agree with recreational use' of cannabis"', Reuters.com, 15 September 2023, < https://

www.reuters.com/world/asia-pacific/thai-pm-i-dont-agree-with-recreational-use-cannabis-2023-09-15/>.

281 Voices of concern were raised globally: 'Singapore Sentences Man To Death Over 1Kg Of Marijuana', *NDTV*, 21 April 2023; UN Human Rights, X, 25 April 2023, <https://x.com/UNHumanRights/status/1650803905998082048>; Richard Branson, 'Why Tangaraju Suppiah doesn't deserve to die', Virgin.com, 24 April 2023.

281 Singapore executed Suppiah by hanging: Heather Chen, 'Singapore executes man for trafficking two pounds of cannabis', *CNN*, 26 April 2023.

281 Singaporean authorities have argued: 'Singapore chides billionaire Richard Branson over call to spare cannabis trafficker', *Times of India*, 25 April 2023.

281 'It is just illogical to know that countries': Kelly Ng, Frances Mao, 'Tangaraju Suppiah: Singapore executes man for supplying cannabis', *BBC*, 26 April 2023.

282 In August 2021, The Borgen Project: Zoe Tzanis, 'BENEFITS OF LEGALIZING MARIJUANA IN URUGUAY', BorgenProject.org, 20 August 2021, <https://borgenproject.org/legalizing-marijuana-in-uruguay/#:~:text=The%20decision%20to%20legalize%20marijuana,the%20path%20of%20illegal%20consumption.>.

282 Since alcohol is the most prevalent: Philippe Lucas, Susan Boyd, M-J Milloy, Zach Walsh, 'Reductions in alcohol use following medical cannabis initiation: results from a large cross-sectional survey of medical cannabis patients in Canada', *International Journal of Drug Policy*, Vol. 86, December 2020.

282 In the United States, President Joe: Michael D. Shear, Zolan Kanno-Youngs, 'Biden Pardons Thousands Convicted of Marijuana Possession Under Federal Law', *New York Times*, 6 October 2022.

282 Biden's perspective was affirmed by: Christina Jewett, Noah Weiland, 'Federal Scientists Recommend Easing Restrictions on Marijuana', *New York Times*, 12 January 2024.

282 Biden will face an independent challenger: Kritika Katira, 'Rapper Afroman officially enters 2024 US presidential race; plans to legalise cannabis', WIONews.com, 22 April 2023, <https://www.wionews.com/entertainment/rapper-afroman-officially-enters-2024-us-presidential-race-plans-to-legalise-cannabis-585102>.

283 Annual cannabis sales in the US are: Iris Dorbian, 'Despite Some Stumbles, Total Sales In U.S. Cannabis Market Could Soar To $50.7 Billion By 2028, Says Top Researcher', *Forbes*, 15 February 2023.

283 In 2022, Americans spent far more: Dominick Reuter, 'Americans are buying weed more than chocolate, data shows', *Business Insider*, 13 May 2023.

283 An estimated 55 million Americans—roughly: 'Marijuana Addiction: Rates & Usage Statistics', National Centre for Drug Abuse Statistics, <https://drugabusestatistics.org/marijuana-addiction/>.

283 Now, the US is the leading importer of: 'Hemp Seed', Tridge.com, <https://

www.tridge.com/intelligences/hemp-seed/import>.

283 The population of American cigarette: 'Altria: The Cannabis And Smoke-Free Thesis Are Falling Apart', SeekingAlpha.com, 20 January 2023, <https://seekingalpha.com/article/4571018-altria-the-cannabis-and-smoke-free-thesis-are-falling-apart>.

283 Formerly known as Philip Morris Companies: Chris Roberts, 'How Tobacco Giant Altria Is Becoming A Cannabis Company', *Forbes*, 10 February 2021.

284 In a 2022 cover story, *Forbes* argued that the: Will Yakowicz, 'Weed vs. Greed: How America Botched Legalizing Pot', *Forbes*, 9 August 2022.

285 The Hemp Expo is the brainchild of Indian Vaidyas: 'ABOUT INDIANVAIDYAS', IndianVaidyas.com, <https://indianvaidyas.com/aboutus>.

286 Their associated platform, Hempvaidyas: 'Consultants', HempVaidyas.com, <http://hempvaidyas.com/>.

286 Juneja is a practitioner of medical: Vaidya Piyush Juneja, *Medical Cannabis: A to Z*, 20 April 2023.

288 'is the penance that we as a nation': Khagesh Gautam, *Cannabis Indica: Perception Vs Potential*, p. xix.

288 Specifically, Gautam feels that the ministry's: Ibid., p. 19.

290 In 2017, with a focus on studying the: 'Ratan Tata, Rajan Anandan invests in cannabis research firm Boheco', Business-Standard.com, 21 December 2017, <https://www.business-standard.com/article/companies/ratan-tata-rajan-anandan-invests-in-cannabis-research-firm-boheco-117122100386_1.html>.

290 Some of their most popular CBD: Arirta Ghosh, 'How BOHECO is Revolutionizing Health & Wellness with CBD Clinic and Store', IndianRetailer.com, 8 November 2023, <https://www.indianretailer.com/interview/retail-people/new-commerce/how-boheco-revolutionizing-health-wellness-cbd-clinic-and>.

291 The water footprint (WF) of: J. Aveirnk, 'GLOBAL WATER FOOTPRINT OF INDUSTRIAL HEMP TEXTILE', University of Twente, 2015, <https://essay.utwente.nl/68219/>.

291 The future is bright: 'How Traditional Indian Fabrics Are Reinventing the Wheel of Sustainability', Atmos.earth, <https://atmos.earth/hemp-khadi-sustainable-fabrics/>.

291 In Chennai's Chetpet locality, a company: Shonali Muthalaly, 'Chennai's first CBD clinic focussing on medical cannabis and integrative healing opens. We get a first look', *The Hindu*, 27 April 2023.

291 In a special televised report, CNBC-TV18: CNBC-TV18, 'A Deep Dive Into The Hemp Market | Mad About Markets | CNBC TV18', YouTube.com, 5 July 2023, <https://www.youtube.com/watch?v=YjCPI-cLWoA>.

292 Patanjali Ayurved—a private, multinational: 'Ramdev's Patanjali wants marijuana legalised in India; social media can't keep calm', *India Today*, 9 February 2018.

292 Manufacturers of Ayurvedic medicine, cosmetics: 'Patanjali looks to more than double turnover to Rs 1 trillion in five years', *Financial Express*, 17 September 2022.

292 'We should ponder over the benefits': Suneera Tandon, 'India's cannabis economy has a new hope—Patanjali', QZ.com, 6 February 2018, <https://qz.com/india/1191203/patanjali-the-indian-cannabis-economys-new-hope>.

292 Another major step for the industry: 'FSSAI's new regulations to allow Hemp to be used as a food source', *India Today*, 23 November 2021.

292 Not long after this decision, hemp-based: Jayashree Narayanan, 'Pune opens doors to its first legal hemp-based café', *Indian Express*, 19 June 2022.

292 Patanjali has been mired in a whirlpool: Basant Kumar, 'How Ramdev's Patanjali took control of Dalit lands in Haridwar', *Newslaundry*, 19 August 2022, <https://www.newslaundry.com/2022/08/19/how-ramdevs-patanjali-took-control-of-dalit-lands-in-haridwar>.

292 accusations of sketchy research, and poor: M. S. Nawaz, Anupam Trivedi, 'Ramdev's Patanjali products fail quality test, RTI inquiry finds', *Hindustan Times*, 30 May 2017.

292 In February 2024, nearly four months: '"Taking country for a ride": SC puts temporary ban on Patanjali ads for misleading claims', *Newslaundry*, 27 February 2023, <https://www.newslaundry.com/2024/02/27/taking-country-for-a-ride-sc-puts-temporary-ban-on-patanjali-ads-for-misleading-claims>.

292 BOHECO opened a hemp cloud kitchen: Namya Sinha, 'Hemp Is Happening: Meet The Versatile Culinary Hero', *Hindustan Times*, 29 May 2023.

293 With the FSSAI's new regulations: Raul Dias, 'Hemp is the newest Indian superfood in restaurants and cafés across the country', *The Hindu*, 25 August 2022.

296 There is a report [by Prohibition Partners]: 'Reports show $6 billion potential in Asia medical cannabis market', *Nutraceutical Business Review*, 16 May 2019.

297 Among its missions, GLM hope to 're-legalize': 'The Great Legalisation Movement', GLM.org, <https://www.glm.org/>.

297 In 2017, Vaurora wrote an open letter to the: Viki Vaurora, Facebook, 16 December 2017, <https://www.facebook.com/viki.vaurora/posts/glm_india-our-open-letter-to-the-honble-prime-minister-of-india-shri-narendra-mo/517856548587129/>.

298 I find Vaurora in remnants of his past: VIKI VAURORA, 'Liberate2020 (01) - Reality of the World by Viki Vaurora', YouTube.com, 8 May 2020, < https://www.youtube.com/watch?v=wBFwraQ1dH4>.

298 In a TEDx talk in Bengaluru in 2015: TEDx Talks, 'Medical Marijuana: The Ultimate Disease Defeating Drug | Viki Vaurora | TEDxBangalore', YouTube.com, 5 April 2016, <https://www.youtube.com/watch?v=HA3Ek3T5WEE>.

CHAPTER 10: AMRIT

302 Cannabis is also known to be helpful for nausea: G. Giordano, R. Martin-Willett, L. P. Gibson, D. R. Camidge, et al., 'Cannabis use in cancer patients: acute and sustained associations with pain, cognition, and quality of life', *Exploration of Medicine*, Vol. 4, 2023, pp. 254–271.

302 Surveys have revealed that anywhere: Brooke Worster, Emily R. Hajjar, Nathan Handley, 'Cannabis Use in Patients With Cancer: A Clinical Review', *ASCO Publications*, Vol. 18, No. 11, June 2022.

302 Adenocarcinoma is the most common type: Maurie Markman, 'Adenocarcinoma', CancerCenter.com, 19 July 2022, <https://www.cancercenter.com/adenocarcinoma>.

303 There is no peer-reviewed or: R. Prasad, 'Panchagavya... if cow urine could cure cancer', *The Hindu*, 21 July 2017.

305 In a vast survey of cancer survivors in the: Changchuan Jiang, Haowei Wang, Qian Wang, 'Prevalence of Chronic Pain and High-Impact Chronic Pain in Cancer Survivors in the United States', *JAMA Oncology*, Vol. 5, No. 8, 2019.

305 There is some greater good in the 'munchies': 'Cannabis ingredient can help cancer patients regain their appetites and sense of taste, study finds', Oxford University Press, ScienceDaily.com, 25 February 2011, <https://www.sciencedaily.com/releases/2011/02/110222192830.htm>.

305 He began to incorporate hemp products: Naandika Tripathi, 'Cannabis startups chase opportunities despite low awareness and legal challenges', *Forbes India*, 12 April 2021.

307 Some doctors may consider a patient 'cured': 'Understanding Cancer Prognosis', National Cancer Institute, 29 May 2024.

310 An episode mentioned in scriptures including: The Divine Tree, 'Samudra Manthan - The Hunt for Elixir by Devas & Asuras | The Tale of Churning the Milky Ocean!', YouTube.com, 27 January 2021, <https://www.youtube.com/watch?v=z9xEcTRY5to>.

312 Ayurveda also recognizes cannabis as a: Raghav Priyadarshini, 'Does India Have Patience, Will And Resources To Build World's Top Cannabis Medicine Industry?', *India Times*, 27 March 2022.

312 Bhang shows up repeatedly in the recipes: Parmita Uniyal, 'Arthritis to piles; lesser-known health benefits of cannabis or bhang revealed by Ayurveda expert', *Hindustan Times*, 8 March 2022.

312 In their 1957 paper, Chopra and Chopra: Chopra and Chopra, 'The Use of the Cannabis Drugs in India'.

312 In parts of the Himalaya, there has been: G. K. Sharma, 'CANNABIS FOLKLORE IN THE HIMALAYAS', *Botanical Museum Leaflets*, Harvard University, Vol. 25, No. 7, 1977, pp. 203–215.

312 In a 2018 study conducted on patients: 'Study finds cannabis-based drugs help alleviate side-effects post-chemo AIIMS to research further', TheWeek.in, 4 April 2020, <https://www.theweek.in/content/archival/wire-updates/national/2018/11/25/des7-ayush-cannabis-cancer-aiims.html>.

313 Just two days prior to the CCRAS study: 'CSIR-IIIM, BOHECO to develop cannabis based drugs for cancer, epilepsy, sickle cell anemia', *Times of India*, 23 November 2018.

313 'The drugs would be "natural" instead': Kuwar Singh, 'Modi's love for ayurveda may be just the push marijuana needed in India', QZ.com, 26 November 2018, <https://qz.com/india/1474267/modis-ayurveda-push-may-promote-marijuana-use-in-india>.

313 Researchers at TMH announced that: Malathy Iyer, 'Trials using cannabis to cut risk of cancer metastasis all set to begin', *Times of India*, 25 September 2022.

313 In early 2023, researchers at the National: A. Shehla, G. Pawankumar, G. Preeti, S. Reetu, et al., 'Efficacy and safety of local application of Vijaya oil in the management of Sandhivata with special reference to Osteoarthrosis: An open-labeled single-arm clinical trial', *Journal of Ayurveda and Integrated Medical Sciences*, Vol. 8, No. 2, 2023.

314 Our bodies engender its own cannabinoids: MaryAnn de Pietro, 'What to know about endocannabinoids and the endocannabinoid system', MedicalNewsToday.com, 27 February 2021, <https://www.medicalnewstoday.com/articles/endocannabinoid#production>.

314 The endocannabinoid system assists several: Sanjay Gupta, 'Dr. Sanjay Gupta: Cannabis is having a senior moment', *CNN*, 7 August 2023.

314 This balance can help regulate and control: 'Medicinal cannabis, explained', *NPS MedicineWise*, <https://www.nps.org.au/consumers/medicinal-cannabis-explained>.

314 It has been called a 'bridge' between the: *Mayo Clinic Medical Marijuana*, Mayo Clinic, 7 April 2023.

314 As humans age, we make fewer natural: CNN, 'Sanjay Investigates "Weed 7: A Senior Moment" Pt. 1', YouTube.com, 22 August 2023, <https://www.youtube.com/watch?v=dcLxSCf1jxE>.

314 Research in the United States and elsewhere: Janet Joy, Alison Mack, 'Marijuana as Medicine?', *National Academies Press*, 30 November 2000; Elaine Kiriakopoulos, Anup Patel, 'Medical Marijuana', *Epilepsy Foundation*, 3 July 2018, <https://www.epilepsy.com/treatment/alternative-therapies/medical-marijuana>.

315 Depending on the state, patients in the: 'Medical marijuana', Mayo Clinic, 30 May 2024.

315 In May 2023, a cannabidiol-based product: 'Biophore, Its Subsidiary Zenara Pharma, Receive First Approval For Cannabidiol In India', NDTVProfit.com, 15 May 2023, <https://www.ndtvprofit.com/business/biophore-its-subsidiary-zenara-

pharma-receive-first-approval-for-cannabidiol-in-india>.

315 The virus became the biggest khalnayak of health: Long Chi Nguyen, Haley Gula, Thomas J. Best, Dongbo Yang, et al., 'Cannabidiol Inhibits SARS-CoV-2 Replication through Induction of the Host ER Stress and Innate Immune Responses', *Science Advances*, Vol. 8, No. 8, 25 February 2022, <https://www.ncbi.nlm.nih.gov/pmc/articles/PMC7987002/>.

315 During the pandemic, a mix of Covid anxiety: Luke Winkie, 'How the pandemic created a new generation of stoners', *The Guardian*, 30 March 2022.

316 A 2024 study funded by the National Heart: 'Smoking cannabis associated with increased risk of heart attack, stroke', National Institutes of Help, 28 February 2024.

316 Some studies have theorized that medical: 'Consumer Health', Mayo Clinic, 30 May 2024.

316 A 2020 report in the *Cureus* journal: Shweta Patel, Sahar Khan, M. Saipavankumar, Hamid Pousettef, 'The Association Between Cannabis Use and Schizophrenia: Causative or Curative? A Systematic Review', *Cureus*, Vol. 12, No. 7, 2020.

316 Men aged between fifteen and forty-nine: 'Young Men at Highest Risk of Schizophrenia Linked with Cannabis Use Disorder', National Institutes of Health, 4 May 2023, <https://www.nih.gov/news-events/news-releases/young-men-highest-risk-schizophrenia-linked-cannabis-use-disorder#:~:text=The%20study%20team%20estimated%20that,among%20women%20aged%2016-49>.

316 The environment may benefit, but in the: Sandee LaMotte, 'Marijuana users have more heavy metals in their bodies', *CNN*, 31 August 2023.

316 Research published by the *Canadian Medical*: S. Ilnitsky, S. Van Uum, 'Marijuana and fertility', *CMAJ : Canadian Medical Association journal = journal de l'Association medicale canadienne*, Vol. 191, No. 23, Edition 638, 2019.

317 A report by the Indian Council of Medical: V. Kulothungan, K. Sathishkumar, S. Leburu, Rohit Mohan, et al., 'Burden of cancers in India - estimates of cancer crude incidence, YLLs, YLDs and DALYs for 2021 and 2025 based on National Cancer Registry Program', BMC Cancer, 2022, <https://bmccancer.biomedcentral.com/articles/10.1186/s12885-022-09578-1>.

317 Oncologists have theorized that the increased: Priyanka Sharma, 'BackBack India's cancer burden to rise to 29.8 million in 2025: ICMR report', *Mint*, 13 May 2022.

317 'To combat these new-age forms of mental': 'Cannabis And India: A Promising Future', TheHealthSite.com, 20 April 2023, <https://www.thehealthsite.com/ayush/cannabis-and-india-a-promising-future-971309/>.

317 Rungta has further suggested that part of: '"We aim to work with various state governments to implement cannabis cultivation"', BioSpectrumIndia.com, 10 July 2023, <https://www.biospectrumindia.com/features/17/23315/we-aim-to-work-

with-various-state-governments-to-implement-cannabis-cultivation.html>.

317 In 2020, Dr Pankaj Chaturvedi: Akshat Malik, Khuzema Saifuddin Fatehi, Nandini N Menon, Pankaj Chaturvedi, 'Review of Medicinal Use of Cannabis Derivatives and the Societal Impact of Legalization', *Indian Journal of Palliative Care*, Vol. 26, No. 3, August 2020, pp. 369–380.

317 The concept of palliative care: Divya Khosla, Firuza Patel, Suresh Sharma, 'Palliative Care in India: Current Progress and Future Needs', *Indian Journal of Palliative Care*, Vol. 18, No. 3, 2012, pp. 149–154.

318 Analysis by *ProPublica* in the: Hannah Fresques, 'Doctors Prescribe More of a Drug If They Receive Money from a Pharma Company Tied to It', ProPublica.org, 20 December 2019, <https://www.propublica.org/article/doctors-prescribe-more-of-a-drug-if-they-receive-money-from-a-pharma-company-tied-to-it#:~:text=Dollars%20for%20Doctors-,Doctors%20Prescribe%20More%20of%20a%20Drug%20If%20They%20Receive%20Money,prescribed%20more%20of%20those%20drugs>.

318 Pfizer Inc.'s India unit stopped selling Corex: 'Pfizer stops selling popular Corex cough syrup in India after ban', Reuters.com, 14 March 2016, <https://www.reuters.com/article/india-pfizer-medicine-idCNL3N16M1R9/>.

319 Meanwhile, healthcare providers in American: Ashley C. Bradley, David Bradford, Amanda Abraham, Grace Adams, 'Association between US State Medical Cannabis Laws and Opioid Prescribing in the Medicare Part D Population', *JAMA Internal Medicine*, Vol. 178, No. 5, 1 May 2018, p. 667.

319 In India, there is no formal system to: Shaffi Fazaludeen Koya, et al., 'Consumption of Systemic Antibiotics in India in 2019', *The Lancet Regional Health' Southeast Asia*, Vol. 4, 1 September 2022.

319 A part of me imagines that the plant could: 'Medical Marijuana Global Market Report 2023', The Business Research Company, April 2023, <https://www.thebusinessresearchcompany.com/report/medical-marijuana-global-market-report>.

320 'ayurvedic inspired cannabis medicine': 'Savikalpa Sciences | Buy CBD Oil, Hemp Oil, Cannabis Oil Online India.' Savikalpa Sciences, <https://savikalpa.com/>.

320 In terms of modern medication, India is: *India Pharmaceuticals Market Market Size & Share Analysis - Growth Trends & Forecasts (2023-2028)*, Mordor Intelligence, < https://www.mordorintelligence.com/industry-reports/pharmaceuticals-industry-in-india#:~:text=For%20instance%2C%20as%20per%20IBEF,generic%20medicine%20market%20by%20Vol..>;IANS, '$49 Billion And 3rd Largest In The World — Indian Pharma Industry Likely To Grow To $130 Billion By 2030', India.com, 15 September 2022, <https://www.india.com/business/49-billion-and-3rd-largest-in-the-world-indian-pharma-industry-

likely-to-grow-to-130-billion-by-2030-5633319/>.

320 'India has the necessary ecosystem': Raghav Priyadashi, 'Does India Have Patience, Will And Resources To Build World's Top Cannabis Medicine Industry?', *India Times*, 27 March 2022.

322 Not long after the TMH declared: Akshat Malik, Khuzema Saifuddin Fatehi, Nandini N. Menon, Pankaj Chaturvedi, 'Review of Medicinal Use of Cannabis Derivatives and the Societal Impact of Legalization', *Indian Journal of Palliative Care*, Vol. 26, No. 3, August 2020, pp. 369–380.

323 The paper states that cannabis could be a cause: Ibid.

323 'Till date, no death due to marijuana': Ibid.

323 In his Pulitzer Prize-winning book: Siddhartha Mukherjee, *The Emperor of All Maladies: A Biography of Cancer*, United States: Scribner, 2011.

326 According to the Global Adult Tobacco: Ministry of Health and Family Welfare, *Global Adult Tobacco Survey GATS 2 India 2016-17*, <https://ntcp.mohfw.gov.in/assets/document/surveys-reports-publications/Global-Adult-Tobacco-Survey-Second-Round-India-2016-2017.pdf>.

328 There are some doctors in the US: Beth Cohen, 'Many People Think Cannabis Smoke Is Harmless. Here's How How That Belief Can Put Health at Risk', *PBS NewsHour*, 2 September 2023, <https://www.pbs.org/newshour/health/many-people-think-cannabis-smoke-is-harmless-heres-how-how-that-belief-can-put-health-at-risk>.

330 Medical marijuana has the faculty to: Cheryl Pellerin, *Healing with Cannabis: The Evolution of the Endocannabinoid System and How Cannabinoids Help Relieve PTSD, Pain, MS, Anxiety, and More*, United States: Skyhorse, 2020.

334 '... Next to cure,' wrote O'Shaughnessy: W. B. O'Shaughnessy, *On the Preparations of the Indian Hemp, or Gunjah (Cannabis Indica)*, London: S. Taylor, 30 April 2022.

CHAPTER 11: FOREST OF BLISS

336 'a characteristic set of cultural practices': Bhargava Rani, 'The Night before Bhor Ārti: Play and Banarasipan in the Ramnagar Ramlila', *Performing the Ramayana Tradition*, New York: Oxford Academic, 17 June 2021, pp. 298–320.

337 Forest of Bliss was the title of a 1986: 'Forest of Bliss', EthnoFest.gr, <https://www.ethnofest.gr/film/forest-of-bliss/>.

338 The *Encyclopedia of Religion*: Thomas Gale, 'Encyclopedia of Religion', *Academia.edu*, <https://www.academia.edu/17956166/Thomson_Gale_Encyclopedia_of_Religion_02_En_>.

339 These waters are notoriously polluted: Ellen Wohl, 'River Pollution', OxfordBibliographies.com, <https://www.oxfordbibliographies.com/display/document/obo-9780199363445/obo-9780199363445-0003.xml>.

344 According to the legends, it was: Sonali Pimputkar, 'Maha Shivratri: Lord Shiva's connection with bhaang decoded!', *Free Press Journal*, 30 May 2019, <https://www.freepressjournal.in/cmcm/maha-shivratri-lord-shivas-connection-with-bhaang-decoded>.

346 There have been traffic concerns in gridlocked: Abhishek Dey, 'Violence during Kanwar Yatra: Police in Delhi, UP need new ideas to tackle an old problem', *Scroll.in*, 10 August 2018; 'Madhya Pradesh: Clashes Erupt During Kanwar Yatra In Khandwa; Stone Pelting, Police Lathicharge Reported', *Outlook India*, 8 August 2023.

346 Public fairs and festivals of the past and present: Bhargava Rani, 'The Night before Bhor Ārti: Play and Banarasipan in the Ramnagar Ramlila', in Paula Richman and Rustomn Bharucha (eds.), *Performing the Ramayana Tradition*, New York: Oxford Academic, 17 June 2021, pp. 298–320.

347 This bhang is extracted by crushing dried: Jehan Nizar, 'An edible history of "bhang": How the cannabis derivative made its way into Indian kitchens', *News9Live*, 18 March 2022.

352 In 2023, when the Odisha government banned: Subhashish Mohanty, 'Odisha bans consumption of ganja in Shiva temples, move to curb health hazards', *The Telegraph*, 24 May 2023.

352 India is not the only country where religion: Kyle Jaeger, 'State Department Says Marijuana Reform Helps Address Religious Discrimination In Other Countries, While Ignoring U.S. Policy', MarijuanaMoment.net, 13 June 2022, <https://www.marijuanamoment.net/state-department-says-marijuana-reform-helps-address-religious-discrimination-in-other-countries-while-ignoring-u-s-policy/>.

353 The unconstitutional marriage of politics and: Harish S. Wankhede, 'Parliament Rituals Show Permanency of BJP's Brahmanical Cultural Agenda', *The Wire*, 16 June 2023.

355 I think often of the Sikkim Anti Drugs Act: Neha Singhal, Naveed Ahmad, 'Sikkim stopped seeing drug users as criminals and look what happened', *The Print*, 22 September 2020.

355 In 2021, the Ministry of Social Justice: 'Treat users with small quantity of drugs as victims, not culprits', *Times of India*, 25 October 2021.

357 The Manipur government issued 'shoot at sight': Rahul Karmakar, 'Many killed in Manipur riots; State government issues shoot-at-sight order', *The Hindu*, 4 May 2023.

357 The army and other armed forces created: 'Concerns over armed forces' role in Manipur', TheMeghalayan.com, 18 September 2023, <https://themeghalayan.com/concerns-over-armed-forces-role-in-manipur/>.

357 Curfews emptied the streets. Hospitals ran: Tabassum Barnagarwala, 'HIV patients in Manipur hills at risk as medicine supplies disrupted', *Scroll.in*, 25 August 2023.

357 **Tens of thousands of paramilitary forces were sent:** Alex Travilli, Suhasini Raj, 'Dozens Killed in Ethnic Clashes in India's Manipur State', *New York Times*, 6 May 2023.

357 **Over the next ten months, nearly 200 people:** Krishn Kaushik, 'Manipur: Bearing brunt of violence, Kukis make up two-thirds of the victims, says Reuters analysis', *The Telegraph*, 29 July 2023.

357 **and approximately 400 churches were damaged:** Anugraph Kumar, 'INDIA's Manipur still tense after 400 churches burned and 60 Christians killed', Hrwf.eu, 21 May 2023, <https://hrwf.eu/india-indias-manipur-remains-tense-weeks-after-400-churches-were-burned-60-christians-killed/>.

357 **There were cases of looting, vandalism:** Suhasini Raj, 'Video of Sexual Assault Goes Viral in India, Renewing Attention on Ethnic Conflict', *New York Times*, 20 July 2023.